THE
CONFESSOR

Before writing his first novel, Mark Allen Smith spent ten years as a television investigative news producer and documentary producer-director, and over twenty years as a screenwriter. He lives in New York City with his partner and three children.

ALSO BY MARK ALLEN SMITH

The Inquisitor

THE
CONFESSOR

MARK ALLEN SMITH

**SIMON &
SCHUSTER**

London · New York · Sydney · Toronto · New Delhi

A CBS COMPANY

First published in Great Britain by Simon & Schuster UK Ltd, 2014
A CBS COMPANY

1 3 5 7 9 10 8 6 4 2

Simon & Schuster UK Ltd
1st Floor
222 Gray's Inn Road
London WC1X 8HB

www.simonandschuster.co.uk

Simon & Schuster Australia, Sydney
Simon & Schuster India, New Delhi

A CIP catalogue record for this book
is available from the British Library

Paperback ISBN: 978-0-85720-773-9
EBOOK ISBN: 978-0-85720-774-6

Typeset by M Rules
Printed and bound by CPI Group (UK) Ltd, Croydon, CR0 4YY

To Dodie, Cari Esta, and Liz.
The Hardass Trio.
Faith and love, from Day One.

Acknowledgements

Well ... I did my part, for better or worse. Now, I'd like to give sincere thanks to those who did theirs in helping this manuscript become a book;

Ian Chapman, Chief Executive and Publisher, Simon & Schuster UK – for his unwavering faith and belief in my novel

Emma Lowth & Maxine Hitchcock, Simon & Schuster UK – for their keen editors' eyes and imagination

Steffan Luebbe & Marco Schneiders, Bastei Lubbe, and Joy Terekiev, Mondadori – for their constancy, spirit and generous support

Liz Robinson & Dodie Gold – almost thirty years my partners, protectors, and loving friends

Tony Cartano – for his French translations

and

Nat Sobel & Judith Weber, Sobel Weber Associates Inc. – for being, quite simply, the best, most steadfast and caring agents a writer could dream of having ... anywhere, anytime, anyhow

and

Cathy Nonas – my reader, my editor, my scribbler, my wife, my love.

Prologue

He could see his indistinct reflection in the laptop's screen – a diaphanous face imprisoned behind the dense thicket of words. Playing with the light's angle, tilting his head forward and back a few degrees, infused the specter with depth and dimension. He enjoyed it – making his image wax and wane, bringing himself to the cusp of the living, then sending himself back to the edge of the netherworld.

His right hand rose up, and he began to tap the philtrum in the center of his upper lip with the tip of the forefinger as he read what he had written so far today.

> We're not like other professionals. During a down-time, you can't go to a batting cage to keep your swing sharp or read law journals to stay up to speed. You lose the feel of some things. Most important of all, you lose the feel of another's fear.

A clogged, rheumy sound came from behind him. He had always thought fear made humans sound more animalistic – that there were similarities between the tight-throated yelp of a helpless, scared human and the cry of a wounded dog or a bear caught in the steel teeth of a trap. He didn't turn around. He decided to wait a little longer.

How strange, he thought. In the moment, everything that was measurable, quantifiable, seemed more or less the same – the event, his role, the necessary skills and implements – as if a day had passed instead of ten months of surgeries and rehabilitation. Yet sitting here in this nexus of time, this rebooting – if it had been possible to take an x-ray of himself that revealed his *emotional* terrain, and he could have put it alongside one taken before the events of last July Fourth's, he was certain they would bear little resemblance. Hills would now be mountains, gullies rivers, crevices canyons. Earth, Planet X.

He rose, walked to an old, scarred oak table – for his re-entry into the life he'd wanted something organic, fashioned by man but created by nature – and gazed down at the terrible array laid out on it. The three o'clock sun was strong for early spring, pouring through the room's skylight and coating the instruments with a coppery, liquescent shine.

After the two reconstructive operations, the doctors had told him further procedures would not serve any purpose, the damage was too extensive – but when they'd presented the alternative, he had felt the moment's promise of perfection stir within its black irony. He would be remade, and remake his internal self as well – he would stretch his limits, transfigure his tolerances. Money was not an issue. He'd saved more than he'd ever spend. When he was done there would be no pain too great to bear.

He had it documented, with two cameras to ensure

coverage, and while he healed had spent hundred of hours watching the video, studying each cut, each severance. In the post-op months, he had allowed himself only two 50mcg fentanyl patches daily, and experienced sensory events of such wrenching intensity that his understanding of physical suffering underwent a radical realignment that matched the feats of his surgeons.

He picked up the 1867 Horatio Kern one-piece scalpel from the table. He'd tried the commercial plastic brands with disposable blades but their lightness was problematic, so he had one of the men shop for something more substantial. The Kern's ebony handle gave it heft and a more satisfying grip. He'd begun practicing on rabbits, and once he'd mastered basic skills had pigs brought in from a nearby farm. His surgeons had said the animal's subcutaneous fat and dermal thickness were relatively similar to that of human flesh. It was the closest he would get to the real thing.

A familiar, coarse droning made him look up. A very large hornet, two inches long, had wriggled its way into the room through the hole in the window screen, and now lighted on the slice of white peach he kept on the sill as a lure.

He put the scalpel down and went to the window. He could see the large gray, scabrous nest, bigger than a medicine ball, fixed to the underside of the eave outside, beside the lean-to where the dusty car was parked. The insects' visits had become a useful element in his regimen. While the hornet probed the peach, he reached down, gently grasped its gossamer wings between the tips of his thumb and forefinger, and raised the struggling, madly buzzing creature. This particular action had, over time, helped hone his fine motor skills and hand-eye coordination. As a rule, he would then hold the plump, striped abdomen between two fingertips and slowly squeeze until it burst. That had helped his sense of applied pressure, a facility that had been difficult to reacquire. He had been practicing on grapes when the first hornet had made its way in, and had discovered that animate flesh, sensitive and reactive to his touch, was a distinct improvement on fruit – so he'd started putting a slice of peach on the sill. For months now, the maid would find a pile of wizened carcasses on the floor when she came in.

He watched the beast twitch. Its energy was unflagging. The thick grunt came again. It was time. Time to begin anew. He turned and walked across the room. The subject was in a high-backed chair, draped with a loose-fitting, blue surgical smock that rendered the body shapeless. A makeshift hood of the same material covered the head, with holes cut for the eyes and mouth, which was covered with strips of black tape. Plastic lock-ties secured the body to the chair at the neck, wrists, waist and ankles.

He bent down to the face, and frowned. There was not enough fear in the gaze. He held the noisy, struggling beast up. 'Huge, isn't it?'

The lids of the eyes inside the hood pulled back and the pupils flared.

'My travels on Google tell me it's probably a Vespa mandarinia – the Asian giant hornet. The most venomous there is – they say a swarm attack can kill a man in minutes ... anaphylactic shock – but I'll be damned how they got here.'

He held up the index finger of his free hand. 'Watch,' he said, then moved it beneath the hornet's twisting abdomen and gave the underside a poke. The end of the abdomen immediately curled down and inward, as the quarter-inch stinger slid out and jabbed into the finger. He showed no reaction – not a flinch, or a wince.

The right brow of his audience rose in confusion.

'The most interesting difference between the wasp family and bees is ... bees can only sting once. Their stingers are barbed and get lodged in the flesh and torn off, and the bee dies. But hornets have barbless stingers. They can just keep on stinging, over and over.' He prodded the insect's belly with his fingertip and the hornet stung him again. 'See?' He pulled the bottom edge of the hood a few inches away from the neck. 'This is just to loosen you up a bit. Get rid of some of that adrenaline.' He watched the Adam's apple bob up and down with a tight swallow, then he released the hornet under the hood. 'They aren't particularly aggressive unless provoked, but it's best you try not to move.'

The nasty buzz suddenly stopped. Because of the hornet's size, he could clearly see it moving beneath the fabric as it crawled up the cheek. The eyes in the hood stared straight ahead, unblinking, but unfocused – like the look of someone trying to recall a person's name, or the date of some upcoming appointment. Then, the lids slowly closed and quivered, as the hornet crawled over the left eye and headed upward.

Beyond a window, the wild lavender was in bloom, a waving purple sea. Sudden movement there made the man look up from his captive, and he saw dozens of serpents with brilliant, iridescent scales begin leaping up from the brush in suspended, elegant arcs, one devouring another, opaline fangs glistening red. He watched until one, bloody, victorious creature remained, and it turned to him with a curious gaze.

'That's right,' he said. 'Come to Papa.'

The monster started slithering toward him, and he closed his eyes. He'd learned how to deal with the visions. He had no control over their onset, but had discovered shutting his eyes tightly made the hallucinations vanish. He understood they were graphic manifestations of a kind of madness. To his thinking, the psychopathy was the result of a remarkable catalytic reaction, the gradual synthesis of pain and suffering into a new chemical alloy that now resided in his brain like any other part of his psychological make-up – pleasure, fear, anger – and while those catalyzed adrenaline or serotonin or neutrophins, when this new component flared it triggered the visions.

There had been many. He had seen the clinic's cat sprout steel spikes in its fur; watched Dr. Ling's face explode discussing synthetic-organic polymers; poked through the melted gruyere on his onion soup to discover neon tetras darting about in the broth; and he'd seen an angel fall from the sky, its flaming wings leaving a trail of smoke in its wake. It was a sign that his intuition was not delusional, that his nemesis was, contrary to reports, alive – and that when they met again his extreme choices would be rewarded.

And he believed all this because the falling angel had Geiger's face.

Geiger.

He opened his eyes, raised his hands, smooth and

hairless, to his face – and the events of July Fourth started up in his head. They had become more an ever-present part of consciousness than memory – those hours in exquisite detail flashing by behind his eyes:

The call from Hall ... his pulse amping when he learned he would be working on, of all people, Geiger – the legend, master of their craft, the man called The Inquisitor ...

The session in Geiger's own space ... strapping him into the barber's chair, asking the only question Hall had provided – 'Where is the boy?' ... Invading Geiger's cheek with a white-hot awl ... hammering him with the bat ... slicing his quadriceps – and Geiger refusing to cave, unwilling to betray the boy he barely knew, or beg or even howl, as if he was immune to mortal pain ...

Then Geiger attacking, taking control, announcing that both of them were done with torture – then the smashing and shattering of his own fingers and metacarpals – the crisp, loud snapping of bone and the excruciating, unworldly pain ...

Geiger had become the center of his universe – the sun who ruled every thought, each decision. Geiger had instilled in him a new sense, something he'd never felt before. It had begun as a tiny seed, and bloomed. Now it was a beacon inside him. At first, it was vengeance – and now it had become something beyond that.

The lump beneath the hood moved slightly, just beside the ear. He gave it a tap, the thing buzzed and twitched – and the victim suddenly stiffened in its bonds, a muffled growl rising up from its throat. Tears slid from the corners of the eyes.

'There are questions I have to ask you.'

The eyes in the hood squeezed shut, cheeks tightening involuntarily – and the hornet stung again. The body pulled fiercely at its ties, and another groan pushed its way through the tape like a deeper echo of the first.

'I said try not to move.'

His palm suddenly swung up and walloped the victim's temple. The skull trembled from the shock. The hood darkened with crushed viscera. He brandished the antique scalpel and bent down, face to face.

'I'll be using this as my primary tool.' He put the instrument in his victim's palm. 'Go ahead. Hold it. It has a pleasing feel. Perfect balance.'

The eyes in the hood studied the man, trying to plumb the depth of his madness.

'It's remarkable how fate plays a hand. You see – you and I ... we have a – *common bond*, of sorts.' He grabbed the top of the hood and pulled it off. 'It's quite possible you already know who I am – but let me introduce myself. My name is Dalton.'

LEVEL EIGHT PROFILE

NAME: Unknown. Assumed alias – GEIGER
CLASS: Interrogator
CODE NAME: Inquisitor
AGE: Unknown. Presumed to be between 27 & 34 years
old
ORIGINAL CONTACT: Carmine Delanotte

USAGE:
DATE: 2/16/2004 CASE NAME: Black Nile LOCATION:
Cairo, Egypt
INTERROGATION SUBJECT: NARI KANEESH, 42,
Egyptian deputy minister – suspected of clandestine
meetings with Al Qaeda operatives
COMMENTS: Rating – 9.8. Superior intellect & stamina.
Psychologically-oriented methodology. (See attachment
for case detail – Deep Red clearance reqd.)

DATE: 7/3/2012 CASE NAME: De Kooning LOCATION:
New York, N.Y.
INTERROGATION SUBJECT: EZRA MATHESON, 12,
son of DAVID MATHESON – head of Veritas Arcana,
online whistleblower site
COMMENTS: Rating – N/A. (See attachment for case
detail – Deep Red clearance reqd.)

A slender thumb rose to the monitor and pressed flat
against the octagon at the bottom of the screen.
'IDENT' blinked twice, then a new document appeared.

CASE NAME: DE KOONING
7/3/2012– NYC: Contractors (RICHARD HALL,
MITCHELL CARNEY, RAYMOND BOYCE) seek
reacquire of classified video of CIA interrogs from
DAVID MATHESON (Veritas Arcana whistleblower).
Matheson eludes capture. Hall delivers Matheson's son,
EZRA, to GEIGER for interrog re: father. Geiger
absconds with child.

7/4/2012 Geiger captured. Interrog by DALTON re:
Ezra's whereabouts (significant damage inflicted).
Geiger compromises Dalton (see Dalton Debriefing) &
escapes. Contractors track Geiger, Ezra, HARRY
BODDICKER (aka THOMAS JONES) & LILY
BODDICKER to house of Dr. MARTIN CORLEY in Cold
Spring, N.Y. (No further intel.)

Excerpt from Cold Spring P.D. Incident Report: 'Thomas
Jones & Ezra Matheson stated 2 men committed home
invasion at 29 River Lane, house of Dr. Martin Corley.
During struggle one man fell from porch. Cause of
death: impalement on lawn lamp spike. 2nd man
abducted Ezra Matheson & attempted to escape in
rowboat. Boat capsized. No sign of bodies. Large
amount of blood found on boat dock.'

OUTCOME:
Video not re-acquired. Posted by D. MATHESON on
Veritas Arcana website 8/29/2012
HALL – missing, presumed dead; BOYCE – deceased
CARNEY – deceased.

9/3/2012 Blood Analysis results: Sample from boat dock (Cold Spring, N.Y.) matches sample from gauze in 'session room' following interrog of GEIGER by DALTON.
GEIGER – missing, presumed dead.

Part One

Part One

1

Racing through the night and drizzle, he was more a dark phantom than the living – black pullover and sweatpants, black Ghost GTX running shoes, black hair dyed brown and chopped to a one-inch cut, his beard nearly reaching his sharp cheekbones. To the few who knew him, he would be nearly unrecognizable. Thirty violins sang Mahler's passion and whipped themselves into a frenzy in his head. The streets' wet sheen made them look liquefied, bottomless. You might take a step and plummet, and never stop ...

... He remembered the madness beneath the river, the desperate, clutching bodies. He remembered finding Ezra's skinny arms, pulling the boy free of the scrum and shoving him to the surface. He remembered hands closing round his throat – and the waterlogged *ooof!* as his fist smashed into some boney part of Hall, feeling it break and cave.

He'd come out of the river, dragged himself up the bank and crawled toward a squat, dark outline in the mist. It was an old storage hut for the railroad, with a door hanging on one rusty hinge. Inside, he'd torn the pockets out of his sweatpants and stuffed them in the bullet hole in his chest and exit wound in his back, just below the scapula. He thought it likely he'd lose consciousness and didn't want to bleed out in his sleep.

The magnitude of pain was new, its presence unbordered, so he'd kept his mind drenched with Chopin – *Fantasie Impromptu, Prelude in E Minor* – trying to finesse the pain, negotiate instead of wage all-out war on fronts too wide to control. He slept most of the first two days, and when he went outside on the third night, he found a sleepy town a mile away, vegetable scraps in the garbage behind a diner, and an orphaned windbreaker and bottle of water on a dugout bench at a ballfield. On day five he left at dawn, and it took four hours to walk the two miles to the highway on his mutilated leg. He only stuck his thumb out for trucks, and the first that stopped took him all the way to the city . . .

Brooklyn was a mongrel jumble of edifice, ethnicity and class. Every turn seemed to transport him to someplace unconnected and alien. A shadowed stretch of warehouses and saggy-fenced lots became a well-lit block of townhouses with flat-screens and stuffed bookshelves behind windows, which morphed into a pocket of shabby check-cashing storefronts and grimy bodegas pouring reggaeton into the street, then around a corner came brick and chrome hipster restaurants and bars with neon 'Brooklyn Lager' signs.

He'd considered leaving, starting over. He'd gone to Richmond, Brattleboro, Boston, and stayed a few days – but they never took hold. New York was his planet, its singular gravity kept him tethered. Another place would not hold him in orbit. He could float into black space and drift like a broken satellite. And – he had a task to finish here.

It had taken months before he had healed sufficiently to run again. There was new pain, a prickly burn in the left quad under the fresh scars of Dalton's cuts. Coupled with the old issues in his hips and ankles, equilibrium was at times elusive – but the music, as always, helped the alchemist in him transform pain into pure sensation ... and power.

As the light turned green and he jogged into the deserted intersection, the strings reached their peak, and in his mind's eye strands of sound circled each other in a mating dance, then rushed into an embrace, fusing into a multicolored ribbon. The music was ripe. He tasted spearmint, strawberry – and heard the urgent snarl of the horn one second before the black, speeding mass entered his peripheral landscape, wrenching him around to a head-on view of the Dodge Dakota as it ignored the red light and barreled toward him. The streetlamps shone on the windshield, illuminating the three faces behind it – the widening eyes and stretching lips – then the driver jerked as he hammered the horn again and stomped the brake, and the vehicle flinched on the wet asphalt and went into a skid.

The tires' screech overpowered the strings, and he fought the drift of inner tumult. He'd been here before – caught unaware when the world snuck up on him, slowing the nature of things to an exquisite crawl. Perpetual motion broken into minute segments, falling dominos, connected but separate and distinct. Sounds spread like mercury on tilted glass, then lingered beyond their usual half-life. He put his hands out in front of him.

In the final moment, a thought surfaced that he found unexpected:

He wondered if someone had ever discovered his father's body on the mountain, trapped under the truck's tire, the knife deep in his heart. Geiger could feel the leather hilt in his child's hand as he'd pushed it in. More likely, wolves had devoured the flesh. Mountain lions and foxes had played with the bones, scattering them, the sun had dried the blood-soaked ground, and the wind had scraped the darkened dirt free and swept it away. All that was left of the man was what Geiger carried with him, inside and out – the demented rituals, the elegant circuitry of scars, the kinship of pain, the final declaration from pale, bleeding lips: *The world knows nothing of you. That is my gift to you, son. You are no one.*

The truck was upon him. In the front seat, the young woman between the two men covered her face with her hands. The tortured cry of tires died as the gleaming silver grill met Geiger's upheld palms – and stopped. Had there been witnesses, they might've thought he was some superhero able to stop speeding vehicles with his bare hands.

The door swung open and the driver hopped out. He looked a few hard years past twenty, had a beer bottle in hand, and wore a sweatshirt that read 'STAR SPAN-GLED BANGER!' in red, white and blue letters. He ran a hand across his buzz-cut, then spread his arms like a rainmaker about to pray to the sky.

'What the fuck, man? What the fuck're you doing, huh?'

Geiger straightened up. 'You drove through a red light,' he said.

Something about Geiger's smooth, uninflected tone put a grin on the man.

'Red light? This is fucking *Brooklyn*, man.'

'You should be more careful. It was a stupid thing to do.'

The man's smile held its ground. He glanced at the others. 'He says I'm stupid.'

The other man in the truck laughed, and threw an empty beer can through the open door at his friend. 'He's right, you dumb asshole!'

The driver turned back to Geiger, and held up his bottle. 'You made me spill my beer, man. It was almost full – my last one. Bummer.'

Since his return Geiger had kept face-to-face events to a minimum, but the man's chatter was firing his sensors, probing beneath the surface of words and tone for intent. Somewhere a fire engine was keening for a new tragedy. He took out his earbuds.

'You should get back in the truck now.'

'C'mon, Dougie,' said the woman. 'Let's go.'

'In a sec.' The driver was staring more intently now. 'You're not from around here – are you, man? We, uh – we drive around and, y'know, keep an eye on things in the nabe ... and I don't think I seen you before.' He cocked his head like a Doberman getting a whiff of hamburger. 'Hey ... Are you a moozle? Cuz – you sorta look like one.'

Geiger felt the pulse in his temples ticking like a clock. 'I don't know what a moozle is.'

'Sure ya do. Y'know ... *moozle*. Towel-head. Mosque

rat.' The man shrugged. 'A moozle.' He looked back at the other two. 'Looks kinda like one, don't he?'

'I guess,' said the man in the passenger seat. 'Sorta.'

'I'm not a Muslim,' said Geiger, 'so you can go now.'

'In a sec.' The man started across the asphalt in a chummy shuffle. Geiger's fingers started tapping against his thighs. The breath in his nostrils turned hot. The driver stopped inches from him and held up the bottle. 'Have a drink, yeah? Just so there's no hard feelings. I mean *moozles* can't drink – but you're not a moozle, so you can.'

'I don't drink.'

'C'mon ... not even a swig of Bud?' His grin had a lazy droop to it, like his heart wasn't really in it. His buddy stuck his head out of the passenger window.

'Are we cool here, Dougie – or what?' he asked.

Geiger felt the memory of the hundreds of fates held in his hands – the sweat of fear on skin, muscles tensing in alarm, wills succumbing to his touch. His inheritance, his expertise – the creation of pain ... the construction of suffering ... the extraction of truth ...

'Douglas,' Geiger said, 'get in the truck and leave.'

The last pretense of amity abandoned the man's face. 'Well how 'bout *you* get on your fucking camel ...' He planted his forefinger in Geiger's chest. '... and—'

Movement was so fast it precluded the man from making another sound. Geiger grabbed the collar and pulled him in, while his other hand latched onto a wrist and spun him around as he twisted the arm up behind the man. The bottle shattered at their feet.

Geiger's right arm locked round the neck and they stood pressed together, chest to back. Every time the man tried to move, Geiger hitched the arm higher – and the man stopped.

The young woman jumped out to the street. She wore a powder-blue version of the driver's sweatshirt. 'Dougie!'

The driver started to speak, but Geiger's forearm tightened round the throat and silenced him, and then he spoke very softly into the man's ear.

'Don't talk. Don't move. Relax.' There was a light touch to the words, an almost paternal promise in them. *Don't worry. There's nothing to be afraid of.*

The man riding shotgun got out, nervously grinding a fist into his other palm.

'Let him go!' said the woman. She reached into the front seat, and then straightened back up with an aluminum bat in hand. The green paint was scuffed in places. 'Right now, motherfucker!'

The man in Geiger's grasp chuckled coarsely. 'Meet my girlfriend, Abdul.'

Geiger was studying her – the straightness of her spine, how her fingers moved in a repetitive motion around the bat's neck. She knew the feel of it. She'd used it before.

The woman shot a look at her friend. 'Let's do this, Jamie.' He nodded, and the two started forward. Five strides, at the most.

Geiger leaned to the driver's ear. 'Douglas ... we have a change of plans.'

'Gonna let me go – huh, asshole?'

Geiger shifted his forearm, fingers curling stiffly, and dug into the front of the man's neck above the clavicle. The man's brain received an instant message from the brachial plexus – of a sudden, massive shock to the nervous system – and he blacked out and went rag-doll limp. Geiger's forearm kept him from falling. The others stopped with a synchronized flinch, as if they'd run into an invisible force-field.

'Jesus Christ . . .' slipped out of the other man.

The girlfriend raised the bat. 'Motherfucker! What'd you do to him?!'

'Douglas is unconscious.' He felt the smooth march of blood, saw the darkest part of him watching it all. The Inquisitor nodded at him. *There are numerous applications of pain.* 'You both need to get back in the truck.' *There is pressure, blunt force, application of intense heat and cold, manipulation of joints . . .* 'Do what I tell you.'

The woman put the bat on her shoulder. Confusion and awe tugged at an eyebrow.

'Who the fuck *are* you?'

Geiger parsed her timbre and cadence and found as much fear as fury, which was a good thing.

'Put the bat down, get in the truck – and close the doors. When I've gone, give Douglas a few slaps on the cheeks and move his head side to side. He'll wake up.'

The second man was shaking his head like a bystander at the scene of an accident.

'Did you two hear what I said?' Geiger's voice was that of a patient teacher in a rowdy classroom, and it made his students look at him with something akin to dread.

'Motherfucker,' snarled the woman, and dropped the bat. The second man gratefully took it as a cue, and they walked to the truck, got in and slammed the doors.

Geiger dragged the body to the corner farthest from the truck, watching them watch him. He lowered the driver to the sidewalk and propped him against a lamp-post. He could smell oily smoke starting to crowd the air. A second fire engine's siren called out to the first, like a beast seeking a mate. Something was burning down close by.

Geiger put his earbuds back in place and resumed his run. He took a different route each time – and had another half-hour before he got there. Dylan's sand-paper rasp was in his ears. *'Something is happening here and you don't know what it is – do you, Mr. Jones?'*

2

In this jam-packed, crazy-quilt, rackety part of the city, the *crack!* jolting Harry Boddicker out of his doze could have been any number of things – a car backfire, a shout, a gunshot – but his mind thought the sound was a salvo of fireworks ... because the dream he'd been trapped in, as was often the case, was about July Fourth. He'd fallen asleep in the folding chair on the fire escape outside his fourth-floor walkup on Henry Street in Chinatown – the perch where he now observed life on Planet Earth. He could have been a gargoyle on a ledge peering down at the shifting, joyful madness.

He'd had two reasons for making Chinatown his new home. The density of people on the streets gave him hope that on the rare times he went out his odds for anonymity would be bettered – and his favorite dim sum restaurant was a block away. Still, the world had become much too small a place – so small his hideaway life seemed little more than a futile postponement of the inevitable. They would find him. *They* might change in personage – Hall, Mitch and Ray were dead – but they would all be very good at their job, and someday he'd get a tap on the shoulder or a sap on the skull because, as Geiger had said – *they never stop*. And a day after Geiger had spoken those words he was dead.

Harry's sadness had a sharp, fine edge. For nine months, it had been honed by the loss of Geiger, his partner and only friend, and Lily, his sister. It was a shard lodged within him, cutting him with every movement – even as subtle as a breath. And sleep offered no respite. Awake, he had mastered the skill of squelching the images when they sprang up – but he was helpless in dreams to escape the replays of that July Fourth night ...

... The livid sky punctured by pyrotechnics ... Geiger standing at the dock's end, battered, bloodied, watching the rowboat drift into the Hudson River with Hall and Ezra ... then Lily rising from the depths, grabbing the boat's gunwale, capsizing it ... everyone disappearing beneath the surface ... and Geiger diving in as Harry hobbled down the dock, helpless, useless – watching the union of fate and chaos ... the river foaming with turmoil – then one gasping soul rising up and swimming to shore. The boy. Ezra. With the gym bag of torture videos clutched in his hand ...

Without Geiger to stabilize Harry's orbit, without the work and reason to put on his stickler-for-detail hat – time was thoughtless. It made him vulnerable to pricks of memory, and his exiled past had sensed its chance, mustered its army, and overthrown the present. Now he spent much of his life in the company of ghosts, a melancholy congregation – those who had left by choice, and those who'd had no say in the matter. They looked to him. They asked unanswerable questions.

The buzzer rang inside and Harry leaned over the railing and looked down. The delivery man was on the stoop. He rose with a grunt and stepped through the window, into the living room, went to the door and pressed the intercom.

'That you, Cheng?'

'Yes, Mr. Jones, sir.'

He hit the buzzer. He'd come to the conclusion that mayhem was cheap – the gods had overstocked inventory and tossed it down as often as possible. He lived on the cash in his Citibank safe deposit box, addicted to Pepcids, fighting a return to his pre-Geiger drinking form – and hadn't been back to his apartment in Brooklyn Heights, his cherished sanctum, since the Independence Day massacre. It wasn't a stretch to think there was a file with Harry's name and address in the database of some ice-for-blood honcho in the CIA or NSA or some other lethal three-letter cadre. He could see the lush trees lining his old street, rolling out their thick shadows – and imagined someone standing cloaked within them, staring at his second-floor windows, waiting for his return.

He craved the company of others. Early on he'd considered getting a job, putting himself in the crosshairs of the public eye, just to pass some time with people – but then he'd imagined the job interview, sitting across from someone perusing his résumé.

'You have a BA from CCNY, 1989 – superior skills in computer programming – reporter for the *New York Times* from 1991 till 1997, worked in Obituaries from

'97 until 2001. Very impressive, Mr. Jones. Have you been employed since then?' And Harry could answer – 'Well, yes. I was a partner in a very successful entrepreneurial venture. IR.'

'"IR"? I'm not familiar with that field.'

'*Information Retrieval.* Our start-up capital was provided by Carmine Delanotte, a Mafia don – and I was the business manager for the greatest torturer in the world. So ... do I get the job?'

Harry scratched at his beard – he'd grown it for camouflage, but hated its itch – and looked glumly around the room: the buckled walls, the east-west crack in the ceiling, the meagerly stuffed corduroy chair, the folding card table with his MacBook, the dented Sears minifridge and stained two-burner oven of unknown origin.

'Long fucking way from Brooklyn Heights, Harry.'

Having conversations with himself was another new habit. He missed talking to someone, because being heard was being known. Most of all, he missed Geiger – their diner breakfasts two or three times a week, their mutual, obsessive dedication to detail, the man's unworldly calm, his unknowableness right until the end – a man whose genius was acquiring truth through torture but who gave his life to save a child he barely knew.

Eleven years.

What they had done was always with him now. The list of those who had suffered was long. That most had stepped out of a catalogue of the seven sins, and that Geiger had never shed blood – those facts were only a weak salve for Harry's shame. Still – had anyone asked, he wouldn't have denied he keenly missed the ritual of the work. Being the gatekeeper with those who sought Geiger's gifts ... using his own singular skills to create the dossiers of potential clients and targets – navigating the internet's dark alleys in search of pieces of a life, then stitching them together so Geiger had a detailed picture of who he would be dealing with before accepting a job ... negotiating what price truth was trading at on a given day with the client ... creating transcripts from the interrogation sessions' DVDs, looking away as often as possible as he typed ... and collecting his 25 percent, tax free ...

There was a knock. Harry turned the three locks and opened up, leaving the extra-long chain he'd put on attached. The extra two inches of links allowed a large-enough gap for a bag of dim sum to fit through. He stayed behind the door out of sight.

'Cheng?'

'It me, Mr. Jones, sir.' A brown paper bag came through the opening. 'Usual, Mr. Jones, sir.'

Harry took the bag, fished a five and a ten out of his pocket and held them out below the chain, and a hand took it.

'Thank much, Mr. Jones, sir.'

'You're welcome. So, uh – how's business, Cheng?'

'Deliver all time, Mr. Jones. All time. Never stop. Business good.'

'That's good. Good to hear.' Harry sighed. 'How's Mr. Han doing?'

'He fine.'

'Is the restaurant gonna do that—'

'Must go now, Mr. Jones. Busy. Very very busy. Bye.'

Harry heard footsteps go slowly down the steps, and

smiled. Cheng wasn't in a hurry. He just didn't want to stand in the hall talking to the weird guy who never took the latch off. He flipped the locks, sat at the table and took the Styrofoam box and plastic fork out of the bag. The nightly ritual – closing his eyes, opening the lid, taking in the aroma of his cha siu baau. He was not beyond certain pleasures, few though they might be.

An icon of a washing machine began to glow on his laptop. '*Clean. Dry?*' appeared beneath it. He tapped it and stared at the delicate profile of Ezra Matheson, sitting in his bedroom. Harry could see the boy's violin lying on the bed behind him.

'Hey, kid,' he said.

Ezra's face softened with feeling. 'Hi, Harry.'

A brake pressed down on Harry's pulse, slowing it, giving each beat a richer thud. Each time they spoke, it struck Harry how the nine months had changed the boy. It was more than the unstoppable bloom of youth. The hollow curve of his cheeks looked ill-matched to his widening face. The dark under his eyes stole some of the luster from their bright emerald. Harry was loath to accept it. Ezra looked *haunted*.

'Mom went out to get some stuff. This an okay time?'

'Sure.'

The boy's mother had decreed that he was to have no contact with his father or Harry unless she was present – so the secret chats happened once every two or three weeks, using software Harry had created with painstaking detail fueled by paranoia. It was some of his best work.

July Fourth had all been about getting Ezra back to his mother. Harry, Geiger, Lily and Ezra had ended up at the apartment of Martin Corley, Geiger's psychiatrist – a ragged, besieged troop – and Corley had given them the keys to his car and his home upstate in Cold Spring. That would be the site of the mother-son rendezvous, their 'safe house' – but by the time Ezra's mother had arrived, there was only the boy and Harry alive to greet her.

After the catastrophe in Cold Spring, when the police had run out of questions, Harry, Ezra and his furious, grateful mother had driven back to the city, to Corley's apartment, where Harry had told the psychiatrist a tale of death and watched something wither inside the man. Mother and son flew home to California, only to discover Ezra had brought a flock of stowaway demons with him – nightmares, sudden bursts of tears, hours sitting in silence – and after a month they'd moved back to New York, into the brownstone on West Seventy-fifth Street where they had lived until the divorce, so Ezra could be in therapy with Corley. His mother felt that Corley, having been Geiger's shrink, would create some comfort zone for the boy – and Corley agreed.

The boy let loose with a sigh. 'Good to see you, Harry.'

'You look good, Ez. The stache is coming along.'

Ezra rubbed the paltry wisps of hair on his lip and frowned. 'Oh man ... It looks *sooo* lame – but Mom won't let me start shaving it yet.'

They needed the chats because they needed each other. They shared the loneliest of things – loss and guilt, like the only survivors to walk away from a plane wreck.

'Ez ... talked with Dad lately?'

The boy's face tightened like a fist. 'No. Screw him – and Dr. Corley says I'm allowed to still be this pissed.'

'Gotcha.' Harry had learned to only ask that question once.

'I'm gonna go see a movie tomorrow,' said Ezra. 'Wanna meet me?'

'You know I can't do that, Ez.'

'Yeah, well . . . I keep asking.' The boy's grin grabbed and twisted something inside Harry. 'I figure one of these days maybe you'll stop being a totally crazy person and realize somebody isn't gonna grab you if you walk down the street.'

'Paranoid is the proper term, Ez. I'm not crazy, I'm paranoid.'

'I know what paranoid means, Harry. You are wayyyy past that. But don't worry. I still think you're cool.'

'You playing your axe, kid?'

'Uh-huh. A lot.'

'Guess you'll be hitting the concert circuit pretty soon then, huh?'

'Yeah, right. That's me. Wanna be my manager? Go on the road together?'

'I'm there, kid.' They shared a slow smile, and Harry hid a sigh. His list of small talk had shrunk to nothing. All that was left was the colossal presence hovering between them, the person that would bind them together forever.

'So . . . you're doing okay, huh?' he said instead.

Ezra shrugged. 'Yeah. Sometimes. I still have the nightmare. Y'know . . . in the boat with Hall. Tipping over. Going under. Dr. Corley says they'll stop when I

understand it wasn't – my fault.' The last two words
limped out – wretched, unwanted stragglers, runts of
the litter. 'Only thing is – it *was* my fault.' His eyes suddenly glistened, and tears started down his pale cheeks.
'Shit, I'm sorry,' he said, and tried to wipe them away.

Harry felt the gathering of ghosts again – sad, mute
witnesses. Of all the loss and wreckage, this was the
worst of it – the boy, with a ponderous chain of others'
sins around his slender neck. His father's, Harry's,
Geiger's, Hall's ... and so many others.

'Ez, we've talked about this. Listen to me. Hall *kidnapped* you. You didn't do one single thing.'

They'd been here before. Harry considered playing
the 'if' game again ...

If your father hadn't gotten hold of the torture
videos, Geiger would be alive.

If Harry had read Hall's job request on the website
and decided not to follow it up, Geiger would be alive.

If Geiger had turned down the job when Harry presented it to him, he would still be alive.

... but instead, Harry just said, 'It *isn't* your fault,
Ez.'

'Then why is he dead, Harry?' Ezra looked stricken,
sick with remorse. 'He jumped into the river to save *me*,
Harry. He died saving *me*. God ... I can feel his hands
grabbing me, pulling me free, shoving me up to the surface ...'

Ezra sniffled. Guilt is not something children are
meant to feel in great strengths. They've not developed
antibodies against the virus. They are helpless against
the spread of infection. The boy's shoulders did a slow
rise in time with his sigh.

'I see him, y'know.'

'What do you mean – 'see him'?'

'Happens all the time. He's crossing the street …
walking out of a store. I mean – it isn't *him* – just somebody who looks like him, but for a second I think—'

'Ezra, I'm back! Dinner in ten!' It was a woman's
voice.

The boy's head snapped to the side. 'Shit … gotta go.
Bye.' He grabbed the top of the laptop and swung it
down. The screen went dark.

'Bye,' Harry mumbled, felt the familiar flinch of help-
lessness in his gut, and pushed his dinner away. So much
damage. Pieces of them all, scattered over the land.

Everything was broken.

3

The lights were set on dim. The video freeze-frame on the center screen of the monitor bank was a street study of light and dark grays – looking down on figures waiting to be set loose into action. The rest of the room was a fuzzy netherworld of unknown dimensions. The tech pulled at his moustache while he did a habitual, back-and-forth rock in his task chair. It squeaked with each motion.

'Stop,' she said from the shadows behind him, and put a hand on the top of chair's back, freezing it. 'Do not do that.'

He straightened his glasses on his nose and pointed at the screen. 'Where'd this come from?'

'One of our ex-contractors works for NYPD in surveillance. He saw this, had a hunch – thought we might like to see it.' She leaned down over his shoulder for a closer look.

'Basic urban surveillance setup,' the tech said. 'Cameras on lampposts. Most people don't even notice them. Low-rez. Lots of bleed. You can get this stuff online at Spies-R-Us.' He glanced at her, hoping for a grin. She smelled really good.

'You smell good. Lavender?'

She turned her head the minimal amount of degrees to ensure eye contact.

'Willie, I'm tired. If you hit on me I will hit you back, and it won't be a figurative gesture. It will hurt much more than having to listen to one of your dumb lines. Yes?'

'Yup,' he said, and straightened up in the chair.

She was used to it. She'd always known she was pretty – ripe cheekbones and an aquiline nose framed by wavy, sand-colored hair – but it was her eyes, a rare violet, like amethyst, and bizarrely bright. 'Liz Taylor eyes', her mother called them. They'd been a curse all her life. When she was a child, relatives and friends were forever leaning huge faces down into hers, crunching her cheeks – 'Look at those *eyes*!' When puberty came knocking, every female body in her grade seemed to bend and curve except hers – but her eyes stopped every testosterone-soaked teen in his tracks. Now, in her job, they were an unwanted feature, a marker – and could lead to trouble far more dangerous than wrestling in the backseat of a car. She took hazel contact lenses with her when she went into the field.

'Let's go, champ,' she said. 'Do your stuff.'

The tech punched the console and the surveillance video began to play in slo-mo. A lean figure, dressed in black, jogged into an intersection, his back to the camera.

'He's got some kind of limp,' the tech said. 'Works around it, sort of.'

'Yes, he does.'

They watched the runner reach the middle of the intersection when a truck bore down on him. He turned, face not quite three-quarters to the camera. The tech stopped the video, isolated Geiger's face with a visual grid and enlarged it, bringing it up full-screen.

'Nah,' said the tech. 'We can do better.' He let the event continue at quarter-speed – Geiger center-stage, stock-still. 'So who is this guy?'

'That's why I'm here, Willie – to find that out.'

Next month would be her four-year anniversary with Deep Red. The government had recruited her straight out of college, and she'd gone over to Deep Red sixteen months later. Like everyone else in the group, she had known of Geiger – the best interrogator in the world – but had never worked with him. Last year, after the torture videos disaster, Deep Red had classified him as 'Missing, presumed dead'– but they all knew the label really meant 'We have no fucking idea what happened to him . . .'

In the surveillance video, Geiger grabbed the driver, spun him round and took control.

The tech nodded. 'Nice move.'

She had been the one who debriefed Dalton post-event, she'd read the Level Eight Profile, and she'd talked to one of the team that had used Geiger in Cairo back in 2004 – but she still didn't have a feel for the layers or depth of the *man* . . .

The driver's body suddenly slumped, lifeless, in Geiger's grasp.

The tech sat up. 'Wow! You see that?'

'Play it back and enlarge.'

The tech reversed the video, magnified the men – and they watched again.

'Watch his hand, Willie. See that? Pressure point. Brachial plexus.'

Geiger turned – and the tech stabbed the keyboard. 'There!' He isolated Geiger's face again, blew it up and filled the large flat-screen with it. The slate-gray eyes above the pitch-black beard stared out at them, past them. It reminded her of a falcon's gaze, taking in whole vistas without missing one tiny detail. It belonged up in the sky. She handed the tech a DVD. He slid it into the console and the adjacent screen lit with a freeze-frame:

In a windowless, bunker-like room, a swarthy, bearded man lay strapped onto a gurney, dressed only in soiled boxers, shiny with sweat, his face and body spotted with welts and cuts. A man in a short-sleeved white shirt and khaki shorts stood beside him.

'Hey,' said the tech. 'I've seen this. This is the secret interrogation Veritas Arcana put on the web – right? The stuff in Cairo …'

'Run it.'

The man in the khaki shorts came alive and stroked his clipped goatee.

'Nari … meet your new friend – the Inquisitor,' he said, and Geiger walked into frame in a white T-shirt and slacks. He put two fingers to the victim's neck, as a doctor would check a pulse. The prisoner smoldered as he spoke with a thick Middle Eastern accent.

'I cannot tell you any more than I already—'

Geiger's fingers dug into the flesh beneath the jaw. 'You're right, Nari, you will not tell me anything – now.' His voice had the feel of satin and the sound of dominion. 'Later you will, but it isn't time yet. For now, it's best you don't speak at all.'

Nari's eyes registered surprise and confusion. 'But peace is what I was trying to—'

Geiger's grip tightened, rendering the man mute. 'Not a word, Nari.' His fingers dug deeper, and the prisoner's grimace stretched so wide it looked like a smile. 'Nod if you understand me?'

The prisoner shook his head. 'One question,' he rasped. 'One.'

Nothing moved on Geiger's face – more a painted canvas than body and soul. Then he nodded and removed his hand. Nari cleared his throat. The thin, crooked tendrils of tension at the corners of his eyes straightened.

'Tell me,' he said. 'What else is a man to say when he speaks the truth and is not believed?'

Geiger blinked, once. 'That is what I am here to find out.'

'Jeez ...' said the tech. 'That is one icy dude. What's the name again?'

'Geiger.'

'And you think it's him in Brooklyn? Hmm ... Maybe.' He started toggling the second video, fast and slow, looking for a matching angle. 'Didn't Veritas Arcana say he was dead?'

In the video, Geiger started to walk the room in a slow circle, fingers tapping rhythmically on his thighs. The tech leaned forward.

'Keep going ... keep going ... and turrrrnnn – now!' Geiger came around to camera and the tech whacked a key. 'Gotcha!' He turned the face into a full-screen freeze the same size as its neighbor. 'Which way you wanna go on this?'

'The street shot. Lose the beard and give him back his hair.'

Both heads took on a floating, three-dimensional quality as the tech matched angles, and blue dots started popping up on Geiger's bearded face, white lines connecting them, a malleable web shifting by minute degrees. He played with the lighting, equalizing brightness and shadow. He made Geiger's hair grow four inches in a second.

'Too long?'

'No. But make it wavier.'

She felt the pony-trot kick in her veins, telling her body something before her brain was certain. If it *was* him, she already had her next move. That was her strong suit. Big picture, don't miss the details. He was a runner, and there was ritual written all over his stride, so she'd get all the NYPD surveillance vids for Brooklyn. There were hundreds of cameras, thousands of hours to view – so how far back should she go? It was nine months since Dalton had carved him up ... he would've needed at least four or five months to heal before he could run again. Going back to November would do it. She'd find him on the videos and track him. She might not nail the place where he lived, but she'd get close. A neighborhood. A street. A block ...

The tech raised a finger. 'And now, as they say in Brooklyn – *Voila*!' He tapped a key and Street-Geiger's beard disappeared. Then the network of lines and dots was gone.

She stared at the giant faces. Two Geigers. A match.

It was him. The rush in her pulse became a stallion's kick. She wanted chocolate. Desperately. Her reward.

'Why do you want to find him?' asked the tech. 'They want to take him out?'

'They didn't tell me.' She stretched with a soft grunt. 'Nice work, Willie.'

'Thanks.' He gave her a grin. 'I, uh, always aim to please – y'know?'

She looked down at him, deadpan. Then she nodded. 'I get it. That was a borderline-cute throwaway with some sexual innuendo for a kicker.'

The tech shrugged. 'Sorry. I can't help it.'

She smiled, and patted his hair like she would a puppy. 'I know, Willie. I know.' Then she whacked him on the back of the head so hard it sent his glasses into his lap.

'Owww! Jeez, Zanni—'

'Sorry,' she said. 'I can't help it.' She turned and went out a door. The tech put his glasses back on, and grinned with equal parts admiration and lust.

'Fantastic,' he said.

The tub water was getting cold, but she liked it that way. She'd been re-reading the transcript of her debriefing of Dalton. She'd forgotten it was so long. Dalton had been on heavy painkillers for a day before she could get to him, and his answers had made Hamlet look tongue-tied – but she'd let him huff and ramble because she'd had the feeling he'd completely lose it if she'd tried to rein him in. Both his hands were in casts to his elbows because Geiger had demolished them, and his jaw was wired because Geiger had broken it – and his slurp and grumble added to the bizarre spectacle. She remembered sitting across from him, listening to him, thinking – *This is someone who should be kept away from people and other living things.*

Zanni went back a few pages and scanned one.

SOAMES: All right. You used the awl and the bat on him, to seemingly little effect. Then what?

DALTON: A straight razor. It was his. I found it there at his place before he came to. He had all this stuff — amazing stuff he used in the work. The man's mind was incredible. But the razor — it was beautiful. Antique. Had an inscription — a 'From Jane with love to Jack' kind of thing. I can't remember the real names. But I saw all the scars on him, the cuts, and I started thinking somebody had used the razor on him when he was a kid.

SOAMES: What kind of scars?

DALTON: What kind? Jesus ... You've never seen anything like it. Dozens of them up and down the backs of both legs. Perfect, precise. It was a thing of beauty. Really. A work of art. When I started using it on him, he went into a kind of trance, and said some things. 'Your blood, my blood, our blood' ... 'It didn't hurt, father' — so I think his old man was the one who cut him. A ritual, for years. Maybe Mom watched. Who knows?

```
SOAMES: Anything else?
DALTON: Is there any word on him?
SOAMES: Geiger?
DALTON: Yes. Geiger.
SOAMES: We think he's dead.
DALTON: You're wrong. He isn't dead.
SOAMES: Why? Is there something you know?
DALTON: He can't be dead.
SOAMES: Why not?
DALTON: Because. He's indestructible.
```

Zanni remembered Dalton's smile when he said it. '*He's indestructible.*' It was not something she'd forget.

She dropped the papers to the floor. What does a child do with that kind of suffering and abuse? Do you become an alchemist and turn it into something else? She grabbed a few Raisinets from the bowl on the rim of the tub and tossed them in her mouth. Was it a *What doesn't kill you makes you stronger* thing? Is that who Geiger was – taken to the nth degree? Did anything actually *get* to him?

She slid farther down and turned so her cheek rested against the cool porcelain, and closed her eyes. She wanted the release, but was tired and wished she didn't have to do all the work. It'd been months since a man had touched her, so long that she had gone through her small cache of fantasies three or four times. Her hand slid down into the water, between her thighs. She tried to decide whether Geiger looked sexier with or without the beard ...

4

Geiger stood with his back against the session room wall in overalls, long fingers tapping his thighs like frisky creatures that had crawled up his legs and attached themselves to his wrists. Hidden speakers delivered an audio loop – a snare drum and cymbal in crisp four-four time. On random beats the snare would hit a millisecond early or late, just enough to produce an unsettling mental flinch in the listener. He had brought the lights down to a murky dimness, so the Jones in the barber's chair was a smudged silhouette and, more to the point, so was Geiger. He was dealing with a razor-sharp intellect, and Geiger wanted to blur the edges of things.

'You've been Mr. Redding's financial consultant for how long?'

'Eight years. But you know that.' The Jones's voice had a thick, froggy quality. And he was right – Geiger did know – because his dossier had been extensive. Geiger knew the man suffered from vertigo and acid reflux and had made him drink a potion – 20 percent sodium hydroxide solution mixed with club soda and molasses. Geiger wanted him in a state of familiar distress, only heightened, and had asked the question because he wanted to hear the man speak, to gauge the extent of the irritant's effect.

'What happens when we're done?' asked the Jones.

'When I retrieve the information, you're put back in the trunk and returned to the client.'

'Then what?'

'That isn't my concern. It's not part of the job.'

It was '*Then what?*' that Geiger wanted to hear. He was the master builder, and each response was brick and mortar for the house of fear he was building. Everything mattered in IR, and '*Then what?*' meant the Jones was thinking beyond the present, considering events to come – possibilities more chilling than the now, more terminal in their nature. It was a useful building-block for the construction.

The Jones coughed, which set off a deep wince. 'So when the trunk closes – that's it for you? Out of sight, out of mind. No guilt?'

Geiger's voice was a silk scarf wrapped around his answer. 'About what?'

That brought an elegant curve to the Jones's lips. In another place and time, it might have looked like a wistful smile, but now it struck Geiger as profoundly mournful.

'I had a lot of guilt – at the start,' the man said, 'but you can get used to just about anything, don't you think?'

Geiger homed in on the tone. Ennui? Remorse? Enlightenment? 'It's interesting you say that, Charles – because that concept is crucial to what goes on in this room.'

Geiger hadn't asked where the money was. It wasn't time yet. He pushed a button on the wall. The lights came up full-power, the shiny white linoleum surfaces of the room put out a jarring gleam – and the Jones clamped his eyes shut with a sideways wince.

'"Now is the winter of my discontent,"' he said, and slowly opened his eyes. A flicker of corrupt wisdom flared in them. 'And it's been a very, very long winter.'

His toned body, naked except for plaid briefs, was strapped to the chair at the neck, ankles and wrists with steel-mesh belts. His curled, silver-flecked hair was a crown atop a face that showed more than a hint of excess. Geiger had his take on him: world-weary, a keen intelligence that often complements amorality, and, most importantly – a simmering resignation. Geiger wouldn't have to create that feeling – just bring it to a boil. He walked to him and put two fingers on the jugular. The Jones's heart seemed unperturbed at the situation.

'This where the pain starts?' asked the Jones. 'The laying on of hands?'

'Charles, what you need to understand is – being here is not primarily about pain. A man once said – "Pain is just the messenger. It reminds us of *why* we hurt."'

'Do you think I need to be reminded of why I'm here?'

'I'm not just speaking of your crimes. The more important point is – you put yourself here. Almost every Jones ends up here for the same reason: They want the world to make them more than they are.' Fingers of Geiger's left hand started tapping a triad.

A sigh drifted out of the man's lips. It sounded like the tide gliding up to shore.

'Redding's just one of a dozen,' he said, and the act of swallowing clearly hurt. 'I've stolen almost fifteen mill, all told.' There was no boast in the statement.

'Irrelevant information. I don't need to know that,' said Geiger, and took the Jones's left hand in his. 'It's important you be focused, Charles, so watch closely.' He put his thumb on the fleshy webbing between the thumb and forefinger. 'The thenar space.' He pressed his thumb into it. 'Applied pressure is said to relieve pain in the head and back.' He moved his thumb to the space between the third and fourth metacarpals. 'But move just one inch, to the lumbrical muscles . . .' He shoved his thumb in and the Jones arched violently against his binds as a doggish growl bounced from one wall to another.

Geiger let go. The man was breathing deeply through his mouth, trying to flush the pain away, but it only worsened the fire in his esophagus. Geiger leaned down nose to nose.

'If you offer unsolicited information in this room, it is unacceptable. Focus is essential.'

He gave the barber's chair a push, and it began to whirl round, completing each cycle in about two seconds. The Jones began to moan and squeezed his eyes shut.

'Keep your eyes open, Charles. You are not allowed to close your eyes.'

The man's lids rose over skittish eyeballs. The flush on his face was draining, red turning to stark white. His breath took on a ragged rhythm. His vertigo was kicking in.

'I'm going to throw up . . .'

'If you close your eyes – what follows will be worse.' Geiger's head turned until the vertebrae clicked. 'Keep your eyes on me. The world is a blur, except for me.'

The Jones's chin dipped to his chest like a sad drunk. 'Stop it – please!'

'I need to see that you are focused, Charles. Right now, I am the only anchor you have. Look at me. Find me every time you come around.'

The man's head rose like a puppet's. 'Christ ... I'm gonna black out ...'

'Look at me.'

'Jesus ...' The slow, breathy release of the word stripped it of meaning. It sounded primal, nonlingual. Another revolution finished.

'Look at me.'

'I am!'

Designs of light flashed on his steel-mesh restraints as the Jones spun. The audio loop's drum and cymbal tried to enforce a cadence on the fluid motion, and Geiger considered the flow of time, and man's need to break it down into finite increments – to measure what has no size, to control what has no form, so at any moment he can declare it exactly so many seconds and minutes of an hour in a month of a year – and he thought of his clockless, timeless childhood, when nothing was measured but the precise allocation of pain. He stepped forward and grabbed the chair. The Jones swallowed between short, coarse huffs. The skin of his cheeks and forehead glistened in the lights.

'Do you still feel like you want to vomit?' Geiger said,

and watched surprise and slow realization dawn in the Jones's eyes.

'No,' he said. 'I don't.'

'Good.' Geiger glanced at the chrome cart and its display – a bat wrapped with foam rubber, a Smith and Wesson six-inch Tanto knife, and a SeaChoice air horn. The Jones's gaze followed his. Geiger was certain none of the implements would come into play, but the Jones didn't know that. He began to stroll the room's perimeter.

'We will get to the truth, Charles – perhaps in more ways than one might assume.' He hit a button on a wall panel and the audio ceased. 'You are a highly intelligent man. Has it occurred to you – that what happens from this point on depends almost entirely on you?'

The Jones laughed grimly, and it set off a short hacking fit. 'So I'm the one calling the shots, huh?'

'I wasn't speaking about control. I was speaking of cause and effect. Do you understand the difference?'

Geiger had created categories for everything that occurred during a session. Initial body languages, muscular and facial responses to interrogation, vocal tones and rhythms, emotional manifestations, delay and misdirection tactics, forms of denial – eighteen categories in all, each containing dozens of variations. He was an ever-evolving, living text on torture – student, historian, expert. But as he watched the embezzler's head cock a few degrees, and the emerging smile – he didn't think they fit into a particular grouping.

'I'll make you a deal,' said the Jones.

'Negotiation isn't part of the process.'

'I'm not negotiating. I'll tell you what you want to

know,' the man said. 'I know how this ends. I've known for years. I just didn't know when. That's the tricky part – not knowing *when*. So how's this? I ask a question and you answer, then *you* ask a question and I answer, and so on – and in the end you get what you need. That's fair, right?'

Again, Geiger studied the voice – sifting through it for signs of manipulation. The man had made a career out of duplicity ... But he saw an opening, and a path. Unorthodox, but expedient.

'What do you want to ask me?'

The Jones's smile broadened. 'Have you ever been wrong?'

'In what sense?'

'You finished a job, gave the client the information they wanted – and at some point the client calls and says the information was wrong. That what you believed was the *truth* – was a *lie*. That kind of wrong.'

'No. Where is the money you embezzled from Mr. Redding, Charles?'

The Jones didn't hesitate. 'Falstead Channel Islands Bank and Cayman Royal Bank. Three accounts in each.' He sighed, and his head listed a few degrees. Geiger was uncertain why. Maybe exhaustion – or relief.

'How do you do it?' asked the man.

'How is it I haven't been wrong?' Geiger turned his head to the left until he got a *click*. 'Do you know how a piano is tuned?'

'No.'

'The piano tuner uses a tuning fork, today often an

electronic device, to set one note out of eighty-eight to the correct pitch, usually A above middle C – then, by ear, tunes every other note in relation to that first note. If the harmonics don't coincide perfectly, a master tuner can hear it – can feel the slightest fluctuations in the air. In IR, Charles, truth is A above middle C, and I have perfect pitch. I know a lie when I hear it.' His head turned right. *Click*. 'What are the names and numbers on the accounts?'

'The name on the Cayman Island accounts is Earl Kent. K – E – N – T. The Channel Island accounts' name is Byron Keats. K – E – A – T – S. I don't remember the account numbers, but they aren't necessary. Go online to the banks, enter the account name and the password – Richard The Third – one word, no spaces ... and you're in.'

Geiger stepped forward until his knees almost touched the man's. His gray eyes were still. The whole world was silent. Then his right hand rose from his side and reached toward the man. The Jones's fear reflex pushed him back against the seatback.

'Woah, woah ... I was telling the truth.'

Geiger's hand rested on the man's neck. 'I know,' he said, and undid the strap. The man rolled his head – and Geiger started toward the door of the viewing room.

'That's it?' said the Jones. 'No more questions? We're done?'

'I'm not a confidant, Charles – or a priest.' Geiger reached for the doorknob.

'Maybe you are. Maybe you're my father confessor. Ever think of it that way?'

Geiger stopped. He had never spoken to a Jones after the retrieval, but he was turning round now. 'Is there something else you have to tell me, Charles?'

The man's countenance softened. 'I have a hundred things to tell you. A *thousand* things. And – I have one last question.'

Geiger felt the pull of the supplication, despair tugging at his sleeve, and came back to the Jones.

'All right. Ask me one last question.'

The Jones's eyes suddenly took on a flat gloss of lifelessness – a dead man's eyes, wide open, powerless to ever close again.

'Tell me,' the man said. 'Do you remember *her*?'

Geiger awoke. The muscles in the back of his neck were growing taut, and the dots of light were floating around him. The post-dream/pre-migraine aura had come to call, on schedule. He sat up on the mattress and stood. The floor's concrete was cold, the sealant smooth like new ice, and the planet accommodated his listing as he walked to his desk and sat down. The chair's leather was cool against his bare skin. He clicked on his laptop's icon of a microphone. He didn't know how far he'd get before the storm hit – the hot tendrils were starting to wend their way down from the top of his skull.

'Dream seventeen,' he said.

Since July Fourth his ritual of recurrent dreams had continued, but their nature had changed – no longer a child's quests to unknown destinations where his body ultimately, literally, fell apart. Now, they were authentic replays of past IR sessions – until some demon driver took the wheel and steered them down a route of shadows into another realm, always to the same denouement. The same question. It was as if the river's blunt, cold power had flicked off one switch in his subconscious and turned another on.

He sat back and closed his eyes. Without Dr. Corley in his life, Geiger had been keeping a verbal record of the new dreams in an attempt to simulate the psychiatrist's presence and guidance – as if he was lying on the leather couch with Corley sitting behind him, legs crossed, pen and pad in hand, his questions soft, simple steps down a path.

Was this dream like the others?

'Yes ... another IR session – completely realistic, until it shifts.'

You often use that word – shift – when you describe the dreams.

'There's a point where I can feel the texture starting to change.'

An actual physical sensation?

'Like a pulling. Like changing gears.'

And the Jones asked the question?

'The last thing he said, like they all do: "Do you remember *her*?"'

Can you get back in that moment – and describe your reaction. Anything – physical, emotional, cerebral ...

'I woke up as soon as he said it, before I could have any reaction at all. It's as if the question, in the very asking, demands an answer and denies it at the same time ...'

The hum in his head was rising to a howl. It was time.

He went into iTunes. His eighteen hundred CDs had been destroyed when his Manhattan house exploded last July, but years before Harry had begun storing their data in the cloud – dossiers, session transcripts and video, software, DoYouMrJones.com's website info, audio files, Geiger's CDs – so Geiger had retrieved and downloaded all his music from the cloud when he bought a new laptop.

He chose a playlist that melded dark and light, sublime and brutal – Hendrix, Mussorgsky, Liszt, Coltrane. When the pain burst into bloom, so would the music's color and taste. He'd let the pain grow until it was all he felt – then mount the beast and ride it into the blackness until thought was gone and everything was white-hot sensation laced with a thousand hues of sound. Then he'd pluck a silver melody from the swirl and fashion it into a sword, and plunge it into the heart of the galloping beast – and kill it.

He clicked 'play' and headed unsteadily toward the closet. He knew the tendrils in his brain would turn into lightning bolts and the thunder would send him reeling. He opened the door and stepped inside. The staccato crack of lead guitar poured out of the Bose cube speakers mounted on the walls. *'Purple haze is in my brain ...'* He pulled the door closed, lay down on his side in the darkness and pulled his knees up so he fit snugly against the walls. It would be any second now. *'S'cuse me while I kiss the sky.'*

For a moment, the ancient, dull ache in his iliac crests and ankles yanked him back into his child's mind, to the cabin's closet his father had built for him – curled up on the floor, arms wrapped round the cassette player – and a voice came through the door. But it wasn't Hendrix. It was rich and arctic. His father.

'*You go to sleep now, boy.*'

And then the storm hit – and Geiger reached out and grabbed hold of a golden rope of a guitar's scream and held on with all his might.

5

Harry turned off the shower, and his left hand went to his groin and probed the flesh. The smooth surfaces triggered an exhale. The grape-sized bump he had assumed was cancer, that had taken four months to shrink to nothing, hadn't come back. The fact that he still checked every day told him he expected it *would* – but, as with most things now, even his dread of fated calamities had lost some of its boil. His cell rang and he walked out and picked it up off the folding table. Only one person had his number.

'Hi,' he said.

The voice on the line was measured, but there was a charge in it. 'Something just came in an e-mail to the site. I need you to look at it.'

'So send it. Use the program I installed last month. It's secure.'

'Doing it now. Harry, this is big – if it's real.'

Harry glanced at his laptop's screensaver, the revolving series of Jackson Pollock paintings he'd used as a natural tranquilizer for a decade, and the laptop gave a *ding*.

'I got it,' he said, poking the mail icon with a fingertip; he squinted at its content – a few lines of text.

'Scroll down to the photo.'

Harry did so 'Who are they?'

Two men sat at a table filled with plates of delicacies and demitasses, smiling, hands raised in conversation. One was dressed in a short-sleeved shirt and elegant beige slacks. The other man wore a masqati cap and a keffiyeh over an expensive suit, the classic modern meld of Middle Eastern and Western style, a snake of smoke from his cigarette frozen in the air.

'The guy in short sleeves is the former US Assistant Secretary of State – who now owns a major chunk of Argent Industries International.'

Harry nodded. 'It's good to be king, huh?'

'The other guy is number two in the Afghan Ministry of Economic Development. Now there's an oxymoron for you. Harry ... there's software that can tell if an image is real or fake – right?'

Harry put his nose two inches from the laptop. 'Yeah – but these days the fakes are so good you really need the pro stuff the spooks use.'

'You have it?'

'Yeah, but not here. It's at my apartment in the Heights.'

'Shit.' A deep breath came through the phone, signaling contemplation of a difficult subject. 'You've got to get it, Harry.'

Harry shook his head at no one. 'You know I can't do that.'

'I know you *haven't* – but you could.'

'C'mon, man. The deal was I'd help you with the tech end. I don't remember anything about getting myself killed.'

'You're paranoid, Harry.'

'I'm breathing, too.'

There was a five-second, silent hole in the conversation.

'You're right, Harry. This is my work, not yours – so here's what we'll do: Let's meet tomorrow, I'll come to you, you give me the keys to your place in Brooklyn. *I'll* go – by myself.'

A scowl took up residence on Harry's face. He burped. It burned, a come-to-life ember dead-center in his chest. Harry blew out a weary breath. With Geiger's death and the end of their sordid, lucrative business, his conscience had slowly come out of hiding. He liked having it around again, but not at this particular moment – because he knew he'd be the one retrieving the disk. He was finally going home.

'You're a manipulative prick, y'know that?'

'Harry, I'm not in this business to make friends. On the contrary. If I'm not making enemies then I'm not doing the job right – right?'

'Right,' he said.

Brooklyn Heights felt light years from Chinatown. Remsen Street was a narrow passage and held onto the late-March mist from the East River, muffling the few, scattered 3 a.m. noises that slipped out of brownstone windows. The streetlamps' fan of light made the sidewalks chalky and shadows blacker. Coming down the street, eyes swiveling side to side, Harry's heart had a heavyweight slugfest going on inside it – jabs of fear and counter-punches of anticipation. He felt a touch of fatalism. He was almost home.

If, in fact, there was a 'they' after him, it was the same folks who hired Hall and company to retrieve the torture vids – and they would want him dead. One less loose end. And if they were here now they knew he was, too – and they'd wait till he was off the street, inside. Make a neat job of it. Then again, he was aware of his penchant for paranoia, and that it was quite possible all that life had in store was a future much like the present. Still, his hands stayed in his raincoat's pockets so he could steady the Louisville Slugger concealed beneath it. He had three false front teeth and thirty stitches in his scalp – mementos from the Central Park mugging that had cast a stranger named Geiger as his savior twelve years ago – and he wasn't going down without a fight ever again.

The sight of his darkened, second-floor picture window slowed him. He could see Lily standing at it, her favorite post when they brought her from the home for weekend visits. Nose pressed to the glass, staring at the reflection of Manhattan's skyline lying on the river's surface, singing about the city she could see beneath the water. '*Way down below the ocean ... where I want to be ...*' His anguish caught on the edge of his grief and made him wince. He needed a Pepcid – and a few bourbons to wash it down.

He headed for his front door. He slid the baseball bat out as he neared the step-down recess off the sidewalk where the garbage bins were, peered into its shadows, and went up the stairs. He opened the door, gave the street a final look, and stepped inside. He unlocked the inside door and went to the first-floor apartment's door. He leaned to it, heard nothing, and headed up the stairs.

The old wood still moaned at every imposition. The bulb on the second floor was out and every step took him into thicker darkness. When he tried to fit the key in the lock of his door, his hand shook so it took three tries to open up and go inside.

A musty odor came at him, he waved it away, locked the door and went to the drapes and drew them closed. He put the bat against a wall, took out a penlight and turned it on. A galaxy of dust fairies did a lazy jig in the shaft of light. His large dracaena had died a slow and lonely death, its withered leaves in the pot and on the floor. He lowered the beam, and discovered he was standing on a large maroon stain in the rug. Ray's blood.

The memory rushed at him – the last time he stood here: Hall in a chair, stunned at the gun in Harry's hand … Lily lying where Ray had tossed her like a rag doll … the queasy, thrilling sensation of crushing bone as he smashed his Beretta into Ray's smirk …

He pulled out the desk's center drawer and trained the light, picked out a jewel case labeled 'Video Verify' and slid it in his pocket. He had given himself a talking-to before coming here – get in and out. This was no longer home-sweet-home. That life was gone.

His stomach sent a corrosive comment via his esophagus and he patted his pockets for a remedy, then headed down the hall to the bathroom. He turned on the light and met his face in the mirror. The gray-specked beard still surprised him. He opened the cabinet and the annoying squeak of the hinges brought a grin. No amount of WD-40 ever silenced it. He found some Pepcid Complete on a shelf. The expiration date was six months ago.

'Close enough,' he said, shook out three tablets and tossed them in his mouth. He swung the cabinet door closed – and heard its squeak continue for a second, like a faint, tardy echo that defied the laws of physics ... and realized someone was on the hall steps. He flicked the light off and stepped into the dark hall. All he heard was his own fear-drenched breathing. He turned on the penlight, moved to the living room and pressed an ear to the door. Maybe the old cellist on the third floor was getting home uncharacteristically late. He glanced up at the ceiling and waited – a penitent hoping for a sign from above – but there were no footsteps. They'd seen him come in, and now somebody or bodies stood out there, almost certainly on an errand of erasure, unquestionably proficient at the task.

They had only one way in – through the door – either picking the lock or putting a heavy shoulder or foot to it. Or, they might bide their time and make their move when he opened the door to leave. There was a fire escape outside his bedroom, but he'd put a steel gate on the window years ago and God knows where the key was – and then, Harry thought of Geiger, and saw it all clearly. It hit him head-on, like a punch in the eye.

Geiger's rule number one, in the work, in life, had always been *Never let the outside inside* – until he learned it was utter folly, and that cold truth had gotten him killed. But Harry had forgotten the lesson ... and become a ridiculous man, a turtle of a man – crawling around in a tiny circle, ducking his head back inside his shell at every noise and tremor, as if the world wouldn't notice him if *he* couldn't see it.

He grabbed the bat and faced the door. If someone

was out there, it didn't matter what side of it he was on. He figured he might have an advantage – a half-second's worth of surprise. He wouldn't go left, where the stairs met the landing three yards away. He'd go straight out the door, take a single stride, grab the railing with his left hand and vault over it, and land halfway down the staircase. He played a movie of it in his head – and it looked doable. Whether he'd break an ankle was a question he decided not to address.

He took hold of the knob, blew out a deep breath to cleanse as much roiling stress as he could – then turned the cold brass and flung the door back . . .

He sensed a moving force – shapeless, black – a tenth of a second before it hit him. Strong hands grabbing his arms, yanking him around, pushing him up against the wall and pinning him there, face-first. He was squirming madly, trying to twist free.

'Stop,' said the enemy.

'Fuck you!'

The hands shoved him harder against the wall, knocking the air and resolve out of him, and even with thick fear crushing his senses, he had time to feel incredibly stupid.

'Calm down,' said the voice in the familiar, singular, velvet tone. 'It's me.'

It's . . . me. Two syllables hit him a thousand times harder than the wall. The hands released him, and he heard the door close. He was holding his breath, while attempting the magic trick of turning absurdity into truth. He turned. The figure was a black imprint on the darkness of the room. Harry reached up and flicked on the light switch.

Geiger was dressed in black, and his physical trans-
formation – the severe haircut and beard – added to
Harry's state of shock.

'Hello, Harry.'

The best Harry could do, in a flat, stoned-out voice,
was state the obvious.

'... You're ... alive.'

'Yes. I'm—'

Harry took a step and threw his arms around him in
a hug. Geiger tensed, hands flicking to life at his sides.
Then, slowly, they rose and came to rest on Harry's
back.

'All right, Harry. All right,' he said. He grasped him
by the shoulders, put him at arms' length, and then let
go.

Harry watched the unblinking stare. It was
unchanged. Fathomless, placid, but intent. Without feeling, but not unkind. A flesh and blood sphinx.

'You don't look well, Harry.'

A sharp, short bark of a laugh came out of Harry.

'Y'think?' he said. Geiger was back from the dead –
but the edges of everything still glowed with an aura of
fantasy. Harry's grief was dug in deep. It wouldn't sur-
render its territory easily. 'I have to sit down, man,' he
said. He went to his favorite chair and lowered himself
into it, head wagging slowly like a Parkinson's victim.
His pulse thudded in every cell. 'Sorry. This is tough. I
just need to let this settle in.'

He watched Geiger come and sit on the sofa, and
noticed a subtle new hitch to his gait. They stared at
each other. Harry was used to talking to ghosts, but this
was different.

'Jesus ... We look like the fucking Smith Brothers.'

'Who?'

'The Smith Brothers. Y'know – the two guys with the beards? The cough drops?'

'I don't use cough drops.'

'Never mind.'

Geiger turned his head to the right. *Click*. 'Did Lily come back to shore, Harry?'

'No. Lily's gone.' Harry felt a surge of melancholy coming on, and tried to head it off. He stood up. 'I need a glass of water. You want some?'

Geiger shook his head. Harry pushed himself out of the chair and went into the kitchen. He got a glass from a cabinet.

'Can I ask you some questions?'

'Yes.'

'What happened – after the river?'

'I swam to shore, hid out, and got back to the city. The details aren't important.'

Harry turned on the faucet. The water had a tint of brown, so he let it run. 'Where are you now?'

'Here. In Brooklyn.'

'Yeah? Since how long?'

'Since the end of July. Three weeks after the incident.'

Harry shut the faucet. Some new emotion bubbled up in him, expanding. There was only so much room in him before he popped. He walked back into the living room.

'You've been here for eight months – and you didn't let me know?'

'Harry ...'

'What the hell is that? I mean – maybe you don't

understand the concept of grief – but Jesus Christ, Geiger ... I've been a fucking—'

'*Stop*.' The soft command might as well have been shouted by a staff sergeant. 'Harry ... You shut down the website. You changed your cell number. How was I supposed to contact you?'

Chagrin rushed into Harry's stew of feelings. 'You're right. I'm sorry ... I can barely think straight.' He was uncertain of his balance, and put a hand on the chair. 'Jesus ... what're the odds of you coming here tonight? I haven't been here since July.'

'I've been standing in the shadows across the street three or four nights a week for six months, waiting for you to come home.'

'... You have?'

Harry felt the tears about to bloom, and his hand sprung to his eyes and he rubbed them with thumb and forefinger in a counterfeit display of weariness. When he was reasonably sure he wouldn't weep he stopped, and smiled warmly.

'Thanks, man.'

'Don't hug me again, Harry. No more hugging.'

Geiger's classic deadpan made Harry's smile stretch across his face.

'Gotcha.' Harry definitely had to sit back down, and did. 'Does Corley know?'

'No.'

Harry remembered the *unhhh* of the psychiatrist's breath catching when he'd told him Geiger was dead ... and then the terrible silence. Later, for months he'd thought of getting in touch but was too worried someone might be watching Corley's apartment, or tapping his line, or hacking his e-mails. Geiger probably felt the same way. Poor Martin.

'Geiger ... Ezra lives in the city now.'

Geiger's fingers fluttered to life in his lap. '... Where?'

'In Matheson's brownstone on Seventy-fifth. I have his cell, e-mail. You can—'

'No, Harry.'

'You're not going to tell him?'

'I don't think so, no.'

'But the kid's having a really bad time, Geiger. He sees Corley three times a week – about *you*.'

'I wasn't meant to be part of his life, Harry – and I shouldn't be. And he'll be safer not knowing. Martin will get him through.'

'But he needs—'

'Ezra will be better off forgetting about me, Harry. And over time, he will.'

'But—'

'Harry ... I know what works best for me.'

Harry wanted to push back, but he knew he'd hit solid rock. 'What works best for me' meant *This conversation is over. I have no need to be understood.* So Harry nodded, and sank back into the chair.

'Do you know the Cairo videos went viral? Internet ... TV.'

Geiger nodded. The cool, thoughtful torturer in the videos had made a strong impression on the world, depending on the audience. Villain, madman, patriot. Terrifying, repellent, heroic.

'Harry ... Are you working?'

'Not really. But I'm sort of the unofficial computer guy for Veritas Arcana.'

'You're working with Matheson?'

'I help out here and there. Tech stuff. It felt like the right thing to do.' He grinned sadly. 'Penance for my past sins.'

'Do you want a job, Harry?'

'A job?'

Echoes of the past chilled Harry. He could see Geiger waiting on the sidewalk outside of The Times Building twelve years ago. *I am going into a new line of work, Harry,* he had said. *Illegal. I need a partner.* Geiger had barely known Harry, but had offered him his trust with a paramount aspect of his life ... and Harry had said yes. The strangest of pairs – alone, together.

Harry's face creased in a wary squint. 'What *kind* of job?'

'Don't worry, Harry. It's not IR. I'm done with it. Completely. I make furniture now, Harry – and I need someone to sell it.'

'You make *furniture*?'

'I know a lot about wood.'

'Since when?'

'Since I was a boy. My father taught me.'

Harry's head did a hunting dog tilt. 'Your ... *father*?' Geiger never spoke in any kind of personal mode. 'You *are* Geiger, right?'

'Are you interested, Harry?'

'Geiger, I don't know anything about furniture.'

Geiger rose from the sofa. From this angle Harry thought he looked thinner. Not in the sense of a dedicated dieter, or someone who had come through an illness. It was as if Geiger had shed something beneath the Hudson that night – as if the river had taken something from him.

'You've always been a quick study, Harry. Think about it.' He started for the door. 'My e-mail is Oldwood – one word – at Gmail dot com. Send me your cell number. I'll be in touch.' He reached the door. 'And Harry ... I think you can stay here if you want. I doubt they're looking for you. The videos are out there. Everyone's seen them. You're of little concern to them now.' He opened the door. As with everything he did, the movement had a simple elegance to it. A touch of the dance. A hint of affliction.

'Geiger ...'

'Yes?'

'It's really good to see you.'

Harry was the only person alive who could tell that the nearly imperceptible bend at the corners of Geiger's lips might have been a smile. Geiger stepped out into the darkness and closed the door behind him. It didn't make a sound.

6

The world was in the wood – strength, vigor, decay, texture, aroma – the names themselves a savory, musical pageantry. *Sugar maple, hemlock*. Completion was in the wood, waiting to be found. *Palisander, ironwood, hickory*. Truth was in the wood, and this above all made the work a sister to IR. The prep and strategy for remaking what was already formed, the exploration of characteristics – its strength, malleability, breaking point. Application of methodology – force, patience, finesse. It was all in his hands and vision – seeing the end, but letting the way reveal itself. A way to find a new life. *Spruce, black cherry, tigerwood*.

'Willow, weep for me ... Willow, weep for me ...'

Billie Holiday's slinky voice purred from the Hyperion speakers. Geiger placed the butt chisel against a side of the crescent recess he'd dug out of the mahogany slab. He wore only a pair of gym shorts. When possible, he kept his quadriceps free from friction. The jagged scars left by Dalton were a stark contrast to the elegant tapestry on his hamstrings and calves his father etched for years by the cabin fire. Geiger gave the chisel a tap with the beech mallet, shaving the wood. It would ensure a tight fit for the inlay.

'Listen to my plea ... Hear me, willow, and weep for me ...'

He had been listening exclusively to female vocalists while he worked. Dalton's torture had opened a door and his father had come barging out – and now something else was stirring, barely an essence, like a harbor fog at the edge of his senses – fragile, ghostly, feminine – and he was saturating the air with voices – Holiday, Nina Simone, Bonnie Raitt, Joplin. Perhaps they would help draw the essence out.

The notes drifted to the high ceiling like an angel's lament. His new home had been built in 1912 as a Pentecostal chapel and had changed hands four times. Geiger had seen a picture in a real estate office window when he'd gone to Brooklyn after returning from Cold Spring. The heavy wooden door in a gothic arch had caught his eye. It was set back sixty feet from the sidewalk behind stores, accessible by an alley – a twenty-by-twenty one-room construction of cut stone, the cathedral ceiling eighteen feet high at its apex.

The reason Geiger had been in Brooklyn that day had nothing to do with living space. It was about money and, in a sense, Carmine Delanotte – his patron, mentor and, ultimately, betrayer. When Geiger's house in Manhattan had imploded on July Fourth he'd lost everything, including a key to a safe deposit box at the 96th Street Chase with half a million dollars in it, and the only way to it went directly through questions and gazes from a bank manager, in the company of a surveillance system. But – ten years ago, Geiger had had one of his lunches with Carmine at his restaurant, La Bella, in Little Italy.

'My accountant told me ...' Carmine had said, and taken a sip of his beloved espresso and smacked his lips. He would often start a comment and pause – to reposition a fork, pull his sleeves a half-inch from his suit jacket, comb fingertips through his silver hair. Geiger knew it was part of his situational manipulation. He'd watched others react to the pauses – seen them lean forward, unaware of doing so – as if Carmine's suspension of the moment increased his gravitational pull. To Carmine life meant control, and tipping a conversation or negotiation even half a degree would eventually pay dividends. Geiger had incorporated the technique into his own work since the man had set him up in IR.

'... He told me I'm paying a hundred and twenty-seven thousand in taxes this year. That's what it costs to look like an honest success.' Carmine drained his demitasse. 'You're making real money now. You saving any?'

'I don't spend very much. It goes in the safety deposit box, like you said.'

Carmine wagged a finger. 'Not *all* of it. You need to have a little coffin money.'

'What is coffin money?'

Carmine had smiled, then reached over and patted Geiger's cheek. 'You always tell me you don't know where you came from – but I do. *Mars*.'

That is why Geiger had been in Brooklyn – because buried in Prospect Park, in dense woods between two elms marked with notches, was a tool box with sixty thousand dollars and an extra key to the safe deposit box. At 3 a.m. he'd dug it up, taken forty grand and the key – and stood beneath the indifferent gaze of a million stars and thought of Carmine Delanotte, revisiting the pain in his benefactor's voice as he had delivered Geiger to Hall and Dalton – *You think I'm happy about this? I'm not, Geiger. You're my boy, but I do business with these people* – knowing chance was blind and without fidelity, but convinced certain parts of a life never died unless you killed them, and filled with a sense belying reason that there was a time and place when that theory would be tested.

After moving in, Geiger had brought in a mini-fridge, food preparation table and a mattress. Then he had started purchasing woodworking tools. The first thing he built was his desk, then the five-foot-square closet in the west corner of the space. He bought an Aeron ergonomic chair, a MacBook Pro, and an LG Spyder cell phone – and the first call he made was to Harry, but the recording said the service had been cancelled.

At their reunion, Geiger had been struck by Harry's intensity, his unrestrained joy – by the time he arrived home that night, Harry's cell number and e-mail address were waiting on his laptop. Geiger was a student of feelings – a gauger, an analyzer. This quality had helped make him the master of his craft – the ability to *feel* others' emotions while living in estrangement from his own. Bonds, intimacies – they were for scrutiny and evaluation, not experience. But standing in the eye of Harry's emotional storm, the incongruity of their relationship – that Geiger's presence in Harry's life, and his absence, were so meaningful – had not been lost on him. He had left his mark on someone outside the session room without intent. Jogging home that night he'd summoned a vision of Ezra, and wondered what part of himself might be alive inside the boy.

He slid two fingertips down the side of the cutout in the wood, measuring its slope with an instrument as sensitive as any tool. He picked up the half-moon piece he'd carved out of quilted maple – six inches from tip to tip. The ripple effect in the grain gave it a stunning brightness and three-dimensional quality. It had been one of his best finds – the unscathed back panels of an armoire damaged in a fire. He'd get a dozen more inlays from it. His peregrinations to the reno shops throughout the boroughs were one of the holdovers from the old life – rummaging in the racks and yards for discarded, unwanted treasure. Something warped, damaged, all but useless. His eye never missed them.

Geiger turned to his finished works. Against the walls were two desks, three tables and an armoire – all dark woods, mahogany, black walnut, Indian rosewood. Each had dozens of lighter inlays – elm, red oak, aspen – big as a grapefruit, small as a dime. He was creating a universe. Each piece was a part of the night sky – stars, planets, constellations, nebulae, moons of different phases, all set in deep darkness – the sky he had watched endlessly as a child invisible and unknown to the world.

He stroked the inlay's sides and rubbed his fingertips together, determining how much of his beeswax and chinawood oil blend remained. Before oiling, each piece underwent three sanding sessions to return the surface to its natural state – trance-like procedures. In all the years of watching his father work, the man had never made pronouncements about rules. This was, simply, the way to do things.

He heard himself talking to Harry last night – *Don't worry, Harry. It's not IR. I'm done with it. Completely.* He had come to that decision nine months ago, while Dalton worked on him, but he had never voiced the words aloud. *I'm done with it. Completely.* The statement had a cleansing feel to it, like some caustic agent sweeping away the last, clinging remnants of a toxic sludge within him. He would never go back to it.

He fit the piece into the cutout and pressed down until two inches remained, then took a chamois and laid it over the inlay. He picked up the mallet as the cat strolled over, rubbing against him.

'Not now, Tony.'

The cat had adapted. Geiger had put a pet-door in a window and the animal had taken up its nightly journeys, returning around 5 a.m., as always. It peered up at him with its one eye and started scratching at Geiger's calf. Geiger picked it up and draped it on his shoulder. He gave the scar where the right eye used to be a few scratches and the animal settled on its perch, its purr an engine in Geiger's ear.

He had begun calling the cat 'Tony' after they moved in here. It had been Ezra's suggestion – one of a million things Geiger kept from their twenty-four hours together. The boy had immediately taken to the cat.

'What's his name?' he had asked.

'Cat.'

'That's what you call him? "Cat?" You should give him a real name,' the boy had said. 'Hey, you could call him Tony – after Tony Montana.'

The name had meant nothing to Geiger. 'Who?' he had asked.

'Tony Montana – you know? Al Pacino in *Scarface*.' Geiger had stared back blankly. 'Get it? *Scarface* – the movie?'

'I don't go to the movies.'

'Well, you ought to name him *something*. "Cat" is kinda dumb.'

And these days, every time Geiger spoke to the cat, the boy was with them.

Geiger raised the mallet and struck the chamois with just enough force to push the piece downward – once, twice – then removed the cloth and ran his hand over the wood.

A smooth fit. Flush. Perfect.

7

Harry was heading east on 125th Street, buffeted by the boom boxes' output, watching deals go down with the sidewalk vendors – fake Rolexes, sunglasses, something to smoke – past a soul-drenched sax player and three silent, suited men offering their pamphlets. He was experiencing sporadic moments of something that bordered on giddiness. He was out in the world again, on the street, *going* somewhere.

Geiger's resurrection had been a kind of rebirth for Harry. That night, he'd returned to Chinatown, grabbed his laptop and a few disks, and left without closing the door. In the cab back to Brooklyn, he'd caught sight of himself in the rearview mirror with a grin so wide he looked like a lunatic stranger. When he got home, he'd taken a long shower and shaved off the unwanted beard. Then he'd gotten into his own bed, made a note to buy a new dracaena, and fell into lush, dreamless sleep.

He turned left at Second Avenue and headed north. The street level of the three-story building housed a West African clothing store. It was Harry's first time here – the work he'd done until now had been from his

Chinatown hideout. The building's side door was in a narrow alley – pocked, gray steel with three locks, two steps down. Harry pushed the button on the intercom panel. Above it was a small, recessed lens.

'Coming,' said a voice.

There were motion-sensitive lights and two round, metal reflectors mounted on the opposite wall to afford a view of both ends of the alley from inside the building. He grinned at the irony, because obsessed as Matheson was about detection and invasion, in this town his setup was business as usual. From Harlem to Soho, you could have a dozen locks, mirrors and security cameras and no passer-by would give it a second's thought – and that made it perfect for Veritas Arcana. In a world where every day less could be hidden and more was revealed, the paranoiac was the sanest man in the room. He heard the locks being turned, and the door creaked opened on cranky hinges.

David Matheson looked like hell. It had been two months since Harry had seen him – when Matheson had come to him for some software installations. Raccoon eyes stared from a pale, unshaven face, his tall, muscular frame in rumpled Dockers and a tan hoodie whose sleeves were dappled with coffee stains. He pushed his long, dark hair back from his forehead and took a drag of his cigarette.

'Hi,' he said.

Harry stepped into the dark entry. It smelled of smoke and popcorn and stale, imprisoned air. Matheson closed the door, turned the locks, and went down a short hall toward a spill of light. Harry followed.

The world had taken a heavy hammer to Matheson.

His reckless passion for truth and disclosure had put his son in grave danger, unknowingly delivered the boy to violence, and in the end, been the blade that severed all but minimal contact between them. His online release of the torture videos had elevated Veritas Arcana, in the eyes of some, from a second-tier whistle-blower to an entity worthy of eradication. Now he was the *enemy*.

Harry turned the corner. The small, windowless room was part of a converted basement, bald concrete melting into shadows – trapped, hovering smoke lending it a Stygian mood. Jammed against a wall were a cot, mini-fridge, two dinged-up file cabinets with a microwave and lamp on top, and five plastic bins filled with tossed clothes. On the opposite wall were a laundry sink whose porcelain had once been white and a network of sweaty pipes that snaked from floor to ceiling. Matheson turned to Harry.

'Welcome to my living room-kitchen-bedroom-dining room. *Mi casa es su casa.*' There was a wrinkle to his smile that Harry had always liked – a meld of loathing for his between-a-rock-and-a-hard-place existence and a dark appreciation of it.

'Not real big on the feng shui thing are you, David?'

Matheson took a pull on his butt and flicked it into the sink. 'On the contrary. It took me months to work out the proper ... *flow*.'

Harry waved the smoke away as he stepped inside. 'Jesus ... You're gonna die from your own second-hand smoke. Can that happen?'

There were Xeroxes of Veritas Arcana web pages

taped on the walls: 'US assault rifles found in Taliban hideout in Kandahar' ... 'Classified US Department of Defense memos discuss secret bid-rigging in Iraq' ... 'Secret CIA torture of Egyptian cabinet minister'.

Harry strolled, leaning in, reading them. 'The Veritas Arcana Hall of Fame?'

Matheson went to a door and pushed it open. 'Let's get to work. And close the door. Keeps the smoke out.'

Harry followed him inside. This room was twice as large as the first, smoke-free, and ten degrees colder. A row of four web servers went down its middle, and six laptops sat in a row atop a twelve-foot aluminum table. There were three wall-mounted monitors with CNN, MSNBC and FOX on and the sound muted. Matheson sat down at a laptop.

Harry took a seat beside him and got the disk out of his coat.

'Thank you for this, Harry. I know you didn't want to go back to Brooklyn.'

'I'm glad you asked. It was good for me.'

'No bad guys waiting for you?'

'Right. No bad guys.'

Harry tapped the space bar and the desktop came on – a picture of Ezra, green eyes locked on the neck of the violin wedged under his chin. It wasn't a recent image.

'You speak to him lately?' asked his father.

'Uh-huh.'

Matheson let out a clipped, bitter chuckle. 'So you know I haven't.'

The emotional geometry of the three of them made Harry antsy. 'He's okay. Not great. Still pissed at you.

Still in therapy. A lot of guilt about Geiger.' Harry's pulse did a short jig. *I wasn't meant to be part of his life, Harry – and I shouldn't be.* Geiger was wrong – but it wasn't Harry's secret to tell.

'Christ, I miss him.' Matheson sighed, but there was no trace of self-pity.

'Well ... I think he misses you too. He just also hates your guts.'

Matheson nodded wearily. 'As he should. Right?'

Last 3 July, with the secret CIA torture videos finally in his possession, he had told his son to lock the apartment door behind him and then gone uptown, to this room, to prepare the disks for online access. He was pumped to the max. He knew the bad guys were close – but it would only take a few hours, and Ezra was safe at home ...

'David,' Harry said, 'you do good work. Important work.' He slid the disk in the drive. 'You made a decision because of the work. You didn't think Ezra'd get snatched. Maybe you didn't think long enough. I don't know.' The screen filled with a spyglass logo and *VIDEO VERIFY* in a chrome font. 'Did you fuck up? Yes – and now you're paying for it. That's what usually happens, David. We fuck up and then we pay for it. Maybe when Ezra gets older he'll see a bigger picture.'

Matheson's wistful smile returned. 'How'd you get so wise, Harry?'

'By fucking up – a lot. Where's the e-mail?'

'V–A–3 inbox, labeled X – X – X.'

Harry clicked on the e-mail's icon, clicked and it came up on-screen. There were six lines of text:

Copy of email from Argent Industries to Kabul.
Secret milions for gov contracts. email is one of 4.
foto is 1 of 6 from cellfone on 24/2/2013. I am hide
now neer paris. No mony. need mony to get wife
and child out from Kabul. You want all fotos and
emails must arang and come. Is 7000 euro enuf?
you do good work. Seek truth. answer please.

Harry scrolled down to a photo of two men. Beneath it
was a copy of another e-mail, in a different font, below
it. It read:

Outlays to Sp and Gr shellcos will be substantial,
so 600m is high as we go if still just talking o & ng
lines & refi. If you reconsider pops we're at 9. We
feel it is important this be resolved before next
election, for obvious reasons.

Harry finished reading. '"600 million for rights to oil
and natural gas pipelines and refinement"?'
  'I guess.'
  '"If you reconsider pops we're at nine"? What's that?'
Matheson smiled faintly. 'Poppy fields?'
  'And "S-P and G-R *shellcos*"?'
  'Shell companies. Spanish? Greek?'
  Harry sat back. He finally nodded. 'Argent Industries
is buying Afghanistan. Wow.'
  'Sounds like it.'
  Harry straightened up and cracked his knuckles.
'This is gonna take some time, David. Pixel by pixel
examination and comparison.'
  Matheson put a cigarette in his lips. 'Gonna have a

smoke.' He opened the door, stepped out and closed it behind him.

Harry's fingers settled on the keys – and something made him stop. It was the click in his brain – a slow, rhythmic ticking – pleasing, familiar, long absent. He had the look of someone who'd remembered a favorite song he hadn't heard in years. It was the sound he heard when he was a *Times* reporter – the click of his lens focusing, locking on to something whose meaning might outweigh the common and mundane. It felt good.

Matheson lit his fourth cigarette with the butt of his third and paced slowly, leaving a white, wafting tail in his wake. These days, if he was standing up he couldn't stay in one place. A medically informed observer might have surmised he suffered from a moderate form of akathisia, or perhaps ADD – but the motor of Matheson's restlessness was in his soul, not his brain or muscles, and it ran on a high-octane blend of zeal, out-rage and remorse. The first two were ammunition for his online crusades ... and the last a constant flow of melancholy – blood from an open wound, the severance from his son.

He'd grown up rich and rootless, dead-on aware of his lack of skills and desire for any. His sole passion, art, finally eased him into a profession – middle-man for the buying and selling of paintings and antiquities. It suited him – exotic travel, short episodes with people that didn't require an effort at intimacy, and a modest sense of accomplishment – even though nothing was actually ever created or produced. Then, like so many others on the planet, the concussive waves of 9/11 swept him off his path, and he found himself on another.

Veritas Arcana was born, Matheson was reborn.

And the quest consumed him. His secret life casting shadows on his old one. A growing estrangement from his family, divorce, a creeping separateness and seclusion, Christmas and two summer weeks with his son – and then the Geiger incident and the break with Ezra. Matheson was not one for introspection, but he carried his son's sense of betrayal with him, always. He had shattered the boy's trust, and heart. He had no illusions about what he'd become – a slave to his obsession, ridden by it like a horse and master, waiting for the next secret to show itself . . .

'David! C'mere!'

Matheson tossed his cigarette and swung the door open.

Harry watched the gold, pentagon-shaped icon blinking on the screen. 'Done.'

'And . . . ?'

'Real. Probably.'

'Probably? What the hell does that mean?'

'It means the program found minimal anomalies – but this is *one shot*, David. So that's why the "probably". This software isn't perfect. If you want closer to one hundred percent certain "it's real" – you'll need all the photos and docs.'

Matheson scowled. 'What do you think?'

'The right side of my brain says it sounds and reads legit. Non-American. Limited English – the misspellings, grammar, syntax . . .'

'And putting the day before the month in the date . . .'

'That too. But the left side of my brain says "setup". This is tailor-made to burn your ass. Lots of people would like to do that.'

Matheson was nodding. 'They certainly would.' He took out his cigarette pack. It was empty. He crumpled it up, pulled a new pack out and started smacking it against his palm in the addict's ritual.

Harry sighed. 'And you're gonna do it – aren't you?'

'I've been here before. This is what I do.'

'If it's a trap ... Is it worth a bullet in your—'

'Harry, when you were at the *Times* ... Maybe you got a tip on a story, something that *mattered* – but it might be dangerous. Would that've made you walk away?'

It was one of the last places Harry cared to go. 'That was another lifetime.'

'Look at the way I live, Harry. *My* choices, yes – but all I've got left is the job ... this is it – so it wouldn't make much sense if I just hid down here and waited for things to happen. That would make me a pretty ridiculous man, wouldn't it?'

He lit up again, stepped out and closed the door – and Harry stared at the letter-size paper taped to it. It had a quote printed on it in large, italic font: *TRUTH IS LIKE THE SUN. YOU CAN SHUT IT OUT FOR A TIME, BUT IT AIN'T GOIN' AWAY – ELVIS PRESLEY.*

Harry grinned. He had written off God and his faithful stooge, fate, seventeen years ago, leaning against a wall in an emergency room – but he'd accepted that life had a chaotic but causal flow – and that a random event did, at times, push others into motion.

'Elvis?!' he hollered. 'The King said that?!'

'According to Google, yeah!'

The world had become a reality-show version of itself, where truth and lies and spin all mingled around the prizes like ruthless contestants – and he could feel mayhem's finger tapping him on his shoulder again – *Psst ... Take a look at this.* The click in his brain wouldn't stop, and when he'd read 'Paris' in the e-mail his insides had tightened.

'David ...!'

'Yeah?!'

'I want to come with you!'

The door opened. Matheson's lips were tangled up between a faint smile and a curious frown. 'Why?'

Harry shrugged. 'Isn't that reason enough?'

8

Geiger was deciding where his run would take him tonight. As he jogged out of the alley to the sidewalk he slowed to a stop, running in place, watching an antsy man in baggy jeans and a North Face coat stride back and forth in front of the bodega, stalking his own shadow, sharing his message as fast as his tongue would let him.

'I am the agent of the Lord God Almighty – *Whoa!* – but I don't take no ten percent! *Whoa!*' Each punctuative *whoa* fell somewhere between an Otis Redding grunt and a Tourette's bark. 'I'll get paid in full later – when I'm done! *Whoa!*' He shook his head back and forth without pause, like a wind-up toy whose mechanism had gone awry.

Geiger wasn't listening. He wasn't looking at him, either. He was looking at the pane glass of the bodega behind the man that held the reflection of the laundromat across the street – and the figure standing inside at the window. When Geiger came down the alley he'd seen the figure, in a long overcoat, drinking from a coffee container – and lowering it the moment Geiger came out of the shadows. It was an ordinary gesture but the timing caught his eye – meaningless coincidence, or a signal to someone on the street.

God's messenger wagged a bony finger at the world's inexcusable ignorance.

'Don't matter to the Lord if you're scumbag or saint – *Whoa!* – rich man or smack-shooter . . . I am here to tell you – you are *his*! He owns your miserable ass . . .'

In tiny increments, Geiger drifted two feet to his left, where the angle endowed the reflection in the glass with greater dimension. The figure in the window was still.

'. . . and he will call you home when it goddamn suits him! *Whoa!* One by one – or by the trainload – or a million at a time.' He eyed Geiger. 'You hear me, brother?!' The apostle came up to Geiger, close enough that he smelled the whiskey on the man's breath.

'Do you hear me, brother?'

Geiger took his earbuds out. His gaze stayed on the reflection. 'Yes. I hear you.'

'No, brother – not like that. I know you can hear me – but do you *hear* me?'

Geiger met the man's bright, dark eyes. 'Step back. You're too close.'

The man smiled. 'You can never be too close to the Lord, brother.'

Geiger's focus shifted back. The figure in the glass was gone – and Geiger kicked into a slow jog. The preacher's call chased after him.

'Remember that, brother! You can never be too close to God! *Whoa!*'

Geiger checked out the block with casual glances.

Despite the late, cold hour Avenue X still had diehards, drunks and late-shifters walking about, and hopeful lights shone in the pizzeria, the Hunan restaurant, the video store, the organic café.

From his perspective, his steady glide down the street had the effect of slowing those around him, almost to stillness, as if he ran through a photograph. He would always be defined by his separateness. He was a sailor navigating treacherous waters, but without desire or need to find land. His solitude was his home. Still – his sensors' messages were clear: someone had found him, and was near. At the light, he turned left and used the moment to look down the street. Most likely, it would be the spooks who had employed Hall. Deep Red. They had discovered his survival and decided to reverse it. One of the tenets of their mindset was the 'clean slate' concept – a job was stamped 'completed' only when there was no reason to consider any element of it again. They hated loose ends. The fact that Geiger, in his own mind, posed no threat to them was irrelevant.

His brain's mode clicked a few degrees, like the chambers of a gun, and took aim. He was never far from the Inquisitor's methodology, and this scenario was a first cousin to an 'asap' gig – a ticking clock, little or no knowledge of the Jones, working more on instinct and reaction than preparation. He was keeping his pace to a moderate speed. He didn't know what kind of shape his pursuer was in, and he wanted to be sure to stay in his view, for now. He needed a destination that would provide privacy – a session room, of sorts. Two blocks away they'd gutted a building for renovation and a scaffold's canopy spanned its sidewalk like an eight-foot-high tunnel. He'd turn right at the light so he'd be coming at it from the east and be going round a corner – and that would take him out of his tail's sight for a few moments. It would be all the time he'd need. And the last consideration ... What to do with the Jones after the capture. Much as it went against his grain, he'd have to be reactive: ride the moment and use what it gave him.

The three-story reno was up ahead at the end of the block, with a few bare bulbs on inside to discourage the homeless and scavengers. Geiger increased his pace slightly, and as soon as he turned the corner, leaving the view of anyone behind him, he dashed into a full run beneath the scaffolding. On his right, at a break in the criss-cross of support piping, he darted through into the building's dark, six-by-six entry. The door-frame had a steel-barred gate in it. A faint wash of light from an interior ceiling bulb came through it. Geiger pressed up against a wall, dissolving into the shadows, and began to count. If someone was following, he estimated twelve to fifteen seconds till arrival.

Three ... four ... five ... His fingers were flicking to the faint whisper of a beat hissing out of the earbuds dangling at his waist. *Eight ... nine ...* He moved a foot closer to the gap in the scaffolding. Step all the way out when the time came – or try and make a grab from where he was? *Thirteen ... fourteen ...* He'd wait till the last second to decide, depending on the runner's speed. *Eighteen ... nineteen ... twenty ...* The dance of his fingers slowed. He stopped counting. He was a stranger to inaccuracy and this was a new, unsettling sensation. He considered the rare possibility of his instincts failing him ...

Then he heard the huffs of a finely tuned body ... rubber soles touching lightly on asphalt – and as the runner reached the opening Geiger's hand shot out, snared a wrist and pulled, using the body's momentum to swing it round into the space and shove it up against the wall, chest first. Flesh and bone meeting concrete produced a purging *ooof*.

Geiger spread his legs for balance, anchoring all his weight against the stunned figure while one hand held the back of the knit-capped skull and his other slid around the throat and jammed up under the jaw in a tight C-clamp grip.

'Who are you?' he said.

'My name is Rosanna Soames. I'm not armed.'

Geiger pulled the cap off and Zanni's sandy hair fell to her shoulders. Geiger patted down the sides and back of her thin Gortex jacket, then the stomach, then the chest. The body was lean, the stomach flat and hard, the breasts small and round.

'Who do you work for?'

'The government.'

Geiger's grip tightened round the soft flesh beneath her jaw. 'The ones who sent Hall out for Matheson and the disks?'

'Yes. Deep Red.'

He smelled a faint hint of flowers in the air.

'Geiger, I'm not here to hurt you – but if you don't let go of me I will.'

'Turn around, slowly,' he said, and took a half-step

back, far enough for her to revolve but close enough to keep his grip on her throat. 'Is there anyone else with you?'

Zanni's violet eyes flashed at him. '. . . No.'

Geiger homed in on the blip of silence before her answer. Perhaps her natural cadence, or breathlessness, or a tell of lying – or she might have wanted him to notice the pause, to keep him wondering. One thing was clear – it wasn't fear. She was a pro.

A bright light suddenly settled on them – and he grabbed Zanni and spun round, holding her against him. It was a harsh, blinding beam. All Geiger saw through his squint was a hot, white void. It occurred to Geiger that she had played him – from the start. They'd let him find his own, private place of execution. He'd done all the work. One less loose end. There was the rasp of old hinges turning, the bar gate swinging open . . .

'Let her go!' The voice was gruff and deep. 'I said let her go – *now*!'

'Jesus,' said Zanni, 'can't a working girl get a little privacy – huh?' Her delivery had a perfect meld of street cool and weary umbrage.

'Oh . . .' the voice chuckled, 'so that's how it is, huh?'

The beam of light was lowered. A man in an AJAX SECURITY cap stood five feet away at the opened gate, billy club in his other hand, forty years of junk food testing the limits of his belt and shirt buttons.

'Well . . . sorry, doll,' he said. 'You're the best-looking hooker I've seen in a long time, but get a fucking room before I call the cops.' He pointed the club at Geiger. 'Take a hike, Romeo. Try and keep it hard till you get there.'

'Okay,' Zanni said, and looked at Geiger. 'Let's go, sweet thing.'

Geiger was studying her performance. The best liars were those most experienced with the skill. They shared traits of other artists – actors, singers and musicians, jazz players in particular – those with the uncanny ability to improvise, to feel the flow in a given moment and add to it spontaneously, and never have the audience question its *trueness*. He decided he couldn't believe anything she said.

Zanni put a hand on his forearm. 'C'mon, hon.' She started drawing him out, and when they reached the sidewalk they took two steps back from each other – movement without thought – a chemical reaction between non-binding molecules. It was starting to rain, and there was a crisp, tinny tympani on the corrugated steel above them.

'Do I look like a hooker in these clothes?' Zanni asked.

Geiger took a slow, even breath. 'I'm not interested in the job.'

'You don't know what it is.'

'That's true, but irrelevant.' He jogged away. He needed to run – to stretch the world out, to push back against the shrinking feeling around him. As he crossed the intersection at West Eleventh she came up on his right and settled into his pace.

'Could you stop for a minute so we can talk?'

'No.'

'Geiger ... I'm not a contractor – I'm not Hall, and I'm not here to lie or play head games with you.'

Geiger looked over at her. She had the lope of an

athlete, the mindless grace and muscular spring, matching him stride for stride. He measured her at five-eight or -nine, one-twenty-five to thirty, mid to late twenties. Her persistence was not unexpected.

'My job was to find you and ask if you'll work again.'

'You did your job.'

Geiger did not want to speak anymore. The outside was too full of unpredictable, shifting elements – and the woman's presence and interactive demands felt like scale-tippers. They went under the elevated subway tracks and he slowed to a halt, out of the rain, jogging-in-place – and Zanni came to rest.

'Just think about it, Geiger. Price is negotiable, to a degree. All you need to—'

Geiger stuck a palm up in front of her. 'I don't want a job.'

A train was approaching overhead, dragging its escalating clatter along the tracks. Zanni decided to wait until it passed by. It would give her a moment to recalibrate. His attributes were far more striking in person. His satin tone and uninflected flow of words, the stillness of him even as he remained in motion, and a calmness that was, paradoxically, intense to witness. They stared at each other without expression until the train passed and the street stopped vibrating beneath them.

'Geiger ... If you—'

'You need to stop talking.' Geiger turned his neck till he got the *click*. 'You are working from a scenario built on comparative thinking – one that assumes I will react in ways that most others in this kind of scenario do. If

I say "No", you will increase the offer of financial reward … you'll consider introducing elements of patriotism, acting for a noble cause … you'll also consider threats, and blackmail …' His head slued back to the right. *Click*. 'But, for various reasons, I do not fit the profile of most others, and because of that, I am irrelevant to the scenario. That's what you need to understand.'

A bus was coming up from the east beneath the tracks. The driver gave the horn three sharp jabs as it neared and they moved away. Zanni followed Geiger until he stopped beside a massive steel stanchion.

'What is relevant,' he said, 'is that I don't work in IR anymore. You need to tell your bosses that, and tell them nothing will change that.'

Zanni watched his tunnel eyes. She was looking for something behind his stare, but he was either a master of concealment … or empty inside. Still – the fact was that last summer he'd run off the tracks. Three pros had been sent to deal with him and were dead. Dalton had been brought in for interrog and ended up crippled. And now she was suddenly aware how little traffic there was in Gravesend this time of night, and that Geiger, by chance or design, had led her into the stanchion's wide, black pillar of shadow.

'When you return to your office, Soames, access my file. I'm sure there is a category for "Status". Delete whatever is there and put in "Permanently unavailable".'

Geiger leaned in closer. She held her ground, but wasn't happy with how much of her focus she was using to keep her adrenaline in check.

'Rosanna ... I'm sure you've done your due diligence ... and you know as much about me as there is to know. You know that they sent Hall and two others out for me ... and that they're all dead – and you've wondered about that.'

Zanni had the uneasy sense that he was one step ahead of her in every aspect of things – action, feeling, thought – and it made her furious.

'I do not want to be asked again. I do not want to take this to another level. Do you understand, Rosanna?'

'I understand,' she said.

Geiger's hands started to come up from his sides – and sinew and joints immediately tightened in Zanni, training and instinct and adrenaline kicking in as one – as she watched his fingers find his earbuds and put them back in place. His right brow rose imperceptibly, just enough to let her know he'd seen all the way in, through the lie of her placid exterior to her moment of alarm. Zanni tamped down a hot simmer. She didn't like being read. What had been her tell? A flare in her irises? Nostrils? Lips?

'Goodbye,' said Geiger. He started off in an easy jog.

Zanni studied his odd grace, his constant adjustments to damage and gravity. She knew what Dalton had done to him, had heard him say it in his own words, and one quote stayed with her: '*It wasn't that he didn't feel pain. He did. I just don't think that it hurt.*'

Geiger leaned against the running path's railing, hands wrapping round the cold steel. The water's face on Gravesend Bay was pocked by a million drops of rain.

Most things had singular meanings to Geiger. It was a stripped-down response mode Corley called 'essential perspective' – experiencing and defining things in the most basic terms and relevance to one's existence. Food was sustenance – pleasure, taste and variety were not part of the equation. Clothing was utile – style, tailoring and color had, if any, minor significance. Housing meant simple shelter and separation – an inside independent of the outside – and now that had changed. The facts of how they'd found him were unimportant. They knew where he was.

Lights twinkled on the other side of the bay – white, pale yellow, paler blue – and snakes of smoke and heat trails rose from buildings and chimneys, wooed by a heavenly charmer. A woman sang, very softly, a feathery lilt, without accompaniment. '*You are the sunshine of my life* ...' Geiger's hands rose to push the earbuds in more snugly – until he realized they hung loose at his sides.

'Go on, Soames,' said Bowe.

Her boss already had his 'I won't like the news' look on, and Zanni was certain the other three of the crew sitting behind her wore the same expression.

She shifted in her chair. The strobe ache from her encounter with the wall last night had kicked in hours ago, from her knees to her collarbone. She wore a long-sleeved pullover to hide the swelling in her wrists. She had a straight-A record, but the alphas were always waiting for her to fall on her perfect butt. Boys will be boys ... and assholes. Her career meant doing two jobs for one salary – being an agent twenty-four seven, and spending the rest of her time proving that possessing a clitoris was not a sign of weakness ... or as she had put it more than once: Having a vagina doesn't mean you're a pussy.

'I walked up to him on the street and identified myself. He didn't seem surprised. I told him we wanted to bring him back in – that there were no hard feelings. He said no. And that was that. It didn't last more than two minutes.'

She'd spent the flight back and half the night going over the episode – how Geiger had played her, reeled her in – and how he'd seen her inner flinch. It wasn't like her – at all. She saw the unbothered ash eyes, heard the smooth-as-ice voice in her ear ...

'So – no chance?' said Bowe.

As he often did, Bowe framed the words in the form of a question when it was actually a conclusion he was clearly displeased with.

'I believe that's right, sir. No chance.'

'His exact words were ... ?'

'His exact words were – "I don't work in IR any-more. You need to tell your bosses that, and tell them nothing will change that."'

'His demeanor?'

'Demeanor? Geiger's hard to describe, sir.'

'So I've heard. Try.'

'Cool. Unaffected. Kind of ... disconnected.'

The man's forefinger did five staccato taps on the desk, and then he leaned back in his chair. She could hear the others shift in their seats.

'So ... for the record,' said Bowe. 'Your conclusion is that further overtures will be pointless?'

There it was again – statement as query. The sideways approach of it irritated the hell out of her.

'Yes, sir.'

'Not good, people.' Bowe suddenly slammed his palm on the desk. 'Has anyone noticed lately that enhanced interrogation has taken a little *dip* in the fucking polls?!'

He swiveled in his chair until he faced the wide window and starless night. Zanni was relieved. The maneuver always meant a meeting was close to an end.

'This division cannot function without highly skilled interrogators, professionals who aren't going to fuck up and put us on Veritas Arcana every month – and we're seriously short-handed. Dalton has disappeared, we don't know where he is. Geiger says he's out of the game. The guys we have coming off the bench – I don't love them.'

Zanni's jaw tightened. Another sports metaphor. Why did they do that?

'Soames ... Now that Geiger knows we've found him, you think he'll go off the grid?'

'I think it would be foolish for anyone in this room to guess what Geiger might or might not do.' She hoped that would keep the rest of them quiet. She wanted to go home.

'Sir ...' came from behind her. McCormack. He subscribed to the 'last heard, first remembered' school, often waiting until he sensed he might have the final comment. Its content was of secondary importance. Its placement was what he thought had value.

'Go on, Mac.'

'The Russians said Vasillich did a decent job for them last month.'

'He's too green for us.' Bowe stood up and stepped to the window. 'I want you all thinking about leverage – ways to get Geiger back in. Starting *now*. I don't want to wait until we need him yesterday. Good night, people.'

Zanni stood up. 'Good night, sir.'

'Soames . . .'

She did her best to bury a sigh. 'Yes, sir?'

'You're taking next week off?'

'Yes, sir.'

'Enjoy yourself.'

'Thank you, sir.'

She headed out and down the hall. A drink was going to do wonders. She punched the elevator button – but the transport was in an uncooperative mood, and McCormack arrived before it did.

'Hey,' he said.

'Hey.'

The elevator's down button was already lit up, but he pressed it a few times. She bit her tongue.

McCormack smiled. 'So you just walked up and introduced yourself . . .'

'Yeah.'

'And the infamous Inquisitor said what?'

'"Who do you work for?"'

'That's it?' He reached out and punched the button again, twice.

'Mac . . . It doesn't come any faster if you keep push-ing it.'

'Habit. So where you going on vacation?'

'None of your business.'

'Relax – just asking.'

'Meeting some family. Big, big fun.'

'Get a drink?'

'No.'

'C'mon ... We'll kick back.'

'No.'

'How come?'

Zanni took an even breath. It hurt. 'Mac ... Twice was enough. I'm not crazy about the way you kiss – and you don't last long enough for me.'

McCormack took a step back, but she didn't think he was aware of doing so.

'Jeez, Zanni. Wow ... Pretty fucking cold.'

'I guess, yeah.'

The elevator came and she stepped inside. McCormack didn't.

'Sorry, Mac,' she said, and shrugged as the door closed.

9

The clink and clack of silverware and plates, the waitresses' barked orders, the farrago of conversing voices ... It was all a splendid symphony to Harry. He had called Geiger about having a meal, then found a diner a few blocks from Prospect Park – busy enough that two faces would be undistinguished but not so crowded they might have had to stand around and wait for seats. His cheddar omelet was not the equal of their old place on Columbus, but the bacon was crisp and hot, and the coffee had body.

He watched Geiger's eyes move across a line of print on the Op-Ed page of the *Times*. That had always been the ritual. Harry would get his usual – and Geiger, black coffee. Harry would bring the paper and start with the arts sections, because Geiger only read the letters to the editor. Harry would do almost all the talking – about the work, the turnings of the planet, the remarkable, ridiculous acts of the people on it – and Geiger would respond with an olio of 'yes', 'no', and 'I see'. It had taken Harry a long time to understand the man was neither aloof nor uninterested – and that his presence was, in fact, proof of some inexpressible form of commitment. They were a child god's play-room creation – ill-formed clumps of clay, randomly mushed together, that had solidified into a single entity over time. Two hearts, two minds, a shared need.

'Still just read the letters to the editor?'

'I haven't read a newspaper since our last breakfast,' said Geiger.

Harry nodded. 'And we went over my dossier for the Matheson job. Who knew, huh?'

Geiger looked up. 'Who knew what, Harry?'

Harry sighed. 'Never mind. Figure of speech.'

Geiger had read Harry's research that day, and decided to take the job. Ten hours later, Hall had shown up with Ezra instead of his father – Geiger had knocked Hall out and taken Ezra away – and the back door of the universe was blown off its hinges ...

Geiger picked up his coffee cup and held it before his lips in both hands with his fingertips, as was his custom.

'They found me,' he said.

'*They*.' Harry said it like the name of someone they both used to know. His tremors of surprise were minimal. 'Fuck. How?'

'It doesn't matter. Don't worry, I made sure no one followed me when I came here.'

'What're you going to do? Disappear?'

'I haven't decided yet.' Geiger took a measured sip. 'They wanted me for a job. They'll be back. It may come down to how many times they'll take no for an answer.'

'Before what? Before they find a way to make you say yes?'

'That won't happen, Harry. I told you. I'm done. For good.'

Harry tapped the fork's tines on the plate's edge a few times.

'Geiger ... If you leave, I want you to—'

'There's no reason to discuss it now.'

Harry started making a circular sculpture of the remains of his home fries with his fork. Nothing seemed to possess a dimension of length anymore. A life, a doctrine, a relationship, a conviction. The assumption of a thing's continuance was foolhardy.

'Listen, Geiger ... I'm going out of the country for a while. For a week, maybe. Leaving tonight – with Matheson. Veritas Arcana stuff. We got an e-mail with—'

'Harry, I don't need to know what it is.' Geiger took another sip, then put his cup down. 'You said "We".'

'Huh?'

'You said, "We got an e-mail ... "'

'Did I?' Harry broke off a small chunk of bacon and popped it in his mouth. 'Guess I'm kind of jazzed. Feels like the old days.'

'When you were a reporter.'

'Yeah. Haven't felt like this in a long time. Matter of fact ... I think you coming back from the dead has something to do with it.' Harry took a swig of coffee. 'Listen ... this trip ... Hard to tell what it might be like.'

'You mean dangerous. A setup.'

'Maybe.'

'Then why are you going, Harry?'

When Harry's blue smile came out, Geiger was waiting for it. It was the emblem of his bedrock sadness, the thing always hovering about him like cobwebs in an attic. Harry reached down to the seat and then put an eight-by-ten manila envelope on the table.

'If anything happens to me. The keys to the apartment and my safety deposit box, copies of the title to the apartment, names and instructions on what to do with it all. Just in case.'

Geiger opened the folder, pulled out a few papers, put them down before him and stared at the top sheet. It had a few typed paragraphs on it. His fingertips began a syncopated roll on the sides of his cup. He looked up at Harry.

'Who is Christine Reynaud?'

Harry felt as if he was watching a DVD from one of Geiger's sessions. The unchanging stare, the calibrated cadence in the question. The utter stillness of the man.

'We don't have to go into it now.'

'If you might not come back, then I think we do.'

Harry sat back. 'Remember the first time we sat and talked? The bar on Broadway?'

'Yes.'

'I had a hundred Wild Turkeys and told you my life story.'

'Some of it, Harry. Not all of it.'

Harry sighed. 'Right.'

Geiger's fingers finished their dance and settled on the tabletop. 'You told me about growing up, being a reporter at the *Times* ...'

'Uh-huh.'

'Then you talked about your drinking, your demotion to the Obituaries. But you didn't talk about what happened in between. All you said was – "You know that sensation ... when you feel like you've hit bottom, and you realize you're right where you belong?'"

Harry grinned – but there was nothing funny about it. His stomach started up like a clothes washer. He patted his pockets for a Pepcid but found none, and took a long slug of water to try and pre-empt the acid's ascent – but he had no strategy for fending off the vision. As is so often the case, the gods had decided to dabble in mayhem on a most ordinary day ...

He had been at his desk in the old Times Building when she'd called. After a moment checking the elevators' status he'd raced down eleven flights, five steps at a leap. The traffic in Times Square was a fused chunk of honking steel and rubber. He'd stood paralyzed, considering the capriciousness of rush-hour subways, and then gone into a mad sprint – west to Ninth Avenue, then north sixteen blocks, gasping 'S'cuse me!' and 'Outta the way!' He remembered the explosive backdraft of scorched air in his lungs as he skidded to a stop inside St. Lukes-Roosevelt and took in a huge breath ...

Harry put down his glass and met Geiger's gaze.

'I had a child once,' he said. 'A little girl. With Christine.'

The only movement in Geiger's face was an involuntary dilating of the pupils. Harry sighed again. It was the sound a priest would hear through the curtain of the confessional. He shoved the image back into the past, and leaned forward.

'I've been thinking a lot about something the last few days. About Ezra. He's hurting. He needs to know, Geiger. He really needs to know.'

'We talked about this. In the long run, he'll be better off not knowing.'

'I don't agree.'

Geiger's hand started up again – a finger-roll on the table, pinkie to thumb. 'Harry ... I know what works—'

Harry's hand suddenly shot out and smacked Geiger's flat.

'Don't say you "know what works" best for you! I've heard you say it a thousand times and I still don't know what the hell it really means! Jesus ... Just once – just once I wish that you'd ...'

Harry slid his hand away and sat back, shaking his head. Geiger remained exactly as he was. It was Harry who seemed surprised at the outburst.

'Go on, Harry. What is it you wish that I would do?'

Quintessential Geiger. Uninflected, a stranger to attitude, a living Rorschach blot to the listener. To a Jones it could paint Geiger shades of ominous, patient, arctic, wise. To Harry, it had often felt like a glimpse of a child lurking beneath the surface.

'Listen ... Maybe it works best for you – but it doesn't work best for Ezra.' He tapped the envelope. 'His iChat is Zman. One word, Z – M – A – N. It's in here, with his address and cell. You saved his life – but he thinks you sacrificed *yours* to do it. He needs to know you're okay. So ... Either you tell him, one way or another – or I will when I get back.' Harry stood up. 'Time to go. Got things to do. I'll be in touch when I get back.'

Geiger nodded, once – and watched Harry walk to the door and step out of sight. His eyes shifted and fixed on the shiny nebula of oil that floated on the surface of the coffee left in his cup. The diner suddenly seemed louder, and each clink and uttered word etched its distinctive mark on the aural swirl. Some tiny filament fired in the part of his brain that sheltered its unremembered secrets – and he heard a sigh, dulcet, mournful – but couldn't be certain whether it came from a nearby table or booth, or a place that defied concrete definition. Then the waiter was at his side.

'Would you like something else?' asked the waiter.

Geiger's right forefinger started a solo tap on the table, as if he had found a beat within the sound. He closed his eyes.

'No,' he said. 'Nothing.'

10

The early morning lines for non-Europeans at Paris Orly passport control were long. Harry still had half a dozen weary travelers in front of him while Matheson had already breezed through the section for nationals with a phony French passport, a perfect accent, short gray hair and a salt and pepper goatee. Harry had a carry-on duffel, and his laptop and private software – on disks sporting labels of albums by the Allman Brothers, R. Kelly and Coldplay – were in the scuffed leather portfolio he'd had since he was a reporter at the *Times*.

He looked at the 'Thomas Jones' passport in his hand. Six years ago, Geiger had taken a gig in Cancun – some bad blood in the luxury condo business – and they had acquired quality forgeries for the trip through Carmine. He remembered Carmine handing him the documents, patting him on the back and saying, 'Harry ... take good care of my boy ...' – as if Geiger, the man who broke the wills of killers and kings, was a naïf who needed looking after. And Harry remembered looking at Carmine's hard, cobalt eyes and thinking – *If anything happened to Geiger, this guy would rip out my liver and make me eat it.*

The immigrations official was a woman in her twenties – pale and stiff-backed in her crisp blue shirt, with a short frown she clearly hadn't had much time to earn. Maybe they taught you how to wear it at border police school. Harry handed the passport to her.

Her eyes went from his picture up to Harry's face, then back down.

'Monsieur Jones . . . visit in France why?' she asked in poor English.

'To see an old friend.'

'In Paris?'

'Yes. That's right. For a few days, maybe a week.'

He faked a yawn and sneaked a glimpse at the security camera on the cubicle wall behind her.

There was a fuzzy squawk that seemed to come from a few spots simultaneously. Harry's head did a ninety and saw a uniformed man across the area put his two-way radio to his ear. Then Harry picked out two other blue-shirts doing the same. The men looked up as one – directly at Harry – and started walking toward him. He tried to turn off the spigot flooding him with fear.

'Ne bougez pas, monsieur,' said the police woman. And she made a gesture commanding him not to move.

Harry turned back to her. The frown did a little twitch, and caused Harry's internal screws to tighten from head to foot.

The trio were five feet away and there was no place for Harry to go. He watched them coming for him, one stride quicker than the last, and the tallest brushed against him as they went past. Harry turned and watched them stop at the next line and kneel around a silver-haired old woman who was lying on the floor. She might have been a fainter. Or maybe she'd suffered the heart attack Harry was certain he was about to have. The men exchanged comments, then gently helped the woman into a sitting position.

'Bon,' said his official. Harry's sweat had glued his shirt to his back.

'Bien, monsieur . . .' She stamped the passport, held it out to him, and her lips curled upward into one of the sweetest smiles Harry had ever seen. 'Paris! Ah, Paris!'

'Thank you,' he said, took the passport, grabbed his belongings, and walked through. Matheson was leaning against a wall twenty yards away waiting for him by the baggage claim area. He picked up his bag and they headed for the exit through the 'nothing to declare' customs gate.

'We check into the hotel, then I'm going out to look at places for us to meet him. Give him some options, let him choose – so he doesn't get spooked.'

The anonymous e-mailer had responded within an hour to Matheson's message. He would meet them in Paris. Matheson had made plane and hotel reservations – coach and three-star. Not that money was scarce – nine years ago Matheson had inherited sixteen million dollars when his hedge fund manager father suddenly dropped dead – but except for Ezra's child support every penny was considered part of the Veritas Arcana budget, and first-class seats and luxury suites were not only expensive, they were conspicuous.

Glass doors sensed their approach and slid apart, and the two men stepped outside toward the long line of cabs. Matheson checked out the sky. The early morning sun was a white smear behind a slow-marching phalanx of clouds.

'Sixty percent chance of rain tomorrow,' he said.

'Does that matter?'

'It might.' Matheson moved on towards the cab at the head of the line. 'Taxi!'

The man lowered the *Herald Tribune*'s crossword puzzle and watched the men get into the back of a cab. He brought his cell phone to his lips.

'They are getting in a taxi. Come up, not too fast.' His English had a creamy gloss of a French accent on it.

'On my way,' came the reply.

As the taxi pulled out from the curb a silver Citroen DS4 glided up past the row of cabs and pulled over, and the Frenchman slid into shotgun.

'You have them?' he asked.

The driver nodded. 'Blue Opel. License number BD – 611 – AX.' His accent was flat and nasal, an echo from a Bible-belt wheat field, and his face was straight out of a Boys Scouts poster. 'There's two of them?'

'Yes. Not sure how that will sit. I will call. Go.'

The driver cracked his knuckles, curling each finger inward toward his palms, and then swung into traffic, three cars behind their quarry. The cab was following signs that read 'PARIS – A6B'.

The Frenchman tapped at his cell, and while he waited glanced at the driver, who was less than half his age. It seemed they were all half his age these days. This one was two years out of the army, a year into freelance, full of brass and questions – gung ho, as they liked to say in the States.

'We are leaving the airport,' he reported to the cell. 'Matheson is here. Disguised. And he has another man with him.' He drew the edge of his thumbnail slowly up and down the deep cleft in his chin. It was an old habit, proof of deep focus. 'All right,' he said, and clicked off. 'If they split up we each take one.'

The driver kept his gaze on the road. 'Yessir.'

The Frenchman took a pen from behind his ear and looked at the puzzle in his lap.

'Dewey ...' he said. 'A favor, please. Do not call me "sir". You are not in the military anymore – and I feel old enough as it is.'

The driver gave a quick nod. 'Right,' he said.

The Frenchman checked his watch, and wrote the time down on the newspaper's margin. Dewey glanced over.

'That is one excellent watch, Victor.'

Victor raised his wrist. 'A Zannetti Dragon.' He looked at the large facing – a gold and green Chinese dragon made up of thousands of tiny impressions. He thought back. Milan ... 2003 ... the race car driver who raped the girl ... delivered to her family. 'When a job is done, I always buy something in that city before I leave. A ritual, I suppose.' He looked back down to the puzzle.

'I get that,' said Dewey. 'Cool.'

Dewey was jazzed to the max. The job was a real step up – the money, the action – and working with the Frenchman was like winning the lottery. The dude was the pros' pro – he could teach him a lot – and if Dewey didn't screw up maybe Victor would hook him up with another gig. It was as good as it gets. Put some more coins in the jukebox, ladies. Dewey's gonna dance with every one of you tonight.

'Question,' he said.

'Yes?'

'Have you ever killed someone in the job?'

The Frenchman filled in an answer with neat, block letters. The only ability that had improved in the last ten years was his crossword puzzle skills. Everything else was in a lessening mode. Not at a high enough rate or degree that anyone else was aware of it – it was still his secret, and cunning and experience still masked a host of things – but in his profession, the first time someone noticed would likely be the last. *C'est la vie.*

'Why would you want to know that, Dewey?'

'Professional curiosity, I guess. I mean ... You being a heavy hitter so long ... I was just wondering about it – what it feels like. That's all.'

'I'll give you two answers. Yes, I have. And – it doesn't *feel* like anything. That's why I've been able to do this for so long.'

Dewey nodded. 'Right. I get that.'

The Frenchman doubted the declaration. Dewey was a kill virgin who probably assumed there was little or no difference between lobbing a grenade into a dark, open door – and putting the nose of a gun to the back of a skull and pulling the trigger. The Frenchman knew the difference, and he also knew the folly of trying to describe it to someone who didn't.

Harry stood on the thin mini-balcony of his room at Hotel Littré, leaning on the wrought-iron railing, looking down at Rue Littré – a narrow, one-way, single-block street. Except for two riders on motor-scooters, there'd been no traffic for ten minutes. The hotel, off

Rue de Rennes, was a small, gray-stone, five-story accommodation. Their adjoining rooms were on the second floor – high ceilings with ornate molding, bathrooms with cream-colored pedestal sinks, and a mini-bar with Bonnat chocolates, half-bottles of red Bordeaux, and some packs of flatbread and brie.

'Harry ...'

Harry leaned back inside. Matheson was in the doorway that linked their rooms, dressed in jeans and a sweatshirt.

'I have to get going. I'll be all over the city looking for spots. And I've been thinking ... It might be better if you aren't at the rendezvous – so it's just a one-on-one. Keep his stress down.'

'Well ... He doesn't have to see me – but I want to be there. I can be nearby.'

Matheson played with it. 'Okay. That'll work. You staying in or going out?'

'Probably out. Wander around. Be a tourist.'

Matheson headed for the door. 'I'll call when I'm heading back.'

'David ... Wait.'

Matheson glanced back. 'What is it?'

'Geiger's alive.'

The words pulled Matheson to a full stop and spun him around like a top.

'*What?*'

'I found out two days ago.'

'Jesus ...'

'He's in Brooklyn. Making furniture. The feds know too.'

'Jesus Christ ...'

'Yeah.'

'*Jesus – fucking –Christ* …' Somewhere in Matheson's astonishment was the start of a thought …and then it kicked in. 'Does Ez know?'

'I told Geiger he had to tell him – so Ezra knows by now or *I'll* tell him when we get back.'

Matheson was nodding very slowly, like a man getting a first, sweet taste of clemency. 'This will change Ezra's life.'

Harry nodded.

'Thank you for telling me, Harry.'

'I probably shouldn't have – but I figured Ezra would tell you, eventually – so …'

Matheson took in a deep breath, to keep things from spilling out. 'Gotta go. See you tonight.'

'Right.'

Matheson stepped out into the hall and closed the door behind him.

Harry turned back to the view. He'd stayed awake the whole flight but wasn't sleepy. His body's clock had adjusted itself – not to the time difference, but to the anticipation of events. Harry had a picture in his mind, of his passion – shattered long ago, pieces flying like shrapnel, embedded in him all these years – and now some magnet was alive at his center, pulling the shards free and drawing them back together …

The concierge looked at her computer screen. 'Pour une nuit?'

'Oui.' The Frenchman handed her a credit card.

'Merci, monsieur.'

He didn't turn around when Matheson came out of

the elevator into the lobby and headed for the front door.

'Bonne journée, monsieur,' said the concierge, but Matheson either didn't hear her or was too wrapped up in his own thoughts to answer – and went out the door.

Harry watched Matheson come out of the lobby and head toward Rue de Rennes. Overhead, the clouds were sliding by in blockish clumps, and every so often the sun's rays slipped through and lacquered the buildings with the diaphanous shimmer that had brought thousands of painters to the City of Light like believers trekking to Mecca.

11

The café was on Rue St Jacques, the street-level space of a three-story residence whose apartments' tall, white shutters were in serious need of a coat of paint. The last time Harry had stood here, the place had been a noisy, family-run boulangerie in its third decade, known for its croissants and brioche. The tinted-glass frontage and red door were the same, but now there was an oval, wooden plaque above them with an engraved name: SOLEIL COUCHANT. On his last night in Brooklyn, Harry had gone on Google Maps, found Rue St Jacques and strolled digitally down the street till he found the storefront. He was an amateur with the language but he knew the word – 'Couchant' was French for 'sunset' – and he knew why it had been chosen.

He stepped to the door's glass to get a better view inside. Half a dozen patrons sat at tables beneath the spill of pin-spot pendants hanging from the high, pressed-tin ceiling.

'Excusez moi ...'

Harry turned to a man in a turtleneck and winter vest. The Frenchman had raised one patient brow.

'Après vous?'

Harry's mind stuttered for a moment at the decision. 'Oui,' he said.

The Frenchman made an elegant after-you gesture. Harry turned the knob – and when he opened the door a sweet, crisp jingle of an overhead bell sounded. He went inside.

The smell of rich, potent coffee was as seductive as the nymph Calypso. Renovative sleight of hand had created extra space without any actual expansion. There were fifteen small tables with beige granite tops and deco-style bistro bases. The floor was dark slate, the walls paneled with old-fashioned wainscoting. On the left was a mahogany bar with leather and brass stools, and Miles Davis floated through the air leaving a honeyed aural coating on everything. The overall effect was as close to time travel as one could achieve, and the owner's opinion was clear: If you were looking for coffee and a few moments of peace, or sought a stronger libation and a state closer to thoughtlessness – the past was preferable to the present.

Harry sat down at the bar. The bartender and the waitress – in their twenties, lean and attractive in black dress shirts and gray slacks – were huddled at the wide, three-tap espresso machine. She pushed a square white button and they waited. The machine began to grumble unpleasantly, then gave out a wet belch and went silent. The pair looked at each other and frowned, then noticed Harry. The bartender came over.

'Bonjour, monsieur ...'

'Café crème, please.'

'Très bien.' The bartender turned round and went to

work, pouring coffee into a large cup. 'Where are you from in America? New York?'

'That's right.'

The bartender grinned over his shoulder. 'I like to try and guess.'

'*Merde! Je m'en fous, Marcel! Il est encore foutu.*'

It was a woman's voice, ripe with righteous anger. Harry had always felt French made cursing something of an art form, and he knew a few. *'Shit! I don't give a fuck, Marcel! It's fucking broken again!'* she had said.

A slim woman in an oversized, long-sleeved, cream-colored blouse and pleated slacks marched out of a back room, cell phone to her ear. Her hair was the color of a penny and rested in waves on her shoulders. Her face had striking, wide planes. If someone saw her, they would remember her.

'*Faut résoudre le problème, Marcel! Fix it! Now!'* She punched off the call, sat down at the end of the bar, and slammed her palm down. Her two employees flinched. '*Trou du cul!*' she growled, elevating 'Asshole!' to a poetic realm.

Then she glanced up and saw Harry staring at her. The sudden outbreak of so many feelings at once made the woman's expression a spectacle – shock striking the forehead and etching three stiff lines across it . . . recognition widening the pale blue eyes as the pupils flared . . . something lighter-than-air raising the ends of her lips up an infinitesimal degree – and ruling over it all, a sorrow instantly rekindled.

'Hello, Chris,' said Harry.

He'd always been able to read her moods, no matter how subtle, but not now. And she seemed to be in the same state – caught up in the swirl of her feelings and uncertain where she was going to land. She stood up and walked to him, close enough that he could smell the single drop of Chanel No. 5 she always dabbed behind each ear.

'Hello, Harry,' she said.

The inches between them could be measured in years. They could be measured by the slow, crawling ebb of intimacy in spite of love and want – and by the unstoppable, off-kilter turning of lives – when winter had come but never left, and the chill and inescapable shiver finally became too much to bear.

'This is very strange, right?' said Harry.

'Yes, it is. Very.'

'You think a hug is doable?'

He opened his arms. It might have been that she agreed, or perhaps just needed some kind of anchor in the vertigo of the moment – but she leaned into him, and their arms gently closed round each other. She hadn't put on any weight.

He put his lips to her ear. 'How do you say "I've missed you" in French?' He felt the muscles in her slim back beneath the silk tense, and then soften.

'Tu m'as manqué,' she said, and took a step back. Seeing her faint smile rise was like watching a memory come back to life. 'You know how to say that, Harry. You heard it every day when you came home.'

There was a dreamy buzz seeping into the whole event – the throwback look of the place, the waitress and bartender in Harry's line of sight staring curiously, the soul-chilled jazz, the rickety rope-bridge between them that spanned thirteen years and a deep, mist-filled crevasse where joy and hope lay.

Christine turned to her employees. 'André ... Nicole ... This is Harry Boddicker. We used to be married.'

First came the widening of eyes at the news that their boss had ever had a husband, then the intensified refocusing on Harry with that new knowledge in mind.

'Yeah, I know,' Harry said to them. 'I got that look all the time. Kind of a beauty and the beast thing – right?' The bartender and waitress managed grins to try and mask their embarrassment. 'Feel like a walk, Chris?'

The simplest of questions seemed to have her stumped. Her gaze drifted to the floor, as if the answer might be written on it. She sighed so deeply that the sheer silk of her blouse fluttered, then she turned to the bar.

'André,' she said, 'call me when Marcel is here.'

The bartender nodded, and Christine picked up her cell phone.

'Yes, Harry,' she said, 'let's walk,' and they headed for the door. She grabbed her coat off an antique rack and they went out.

The man in the turtleneck was sitting at a corner table, watching them over the rim of his teacup. His thumbnail played at his chin's cleft and his eyes never left them until they had turned right and walked out of sight. He put a few coins on the table, picked up his *Tribune* and walked out to the street. The couple was strolling slowly, and as he headed their way he took out his cell and made a call.

'The second man's name is Boddicker,' Victor said. 'Harry Boddicker.'

'Boddicker?' came the response. 'I know that name. Wait.'

The Frenchman heard the phone being put down – then the crisp *click-clack* of fingers on a keyboard. Then silence.

'Stay on him at all times.'

The call was ended, and the Frenchman's cell went back in his pocket. He zipped up his vest. It was a bit cooler than he had expected. Not that he minded – he'd come from Singapore where the air had been hot and damp. The combination always riled his sinuses – and he hated using a knife with sweaty hands.

They crossed at Place Edmond Rostand, the rotary where Boulevard Saint Michel, Rue Gay-Lussac and Rue Soufflot converged, and walked through the eastern gate of the Luxembourg Gardens. There had been more steps taken than words spoken since they left the café, the adjustment to each other's presence taking precedence over the swap and updating of biographies – and Harry was content with that.

'You look good,' she said. 'I always thought you would age nicely.'

'You look great, and you aren't aging at all. How exactly does that work?'

'I sleep with lots of young men,' she said, 'and then murder them and drink their blood.' The warm winter had rescheduled the bloom of things. The grass was already a brazen green. Tulips swayed in pastel congregations. She slid her arm inside his as they walked down the wide, treed promenade.

'Why are you here, Harry?'

'I'm on a job.'

'That's not what I meant.' She glanced over at him. 'You know what I meant.'

Some human elements prove indestructible, armored against tragedy, and guilt – even the dispassionate abrasion of time. She'd never steered round a conversational corner, never put off stating what was on her mind to preserve a moment's lightness. Harry was glad to see some of the old her was still calling the shots.

'Listen, Chris ... I've been through a lot of stuff ... and come out the other end. The job was here – and when I thought about coming, I thought about seeing you, and that was more of a reason to come. I mean – this doesn't feel crazy, does it?'

The view on their right opened up to display the massive Luxembourg Palace – a stately, three-tiered chunk of seventeenth-century majesty.

'No. It doesn't feel crazy,' she said. Harry heard her sigh, and watched her small, elegant shoulders rise and then slowly descend.

They stopped at a pair of garden chairs and sat down. Sunshine was a sparkling gilt atop the surface of the gardens' large, central pool, and parents kept watchful gazes on their children as they leaned over the rounded marble rim, sailing their toy boats on the water. Their bursts of sweet laughter were jazz riffs amid the birds' steady melody.

'You don't drink anymore, do you?' she asked.

'Not for almost twelve years.'

'I can tell. Isn't that odd – after all this time apart?'

The Frenchman watched them from the opposite side of the pool as he made a cell call.

'Hi,' Dewey answered.

'Where are you now, Dewey?'

'Notre Dame.' He pronounced it like the American football team. 'Matheson went inside for a while and now we're walking around outside. Before that he went into a big McDonald's on Boulevard Saint Germain, then walked along the river for a while.'

'This second man seems to be of significance. For now, I am to stay with him and you remain with Matheson.'

'Got it. Listen ... Can I ask you a question, Victor?'

'Yes.'

'Seeing as how we're dealing with *two* guys now ... Shouldn't we, y'know – do you think we should get more money?'

'Perhaps you should bring that up.'

'Well ... I thought, y'know, cuz we're partners, and you're senior, maybe *you* should bring it up.'

'Dewey ... I have worked with many people, but I have never had a partner.'

There were a few ticks of dead air. 'Okay. Right – I get that.'

'You should consider how you wish to deal with that by yourself. You see?'

'Got it. Later.'

Dewey's end went dead. The Frenchman took a pull on his Gitanes and ground it out. His father had told him, twenty-five years ago, sharing a bottle of Côtes du Rhône, that if you lived long enough life provided you with a surprising kind of inverted wisdom – of how few truths there actually were in the world. The son was now as old as the father had been and had come to be of the same mind – and the list was a short one.

Wine is the only thing in life that gets better with age.

Smart people are never quite as smart as they think they are.

No one in a lucid state of mind dies without regret.

The job was always easier when he was on his own.

Christine put her face up to the sun and closed her eyes. The sight of her that way made something in Harry ache. He used to lie in bed and watch her while she slept. It was something about the simple quiet in her face.

'Papa died eight years ago,' she said, 'and I turned the shop into the café. There are a thousand things to do, and I keep a small staff, on purpose, so I barely have time to take a breath. I get up at five and go till eleven, then I go home and sit with a book and a glass of wine, and when my eyes start to droop I go to bed. I make sure I never have time to just *think*.' She opened her eyes. 'That's how I do it, Harry.'

He could see her standing alone at the end of the hospital corridor, its cold whiteness casting her as a waif on a deserted winter street. She had sensed him there, and her head had come up to look at him, but she hadn't moved to him. Her stillness had been a bipolar magnet – pulling him toward her and at the same time repelling him, keeping him distanced from the possibility of some awful utterance, some bare, unbearable, annihilating fact ...

'But you named the place "Soleil Couchant",' he said. 'Not exactly the best way to keep a memory buried.'

'No, never buried. Always in my heart. I just try and keep her out of my head.'

'Plus facile à dire qu'à taire,' Harry said softly, uncertainly.

Christine grinned. '"Easier said than done" is "C'est plus facile à dire qu'à *faire*".'

'What did I say?'

'You said "Easier said than *keep silent*," sort of.' Her eyes suddenly glimmered. 'It was always so sweet when you tried to talk French.' Her cell rang – and Christine looked grateful for it. She answered. 'Oui?' She listened, and then stood up. 'Harry ... I have to go. The repair man ...'

Harry got to his feet. 'I'll come back with you.'

'Maybe you shouldn't, Harry. Maybe we should just say goodbye now.'

'We could do that – or I could come back and sit in a corner and read the *Trib* until seven or so, then you could have dinner with me – and *then* we could say goodbye.'

She had always looked younger to him whenever she tried to make up her mind about something difficult. The shoulders shrugged downward, the head tilting to one side, the arms coming up and crossing. Like a child. Then a long sigh before she answered ...

'Not until nine. Then we'll go home. I'll cook,' she said.

Notre Dame's gargoyles looked down at the crowd in Parvis Notre Dame, the public square at the entrance to the cathedral, with their frozen, timeless glares.

The rose peddlers were out in force. Dewey had seen them in Rome, Florence, Barcelona – toting long-stems in cellophane. Fleece vests and khakis, swarthy, jet-black hair and clipped staches – they meandered through the crowd, their come-on a meld of meek and obstinate. They reminded him of worker ants back on the farm – one-minded, determined, their only goal the betterment of the colony. They were creeps but he admired them. If the Afghanis had had some of that, every Taliban prick would've had a 5.56mm in their skull years ago – and a lot of his buddies would still be yanking his chain instead of doing eternity rent-free in coffins. The rest of the guys? Most of them home now, living on food stamps and Mike's Hard Lemonade, waiting for some bow-tie a-hole at the Veterans Admin to read the disability request they sent in a year ago. And whaddaya know? Here's Jefferson High's No-Can-Dewey already with fifty thou in cash that Unc Sam couldn't touch. Go figure.

Matheson seemed intrigued with the square. He'd been strolling for twenty minutes, sitting on the stone edgings of the small gardens, turning this way and that for a sense of positioning. Dewey agreed with him. It would be a good choice for the meet – busy but spacious, flat and without any verticals to block sight-lines, so Matheson would have a three-sixty to see someone approaching, and options for escape to busy streets if he got suspicious ... or it turned bad.

The guy had cojones, knowing he might be walking into a fuck-you – and then it kind of snuck up on Dewey ... one of those thoughts that make you put other things aside for a moment so you have the headroom to step back and take a longer look at it. In a way, Matheson was a sort of soldier, too – in his own volunteer army, fighting for what he believed in ... something bigger than him, and ready to take a bullet for it. A lot of people back home thought the guy was a traitor, an enemy of the good ol' American way – and many of them had 'Support Our Troops' ribbons on their bumpers but never gave one second's thought to the bullshit a warrior had to slog through once he got back ...

They weren't wondering how long it took to get a job, or a prescription, or treatment, or a new leg – and weren't keeping count of how many jarheads ran out of faith and sanity and time and bought a ticket out of this life on the Beretta Express because it seemed to make more sense than anything else. Dewey felt he was cool-ass steady enough to take Matheson down without a blink when it was time – but the dude was okay. He had the right stuff.

Matheson pecked at his cell. 'Hi,' he said. 'I'm heading back. I'm going to set the meet at the square at Notre Dame, for ten. It'll be busy by then. Where are you?'

Harry's answer came through the line. 'At a café on Rue St Jacques. I'm gonna have dinner ... with an old friend. Is that cool?'

'Sure. See you at the hotel later tonight.'

He pocketed his phone and took a final look around. This was the place. He'd e-mail the mystery man when he got back: The man would buy a rose and sit on the northeast corner of the garden closest to the cathedral, with the flower on his lap, petals facing the doors. Harry would mingle with the tourists. At any given moment there would be dozens of people taking video and photos – so if it *was* a setup, that would discourage action out in the open.

He felt the blues coming round – his own, minor moon in its slow, solitary orbit, circling into view once or twice a day. The nearness of people often brought it on. The sweet, human medley of faces and voices. Intertwining hands and arms round waists, lips close to another's ear murmuring secrets, a child saddled up on a father's shoulders. A thousand simple intimacies. At these times, he did a quick self-examination – checking for hints of bitterness or self-pity, but there were none. He knew his choices had made him who he was – you didn't meet many others in the shadows, searching for things that others had hidden there. And if you spent most of your life there, then the ties to those you loved frayed … and snapped. It was his doing. So be it.

He headed for the Pont au Double, to cross over the Seine to the left bank.

Dewey watched Matheson start through the crowd. He came out from behind the statue of Charlemagne to continue the tail – and a rose peddler stepped in front of him and held out his wares.

'Une fleur, monsieur? Une rose? Deux euros. Pour une femme ... ?'

Dewey gave the man a slow smile, then dug two coins from a pocket. 'Sure.'

'Merci, monsieur.'

Dewey took a flower. 'You guys're all totally fucked – y'know that, right?'

The peddler cocked his head. 'No English, monsieur.'

'Your life, man. You'll always be second-class this way. Stoke up your pride, dude. Be smart. Go back home.'

He started away. As he passed a young woman in a tight jacket that announced the curves beneath it, he stopped. She was taking a picture of the cathedral.

'Hey babe ...'

She lowered her camera. 'Oui?'

He held out the rose. 'Here.'

She hesitated, and then took the offering with a grin. 'Merci.'

Dewey tipped an imaginary hat. 'Now you'll never forget me,' he said, and walked off.

12

'*You are the sunshine of my life ...*'

He had the song on 'repeat' – and it had been his accompaniment for the long hours – a slow, acoustic version he'd found on iTunes by a woman, a Norwegian named Vedvik, that came close to the feel of the voice that he'd heard half a dozen times now. He was using the song as a musical magnet – to try and pull something out of his depths.

The first time he'd felt the presence it had been the late arrival of an echo, a sense of something in the air brushing his skin. Softer than a breath, like the scent of a woman's perfume reaching you three strides after she's passed by. Now it had become a visitor, with a reason to come calling.

Geiger worked the chamois over the gleaming mahogany in a circular motion, expanding the circumference with every cycle. He'd gone round the clock to finish the piece. Everything needed to be finished, to be done – because he was going to leave. To his mind, Deep Red had already moved into his home. So he was going, and there would be nothing left undone, nothing that could ever come to mind – next week, next year –

that would feel incomplete. There would be a hard line of demarcation drawn between now and what would come next, between an end and a beginning.

It was clear now, though he'd not seen it taking shape. It had come to him fully formed. He would make his father's choice – the very same one. He would live with the wood, carve a life out of the forest, high and silent, somewhere only the clouds touched. There would be no words, no signals or messages or pulsing images. *This is my gift to you. You are no one.* And there would be no one else. He would be alone, with her voice.

The to-do list for his departure was a short one. A trip to the bank and safety deposit box, packing a duffel's worth of clothes, an e-mail to Harry, the destruction of his laptop and, lastly, a final errand in the city – then on to the Port Authority Bus Terminal where it had begun sixteen years ago. The bus driver's hand nudging his shoulder – '*End of the line, son …*' – waking him, without memory or identity, without need of communion, sealed within himself like a chrysalis with no urge to open.

He stepped back from the table. He could see his reflection in the buffed surface, but the nature of the wood masked all detail. It could have been anyone.

Christine watched him scoop up the last of the coq au vin and finish it. His favorite dish. Harry leaned back.

'Never better. Magnifique.'

'Haven't made it in years.' She picked up her water and had a sip.

'You can have wine, you know,' he said. 'It's not a problem for me.'

'Yes?' Harry nodded, and she got up and left his sight, into the kitchen. He took in the room. The one-story, two-bedroom house was half an hour north of the café, in a quiet neighborhood on Rue Antoine de Saint Exupéry, bought by her parents thirty years ago – and she hadn't done much to it since her father died. The sofa and dishwasher looked new, but the rest looked familiar, endlessly lived in, and the radiators still complained loudly of neglect. He heard her pull a cork from a bottle. He'd told her about Lily's death, but not the how and why – and for whatever reason, Christine seemed to think he'd stayed on at the *Times* all these years – and he had said nothing to correct that assumption. She returned with a glass of red wine.

'Outside?' she said.

Harry got up and they walked through the living room. He realized he'd not seen a photograph anywhere, of anyone. Christine opened a set of glass doors and they stepped outside, onto a semicircled stone patio. The dampness in the night was keeping a touch of the day's warmth from dying. The wash of light from inside painted shadows blacker than the dark on the small backyard. He could make out the silhouette of the fence-top and the oak bench where they had made love sitting up after her parents had gone to sleep – silently, his hand over her mouth when she came – because Christine's bed-springs squeaked too loudly. They'd had no real way of knowing for certain, but later on, they had decided it was the night Sophie had been conceived.

Christine sipped her wine and studied Harry's profile. Its gentleness had always fit his manner, but his presence was like a whirlwind, whipping things up inside her and tossing them about.

'How did you get the scar?' she asked.

Harry turned to her, and his hand went to his forehead – fingertips on the thin, two-inch seam that ran out of his hairline. Carmine called it Harry's mark of Cain.

'Everybody should have one,' he'd said. 'Tells the world you paid your dues – so *do not fuck with me*.'

Harry grinned. 'I thought about telling people I got it in a sword fight over the honor of a fair maiden, but I got mugged in Central Park. A year after you left. I was drunk. They would've killed me – but someone came by and beat the hell out of them. Man named Geiger.'

'Jesus, Harry ...'

'Saved my life.'

'Geiger? Like the counter?'

'Uh-huh. We became friends. Close friends.' A window in a house beyond the fence went dark, and it pulled him back toward another time when he felt lighter, free of weariness, without a coterie of ghosts following him about. 'This is pretty nice.'

'It's been years since anyone's been out here with me.'

His head slowly leaned toward her. She didn't move to meet him, but she didn't lean back, either, so he continued in – and their lips met in a kiss. Halfway through its five-second life, Harry's mind tapped him on the shoulder. He straightened up. A gloomy little grin came out.

'No, huh?'

Christine shook her head. 'I'm sorry, Harry.'

'It's okay. It was a very nice kiss.'

'Yes it was.'

Every heart has both warden and prisoner – tasked with keeping the dreadful and cruel under lock and key while they try and escape. Christine's diligence failed her for a moment – and her eyes welled with tears.

'Harry ... This isn't good for me. I keep everything in its place, nailed down tight. You being here – you bring her with you.' She blotted her eyes with the heels of her palms before the tears could fall. 'Seeing you ... It's wonderful. But I can't have you here. I need you to go. Please don't be angry.'

'I'm not angry.'

'But you wouldn't tell me if you were.' She smiled and then softly stroked his cheek. 'Those last years ... your drinking ... How terrible for you – to love me so, and suddenly hate me at the same time. And you never said a word.'

There were times when Harry could still feel the bourbon's burn at the back of his throat – the booze's opening act making its announcement: 'It's on its way. You'll be cool in a minute. We're working on it.'

He shook his head. 'Chris ... That's not what happened.' He walked out into the yard, out of the light. Some things were easier to say in the dark. 'You left Sophie for *a minute*, something every parent does a zillion times a day – and something terrible happened. And you, being you ... you had to find a *reason* – something to grab hold of so you didn't go under. Something to try and make sense of it. And I always understood that. I got that. The "Why didn't I ...?" The "How could I have ... ?" The "If only I had ..."' He heard himself sigh. 'But because there *was* no reason, you latched on to guilt and held on for dear life – and you couldn't hold on to anything else … including me.'

Christine felt the old chill – the shiver that slid quickly down her arms into her hands, the ague when there was no fever. She watched Harry step back into the light, and his blue, yearning smile broke her heart again.

'I didn't hate you, Chris … I *missed* you – and after a while I found out that when I was drunk I didn't miss you as much.' He shrugged. 'We *both* found something else to hold on to … instead of each other. That's what happened.'

She opened the front door. 'I used to wonder – maybe we didn't love each other enough to get through … to hold us together.'

Harry zipped up his coat. 'I don't think that's true. Do you?'

'I don't know, Harry. These days what's true or not doesn't seem as important to me as it used to. Shall I drive you?'

'No. I'll walk to the metro.'

She leaned to him and brushed his lips with hers.

'Goodnight, Christine.'

'Goodbye, Harry. Take care.'

He hesitated, wondering if he had anything else to say – words worthy of a last goodbye to someone you once adored – but she closed the door softly and stepped back into the dark.

Through a window, Christine watched him turn and walk away, then went to a small breakfront, took out a bottle and poured a generous helping of cognac into a

snifter. She sat down in a chair, and the tip of her forefinger began to slowly circumnavigate the glass's rim,
sending a low, mournful trill around the room. It suited
her mood. He was right about the guilt ... and all that
came after. When you're drowning, you grab hold of
whatever a desperate hand finds and don't let go. She
rolled the glass in her palms. He was still the sweetest
man she'd ever known – and she prayed he didn't come
back. She sniffed in the liquid's fragrance. She was going
to need all of it tonight.

There were faint priestly collars of fog round the streetlamps and Rue Antoine de Saint Exupery felt like a
Hollywood backlot – a perfect replica of the real thing
where the short, square, whitewashed houses were plywood facades with nothing behind them and no one
inside. Harry had sensed the possibility of a new beginning in Matheson's basement – and this felt like part of
it. Perhaps a beginning meant laying lingering things to
rest – things torn loose from their natural place that
drifted from past to present and back on the breeze of
a whim ...

   Most likely because his head was full of thoughts, as
he neared the white van parked at the curb with the side
door wide open his notice was cursory. Someone has
forgotten to lock up, he thought – perhaps a drunkard
or daydreamer or sad, preoccupied soul – and the possibility it was anything more did not occur until two
hands grabbed him from behind and shoved him down
and into the van. When his face and chest met the backseat two other hands grabbed his shoulders and dragged
him in deeper. He felt the full weight of the first

assailant coming down on him, fixing him there. There was that rental car aroma – the mild mint they sprayed in the interior for the next customer.

'Now,' said a man with an elegant French accent – was there any other kind? – and as the needle plunged into his neck Harry got a whiff of a familiar, singular chemical odor. It was propofol. Over eleven years, he'd injected dozens of Joneses with it. In another time and place, he would have appreciated the sublime irony. As it was, the stickler-for-detail in him started counting off the seconds of consciousness he knew he had left – no more than seven or eight, but more than enough to consider the astonishing depth of his stupidity. And then – he wasn't there anymore.

As the Frenchman came in from outside, the young night clerk looked up from the anatomy textbook on the counter and rubbed his tired eyes. 'Bonsoir, monsieur ...'

Victor pointed at the rows of door keys. 'Quarante–huit.'

'Ah. Monsieur ...' He glanced at the computer monitor beside the tome. '... Fontaine.' He took a key off the rack and handed it to the Frenchman. 'Bonne nuit, monsieur.'

'Bonne nuit.'

The elevator was waiting. He stepped in and pressed '4' and began his ascent. He yawned, and checked his watch. One-twenty. When he was young and worked the docks they called him 'Diamant' – because he was harder than a rock and never wore down. Now, he could still go round the clock with a clear head, but his body sent him messages – yawns, and twinges and spasms in muscles that protested the mind's disregard for their age. He looked up, and in the burnished brass wall saw his reflection – a slight tilt of a frown, the raised right brow a crescent moon hovering over an eye. A woman in Cologne he'd had for a week once told him he always looked puzzled about something – and displeased that he was. She'd been closer to the truth than she knew – but this job was proceeding well. Step one, done. Step two, now. Step three would be the most difficult, but its unique elements were appealing. After all these years, that was a plus. The elevator opened and he walked out toward his room.

Matheson sat at a desk before his laptop, reading the whistleblower's original e-mail for the hundredth and last time, trying to soak up any more sense of the writer. He'd sent the rendezvous info two hours ago, and received a response ten minutes later. *I think 12.00 more acceptable for me, no? more of crowds there then. More people, I feel safer. Tell me.* Matheson liked the logic and anxiety in it. It felt sincere. He'd written back in agreement and received a reply in a few minutes. *Much thanks. I be there 12.00.*

He closed the e-mail and stared at the desktop image – eight-year-old Ezra smiling, violin under his chin. Matheson stubbed his cigarette out and took a sip of Grey Goose. Every time he looked at the photo he felt a hollow thud in his chest. His rough sigh was like a trigger bringing his hands to the keys, and he opened up the special e-mail system Harry had created and started to type.

> Hi. Just saying hello – and I miss you. I hope you're
> doing okay.

He picked up his vodka, sat back, and frowned.

Victor came out into the hall with a black tote bag,
walked to a door marked SORTIE, and headed down
the stairs. At the third-floor landing he stepped into the
hall and walked to an unnumbered door. He stood for
a moment, until he trusted the silence, then opened the
door and went inside, and came out pushing a three-
foot-square laundry cart with a large canvas bag
hanging from the frame. He rolled it down the hall to
the door marked 3B and put his ear to it – then took out
Harry's room key . . .

Matheson leaned back to the laptop and typed again.

> I'm just going to keep telling you I'm sorry, and that
> I love you, very much. I would have tried you on
> Harry's vidchat – but I'm out of the country and it's
> 7.30 AM where you are, so I figured Mom was still
> home and you were getting ready for school. Love
> you, Dad.

He heard Harry's door open and close. 'Hey . . .' he said,
clicked 'send' and stood up. 'We're set for tomorrow.
Noon. Notre Dame.' Their rooms' adjoining door was
open. 'So you wanna tell me who this dinner date was?'
He came through the doorway. 'This being the City of
Love, I'd like to think it was—'
    A fist swung around and slammed into his stomach.

He doubled over and crumpled to the carpet on all fours. Matheson's head drooped, rasping, sucking for air, all pure reflex now.

Victor knelt beside him. "Breath slowly."

'... Whaaaaaa ...?'

'It is safer for when I inject you.'

Matheson's head slowly cranked ninety degrees till he could see his attacker. In his expression, Victor saw confusion, and pain, but no fear. And perhaps a hint of a grin that appreciated the truly absurd moments of life.

Victor nodded. 'Good enough,' he said, grabbed Matheson by the hair, and emptied a syringe's milky contents into his neck. 'Relax.' Matheson's lids stretched open to their max in an attempt to fight the drug's power – and Victor saw new anger in the eyes, and nodded. 'I understand, my friend.'

Victor pressed the basement floor button – 'SS' – the elevator doors closed and he watched the floor numbers light in descent. 3 ... 2 ... Matheson was in the laundry cart beside him, the sheets from his and Harry's beds piled on top of him. He reached down and fluffed them up a bit, then eyed his watch again. Night was always preferable for the work. Darkness, far fewer people to deal with, less traffic ...

He heard the elevator's *ding* before he felt it stop – and looked up. 'RC' was lit. 'SS' – basement level – was still dark. The door slid open and a silver-haired woman in an evening gown stared back at him. Victor had a partial view of the night clerk at the counter behind her, across the lobby, bent over his textbook, chin in his palm.

The woman glanced down at the laundry cart. 'Going up, dear?' she asked.

'Going down. I shall send it back up,' he said, and smiled – until the door closed.

The woman turned to the clerk. 'You clean the rooms here at this hour? My ... I hope you pay the poor things overtime.'

The clerk looked up wearily – and watched the 'SS' symbol light up above the elevator. His brow became a field of furrows ...

In the alley, Dewey leaned against the van's hood. The engine was running and he liked the feel of the vibration against his lower back. It hadn't been the same since the IED on the road out of Kandahar. They had told him he'd need two weeks in a brace, but after three days in traction he'd started worrying that the worse-offs thought he was a weak dick – and he was going stir-crazy anyway – so he said he wanted to go back out.

The hotel's side door was a metal roll-up. He'd sprayed it with WD-40, so when it started to rise the noise was minimal. Victor came out pushing the cart.

'Let's move.'

Dewey nodded, but he was looking at something inside the basement. 'Victor ...'

'Hey! Attendez!' demanded a voice – and Victor whirled around and drove his fist into the night clerk's throat – two hard, rapid, left-handed jabs. The clerk made a single harsh, cloying sound – like a cat trying to spit out a hairball – but didn't even have time to raise his hands before he hit the ground like a bag of bones.

Dewey stared at the body. The hair was up on the back of his neck. It had looked so cool. Like a movie.

'Move, Dewey,' Victor said, as he leaned down and grabbed the clerk's arms and started dragging him back inside.

Dewey wheeled the cart to the back of the van and opened the doors. Harry lay inside, motionless – silver duct tape across his eyes and mouth and securing his ankles and wrists together. Dewey pushed the bed sheets aside and grabbed Matheson, who was taped in the same fashion, lifted him out and shoved him in beside Harry. He closed up and got in the driver's seat. He was replaying the short scene of crisp, cool violence. Victor pivoting, the left springing out – wap! wap! – the guy going down ... Perfection.

Victor came back out, eyeing the van with a frown. He came round and slid into the passenger's side.

'You should have backed it in,' he said.

'Huh?'

'The van. You back it *in* when time is not an issue – so you don't have to back it *out* when it may be. Stupid mistake. Drive.'

Dewey had the wince of a scolded pupil. 'You're right. Sorry.' He put it in gear and backed down the alley with a pro's skill, smoothly shifted on the street and headed uphill for Rue de Rennes. 'Just so you know, man ... I could've backed out of there with my eyes closed doing ninety if I'd had to.'

'I understand, Dewey – but you realize that's not the point.'

'Yeah. I do.' Dewey stopped at the red light. Victor took out his gold lighter, and rubbed away a smudge.

Lausanne … 1994 … a tobacco store on the Grand Pont … the South African arms dealer … snatched from a parking lot and delivered to the NIA. He lit a cigarette, lowered his window and stared out. In one of the hundreds of nearby apartments 'Hey Jude' was being played very loudly.

Dewey watched Victor flex the fingers of his lethal hand a few times. 'He saw the van,' said Dewey. 'Won't he call the police when he wakes up?'

Victor took in a long pull of smoke. 'He is not going to wake up.'

There was a sudden ping in Dewey's brain – like a sonar pulse suddenly detecting something massive, unseen but very near. Dead people hadn't been mentioned as part of this job. He'd had four gigs. No one had died.

'Green,' said Victor.

Dewey hit the gas and turned left, south. The air held the promise of rain, but was holding back, waiting.

'Question,' Dewey said.

Victor sighed, and turned to him. 'Ask.'

'Why the Adam's apple? Not so easy a target. Why not hammer him in the face?'

'Because you're more likely to break your hand doing that.'

Dewey nodded. 'Got it.' He settled back, letting the feel of the car rule his movements. The biggest issue he'd had in the job was chilling on the machine. He liked speed, torque, *using* the vehicle – but in this line of work, it turned out that driving was 90 percent layback.

Victor made him nervous. He'd known guys back in

the unit who were good at killing – who didn't blink at it – but Victor was so ... *smooth*.

'Dewey ...'

'Yeah?'

'How did you get into this business?'

Dewey thought he heard a touch of something in Victor's voice – like someone trying to sound polite asking a garbage man how he became a philosophy professor.

'You know ... I knew somebody who knew somebody. Like that.' He cruised past a car and got back into the right lane. 'Listen, man ... I don't want to piss you off with my questions. I'm not gonna do this as long as you – I'm only in till I'm flush enough to get out – and I'm just trying to pick your brain is all. In the Army, you figure out once you're in the shit that learning from the timers is how to stay in one piece – so that's why the questions. You want me to stop – just say when.'

Victor turned round and flicked on the overhead light to check on the cargo. The bodies were still. He killed the light, faced front, and his thumb went to his cleft.

'Les loups ne lisent pas,' he said.

'What's that mean?'

'*Wolves don't read.*'

'I don't get it.'

'It's a saying, Dewey. My father worked for the mob in Marseilles. He'd say it to me.'

'Okay – but I still don't get it.'

'Your thoughts are always about the prey ... and those around it. You act on instinct, and as you move on – *if* you move on – experience. You cannot be *taught* the important things. The only manual is what you have *done.*' He tapped his forehead with a finger. 'In here.' His hand went back into his lap. '*Les loups ne lisent pas.*'

'Wolves don't read. I got it.'

Dewey let a Fiat cut him off without a response and made a right. Victor held the cigarette up before his eyes and studied the tip's pulsing glow, as if all one needed to know was locked inside the fire.

'And something else to understand,' Victor said.

'Okay ...'

'Do you remember I told you I had no *partners* ... ?'

'Yeah.'

'This is to say ... in this job, *trust* makes things very – how do you say? – complicating?'

'Complicated.'

'Complicated. So you just hope for loyalty. That is all one can ask. In the rest of life, disloyalty is a common sin. In the job – it is ... unacceptable to me.'

'Kind of weird, isn't it? To split it up like that?'

Victor sucked in a hit of smoke. His lips had a slight grin when he took the cigarette away.

'If a friend betrays me, maybe I am sad. If *you* betray me, maybe I am dead.'

Dewey gave him a quick glance. He was wondering if Victor actually *had* any friends. He turned into a vast square, Place Denfert Rochereau, a roundabout where six streets converged – on every corner, a massive, ornate six or seven-floor building like V-shaped stone layer-cakes. In the center of the square stood a large statue of a lion, regal in its repose, its black copper gleaming with a coat of rain. Victor pointed his cigarette at it.

'The Lion of Belfort. Beautiful, no?'

'Lions are cool.'

'Bartholdi. The same sculptor who made your Statue of Liberty. You have seen it?'

'Just pictures. Never been to New York. Long way from Oklahoma. I never crossed the state line till I joined up.' He turned off onto Avenue Rene Coty, going south. 'Okay if I ask how your old man ended up?'

'At sixty-one he retired to a small house with a garden in Provence ... and died twenty years later with a bottle of wine in his lap.'

Victor flicked his butt out the window and watched the burst of sparks tumble down the street like a troop of golden pixies, each with its own precious moment of birth, each dying at its own singular time.

The drive took six hours.

In the sweep of the headlights, the bend in the gravel road ended and revealed the silhouette of the farm-house, one hundred yards away. Cold, white light shone in two of the windows and bled out onto the ground. Dewey was not one for drama – but it was his first time here at night, and in the dark the place looked mean.

Victor pointed. 'Go around and back it up to the door.'

Dewey slowed, and as they went past the front door it opened – and a figure stood in the doorway, made black and featureless by the interior light behind him.

'Keep driving,' said Victor.

'Got it,' said Dewey, and kept going.

Harry was clear-headed – one of the reasons surgeons liked propofol was because you came out of it fast, with hardly any fuzz or hangover. He knew he was strapped to a chair. He had watched dozens of Joneses twist and turn and suffer in one – and the full-circle, payback irony of it all was priceless. The gods had outdone themselves. Congratulations were in order all around.

He was wearing a smock and hood with holes for his eyes and mouth, which was taped shut. And he had no idea who the guy holding a large, angry hornet between two fingers was – but you didn't need to be a shrink to see he was crazy.

Dalton bent down to him, 'Huge, isn't it? My travels on Google tell me it's probably a Vespa mandarinia – the Asian giant hornet. The most venomous there is – they say a swarm attack can kill a man in minutes … anaphylactic shock – but I'll be damned how they got here.' He held up the index finger of his free hand. 'Watch,' he said, and moved it beneath the hornet and gave its abdomen a poke. The beast jabbed its stinger into the finger. Dalton showed no reaction.

Harry tried to tune the guy out so he could think. He didn't know where he was, but he could see a field of wild lavender beyond a window of the room, which was old, wide-plank wood. It didn't feel like Paris. He was clueless – but somebody had gone to a lot of trouble. This was pro from start to finish.

'They can just keep on stinging, over and over.' Dalton prodded the insect's belly with his fingertip and the hornet stung him again. 'See?' He pulled the bottom edge of Harry's hood a few inches away from the neck. 'This is just to loosen you up a bit. Get rid of some of that adrenaline.' He released the hornet under the hood.

'They aren't particularly aggressive unless provoked. Still, it's best you try not to move.'

Harry felt the creature on him. The nasty buzz stopped and the thing began to crawl upward, and Harry's hands fisted up as he tried to keep his facial muscles from twitching. He closed his eyes as the hornet crawled over them. When he opened them, he saw the man's pale, smooth finger reach toward him and prod the hornet – and it was as if lightning struck him in the cheek. It brought tears to his eyes.

'There are questions I have to ask you.'

Harry's involuntary wince tightened his facial muscles – and the hornet took umbrage ... and stung him again. His body went into a full electric-chair twitch, and a groan struggled to come out of his taped lips.

'I said try not to move,' said Dalton, and his palm swung up and smacked Harry on the temple, crushing the hornet. He took out his antique scalpel. 'I'll be using this as my primary tool.' He put the instrument in Harry's palm. 'Go ahead. Hold it. It has a pleasing feel. Perfect balance.'

Harry's face was on fire. He wished he could cry more ... to douse the flames.

Dalton leaned down to him. 'It's remarkable how fate plays a hand. You see – you and I ... We have a – *common bond*, of sorts.' He grabbed the top of the hood and pulled it off. 'It's quite possible you already know who I am – but let me introduce myself. My name is Dalton.'

The name cut through Harry's anguish like a scythe. Dalton the torturer, the man who cut off people's lips with a rotary knife, IR's ying to Geiger's yang. Now he knew why he was in this chair – and for more reasons than he could count, he was okay with it.

'I must tell you, Harry ... your presence is unexpected – you weren't part of the plan – but here you are, and you're the best present under the Christmas tree.'

Dalton's forefinger began to slowly tap at his upper lip's cleft, like a metronome for thinking. It was a simple, habitual gesture – but something about its methodical, wind-up-toy action gave Harry the cold creeps.

For Dalton, acquiring Harry as an added element was serendipity at its most thrilling. It created an extra dimension to the scenario without having to change the mechanics in any way, and would amplify Dalton's gravitational pull without any effort on his part. He would become the sun and Geiger the moon. Right now, he was conjuring Geiger's face at the moment when he would first have a sense of the beautiful, secret structure that had been built around him. No one would appreciate it more than Geiger, but even the Inquisitor wouldn't see what waited for him at the center of the game. Tap ... tap ... tap. *Come to Papa.*

Harry realized the utter bizarreness of things was actually buffering his fear. The monster bug out of a 1950s sci-fi film ... the madman and his pet scalpel ... There was a deep-sleep nightmarish feel to it all. But, Harry knew too much. He'd watched all those DVDs of Geiger's sessions, dutifully transcribing – and he knew that pain had a way of making things very real. It was a fast-acting agent – and he knew it was on the way. He made as loud a mushy mutter as he could.

Dalton cocked his head. 'Hmm?'

Harry did it again, and Dalton pulled the tape from his lips. Harry opened his mouth as wide as it went, loosening the jaw joints. His face had a constant little-drummer-boy throb of heat.

'Something on your mind, Harry?'

'Yeah. Bourbon – big glass – no ice – and then let's get this party rockin'.'

Dalton looked like he had fallen in love for the first time in his life. 'You're sure about that?'

Harry nodded. And then – though he knew it would hurt like hell – he smiled, ear to ear.

Part Two

13

ZZ Top slashed through some hardass blues – and Geiger's right fist slammed into the tough, blue leather, hammering the downbeat – then his left followed. He'd started working on a heavy bag in the fall, before he'd been able to run again. He'd thought it could be a way to keep his body loose and pump his blood without threatening the scars on his quads. He had the back door open and the music inside pumped high.

Years ago, Harry had told him something Carmine had said. After one of the many times Carmine had sat in the viewing room, watching Geiger in a session through the one-way mirror, he had remarked to Harry:

'Our boy's a thing of beauty, isn't he? It's like watching a chess match in a boxing ring. Kasparov and Ali rolled into one.'

Never having seen a boxing match, Geiger had gone online, found videos of Muhammad Ali, and studied them – the calm predator's prowl, the choice and change of position, the cool appropriation of the ring. And he'd studied the lesser opponents – the shift and dip of a gaze, the reactive calibrations, attempts to mask fear of pain. As always, Geiger had taken what was relevant and brought it to the work – and last fall, when he'd seen the blue Everlast bag at a flea market, he'd brought it home and hung it from a hook on the concrete wall that surrounded his twenty-by-fifteen-foot backyard. He'd put down sod in October, and now his place before the bag was a circle of dirt surrounded by green.

It was in the fifties outside but he was naked except for gym shorts and gleamed in the pale sun like a stripped-down, steel machine. His movement was a precise accompaniment to the steady bass and snare and, behind closed eyes, in an endless blackness, the music bloomed in gold and red novas with each punch. His duffel was packed. He had more cash in a money belt than he'd ever spend. There was nothing that was not finished. The music stopped and Geiger came to rest, drenched, pulse thumping from toes to temples. He walked back inside.

Zanni was sitting at his desk, the cat in her lap. Her presence immediately turned his heart-rate down like a ratchet. The swiftness of it caused a slight tinging in his ear.

'Sweet cat,' she said. 'I knocked. You don't lock your door.'

'No, I don't. Not since I left IR.'

Her eyes calmly took in his near-nakedness. Zero body fat, tight flesh over hard muscle, and with the workout stoking his heart, the gorged veins were like cords beneath his skin. His body reminded her of drawings in an anatomy textbook, except for the scars. They were as Dalton described, though the star cicatrix in his chest was a surprise, and looked recent. When he went to the shower and took a towel off a hook she had a glimpse of the exit wound. Thirty-eight caliber, or close. Is that what all the blood on the river dock was about? She tried to see it – Hall firing from fifteen, twenty feet away ... Geiger going down in a massive spray ... major bleeding out the back ... *How did he even get up?*

Geiger started wiping himself down. 'This is sooner than I thought,' he said.

'But not what you think. There's something you need to see, Geiger.' She held up a jewel case. 'It came to us this morning in an e-mail – but it's for you.'

'Other than you people, only one person knows I'm alive – and he wouldn't be sending you an e-mail.'

'Like I said – you need to see this. May I?'

She wiggled the jewel case and the dying light spilling through the skylight cast it in gold – like some relic Geiger sensed had the power to bend north into south and the promise of solitude into tumult. To watch it would be an act of abnegation, and it would be irreversible. He was certain of that. He could feel his inner compass tilt.

He nodded. 'Go ahead,' he said.

Zanni took out the disk and slipped it in the laptop. She got up and Geiger came and took her place. The black of the screen lightened and 'CLASSIFIED – DEEP RED' appeared in bright crimson font – and something in the air touched him. A scent. Proustian. Cool fingertips on a fevered brow.

'What am I smelling?' he said.

'Lavender,' said Zanni.

Another's voice sang to him. *'You are the sunshine of my life ...'*

Geiger resisted the pull, the urge to drift. He turned round to Zanni. 'What did you say?'

She cocked her head at his expression. 'Lavender water. You smell *me*.'

'Hello,' said someone else – the effect as cold as the spirit's voice was warm. Zanni pointed at the laptop – and Geiger turned back to it. Dalton, in close-up, stared at him.

'I learned recently that Geiger is living in Brooklyn, New York, and that you have made contact with him. In all honesty, I always assumed he was alive – I saw it in a vision – but still, I was thrilled to have it confirmed.'

'He's way out there now,' said Zanni.

Geiger's mind was autumnal – carpeted with crisp, dead leaves, thoughts meandering through them, kicking them about, revealing what lay beneath, warm, moist . . .

'So,' said Dalton, 'I request that you get this video to Geiger immediately.' The camera began a slow pull-out. 'Geiger . . . I'm speaking now with the assumption that you are watching.' He held up his hands. 'I'm a new man, Geiger, inside *and* out – and I owe it all to you. I am in your debt . . . and I wish to repay you – so here is what I propose. Come see me. We have much to talk about. Come to Paris.'

Geiger stared at the face. Dalton had lost a good deal of weight. The frame continued to widen. Dalton was sitting in a chair, dressed in a checkered flannel shirt and khaki slacks, flanked on both sides by a slumped, hooded figure in a blue hospital smock, strapped to a heavy wooden chair.

Dalton grinned. The Cheshire Cat in a child's nightmare. He reached out to his sides and patted the forearms of the two figures.

'David Matheson – and Harry Boddicker. They are both sedated.' He reached in his shirt pocket and took out the antique scalpel. 'Horatio Kern, eighteen sixty-seven. Beautiful, yes?'

He leaned to the figure on his right and took the left hand in his. The pinky and fourth finger were wrapped in gauze, and looked shorter than normal. With three precise cuts, Dalton severed a third of the forefinger at the top knuckle. The body showed no response.

Zanni made a sound like air bleeding from a radiator. 'Jesus ...'

'I have a confession, Geiger. The plan was to lure Matheson. He was the only possible connection to you that I had, and a questionable one at that – but beggars can't be choosers. Not that I thought the two of you were in touch – but he *is* the father of your dear Ezra, and I hoped that you might be communicating with the boy – and perhaps the father knew that, and had learned of your whereabouts from his son. Harry was pure chance – or fate, if you believe in that sort of thing.'

Dalton placed the digit in the body's lap. 'When you arrive, go to the Hotel Maroq in the sixth arrondissement. There will be instructions for you at the desk, under the name "Dalton".' He grinned. He seemed to like that detail. 'When you make your way to me, you will have the choice of taking their place – or not.' He leaned forward – and Geiger flashed on the same image he had on July Fourth. The bulbish, balding head ...

distorted eyes behind the glasses ... the pointed chin. A praying mantis.

'One more thing: For those of you in Deep Red ... Some words of caution. This has nothing to do with you. Stay out of it. This morning I videotaped a session with Matheson. I played Dalton, the ruthless torturer who is working for *you*. He played the US citizen undergoing government-sanctioned extreme interrog.' He took his glasses off and began cleaning them with his shirt-tail. 'Have a look.'

The shot cut to Matheson, strapped to a chair under unseen bright lights – head drooped, bare-chested, shiny with sweat.

'Matheson ...' It was Dalton's voice, off-camera, close by.

Matheson looked up a bit, hair hanging down in his reddened face.

'Is your name David Matheson?'

Matheson's head rose and fell in a sad little nod. 'Yes.' His voice had a scratchy, tired hiss, like an old LP.

'Do you run the organization called Veritas Arcana?'

Matheson's head bobbed again slowly. A hand came into view and gave him a crisp short slap, jolting his eyes open wider.

'Answer, please.'

'Yes. I run Veritas Arcana.'

'Mr. Matheson ... You have illegally acquired and released to the public classified property of the US government – videotapes, documents, e-mails ... Among them were the videotapes of the C.I.A.-sanctioned torture of Egyptian Deputy Minister Nari Kaneesh – correct?"

Matheson let out a slow sigh, and nodded.

"Mr. Matheson ... You are going to tell us the names of the people who provided you with them. That is why you are here.'

The tip of Matheson's tongue came out and ran across his lips. 'Thirsty,' he rasped.

'All right,' said Dalton's voice. 'One moment.'

Geiger was locked into Ezra's father's face. He'd only met the man once, on July Fourth in Central Park, for no more than five minutes. The man whose obsession for truth had put everything in motion. Geiger studied the unfocused gaze ... the throb of the carotid artery ... the potent melancholy of the man. It was like watching a play he'd seen a hundred times, but from a very different seat. He was aware of a heavier ping in his pulse. *This is what I did*, he thought.

Dalton's voice returned. 'Here is some water.' A hand came into frame with a glass of water – and tossed the liquid in Matheson's face. Then the scene cut back to Dalton, sitting in the barber's chair.

'Well done, right? Simple, not over-the-top. I think it's quite convincing – and if you involve yourself any further in this matter, if you attempt to find me, if you send someone here with Geiger and I become aware of your presence, the video goes to all the usual suspects. MSNBC, CNN, Fox, the networks.' He put his glasses back on, and toggled them a few times before satisfied with their perch on his thin nose. 'I hope to see you soon, Geiger. As I said – there is much to talk about. If you aren't here in, say – four days – I'll assume you aren't coming, and I'll kill these two.'

The screen went black. Zanni ejected the disk and sat

on the desk. Geiger looked different to her, somehow. With the way he sat slightly atilt in the chair, now his nakedness and wounds made him seem younger, vulnerable.

'Did either of them know you were alive?' she asked.

'Harry did. And they work together. So he may have told Matheson.'

'Cards on the table, Geiger. Yes – we want him dead. We can't have him running around loose in the funhouse. Yes – we have no idea where he is, and following you is probably the only way for us to find him. We'd get you a ticket, passport. You'd fly to Paris on a regular airline ... so it looks like you're on your own – in case they start a tail. I'd be there before you and hook up with a contractor. We'd play it by ear – stay out of sight, but be close. We'd be your cavalry – move in when it was time.' She shrugged. 'I just need an answer.'

The cat jumped into Geiger's lap and started kneading his stomach. Geiger's hand went to the animal's head and began scratching the scar. The action looked reflexive, comforting – a thoughtless response of an otherwise occupied mind. There were hands and voices reaching for him, from within and without. He was a magnet, powerless to turn off the force at his core that drew them near.

'I need time before I go,' he said. 'A day ... to take care of some things.'

Zanni nodded. 'I don't suppose you'd come to DC for a briefing ... '

'No. I don't feel that's necessary.'

'All right. I'll be back here morning after tomorrow.' She slid off the desk. 'I'm sorry, Geiger.'

'What are you sorry about?'

'That he's put you where you are. I'm the one who debriefed Dalton. I know what he did to you.'

He looked up at her.

'You debriefed Dalton?'

'Yes. You made quite a mess of him, Geiger. You know what he said about you?'

'What did he say about me?'

'He said you were *indestructible*.'

Geiger's gaze was glass, a mirror. Zanni saw nothing of him, only herself, and she walked to the door and went out.

There had not been any portion of any moment when he'd felt himself in a decision-making mode. Information had been received, and the result was the instant ignition of a plan. And it was not, foremost, about saving Matheson's life ... or even Harry's. It was about Ezra's life, and what the rest of it might be like without a father. Dalton had bet everything on that, and he had been right.

Geiger and Ezra had spent twenty-two hours together. Less than a day.

Midnight, 3 July, in the session room ...

Geiger, prepared to work on Matheson, had opened the trunk to find that Hall had delivered Ezra instead, bound and taped and terrified. He'd knocked Hall unconscious and brought the boy home – the first person to ever share the space with him.

Ezra's melancholy and candor and growing trust had been like a crowbar jammed into a crack in Geiger's shell, slowly prying it open. Their shared hunger for music, their tenuous, solitary places on the landscape, and ultimately traveling partners down a road of violence and death that ended the next night, at ten o'clock, in a desperate tangle of bodies beneath the river.

In the following months, Geiger had come to suspect that in saving the boy he had unknowingly tried to save himself – to resurrect the buried child in him so he might heal and change – and he came to realize that, in a sense, Ezra had rescued him. In that way, the two were inseparable – and so there was no choice to be made now.

Geiger leaned to the laptop and went to Google Maps, typed in Hotel Maroq, Paris, France – and changed the view setting from 'map' to 'satellite'. Slowly, he zoomed in like a pilot coming in for a rooftop landing. He knew that once he walked into the building, there would be eyes in place to watch him if he came out – on the street corner, or inside a parked car, or in a room in the hotel he could see was across the street – whose windows had a view of the Maroq's lobby. It would be one of Dalton's men, or one of Soames's, or perhaps both – and he would have company wherever he went.

He stopped the zoom when he was 'hovering' above the hotel roof. It was flat and non-reflective – likely tar-covered or concrete, which would suit his plans perfectly. The buildings to the left and right were each separated from the hotel by alleys Geiger guessed to be about eight feet wide. He would have to make it across one of the chasms. Jumping from a running start would be an option, but that kind of torque on his hips could be problematic.

He clicked on iTunes and chose Ravel's 'Bolero'. Its foundation of a clean, repetitive melody, upon which a new instrument was added each time the motif came round, would help – a conducive accompaniment to the construction of a plan he could build on, layer upon layer. Long ago, he had learned how to slip inside the music in his mind – the downpour of notes like colored rain on a lake, each drop's impact sending circles spreading out on the surface, meeting and mixing into each other, turning orange and blue and green into purple and violet and brown. He would float there and drift on the rainbowed water. Or dive down, to the bottom.

He walked to the closet, and as he entered the flute slinked inside with him. He pulled the door shut and assumed his position in the darkness, a fetal curl on the cool floor. The snare drum crackled out of the speakers, and laid down a foundation. Focus was crucial. So many elements to weave together into a whole. He closed his eyes. The bassoon joined the melody on its third pass – rich blue, mint-cool swaths washing through Geiger's brain. It would be like composing a symphony.

14

Geiger pulled the baseball cap down low on his fore-head. He never wore hats, but back at Columbus Circle he'd passed a sidewalk vendor and decided an extra piece of camouflage could be useful. He had taken a cab across the Manhattan Bridge and then switched subway lines twice, and was certain that at this moment no one in the world knew where he was – on an upper West Side street, standing in a narrow space between an alley wall and a Norway maple, masked from view but with a wide sight-line.

Morning had commandeered Seventy-fifth Street. Small children were marched out of front doors like prisoners of war to a waiting convoy of school buses. Women of color, in talkative brigades of three and four, weaved their way toward apartments they would clean. Warriors, girded in suits and skirts, tightening neckties and scarves, waved and hollered for their steel, yellow steeds.

Ezra looked around his room. Lately, he forgot things. He pushed some sheet music on the desk aside and found his cell phone. He picked his backpack up from the floor and walked out down the hall. The shower was running in the bathroom.

'Going, Mom!'

The water was turned off.

'Don't forget your money!'

Ezra winced. 'Don't worry – I didn't! Already got it!' The water went back on and he went into the kitchen, took the ten-dollar bill off the counter. He knew she spent her life worrying about him now – if he didn't call when he got to school … and when he left, if he didn't have some breakfast … or finish his dinner, if he was getting homework done, if he was making friends, if he was getting enough sleep … or sleeping too much. When they were together he read her thoughts – she was wondering what to say, what to ask, what to leave unspoken. Try as she did, she was inept at fakery, and her smile had become an emblem of sadness. She loved him fiercely – and she made everything worse.

He went to the door, patting his pockets to make sure he had his keys. As he reached for the knob he heard it, out in the hallway – more blunt complaint than plaintive.

There are known things, certainties – of an empirical essence, or experiential proof, or historical consensus. And there are other things known, heartfelt – born in an instant. Ezra flung the door open. At his feet was a pet carrier, its price tag still attached by a string. Another meow came from inside. He knelt down and opened it, and the cat jumped out into his arms and burrowed into his chest. He thought he might burst into a trillion molecules … or dissolve into a puddle. He had lost the power of speech. He could not move. All because of this new known thing.

On the bottom of the carrier lay a white envelope.

Number sixty-four was three buildings down, and Geiger had an unobstructed view of Ezra barging out onto the stoop, the envelope in his hand, whirling in semicircles, clockwise – pausing to survey the street . . .

'Geiger!' Then spinning back the other way. 'Geiiiiger!'

Geiger had Ezra's iChat name, and had given thought to making contact that way but dismissed the option. This way was cleaner. Information and nothing more. He saw flashes of light on the tearful eyes, and he could see joy in his face. He'd grown – he was at that scarecrow stage when the torso plays catch-up with dangling arms and gangly legs – and his voice had deepened. Geiger could see him – last July, on the couch, scratching the cat, and asking – '*What's it feel like to hurt somebody?*' – and Geiger had answered – '*I don't feel anything on a job. It isn't about me.*'

Ezra sat down on the top step. He had been changed, delivered to some vibrant state of grace. He looked at the hum and rush around him, peered into the shadows and nooks. You're out there, he thought. I know it. I can't see you – but you can see me, and, as you would say – if that's what works best for you, it's okay with me. You're alive.

He opened the envelope and pulled out a sheet of paper. The text was typed, double-spaced.

Now you know.

Tomorrow I am leaving here, going out of the country, and will not return.

I am going to try and help your father and Harry. They are in trouble.

I do not want you to think you have been abandoned by any of us.

Do not show this letter to anyone.

I call the cat Tony now, as you suggested. I saw that you have a fire escape outside a window of your apartment in back. Leave the window open so he can go out at night. As you know, he will always come back.

He was the strangest person Ezra had ever known. A jumble of opposite and inexplicable traits, an emotional Frankenstein – as if a mad psychic surgeon had taken feelings from different people and stitched them all together inside Geiger's mind. And now … What was happening now? The boy's eyes went back to one line of the letter, and its cold, blunt force hit and chilled him again. *I do not want you to think you have been abandoned by any of us.* For a moment he was back underwater, in the river's black, blind turmoil, others' hands clawing at him – then someone had pulled him free and pushed him toward the surface, and life. A tear plopped down onto the paper.

Geiger watched Ezra put the letter back in the envelope and stand up. The boy didn't bother to explore the street again. He just turned, opened the front door and walked back inside. When Geiger was sure Ezra wasn't coming back out, he left the shadows and walked away.

Those who dealt with Carmine Delanotte were likely aware his doctor made him quit smoking fifteen years ago. Those close to him knew temptation still beckoned, and that he went to great lengths to minimize its siren call. These measures included no smoking in his presence, restaurant, homes, and the Cadillac. Geiger knew that his driver, Rollie, was a chain smoker – and while he waited down the block from La Bella Ristorante in the black CTS-V sedan with tinted, bullet-proof windows, he would get out of the car two dozen times a shift to have a cigarette. And, Geiger had often been in Carmine's presence when he'd told Eddie to have the car brought round and Eddie had repeated the order into a Nextel – so he'd heard Rollie's gravel-voiced response. The same four words, every time. Geiger also knew that when it was time to go home, Carmine would come out with Eddie – Eddie would open the passenger-side back door and step aside while Carmine got in, then close the door and go around the back of the car to the driver's side and get in beside the boss.

Geiger knew more than enough for what he needed to do. The last thing Carmine had said to him, nine months ago, before he betrayed him, was: '*Life owns your ass – from day one, cradle to grave. You don't get it, Geiger. You think you can choose whether you're in or not, but you can't. If you come out of this alive, you remember that.*' And Geiger had remembered.

*

Mulberry Street was sleepy. The Cadillac was parked by a liquor store that had been closed for hours. The driver's door opened, Rollie's feet swung out, and when he was nearly erect, an unlit cigarette in his lips, the door was shoved closed, pinning him at the calves and neck. He managed a dismayed gurgle before an elbow smashed into his temple, his chauffeur's cap went flying, and the light in his eyes went out.

Carmine took a last sip of his double espresso, then sat back, drawing lines in the tablecloth with a fingernail. The broccoli rabe hadn't felt fresh. He'd make a call tomorrow and put the hammer down. He picked up his copy of the *Wall Street Journal*.

'Eddie ... Time to go.'

The man in the black suit standing behind Carmine unclasped his hands from in front of his belt buckle and took out a Nextel push-to-call. 'Rollie, bring the car up.'

The rough voice crackled back. 'On my way, boss.'

Carmine's deep blue eyes took a final look at the elegant, emptied restaurant, and then he rose from his chair with a throaty grunt.

'Jesus ... How old am I, Eddie?'

'I dunno, boss.' Eddie's face remained a death mask. 'I lost track.'

Carmine chuckled, shaking his head like a man who has done many remarkable, terrible things ... and remembers them all. He was aware of the soft weariness settling down on him, day by day. The wisdom born of wicked things was a cold, grim companion, but he still kept it close, just the same.

The two men walked to the door, where the maitre d' held it open.

'Goodnight, Mr. D.'

'Goodnight, Kenny.'

The Cadillac idled at the curb. Eddie moved ahead of Carmine, opened the back door and Carmine got inside. Eddie closed the door ...

Carmine settled back into the soft taupe leather. 'How are you, Rollie?'

The driver waited until Eddie showed up in the rearview mirror and hit the gas.

Carmine perked up, and glanced out the back window. 'Rollie ... Hey. You forgot Eddie.' He watched Eddie recede, his hands rising in a *what-the-fuck?!* exclamation.

'Hello, Carmine.'

The cold, satin delivery slid into Carmine's ears like an ice pick. 'Jesus fucking mother of Christ ...' Each word came out more slowly and softer than the one before, until the last was no more than a whisper.

Eddie's voice barked from somewhere inside the car. 'Boss?! Boss?!'

When Carmine turned back around, Geiger saw his reflection in the mirror. He was smiling. He looked absolutely delighted.

'Okay ... Shocked? Yeah, to my bones,' Carmine said. 'But why aren't I surprised? Jesus, it's good to see you, Geiger. Really. It's *wonderful*.'

Geiger turned east on Canal Street, and took off Rollie's cap and put it on the seat.

'I wasn't certain you'd feel that way.'

Carmine's grin stretched out even more. 'No? Why not? You're my boy.'

'That's what you said just before you drugged me and gave me to Hall ... and Dalton.'

'I mean it now and I meant it then. Broke my heart handing you over. God's truth.' He shrugged. 'Business is something else entirely. You know that. You know what I have to deal with sometimes. The government spooks ... They want something from me – I can't say no.'

Eddie spoke up again. 'Boss! What's going on?!'

Geiger tossed Rollie's Nextel in the backseat. 'I'd prefer he didn't over-react.'

Carmine picked up the phone and punched in. 'Relax, Eddie. Nothing to worry about. I'm fine. I'm with Geiger.'

'With *who*?! Did you say *Geiger*?!'

'Yes.' Carmine punched off and sat back. 'Am I fine, Geiger?'

Geiger turned left. Carmine lowered a window and looked out at the street sign.

They were on Ludlow Street. Geiger's old session house was fifty yards up the block. Carmine nodded to himself. Returning to the scene of the crime. It was a nice touch.

Geiger started to slow. 'I haven't been back here since Dalton worked on me.'

'I have it rented out – for photoshoots. Fashion, mainly. I have your barber's chair, though. In my rec room. Works beautifully there.'

Geiger pulled over and put it in park. He lifted his eyes to the two-story building's square, black windows, coated with the sole streetlamp's glare. He was still inside. Part of him would always be inside there.

'You taught me a lot, Carmine.'

Carmine smiled warmly. 'This kid comes into the restaurant – doesn't know who he is or where he came from … I'm thinking this is the weirdest guy I'd ever met – and that's saying something.' His shoulders rose in a shrug. 'We did okay, you and me.'

Geiger turned round to face him. 'What are your thoughts on vengeance?'

Carmine had been waiting, and he didn't try to hide his sigh. 'Generally speaking, I'm in favor of it. Very biblical. Black and white. Black and white is always good.' He ran a hand through his regal mane. 'Just so we're clear. I meant what I said. I wasn't happy when it happened – and I've been sorry ever since.'

Geiger's hand slid inside his jacket. 'I'm not here for an apology.'

'I didn't think you were.' Fear was not a word in Carmine's emotional dictionary. He'd erased it long ago. So now, instead of fearing death, he wondered *how* he was going to die. What did Geiger have? A gun? A knife? 'It's late. Do what you came to do.'

Geiger's hand started back out into view – Carmine's brain failed to stop every muscle in his body from tightening – and Geiger tossed an envelope in Carmine's lap.

A slow, thick breath bled out of Carmine's lips. His body uncoiled. 'Jesus …'

'Carmine … If I wanted to kill you, why would I have waited this long?'

Carmine watched the face for some expression, an

arch of a brow or turn of a lip that might hint at the feeling behind the question, but there was none. He remembered the first time they met, when Geiger walked into La Bella. At one point, Carmine had said – *'Has anyone ever told you that you are one very strange motherfucker?'* and Geiger had answered in the same calm, stoic way – *'Yes. A number of people.'* If Geiger had changed in any way these twelve years, Carmine was at a loss to put a name to it.

'Do you still smoke?' Carmine said.

Geiger brought out his Luckies and Bic lighter, and Carmine took them.

'That's my boy.' He shook one from the pack and lit up. There was an audible *whoosh* as he drew in the smoke, let it sit in his lungs, nodding with approval, and then sent a cloud of smoke swirling around the car. 'What's in the envelope?'

'Seventy thousand. I'm leaving for Paris soon. I need some things waiting for me when I get there. There is a list with instructions. A few calls should be all that's necessary from your end, but there isn't a lot of time. I estimated your costs at ten to fifteen thousand – so you should more than meet your profit margin.'

'That's very generous. This have to do with IR?'

'I'm not in that business anymore, Carmine. You know that.'

'But your ass is going on the line. Why?'

'There's something I need to do.'

Without looking in it, Carmine put the envelope on the seat next to him. 'Why are you so sure I'll take care of things?'

'I didn't say I was.' Geiger opened the door. 'Rollie's in the trunk. Goodbye, Carmine.'

He got out and the door closed softly. Through the tinted windows, Carmine watched him move off until he left the splash of the streetlamp and seemed to simply disappear.

15

Zanni put the items down on the desk one at a time. 'Passport – Mr. John Grey. Plane ticket – Air France, JFK to Paris Charles De Gaulle, ten p.m., Customized iPad, customized cell – press-to-talk, direct to me ...'

Geiger's home was awash with pure light. The copper sunbeams coming down through the skylight made electric illumination unnecessary.

'Just to you?'

Geiger was facing her from across the room, putting clothes in a small canvas suitcase.

'Just to me.' She put down a packet of crisp bills. 'Two thousand euros.'

He was watching her, putting together a profile. Right-handed, but not un-confident with the left. Possible astigmatism – but not to a significant degree.

'Why would I need two thousand euros?'

'You may not.'

She picked up her Starbucks grande and had a sip as she strolled. She was, he decided, dedicated to workouts – for tone, not bulk. Most likely she wanted her body lean for the work, but there might also be an element of vanity in her choice – about her shape, her sexuality.

'All right . . .' she said. 'We assume you've considered a number of scenarios – one of them being that after you pick up Dalton's instructions at the hotel you give us the slip, we never hear from you, and you do this alone.' She turned to him, and waited.

Geiger did his neck turn, to the right. *Click*. 'And why would I do that?'

'Because you don't trust us – and we get that – but in this particular case, we're not the bad guys. The truth is we can't afford another public disaster, and Dalton has to be removed. Do we need you more than you need us? Probably – but if you're doing this to save lives, then we could be of value to you. We just want you to think about that.'

'I have thought about that.'

She kept listening for some tilt of irony or games-manship, waiting for the slightest curl at the corners of his lips. But it never came. Not even a blink.

'Rosanna . . . Are you solo on this job?'

She couldn't get a take on his tone – he didn't really *have* a tone – but the question still pushed one of her buttons.

'Does that make you nervous?' she said.

'I don't get nervous,' he said.

'There is never more than one of us from the division on a job. That's standard Deep Red protocol. On this one – there's me, and the contractor in Paris. He's worked for Deep Red a dozen times.' She drained her coffee, and frowned. 'You know what, Geiger? I'm sup-posed to be on vacation now. They gave me this because

I did the Dalton debriefing . . . and I know more about both of you than the others . . . and, I've already dealt with you.' She stopped at one of the armoires. 'So if you have an issue with me – you should say so now.'

'What kind of issue?'

'This may come as a shock to you – but some men in these scenarios have a problem with the fact that I'm a woman.'

Geiger put two neatly folded black pullovers in the suitcase. He was certain she monitored her conversational tone at all times – and likely had a penchant for sarcasm that she'd had to learn to keep under control.

'Rosanna . . . Your sex is of no interest to me.'

Zanni wanted to turn around to see the look on his face – but she wasn't certain what her own expression looked like, so she ran her fingertips over the smooth, lustrous wood instead. One thing she was certain about: she didn't know another man who could have pulled off that statement.

'Good,' she said. 'Just so we're clear.' She studied the fabulous designs in the wood. 'You restore these?'

'No. I make them.'

'You *build* them?'

'Yes. From old wood.'

She stepped back to get a better look at the entire menagerie. 'This what you've been doing?'

'Yes.'

She turned to him. 'They're beautiful.'

He looked up at her. He gave away less than a sphinx – and Zanni felt an itch, an urge. She wanted to walk over and punch him in the face. The impulse had no anger in it. She just wanted to see what his reaction

would be. She needed to get a feel for a rough edge –
anything other than the unrippled surface. He was,
hopefully, going to be her belled cat – but she still didn't
really know whom she was dealing with. He zipped up
the suitcase.

'You travel light,' she said.

'Just a few days and then I'm back here – or dead.'

'You know, Geiger, you have a way of ... *distilling*
things.'

Geiger's head turned left. Another *click*.

'Okay,' said Zanni. 'I have to ask. What's the neck
thing about?'

'Cervical damage. When I was a boy I slept on the
floor of a very small closet ... for years. It was
cramped.'

Behind her eyes she saw a photo-flash of the soul-
crushing scene, catching her off-guard – and she
squelched it. She looked at her watch.

'I leave in two hours. The contractor's already scoped
the hotel lobby – entrances and exits. We'll be close by.'

'Goodbye, Rosanna.'

She chose not to explore the various interpretations
of the salutation and headed for the door.

'One request, Geiger,' she said. 'Don't call me
Rosanna. Call me Soames, or Zanni – but not Rosanna.
My parents named me after the song – by Toto?'

'I know the song.'

'Well, I hate it.'

'The song or the name?'

'Both. I spent junior high and high school hearing ten
thousand idiots sing it every time I walked down a hall.
So don't call me Rosanna.' She opened the door. 'See

you in Paris, Geiger,' and she walked out, closing the door behind her.

Geiger's fingers started an unrushed, shuffling roll on the suitcase. His mind locked her profile into place. At their first meeting, on the street, he had decided it would be best that he not believe anything she might say. Now, his analysis had shifted a few degrees – and he was emending his perspective. What he had first deemed falseness had more than guile in it. There was a dose of ambivalence in the poison.

It was two hours into the flight. Business-class seats were wide and plush, but he still needed to stand and walk the aisle every fifteen minutes to prevent the 'deadfoot' from kicking in – the pins and needles that started in his left hip and spread down to his toes. There were two seats per row, and he had originally been at the window. After the fourth time he'd gotten up and silently squeezed past the portly, middle-aged man in the aisle seat next to him, upon his return the man had asked politely:

'Are you going to do this the whole flight?'

'Yes, I am.'

'Would it be easier for you to sit on the aisle?'

'It doesn't matter to me where I sit.'

'Then how about we switch?' Without waiting for agreement, the man had moved over to the window seat, and waited for Geiger to sit down before he gave conversation a shot.

'Just need to stretch, huh? Sure. Long flight.' Then he'd answered Geiger's silence with a nod. 'Business or pleasure?' He'd given Geiger a grin. 'Or both?' And he'd added a wink, like a new pal.

Geiger had turned full-face to him, and his blade of a stare had pinned the man to the back of his seat.

'It's best that you don't talk to me,' he had said.

The fellow traveler, tasked with responding to a statement that, wrapped in its indecipherable delivery, lent itself to a dozen interpretations, had chosen an uncertain smile and a soft chuckle – as one might do to a joke whose punch line failed to hit home.

'I mean that,' said Geiger. 'I don't want to have a conversation with you.'

The man had nodded a few times, quickly, like a bobblehead doll, and then turned to the window and not said another word since.

Geiger had run through it all thoroughly, and now his mode of thought was fluid – a river without bends, its surface untroubled. Everything that pertained to precision and detail had been dealt with, and all other possibilities in the future existed in a shifting, minimally defined plane. He was in a free-fly zone. From here on, what happened in one moment would define the next. This was the ultimate asap – with a ticking clock louder than any he'd ever heard in an IR session.

The sound of a young, wet sob pulled at him. He opened his eyes to see a boy – five or six – tugging back against the grip of his mother as they came down the aisle, announcing his feelings in something just short of an all-out plea.

'I don't wanna.' He jabbed a small finger at the lavatory door.

His mother stopped. 'But you said you had to *go* – right?'

'But what if I'm in there and the plane crashes?'

'It's not going to crash, sweetie. Everything's going to be all right.'

Geiger felt a sudden, short-lived yank – but he was uncertain whether the turbulence came from without or within.

The kid shook his head, and that set off his tears. 'Come in with me.'

The boy's mother smiled, and opened the door. 'Look – see? It's awfully small, right? Where am I going to fit?'

The cabin's hum and rumble started to soften, the volume sliding – as if Geiger's brain was turning down a dial – and the human voices swelled.

'Then I wanna stay with you.'

'Sweetie, I *am* with you.'

The muscles at the back of Geiger's neck grabbed at his spine, and he tilted back against the seat.

The mother knelt beside her son and took his face in her hands. 'I'm right here. I promise. *Always.*'

Geiger's eyelids fell shut. There was a slow roll of feelings inside him, creeping up, then slipping away – the gravity of memory pulling them back and forth like a tide under the spell of an ancient moon. He sensed an earthy redolence ... '*You are the apple of my eye ...*' A pulse inside a pulse ... A hand within a hand ...

Geiger opened his eyes. The boy and his mother were gone.

The train ride from Charles de Gaulle Airport to Paris took half an hour. He chose the train and its crowded cars instead of the solitude of a taxi, to begin the process of watching and cataloging faces in case one should reappear later on – standing on a street corner, sipping something at a café table, staring out the driver's window of a car. The odds were slim, but still measurable. For the same reason, when he arrived at Gare du Nord, he took the B line south.

There were empty seats, but he chose to stand in the middle of the car, with a view to both ends. He'd not been to Paris before, but geography would not be of primary importance. This could be Rome, London, Prague, Madrid. Cultural mores, languages, urban habits – they could have some potential impact, but were unlikely to play a significant part in strategic decisions. Riders' gazes were tilted down at PDAs and newspapers, wires dangling from ears – the modern android, rapt and insulated, incurious about the flesh around them. Few looked up from their portals, and no eyes turned his way.

This would not be about the place, but specific agendas. It would be about forces playing off each other – navigation, instinct and execution, flexibility and reaction. He would be – in various perspectives – prey, pawn, helmsman, conductor ... and the very nature of the construct and desires of those involved ensured that people would die.

16

Hotel Maroq was a plain, gray-stone, four-story build-ing wedged between two apartment buildings, their facades adorned with stretches of classic Parisian wrought-iron terraces. Directly across from it was another small hotel, Hotel Estival, with sixteen win-dows that offered occupants an unobstructed view of the Maroq's entrance. The one-way street had parking on one side, and every spot was taken.

Geiger stopped outside the entrance, and studied his reflection in the glass. In this single moment he sensed the domino power behind his potential choices. He was the king of fates. He could continue down the sidewalk, turn a corner, hail a cab to the airport, and get on a plane to anywhere in the world. Or, he could open the door that held his image and go inside – setting in motion forces that would fan out, picking up speed and gaining power as they moved forward, taking anyone and all in their path to some final terminus where lives would end. The former offered utter control, the latter a ride with chance ...

He glanced back at the hotel across the street. The angle of the sun painted the windows gold and denied him a glimpse beyond their glass. They were here, some-where – working for Dalton, working for Soames. He grabbed the door's handle and walked into the lobby.

The floors were old stone, the walls alternating sec-tions of floor-to-ceiling darkened oak and smoked mirrors. On the right was a sitting area – a glass-top table surrounded by three high-backed Chantilly chairs, one of which was occupied by a man in slacks and a sports jacket, one leg crossed over the other, reading a news magazine, *L'Express*, raised high enough that it hid his face. His dangling, tassel-loafered foot bounced continually at the end of his ankle. By the way he was flipping through the pages, he was either looking for something in particular, or bored. Or not reading at all.

Geiger went left, to the marble-topped counter where a short, proper man in a gray suit awaited his arrival. The silver plaque on his lapel said his name was Claude. The way his thumb and forefinger tugged at his clipped moustache said that he had never gotten over his anxi-ety with face-to-face human interactions.

'Bonjour, monsieur.'

'My name is Dalton.'

'Ah ... Mr. Dalton. Welcome to Hotel Maroq.' He punched at his computer, turned round to the grid of room boxes on a wall and took an envelope from one of them, then grabbed a key ringed to a card-sized wooden plaque with a gold-embossed '203' on it from a rack.

'You are in room two-o-three. It is in the back – very quiet.' He gave Geiger the key and envelope. 'If there is anything you need, monsieur, do not hesitate to ask.'

Geiger was eyeing a section of mirror, looking at the reflection of the man with the magazine seated across the lobby, the loafer's tassel swaying like a tiny dancing figurine. Dalton's man? Soames's? Right now it didn't really matter. Geiger walked to the elevator, stepped inside, and hit the '2' button. As the door slid closed, he watched the man turn another page.

When the elevator stopped at the second floor, he watched the door open – and then pushed '3'. The door closed, the elevator ascended, and when it stopped at the next floor and the door opened again, Geiger stuck his hand deep into the narrow, open space of the elevator shaft and pulled out the manila envelope that had been taped there for him. He left the elevator, went into the stairwell and started down.

Room 203 was like a million other hotel rooms. Its two square windows faced those of another building, with a pale, meager portion of light, and Geiger drew the curtains, went to the small desk and sat down. The manila envelope retrieved from the elevator shaft was blank. The envelope from the front desk had 'DALTON' written on it in block letters, and he opened it and took out a sheet of paper with typed text. It read:

Dear Geiger,
I will know what day you are reading this. Tomorrow, take the train from Paris to Avignon – the TGV station, Gare de Lyon. The key is to a storage locker at the Avignon train station on the main level. Inside you will find further instructions.
Sincerely,
Dalton

Geiger shook the envelope and a small locker key dropped into his palm. Its red plastic nub had a '27' on it. He put it aside, opened the manila envelope, and removed another hotel room key embossed with '404'. Carmine's man had rented him a second room, as requested. The rest of what he required would be there, hopefully.

He was being careful to ration focus and awareness – there was much to keep track of. On one flank – Dalton and crew. Dalton had lost some of his sanity, but the madness that had blossomed in its place was cunning, with a devoted purpose. On the other flank was Soames and the string-pullers at Deep Red. Less personal – but just as dangerous, because they had no investment in Geiger's survival. Politics and pragmatism were of the first order, as with most structured entities in the world – governments, corporations, religious bodies, even revolutionary groups. Geiger had dealt with them all. Individuals and lives were not a primary concern. The protection of the foundation and agenda was always paramount – and Geiger knew this was the case with Soames. She couldn't do her job if it weren't so.

And there was one other important element to monitor – himself. He hadn't slept on the plane – to ensure he had no visits from a dream and its migraine companion. He knew he carried a time bomb without an audible ticking inside him, and he'd learned it could explode at any time – and that, in a way, made him the most volatile variable in the scenario. He reached to his bag and took out the cell Soames had given him, pressed 'send' – and Zanni came through instantly.

'Hello, Geiger.'

'I'm in my room.'

'I know. We saw you. We're in a room in the hotel across the street. Turn on the iPad.'

Geiger took the iPad out of the bag and powered up. A corner icon lit up on the screen – the crimson octagon logo of Deep Red. Geiger tapped it – and Zanni was staring at him, the cell phone still to her ear. She lowered it.

'Hi,' she said.

He nodded at her. He was all but certain both devices had tracking systems in them, but that was of little concern. It might even play to his advantage down the line.

'Did you get instructions?' she asked.

'Yes. At the desk when I checked in.'

'Let me see them, please.'

From here on in, everything would be for show, on both their parts. He knew it, Soames knew it – and they both knew the other knew it. They had a union of purpose, with the ever-present assumption of deceit, while holding out hope that in the end they might provide aid to the other. As Carmine liked to say – *Never trust your friends more than you think they trust you*. He held Dalton's note up for Soames's eyes.

Zanni nodded. 'Got it.' Geiger lowered the paper. 'Geiger ... I want you to meet our contractor. You should know his face, and his voice.'

Her image slid away from the screen as she handed off the device ...

'Geiger,' she said, 'this is Victor de Bran.'

... and Victor's stolid face came into frame. 'Good afternoon,' he said, and nodded.

Geiger watched the lips purse slightly into a modest smile. When and if the time came, this was the man who would kill Dalton ... and anyone who was a hindrance to that end. It was the face of an artisan, a maitre d', a writer, a cop ... everyman.

'Hello,' said Geiger. He had a great deal of respect for faces – for the versatility of their features, for their powers of deception – and knew the only place to find an unadorned sense of someone was in the eyes. De Bran's were dark brown and glossy, with lazy lids at almost half-mast. An untroubled, temperate gaze, with a touch of the reptilian. An uncomplicated man whose confidence was the fruit of his experience. Geiger had often found that to be the case with men who killed people for a living.

'May I just say, Geiger ... I will do all I can to help in this.'

At the start of his life in IR, Geiger created a list of categories for lies. He kept it in one of his binders, and over the years added to it frequently, refining it for context and levels of sophistication.

'Denial': a simple declaration of innocence or ignorance with a wide spectrum of deliveries – from outrage to bravado to despair.

The 'Drop': where a small amount of truth or fact is mixed into a lie to try and color the whole statement as genuine.

The 'Con': a lie of great detail whose sheer scope works toward creating the effect of truthfulness ...

... and a dozen other types. Some revealed less about a statement's veracity and more about the speaker, such as the 'Hook'. It was, by its nature,

almost always unsolicited. '*May I just say, Geiger …*'
Seemingly spontaneous, it was premeditated and
aggressive in its intent – to portray the speaker in a specific light with future interactions in mind. '*I will do all
I can to help in this.*' And while a hook might not be a
lie, it revealed the presence of a manipulator. The more
amateurish and unconfident the actor, the greater likelihood there would be a follow-up to try and sink the
hook – '*I just wanted you to know that,*' or a plain
'*Okay?*' or '*All right?*' – so Geiger waited, but was
nearly certain de Bran was finished speaking. They
studied each other, as if face to face. They could have
been sitting at a poker table, waiting for the next card
to fall.

'I understand,' Geiger finally said. On the screen,
Zanni took de Bran's place.

'My take is,' she said, 'Dalton will bounce you
around a bit … and when there's contact, it'll be someplace he feels secure you can't be followed – meaning,
by us.'

Geiger nodded. 'I'm going to shower and sleep. I
haven't slept in a long time.'

'All right. You'll be in touch later on?'

'Yes.'

Zanni worked at a casual nod, as if she believed him.
'Okay,' she said.

Geiger turned the iPad off, put all of his things
back in the bag, picked up the key to room 404 and
left.

Zanni refilled her coffee cup – and as she sipped, she
sniffed … and scowled.

'Victor ... Outside – or put it out.'

He was at the window, staring at Geiger's hotel. As he exhaled a plume of smoke he looked down at the newly lit Gitanes between his long fingers.

'Pardon, Zanni. I forgot.' He opened the window and flicked the cigarette out. 'Thoughts?' she asked.

'He is as you described. I think maybe he will try and make his own way without us. But ... Did you ever think Geiger has no plans to go to Dalton? That he is just using you to get away – for good? You gave him a new passport, a plane ticket ...'

Zanni came to the window. Since she'd arrived in Paris, she'd felt the gears in her starting to turn, their teeth meshing, separate pieces coming together and beginning to push things forward. This job was going to change everything – and it was a rush to know that.

'Whatever else Geiger is – he's honest. He's here to save them, and the truth is – there isn't anything we could do or say, not *one* thing, to make him trust us ... and what's weird is – that works for us. Not trusting us will streamline his choices and give us less to guess about. As long as we don't lose him completely – I like where we are.'

The edge of Victor's thumbnail slid up and down the cleft in his chin. He was thinking about Geiger's legendary powers – to see beneath the masks, to decipher meaning in the noise men make – and wondering if Geiger sensed that betrayal was at the core of Victor's purpose. He looked at Zanni. He was probably about the same age as her father. The thought struck him at an odd angle, vaguely unsettling – because he sensed that within it might be the faintest feeling of concern, and that was unacceptable.

'Yes,' he said. 'I like where we are too.'

Geiger opened the door to 404 and stepped inside. It was a front-view room, as he had requested in his list to Carmine, with two curtained windows. Geiger locked the door and went to the bed. Laid out neatly on it were a canvas gym bag, an aluminum attaché, a Canon wide-angle digital camera, an iPad, three neat stacks of euros, a Grand Master lock-pick set, and two keys on a ring with a cardboard tag labeled '315 Rue Questel, back door of store'. A sheet of typing paper had three hand-written lines on it.

Hotel has no back door.
Side door goes to alley, but only exit from alley
is out to street.
Carmine says good luck. Bonne chance.

Geiger opened the attaché. Inside was a two-foot-square device of aluminum tubes. He took it out, released a knob on the side and started pulling the square apart. The telescoping ladder opened to a length of twelve feet, with eight rungs. It was perfect.

The coffee maker had a three-cup pot, so he filled the basin, put in five packets and flicked it on. He closed his eyes, let his shoulders sag and his head droop, and stood perfectly still – so he could get the purest, clearest feel of his pulse and his pain activity. They were both in accept-able ranges.

He went to one of the windows with the camera and

pulled the curtains apart a few inches. He had a view of
the street below and the buildings across from him. It
had begun to drizzle and the street had a faint sparkle
to it. He took a photo of the line of parked cars from
mid-block to the east corner, and then a photo of the
cars from mid-block to the west corner – about two
dozen in all. Then he began shooting individual close-
ups of every car …

The Hotel Littré's cleaning lady wheeled her cart down
the hall to Harry's room and knocked.

'Femme de ménage!' She waited the requisite
moments, then knocked again. 'Come to clean! Oui?!'
She was hesitant to enter, because she heard someone
talking inside. It was an American. 'Monsieur?! Hello?!'

She used her key to open up and rolled her cart
inside. The voice was coming from the adjoining room.
It was younger than she had first thought. She moved to
the connecting doorway.

'Monsieur?'

Matheson's open laptop was on the desk as he had
left it – and Ezra's vidchat face was framed in the screen,
a portrait of fear, cheeks hiked up, words coming out of
tight lips.

'… and this is, like, the tenth time I've tried, Dad.
Geiger left me a note saying something was wrong –
that he was going to find you and Harry. Where *are*
you?!'

The woman took a few steps into the room. Ezra's
gaze shifted as he noticed her at the edge of the frame,
and he leaned forward like a kid pressing his nose to a
toy store window.

'Hey! Hey! Hello!' The woman came two steps closer. 'Who are you?!'

'Je ne parle pas anglais.'

'You're French?'

'Er ...'

'You're in France?'

'... Oui, oui. France.'

'Is there anyone else there?'

The boy's wiggy energy was making her nervous. 'No English. Je ne parle pas anglais.'

'Just listen, okay?!' Is there anyone with you in the—'

'No anglais ...'

'Shit!' Ezra's fist slammed his desk, his image jumped – and so did the cleaning lady. Frustration was pouring into his emotional stew, creating a volatile mix. 'Christ, lady! *Just LISTEN!*'

The cleaning lady didn't need to understand English – she'd had enough – and stuck a finger in Ezra's digital face and let loose with a reprimand in rapid-fire French. Ezra scrambled to put it in reverse ...

'Okay, okay ... Jeez ... I'm sorry, ma'am. Really. I'm sorry.'

... but it was too late. The woman reached out to the laptop ...

'Wait. No! Don't—'

... and she slammed it shut.

Ezra stared at the black screen. 'Shit ...'

The cat jumped up on the desk, and after a luxurious stretch spread itself out, full-length. Ezra's fingertips went to work on its stomach and its motor started running.

'So what do I do now?' He opened a desk drawer, took out Geiger's letter, and reconsidered options for the nth time. 'Tell Mom ... ? She'd kill me – and there's nothing she could do anyway.'

His hand moved up to scratch the scarred eye socket, and the cat's front paws rose and closed around it.

17

Geiger reached the door at the top of the hotel's stair-well and put the gym bag and the attaché on the floor. The plaque said 'TOIT – N'ENTREZ PAS'.

He was well aware he was functioning in a different arena, doing things he hadn't done before, and it occurred to him that he had never approached a task or job in terms of what could or could not be done – only what *needed* to be done – what was necessary to learn, to procure, to prepare, to execute.

He had to get away without being seen. He took the lock-picking set from his bag. Since he stepped off the bus in Port Authority in 1996, without memory or direction or desire, he had followed the headings of some inner compass, and at every point of arrival melded instinct and logic into method and found a way to live in a world where he had no natural place. Life was construction – creating form from nothing, relevance out of separateness. Process was key. As Geiger had often said to Corley in a session – 'Beginning, middle, end. That's what works best for me. Completion.'

He inserted the torque wrench into the lock with his

left hand and slid in a pick with his right. Before leaving Brooklyn he had watched a YouTube video on 'how to pick a lock' four times – and had spent the last fifteen minutes practicing on the inside door lock of his room. He closed his eyes and, one by one, found the tumbler's pins with the pick's hook and nudged them up out of their set position. It took forty-five seconds, and he opened the door, grabbed his bag and case, and stepped out onto the roof. The light rain brushed against him – and the unexpected raced up at him ...

The door housing was set on a flat, ten-foot-square center section beside a large, noisy air-conditioning unit. From where he stood, the roof – smooth, shiny, gray metal sheets – spread out and down sixty feet on all four sides, finished with a three-foot-wide flat ledge. He judged the slope to be forty-five to fifty degrees. The hotel had put in central air and redone the roof, mansard style, in the years since Google's satellite had taken its pictures.

The western edge faced the street. Beyond the eastern side was thirty yards of open air with a courtyard below, and the north and south sides each ended at eight-foot gaps ... with flat rooftops on the other sides that led seamlessly to more roofs – a patchwork quilt of tile and steel and concrete that he could criss-cross to get to the street one block over.

The rain gave the roof the shiny look of a water slide. He slowly moved his shoe back and forth across a wet panel. The sole glided easily on the material, with barely any friction. The simple plan, when he thought the roof was flat, was to place the ladder across the span and crawl to the next rooftop. Now, just getting to the thin ledge was a downhill expedition, and one slip could send him sliding all the way to the edge with no way to stop – and a sixty-foot drop. He made the movie and watched it in his head. It looked quite real.

But the option cupboard was bare. He couldn't go back inside – he couldn't be seen leaving the hotel now. He couldn't be followed – because that would put a chokehold on the throat of his slim chances to take control of his life ... and Harry's ... and Matheson's ... and Ezra's. And every drop of rain that poked his face felt like another second stolen from the time he had left.

Take what you're given. Use it to make what you need. His father's mantra.

He picked up the gym bag, put his head through the handles and centered it against his chest, then walked to the edge of the plateau. He sat down, legs extended onto the pitched roof, and lay the attaché case on his lap. He'd need the ladder on the way back. And then he pushed off – and began slowly sliding down, fingertips to the slick metal for steerage and balance. He raised his feet off the surface to create more acceleration, and at the halfway point his speed had nearly doubled.

His eyes were on the flat, three-foot apron of the roof. He wasn't concerned with the distance of the leap. It would all be about the timing – and he had a highly developed sense for it. IR had demanded it. Split-seconds, inches and instinct ...

As the ledge came up at him, his hands rose and grabbed the attaché. He rocked his body forward, shoes coming down and finding the flat surface – and he sprang up, hurling the case ahead of him as he leapt – arms windmilling, legs pedaling fiercely on an invisible bicycle as he flew through the air ...

He didn't expect the feeling of weightlessness, the sense that gravity had chosen to give him a free pass for this one, boundless moment – and the pure exhilaration was like a rocket booster. It was the closest he had ever come to feeling free – free of body, of mind, of pain ...

He touched down on the other side – and the landing set off hot sparks in his compromised hips, so he went down into a roll and came to a stop sitting up. He stayed still, letting the sensation linger, his tom-tom heart pounding – then got to his feet. He took note of the attaché's location, fifteen feet away, and started off across the roof ...

André the bartender was checking the inside of the mini-fridge behind the bar.

'Nous avons besoin de crème,' he said.

Christine wrote 'cream' down on her list. Odd – after all these years, how her brain still switched back and forth between the two languages. When she raised her head, she realized someone was staring at her. He was at the other end of the bar, with a cup of coffee, and when her eyes focused on him he felt no need to stop. Not even so much as a blink. She found the gaze unsettling because it was set in a handsome, angular face without any expression at all. She put on her café owner's smile.

'Bonjour, monsieur.'

'Hello.'

'Ah ... An American. Is there something else you'd like?'

'No. Are you Christine Reynaud?'

There was something lacking in the question – an attitude, any hint of a reason for the asking. It was strange to hear.

'Yes,' she said. 'Who are you?'

He rose from his stool, picked up the bag at his feet and came over beside her. 'My name is Geiger.'

There was an intensity coming off him – not sexual, not threatening, neither hot nor cold. It seemed more like a natural state. The name fired a synapse in her brain, and it took about three seconds in search mode to find an association.

'Geiger ... You're Harry's friend.'

'Yes.'

'Well, this is strange. Harry's in Paris, too. But you probably knew that.'

'I thought he might have come to see you. Could we talk in private?'

It was like a fuse being lit. She could almost smell the phosphorus. There was a 90 percent chance when someone asked '*Could we talk in private?*' that what followed could likely blow a hole in a life – and that thought straightened her spine.

'My office. Come.'

They walked to the back of the café and stepped inside a small room with two file cabinets, a cluttered desk and chair, and a half-sofa. She turned to him as Geiger closed the door – and she stated what was clearly a fact.

'Something's happened to Harry. Something bad.'

'He's been abducted. Harry and another man.'

Abducted. The word stretched her face. It wasn't

a term heard very often in conversation. The fuse continued to sparkle as it burned down toward the bomb.

'Why?'

'Someone wants to make a trade – them for me.'

The combined effect of bizarre information and its seemingly nonchalant delivery played havoc with her reaction. Things were tilting slightly, long-assumed ninety-degree angles becoming eighty-eight and ninety-two.

'A *trade*? What the hell does that mean?'

'Christine . . .'

'Who *are* you?'

'Explaining this would take a long time, and I have very little time – so I need you to tell me what you can.'

Christine suddenly had company – a little troll in her mind's corner, gnawing on itself, snickering. *I'm back. Time to lose. Time to hurt.*

'Go on,' she said.

'When was Harry here?'

'Three nights ago.'

'Did he say anything about why he was here? Where he was staying?'

'No.'

'Who he was meeting – and where – and when?'

'No. Nothing. He just said he was here on a job.' She was trying to get some feel for the man, but there was nothing about him to get hold of. He was smooth as ice. Harry had called him a close friend. The pairing seemed unimaginable to her.

From his bag, Geiger took out a folder – the one Harry had given to him in the diner.

'Before Harry left New York, he gave me these. A copy of his will ... title to his apartment ... documents for his safe deposit box.' He dropped the folder on the desk. 'Think again, Christine. Is there anything at all you can remember Harry mentioning that might be of any importance? His schedule? His itinerary?'

The speed of things continuing to shift out of commonplace and swerve into preternatural was dizzying.

'We talked about us. The past, mostly. And he mentioned you. But there was nothing more about his being here. I'm certain.'

There is a certain sense of imbalance – almost a kind of loneliness – upon realizing you are in the presence of a complete stranger who is connected to you, who knows things about another dear to you, secrets with the power to alter feelings and long-set assumptions. She felt a twinge of something close to anger – and didn't understand why.

'I have to go,' said Geiger, and he turned for the door.

'Wait!' She reached out and grabbed his arm. He looked back at her, and something in his eyes made her let go of him.

'Just ... just wait,' she said. 'What are you going to do?'

'Find them.'

'What about the police?'

'This is a world you know nothing about, Christine. No police.'

She watched his hands begin a tap dance on his thighs – crisp, contrapuntal steps.

'I have to go,' he said.

'But – but how will I know what happened? I need to know.'

'You won't see me again. If Harry survives, my guess is you'll hear from him. If you don't – then you'll still know what happened. Goodbye, Christine.'

He opened the door and walked out. She watched him move across the café and out to the street. There was something about the way he walked. Some re-invention that accommodated all but a trace of damage. She closed the door and sat down on the couch.

She suddenly wondered if he was crazy. He was talk-ing about crazy things, and it felt contagious. That first stutter when your senses revolt – I can't believe this is happening – and demand a do-over. The troll winked at her. *Long time, no see.*

When Geiger got in the backseat of the cab and gave the young driver the address, he got a tilt of the young man's shaven head and a raised brow in return.

'Rue *Questel*?' He scratched at his scraggly goatee. 'Hmm ... This is sure? You have gone before there?'

'No,' said Geiger, and showed him the tag on the key provided by Carmine's associate.

The cabbie shook his head and shrugged. 'I dunno – but is okay.' He grinned, and pointed at the screen of the dashboard GPS system. 'We get there. Three-one-five Rue Questel.'

He pulled away from the curb and turned east on Rue Claude Bernard, and Geiger sat back and let his head rest against the top of the seat. His gaze volleyed side to side, watching the buildings go by – taller and more massive here, eight stories of very old earth-toned stone and mortar, graced with rows of iron balconies that stretched without end like a Mondrian-made universe. Their changing intricacies rushing past him – spears, filigrees, curlicues, fleurs-de-lis – touched his sense of design and gave him a visual line to follow, but for hours he had felt his upper trapezius stiffening in his neck, very gradually, and now it was starting to tug at the base of his skull like a cranky child demanding attention.

It was because of all the people. There were too many of them. The shifting and balancing of their questions and stares and needs and agendas. Words to parse, expressions to read, sifting through it all on the fly.

The driver turned onto Avenue des Gobelins, and the sight of its queues of trees – thin-trunked with sparkling emerald leaves lacquered with rain – triggered a tactual moment, like a cool puff of wind in his face.

The cabbie found Geiger's stony face in the rearview mirror. 'I'm always liking this street,' he said. 'Is pretty, no?'

The flashing, glossy patches of green raced up at Geiger, surrounding him, whirling his mind round so it caught glimpses of a lost sylvan life, angled soft shafts of light through branches ... woody aromas of sap and fecund soil ... snatches of sound, an avian cry ... the firm but soft touch of his hand in another's ... '*You are the sun—*'

Geiger's hand rose, thumb and forefinger finding his eyes and sealing them shut like a bedside priest with a just-departed corpse.

He was like a novelist writing a story, fleshing out characters, their instincts, choices, and weaving a detailed plot, beat by beat – but resisting the urge to envision an ending to the tale. When Christine had asked '*What are you going to do?*' the spare simplicity of the question made him realize why he hadn't thought about how it all might end, why he had never visualized the possible denouements and played them out.

It was because he already knew.

Geiger opened his eyes. He turned his head to the right. The vertebrae were stubborn – but he got the *click*.

'Can you put on some music?' he said.

'Yes,' said the cabbie. 'What kind?'

'It doesn't matter.'

Carmine's people had done well. The place on Rue Questel was three blocks off the Seine, in a small industrial park-like setting, concrete and gravel and power wires. It was away from two other buildings – one story high, fifty feet square, its blind, glassless windows filled with plywood. Its faded sign – 'Chevier Carreaux Import' – had four letters missing. It had been empty for some time – a dreary monument to failure.

The cabbie pulled up in front and gawked at the sorry state of things. '*Here*? You be sure?'

'Yes.' Geiger leaned forward and held out a fifty-euro note, and the driver's eyes popped. 'Here is fifty now. I'll be inside for about an hour. If you wait for me, I'll give you another fifty. Understand?'

'*Cent* euros?' The driver's grin came out like the sun. 'I understand,' he said, and took the bill. 'I will be here.'

'Good,' said Geiger, and grabbed his bag.

'Mister ... May I ask why you come to this – eh, how do you say ... *dump*?'

Geiger opened the door. 'I do renovation.' He got out and headed for the back.

He stepped inside, found the light switch, then closed the door and stood in the darkness – feeling the space, smelling it, playing the part of the Jones. The aroma of mildew was potent, and he could feel the dust rushing up to him on all sides. He turned on the lights.

It was all pocked concrete – the walls and floor, the ceiling with its two sets of fluorescent fixtures. There were half a dozen saggy shelving units against one wall, and a large, cylindrical hot-water tank high on another wall atop four thin, metal stilts. Every five or six seconds a drop leaked from it and fell into a full pail on the floor beneath it, and the silence amplified each *plop*. The place felt like a dungeon. Or a tomb. And if events played out in a certain fashion, it would become the one place on the planet Geiger had resolved to never revisit. A session room.

But the truth was – the nature of the physical space was irrelevant. Whatever customizing and constructing he might do here, now – what would ultimately define the place was his choice of action ... and already being near-certain what his dreadful choice would be turned the screws in his neck even tighter.

Geiger put his bag down. This would be as bare-bones as he had gone in a long time. Everything on the list was there. On a rectangular folding table were two small Bose speakers, three one-gallon jugs of water and a package of large plastic cups, a Smith and Wesson six-inch Tanto knife, and two dozen rolls of silver duct tape. On the floor were two gooseneck floor lamps, two radiant space heaters the size of suitcases, and a sturdy, un-upholstered wooden chair with arms and a shoulder-level back. He would have preferred that the back had been higher, but all in all, he could make it work. He would have to.

In Dalton's video, he had told Geiger '*I am in your debt ...*' – and the truth was ... it was mutual. It had taken some time for Geiger to understand how deeply Dalton had changed him, and the irony – that after Corley had tried for so long to discover and deliver Geiger's past to him, it had been Dalton's torturing that had unearthed the treasure – a chest of buried memories, Geiger's own Pandora's box. With each of Dalton's cuts the lid had opened higher, until a host of spirits had flown out and shown themselves ...

The ritual of the razor ...

The years of nights on the floor of the small closet his father had built for him ...

That last night on the mountain, his father trapped and crushed beneath the pick-up truck's tire – dying, but too slowly for the man to bear – and his last request ... his command that the boy use the knife. His father's forefinger rising and tapping at his bloody chest.

'*Here.*'

'*No, I won't do it!*'

'*Do as I say, son.*'

The boy's forbidden tears starting to fall. '*Father ... Please!*'

'*Is this what I've made of you? A weeping, useless*

*little boy? Then go! Get out of my sight! I don't want
your face to be the last thing I see.'*

But there was still one spirit who chose to remain
invisible, only giving him her voice ...

Geiger checked his watch. His schedule was holding.
He thought of Dalton – waiting somewhere without
concern, certain that Geiger would come, *knowing* he
would arrive. In a world that very few lived in, it made
a perfect kind of sense that he and Dalton should share
an ending. They fit together like a dovetail joint.

They were made for each other.

Victor had brought the desk chair to the window of his
room and been sitting for hours, glancing down at his
crossword puzzle every so often as he watched the
lobby entrance across the street. He'd never particularly
cared for the stakeout aspect of the job – it took more
out of you than a layman might guess – but he did find
the act of observation worthwhile. For one thing, it had
taught him that people were very much of a kind – that
you could bring certain assumptions to the job – about
a target, about tendencies and reactions – and be on
solid ground. When people came out on their way to
somewhere they moved faster – looking about, steps
firm, more attentive of the world around them – than
when they returned and went inside.

For the past twenty minutes, he'd been listening to
Zanni's short, crisp huffs coming through the open door
of their adjoining rooms, impressed by their precise
timing and replication. If he hadn't known it was her, he
might have thought there was a steam-fueled robot in
there performing a repetitive task. He got up and went

into her room, and resumed his post by a window. She was on the floor, in sweat pants and a T-shirt, doing crunches, each identical to the one before it – the quintessence of the woman. He'd never known an agent more obsessed with control. It was an admirable trait, but double-edged.

'How many do you do?'

She spoke quickly, in between exhales. 'I don't count.'

'How do you know when you have done enough?'

'S'not about that.' She lay back on the floor and let out a deep breath. 'It's just about doing them.' She sat up and wiped the sweat from around her eyes. 'I have to be able to trust my body. Always.'

Victor smiled. 'But no one else . . . ?' It was a question that was a statement.

'I work in a man's world, Victor, and I've never met one who hasn't tried to screw me – one way or another.'

'I see. And me . . . ?'

Zanni's right brow rose like a scythe. 'Let's just say – I don't *mis*-trust you as much as the next guy. How's that?'

'Ah. I am honored. And I need a smoke. Can you watch a few minutes?'

Zanni got up, grabbed a fistful of M&M's from a bowl on the desk and went to the window.

'Go ahead,' she said, and started jogging in place.

Victor headed for the door. 'I think it interesting . . .' he said.

'What is?'

'That you make this difference between men and women.' There was more than wisdom in Victor's hint of a grin. 'Is Zanni to be trusted?'

Zanni turned to him, violet eyes flashing. 'Don't play me, Victor. You remember Zurich?'

'Yes.'

'If I had trusted our two "friends" there, would I be here having this conversation?'

'No.'

'Then end of goddamn story.' She swallowed to soften the hard edge of her voice. 'Go smoke.'

Victor opened the door. 'Zanni . . . It is not like you – how should I say? – to push your buttons so easy. Relax.' He closed the door behind him.

She started lifting her knees high with every jog. He was right. Idle was her worst gear. She needed the sense of movement, of life happening. She fed off it. When she ran track in college, they started her on the eight hundred and fifteen hundred meters – but she couldn't pace herself, she went zero to sixty and stayed there until she flagged at the end, so they moved her to sprints.

She stared at the hotel. He was in there, designing his plans as he would one of his extraordinary wooden creations. The irony of it all was that, in a sense, she could *trust* him. She had no doubt that one way or another he would find his way to Dalton. She just had to pace herself, stay in a middle gear and follow his lead.

18

The cabbie pulled over one block east of the hotel. Geiger handed the driver a fifty-euro note.

'Merci, monsieur, merci beaucoup.'

'What is your name?'

'Rémy.'

'Rémy ... I'll pay you another hundred if you're waiting for me here at eight-thirty tonight. It won't be a long ride. Fifteen, twenty minutes. You understand *eight-thirty*?'

'Oui!' The young man's smile popped open. 'Yes, yes monsieur.'

'Good.'

Geiger stepped out and headed down the sidewalk in the lightening rain. Mingling smells – toasted, pungent, smoked – made him slow at a display window. Inside the small épicerie, people were two and three deep at the counters – pointing fingers, bringing food to their noses. The aromas, when united with the sights of baguettes and sourdough loafs, generous slabs of cheese, the rainbow-colored piles of vegetables, packed an almost tactile kick – reminding Geiger he hadn't eaten in fifteen hours. This would likely be his last chance to do so for some time, so he opened the door and went in.

The place rang with the music of voices – the call and response, inquiries, appreciative murmurs. Geiger moved to the crates of tomatoes – blood-red and bright yellow, striped orange and green, dark purple – against a wall beside the asparagus, lettuce and fennel. He gently squeezed a few between thumb and forefinger.

'Puis-je vous aider, monsieur?'

Geiger turned to an old woman sitting on a stool, leaning on a black metal cane. She wore dark, thick-framed glasses, and over her cotton dress a checked white and sky-blue sweater buttoned all the way up to her wattled neck. She had the calm air of a matriarch who'd been retired – and it crossed Geiger's mind that she must have asked that question almost a million times.

'I don't speak French,' he said.

She cocked her white-haired head. 'Ah. American. Hmm ... my English, monsieur ... comme ci, comme ça, oui?' She smiled, wrinkles in her face stretching like rubber bands, got up off her stool and puttered over on her cane. She studied the multihued collection, picked up a yellow pear tomato and held it out to him. 'Good, very good. Allez, essayez!'

Geiger took the tomato and bit off half. It was firm and tasty.

'Bien?'

Geiger nodded as he chewed. 'It's good. Sweet.'

'Très bien.' She raised a purple-veined, knobby hand and wiped away a bit of juice from his chin with her

thumb. 'Alors …' she said, 'quoi d'autre?' And as she
looked down at the crates, she took hold of Geiger's
forearm – and the flesh to flesh connection sent goosebumps skipping toward his neck.

'Hmm … Roi Humbert – très bon. Noire charbon-
neuse …'

Hers was the softest flesh he remembered ever touching his. Not that there had been many instances. The
doctors' fingers probing and pressing his body years
ago, and, on occasion, Carmine's huge hands affec-
tionately patting his cheeks, and Ezra holding his hand –
but the skin of the old woman's palm was so soothing
he thought he felt his heartbeat slow. He put the other
half of the pear tomato in his mouth.

'Beauté blanche … orange bourgouin …' As she
made her considerations about the tomatoes, she was
running her hand up and down his forearm, a few
inches north, a few inches south. It was the most natural of gestures, like petting a lap-cat, or stroking a
sleeping child's hair – Geiger was certain she was
unaware of doing it – and it brought a sound, a whisper of a song, *her* voice, like a breeze through an open
window rustling a curtain. *Now it's time to say goodnight …*

'Marmande ancienne. Mmm … very good.'

Good night, sleep tight …

As he had in the taxi, he felt the extraordinary
coming closer – the coppery, earthy smell of the past,
the indescribable, the magical, the unbearable …

'I need to leave,' he said.

Dream sweet dreams …

The old woman looked up at him. 'Partir?'

'Yes. To go. Now.' He slowly rolled his head clock-wise, trying to unlock things.

The old wet eyes watched him as he took a ten-euro note from his pocket and put it in her hand.

'You choose,' he said.

'Oui?' She shrugged her frail shoulders. Her smile returned with a crimp of affection, and she patted his arm.

He needed to be gone. To be alone.

Geiger moved quickly down the block, stopping at the doors of small apartment and office buildings and pressing all the buttons on the directories, hoping someone would buzz him in without asking his identity or purpose via intercom. When he finally succeeded, he stepped inside to find it was an elevator building, and he was grateful for that. On the top floor, he unlocked the roof entry with his tools, and when he stepped outside he was met with the sight of the Eiffel Tower rising above the prairie of rooftops. He granted himself a few moments to stand there and gaze at its majesty.

Its lights were on and the molten marvel painted the Paris dusk bronze – standing like a colossal sentinel. The wedding of space and structure, emptiness and elegance, the brazen commitment of design ... It stirred his most constant of urges – to pull something out of the rubble within himself and forge it with hand and heart into a work of beauty – to try and erase all his monstrous acts, one by one, and in the doing remake himself. He could turn and go back through the door, ride the elevator down and take a train or a plane to anywhere. The world was that small – a spinning ball in the palm of his hand – and so immeasurably big that they would never find him ...

Down in the street there was a sudden squabble of horns – then two crunching metallic *clacks*. Geiger looked toward the sound – as volleys of angry French, in loud and dramatic fashion, rose up in the air ... and then a gendarme's seesawing wah-wah joined the ruckus. Chaos was playing social liaison again, making partners of strangers. Geiger glanced a last time at the tower, then started across the roofs.

The gym bag was around his neck again, resting on his back. He pulled the ladder out to its full length, snapped the locks into place, and walked to the roof's edge with it. Geiger got on his knees and slid the ladder across the eight-foot gap until its end rested on the ledge of his hotel's roof. The first thing he'd do when he got back into his room was take a shower and try to unlock his neck.

He started across the ladder on his hands and knees, rung to rung. Grab with the right hand, move the left leg, grab with the left hand, move the right leg ... With each action there was a tiny give to the ladder, a sink of half an inch at the point of pressure. He had to look down as he crawled – his neck was too knotted to keep his head up and looking forward – and staring at the alley below began to put small bends in his vision, slight vertiginous shimmies. He considered whether he should try and get across before it worsened ... or stop and see if it went away.

He stopped.

He closed his eyes and gray-black eddies started

whirling on the backs of his lids – so he snapped them open again. He became aware of how tightly he was gripping the rung, the pronounced thump of the pulse in his hands and the short, snaky trembles come to life in his forearms. The spread of air on his flesh like another skin ... the vestige of the tomato's tart acid in his mouth ... the rustle of breath in the nostrils suddenly a loud sea rush in his ears – his senses were taking hold, over-riding his automatic pilot, telling him this balancing act was just part of a much larger one – a man on a tightrope juggling doubt, and grief, and shame.

He began sucking in deep breaths through his mouth and expelling them, like pumping up a deflating tire – and pushed himself forward. Grab with the right hand, move the left leg, left hand, right leg ...

... and then the hard, cold flatness of the ledge beneath his palm. He crawled on and let his blood come to rest, then pulled the ladder in, telescoped it back down to its compact square and frisbeed it over to the other roof. He sat down, took a roll of duct tape out of his bag and began wrapping lengths of it around his shoes, soles to tops, the sticky side out – and then did the same with his palms. He rose, faced the incline and then bent to it, palms against the surface, for a test. The tape would be of some help. Then he started up – left hand, right foot, right hand, left foot – toward the top.

The water was cold enough. Ideally, at this temperature the shower's spray would feel like needles piercing his skin, zapping the nerve endings, poking holes in the pain – but the pressure was lacking, and he'd had to stay longer than he wanted and settle for a kind of tentative numbing. He turned off the water and came out of the stall. He wouldn't use a towel, so the coldness would stay with him as long as possible.

There was a full-length mirror in an ornate, faux-antique frame on the opposite wall – and the carnage of July Fourth still beckoned to him. The webbed scar reconnecting the exploded flesh in his chest. Dalton's crooked trio on his quad.

Looking at them was not like staring at the vast array on his hamstrings and calves. That display, the proof of his father's method and madness, had always been part of him, emblems of his past – but this damage was evidence that the world had found him, and now, he had finally received a formal invitation. Dalton might be the host, but it was fate who was throwing the party – and Geiger was the guest of honor, no RSVP necessary, come as you are.

Shielded by room 404's curtains, Geiger finished shooting the second set of wide shots and close-ups of the parking situation on the street – over four hours had passed since the first photo documentation – and then he sat down with his iPad, hooked the camera up to it and went through them all, comparing the two sessions. He deleted any vehicle that wasn't in both sets, and that left nine – five cars, two commercial vans, and two motor-scooters. He created a separate file, arranging them in three rows of three, and made the photos as large as possible for easier recognition, when and if the time came.

*

Before the surgeries, he'd never been one for taking walks. Exercise in general had never held much appeal. It wasn't the exertion, it was the sweating. Even as a child, he had found the feel of the clammy dampness on his skin unpleasant – it felt almost unnatural ... the wet, bodily exudation – but after the operations Dr. Ling had preferred to have their discussions during walks around the clinic grounds and Dalton had found early on that the steady pace and conversation honed his flow of thoughts.

It was during one of those walks that Dalton had his first hallucination – watching Dr. Ling's face silently explode while explaining the neural-transmissive potential of synthetic-organic polymers. They had continued to walk on another fifty yards – the good doctor going on in his high-pitched, nasal way, his head a jumble of twisted, bloody debris between his shoulders – before Dalton had banished the figment.

He turned the corner of the farmhouse, heading around back. Lavender and thistle invaders grew wild amid the rows of barren old grapevines, and beyond the field the forest rose up like a ribbed palisade at the base of the hills. There were creatures there – he'd heard cries and songs – though he rarely saw them. A fox in the very early dim of morning, a few hearty feral dogs, a wild boar ...

He felt strong, at ease, in control. The madness was part of him now, to be acknowledged and managed – like a non-fatal disease. History teemed with men whose delusions and raptures were not fetters but fuel for their quests and great deeds. The play was under way. He had no animus toward Boddicker and

Matheson. They were like minor characters used to set up the plot in the first act, or provide the audience with necessary information ... and now their presence in the unfolding drama was no longer required. Shakespeare would send them on some far-away errand – or kill them off ...

He looked to the west. The sun had slid down the wall of the sky far enough to nestle in the trees – and he watched as the fiery globe set them ablaze. The flames swayed, tangerine and hungry, reaching up past the smoking canopy to feed on the sky.

And Geiger was coming. The angel-hawk, circling, each circuit tighter and closer than the last, his wings on fire ...

'Harry ...'

Matheson stared at the unmoving body. In the over-sized smock, it was hard to tell if he was breathing, and the dimness of the light increased the degree of difficulty.

'Harry!'

Harry's mottled head turned half a degree on his neck, and the meager effort brought a wince.

'I'm not dead,' he said, softly.

They were on opposite sides of a fifteen-foot-square room, sitting on thin mattresses, their backs against the rough-hewn walls. Their right ankles were shackled with a steel clamp at the ends of heavy-gauge chains leading to large screw eyes set into the concrete floor. The chains' six-foot length allowed the men access to their own portable toilets, but not the pair of square windows, which were boarded up on the outside with a four-inch opening in the center. Each man had a plastic gallon jug of water beside his mattress.

'Drink some water, Harry.'

The command made Harry swallow involuntarily. 'Too hard to.'

'Do it, Harry. You need to drink some water.'

'No, David. I need to drink some *bourbon* ... from a highball glass ... while sitting in a chaise lounge ... by an L-shaped pool ... that Isabella Rossellini is swimming naked in.'

'Isabella Rossellini. Is that right?'

'Circa nineteen eighty-five. Without question.' Harry picked up the jug with his right hand and brought it to his swollen lips, took a breath, and then got two gulps down.

That they had, from the first night of captivity, effortlessly settled into a dry, sardonic banter was proof of a kinship that might, in normal circumstances, have taken months to show itself. Their fear was as much a bond as a bludgeon.

Matheson brought his left hand up to his face. Three of the fingers were neatly wrapped in gauze, with a tint of pale red at the ends. They were clearly shorter than they had once been.

'I can't believe how little blood there was.' His voice had a limp – a drag to the words that severe pain and drugs will bring, like a ball and chain.

'How's the pain?' asked Harry.

'Bad. Yours?'

'Scintillating.'

Matheson carefully lowered the hand back down. 'What did Geiger do to him?'

'Broke his jaw. Then all his fingers. Crushed them.'

'Well, they work now.'

Harry closed his eyes. The pain was having a field day – the stings on his face, the bruises on his chest and arms, the raw wounds on his palm – but holding the fear at bay was worse. He'd been negotiating with it for a while now – angling to get the best terms possible, trying to close the deal. Everything was on the table. Make me your best offer.

He had spent all those years watching the session videos of Geiger at his black craft ...

'There are numerous applications of pain for specific scenarios ...'

... dutifully transcribing ...

'There is audio ... there is pressure ...'

... doing his very best not to let his mind burrow into that of the Jones ...

'There is blunt force, manipulation of joints ...'

... not allowing himself to sit in that barber's chair ...

'The application of intense heat and cold ...'

... but it occurred to him now – it was almost as if he'd been trained for it. Mayhem's last move. The final joke. Your turn, Harry. Time to get in the chair. *Au revoir.*

'Harry ... Do you think Geiger is coming?'

'I got out of the Geiger-guessing business. I was never very good at it.'

They heard the doorknob turn and looked to the door as it opened – and Dalton stepped inside. He held two paper plates of food, with plastic forks and knives.

'Good evening.'

The prisoners stared back silently, and Dalton walked

to a small black circle painted on the floor, put the plates down on the marker and took one step back. He'd measured it all out. They could reach the plates if they stretched out on their stomachs, but they couldn't reach him.

'Asparagus from the garden, and jambon from a nearby farm. I practiced on the pig with my scalpel, and then cured it myself. A wonderful word to say, isn't it? *Jam-bon*.' He smiled. It was genuine, with a faint curl at both ends. 'A beautiful language. I'm sure you feel that way, Harry – your ex-wife being French.'

Harry wanted to smile back, but it just wouldn't come. 'Question,' he said.

'Yes?'

'What do you want?'

'What do I *want*?' Dalton cocked his head, as if he was unfamiliar with the word. 'Yeah. What's the end game?'

'Ah.' Dalton nodded. 'You play chess.'

'Used to.'

'The *end game*. That's a good choice, Harry.' Dalton's hand rose, and the finger went to tapping his lip. 'End game. Two masters, face to face, with very few pieces left on the board. Wisdom, experience, cunning become key. Very nicely put.' He straightened his glasses. 'What I *want* – is an end to vengeance. An end to the *feeling*. You have no concept of what I've done to make that possible.'

Harry gave him a deadpan nod. 'Uh-huh. That's very compelling, Dalton. Really – I've got goosebumps. But more importantly – think I can get a couple of Pepcids? My stomach's a mess. I'm very gaseous. It's really not fair to David here ...'

'Sorry, Harry. I try and stay away from all commercial remedies. Painkillers, antacids ...'

'You sound like Geiger.'

Dalton grinned. 'Do I? Harry ... I take that as a great compliment.'

'Fuck you,' said Harry.

Dalton's tapping froze – and the hand slowly descended.

'What happens to us if Geiger decides to come, Dalton?'

'Depending on certain variables, I will agree to a trade.'

'For both of us ... or one of us?'

'Let's don't get ahead of ourselves, Harry. It takes the fun out of things.'

Dalton went to the door and opened it, allowing a glimpse of a hallway – bare wooden walls, a time-darkened wide-plank floor, a small table with an empty ceramic vase – and he turned back to them.

'By the way ...' he said. 'Geiger is in Paris. I expect him here sometime tomorrow. Bon appétit.' He stepped out and the door closed.

Matheson let out a breath. 'Think he's telling the truth – about Geiger?'

'I have no idea. But if Geiger is on his way, then I think Dalton's finished with us now. I don't think he'll be working on us anymore.'

Matheson nodded. 'I think you're right. Of course, there's a very good chance now that he'll kill us ...'

'Definitely – but at least we don't have to worry about torture.'

'You're a real glass-half-full kind of guy, Harry.'

'Famous for it. And my timing, too. Exquisite, always.' He took a slow breath, as deep as he could. 'I picked a helluva start to my new career, huh?'

'I'm sorry, Harry. You're here because of me.'

'I didn't mean it that way – and it's not true, either. The feeling that made me want to come ... Haven't felt like that in a very long time. Great feeling, man. And my dinner last night ...? My ex-wife. The love of my life.'

'No kidding.'

'We haven't spoken in a dozen years. It was a good thing to do. So ...'

They shared a look. Dalton had left something in the room. Like a gossamer, settling darkness. Matheson straightened himself up a bit. The chain made a bright jangle on the floor. He sighed, heavily, and the hollow depth of it was something Harry knew well. He'd heard it many times. The prelude to expiation.

'You know it was me, don't you?' said Matheson.

'That you told Dalton Geiger was alive, and that the spooks knew? Yes, I know.'

'Because you didn't tell him.'

'Right.' There was no anger in Harry's eyes, and no judgement. 'It doesn't matter, David. One of us would, eventually. That's how it works.'

'I tried to hold out, Harry – but after the second finger I just—'

'David ... Do you know what I've seen? A hundred men – weasels to guys who made Capone look like a wimp. And every one of them caved. Every one of them told Geiger what he needed to know. Geiger called it the *release point* – and we've all got one. So let it go. We're all the same that way. *All* of us.'

'... Even Geiger?'

'I don't know. Maybe you'll get the chance to ask him.'

Harry let his eyes fall shut. He needed to go somewhere else – if only for a few moments – places he had crossed off the map years ago. But he sensed they would be easy to find.

He heard a voice call to him ...

'Harry ... Come here.'

The music of Christine's voice, the foreign lilt, always made him smile.

He was at his desk in the corner of their bedroom on Eighty-second Street, working on a piece for the Times' Week In Review. *He rose and came down the hall to a doorway. She was inside, leaning against a wall, arms folded across her slender chest, and when she saw him she put a finger up to her smile, signaling not to speak.*

'Have you seen Sophie?' she said, and jabbed a thumb to her right.

The little girl was sitting on the floor in a corner – snug in her red pajamas, head bowed, her three years of caramel curls falling in her face, which she had covered up with her hands. She was trying not to giggle.

'I think she's hiding,' said Christine, and winked a pale blue eye at him. Harry walked to her, and they brushed their lips together. 'I wonder where she could be,' she said.

'Maybe she's using her special invisible powers,' he said.

'Why yes. Maybe that's it. I wonder, wonder, wonder where she could be.'

The little girl lowered her hands. The magnitude of her smile was off the charts.

'I'm here!' she said, popping up laughing, and jumped into her mother's arms. They had the same face – the pointed chin, wide forehead, the pale blue, oval eyes that seemed to widen and gleam when they were happy.

'You were using your special invisible powers. How do you do that?'

'Daddy taught me.'

'I know – but how do you do it?'

'Well ... First I—'

'Sophie, wait,' said Harry, and leaned to her and started whispering in her ear. The little girl nodded soberly as she listened.

'Mommy,' she said, 'Daddy says I can't tell.'

'No? Why not?'

'Because it only works if you don't tell how. It's a secret.'

'Then you certainly shouldn't tell me. I want you to always be able to turn invisible when you want to.' She kissed the little girl, then glanced at Harry, her blue eyes brightening, and mouthed the words – 'I love you'.

Dalton's forefinger slowly tapped at his upper lip as he composed his thoughts, then his fingers clicked on the keyboard as he wrote.

Obsession is a relative state. It is morality that measures and contraposes obsession in our mind. Jeffrey Dahmer and DaVinci. Himmler and Kubrick. Stalin and Curie. The terrorist and the saint.

The madman and the creator. Feeling and harnessing that power is the extraordinary element in it all. I remember the session with Geiger, talking to him about the pursuit of *expertise*, how it is the great definer and equalizer. One doesn't need a degree, or wealth, or privilege – and it tells us much about someone – that they possess a passion that has driven them to a point well beyond where most people would ever go.

After that day's events, through the months of pain, I came to understand I was far from his equal. Where he had been the expert, I had been a journeyman – artless, mundane. But I have remade myself, elevated myself, while he chose to renounce his expertise – so now I will pay my debt to him. I will help him discover who he really is.

Madness is also a relative state – and if obsession is my right hand, then madness is my left.

Dalton rose and strolled to a window, the dried carcasses of the wasps scattered on the floor crunching beneath his shoes. Outside the glass, beneath the farmhouse's eaves, a few of the giant, buzzing insects were in a lazy hover around the huge, pulpy nest. Its twisted, menacing beauty always moved him.

'Not equals, Geiger, no – but certainly, there were no others like us. And you decided we were done. *You* decided, for *both* of us.' He swallowed like an animal with a bone stuck in its throat. 'You thought you'd ended something – but what you didn't understand is – that you'd started something new ... and left it to me to finish it.'

19

Dewey had the side and rearview mirrors set up so he could see the hotel's lobby, a hundred feet behind him, in both of them – and that allowed him to shift every few minutes behind the wheel, doing his back exercises without losing sight of the target for more than a second. The pelvic tilts and side stretches helped keep things from locking up when he had to sit so long.

He liked crunching the numbers in his head. He had all the figures cold by now – down payment, reno and replacement, monthly nuts – even a quote on a neon sign for behind the bar – and he'd had the new name since before he shipped out in '08. 'McFearless' – by Kings of Leon. It'd be the first song out of the speakers on opening night. '*I roll my sleeves and make a better man of me.*' Victor had said he'd give him a name or two if he finished the job solid. Another four or five gigs and he'd be there ...

He straightened up when he saw Geiger come out of the hotel lobby, tote bag in hand, and stop beneath the entry's awning and overhead light – and then Dewey

was answering his cell and talking before the first ring
was finished.

'Yeah, I see him,' he said.

It was Victor on the other end, smooth as a frozen lake.
'Fine,' he said. He was standing by his room window,
crossword puzzle in hand at his side, watching Geiger
through the neon-threaded rain.

'Am I on him?' asked Dewey.

Victor turned and walked through the adjoining door.
Zanni was sitting cross-legged on her bed, hair still wet
from the shower, wrapped loosely in a terry-cloth robe,
the newspaper spread open before her.

'Geiger's out,' he said, and Zanni hopped to the floor
and went to the curtained window. 'You want Dewey
on him?'

Zanni pulled the drapes back a few inches. 'Yes. But
eyes only. No contact.'

Victor brought the phone back up. 'Yes, you are on
him, Dewey – but keep no contact. Yes?'

'I get you.'

'Good.'

Victor came up beside Zanni, and smiled. 'Always
lavender. Do you ever think of trying something else –
just for a change?'

She turned her poker face to him. 'Why?'

Geiger knew exactly what time it was, but he looked at
his watch. However many eyes were on him, he wanted
to make sure they all got a good look at him. There
were moons circling him, orbits shrinking with every
revolution. There would be a precise time for each to

finally reach him, and the cumulative impact would be immeasurable – but until then he had to hold them all in place.

He glanced up and down the street pensively for a few moments, though he knew where he was going – south to the corner – then started off.

Dewey readjusted his mirrors, and slunk down low in the seat. He watched Geiger's reflection approach on the opposite sidewalk – and sat back up once he was past the car. There was something odd about his gait. Definitely some damage there. It reminded him of a sergeant he knew who'd taken shrapnel in a hip and never walked quite the same after they fixed him up. When Geiger was two-thirds down the block Dewey turned the ignition.

'The closest metro station is at the intersection in the other direction,' he said to his cell, 'so he's either walking or looking for a cab.'

'That is likely, yes,' said Victor.

'Can I talk to her?'

Victor handed Zanni the phone.

'What is it?' she said.

'Well ...' said Dewey, 'now that he's out ... I just wanted to know – did you tell him about me? I mean – does he know I'm with you guys?'

'No, Dewey. He doesn't know about you.'

'How come?'

Zanni stared at the phone like she wanted to slap it silly.

'He doesn't need to know, Dewey. We keep this as

simple as possible. Anyway ... The fact is that whatever else he may be thinking, Geiger absolutely assumes one thing: He's being watched and followed – either by us ... or Dalton's people ... or both. So this is *his* game, not ours – right? Keep him in sight, but keep your distance. For now, our job is to stay out of his way, know where he is, and make sure he gets to Dalton. Understand?'

'But what if he—'

'Dewey ... Think of it this way. Right now, we are ... shepherds – and Geiger is our little lamb. Okay? Now just do your job.' She clicked off and shot Victor a frown. He shrugged.

'He is just speaking his thoughts, Zanni. It is indeed a strange situation – no?'

'Listen to St. Victor the Patient.'

She watched the Citroen pull out and start slowly down the street. Her pulse was up a tick. She'd been waiting. It didn't matter what this was about – whether Geiger was playing them, or going out for some foie gras and a nice Bordeaux before he traded away his life tomorrow. What mattered was the *act* – motion and choice as proof of thought and intent, a step taken, a move made – literally and figuratively. The game was progressing, and games only moved in one direction – to an end.

The cab had its roof light off. When Geiger opened the back door he was met by a rush of Coltrane and Rémy's bright smile.

'Bonsoir!'

Geiger slid inside and closed the door. The dip in the movement tugged at his neck, a sharp reminder of certain states. Geiger took a hundred-euro note from his pocket, held it out – and the driver smiled.

'Plus tard. After, monsieur.'

'Take it now.'

The cabbie shrugged and took the money. 'Merci. Where to go?'

'First, move the passenger's side mirror so I can see it from here.'

'Pardon?'

Geiger leaned forward and pointed. 'The mirror ...'

'Ah! *Miroir*. Oui.' The driver used his panel controls. 'Good?'

Geiger settled back. 'A little higher.'

'Up?' The cabbie made an adjustment. 'Oui?'

'Good.' From his seat, Geiger now had a clear view of the street behind them. 'Head toward Rue Saint Denis – and take your time.'

The driver's brows perked up – and he looked to Geiger's blank face in the rearview mirror. A picture was beginning to develop.

He frowned and tapped his forehead. 'How say ... someone is to follow us?'

Geiger's gaze met Rémy's in the mirror. 'Hopefully.' He took his iPad out of his bag and brought up the nine photos of parked cars. 'Drive, Rémy.'

The neon signs of the sex shops and bars filled puddles with drowning, colored strands, and the thirsty and curious moved along with collars up and newspaper hats, but the rain wasn't keeping the hookers on Boulevard de Clichy inside. A few leaned in doorways, stood under dripping awnings, a hip thrust out, a knee-high boot jiggling, a finger tapping ash from a glowing cigarette.

Rémy was hiding a grin. 'Monsieur ... *Here*?'

'Don't talk now,' said Geiger. His eyes were ping-ponging between the rearview and side mirrors. He saw the street about to take a curve. 'Get over to the left. Do you understand?'

'Yes. Left. A gauche.'

As Rémy performed the maneuver, Geiger caught a second's glimpse in the side mirror of a silver car a few lengths in back of them. His gaze darted to the iPad and found photos of two silver cars – a Citroen and a Renault. He started memorizing their license plates ...

Dewey watched the cab pull over at the intersection up ahead – and he parked in a dark spot between two streetlamps, cut the lights and wipers, and cracked his window a few inches. Hawkers outside clubs were calling out to people, trying to wrangle tourists in for some skin and drinks. Geiger got out of the taxi, looked around, and headed down the sidewalk – and stopped at a doorway with a short, canvas awning where a woman puffed on a cigarette. Dewey picked up his cell and hit '1'.

'Yes ...' said Victor.

'He got out of the cab on Boulevard de Clichy. Lots of sex shops and clubs around here. And hookers. He's talking to one now.'

Victor was seated at a small table in Zanni's room, the crossword puzzle before him. He turned to her. She was lying on the bed, watching BBC News on the television.

'Geiger is in the red light district, making a whore's acquaintance.'

Zanni's right brow did a quick jump. 'Really ...'

Victor grinned. 'It would appear the mystical Inquisitor is flesh and blood after all.'

'I guess so – but why do I think there's something wrong with this picture?' She straightened up. 'You don't?'

His grin widened, and he shook his head. 'No, Zanni. I am French.'

Dewey turned the defrost fan up to keep the fog off the windshield.

'Dewey?' It was Victor on the cell.

'Yeah?'

'Continue as you are. Stay in touch.'

'Right.' Dewey punched off and stared at his quarry. 'Wanna get laid one last time, huh? I don't blame you, man.'

Her hot pants were shiny cobalt blue, her boots ended two inches above her knees, her short silver jacket was made of some kind of faux leather, and she wore her brows at a constant, weary elevation. The pale eyes beneath them appraised Geiger.

'Do you speak English?' he asked.

'Un peu.' The sardonic twist to her lips flipped into a grin. 'Oh, baby – sooooo good.'

Geiger watched the grin wane. He was aware of how being so much in the world was rerouting his senses, and energy, and focus – the strategies, the inter-actions, the conversations and explanations. He was navigating in moderate but capricious currents, and it was tiring.

'Does one of you speak English? You'll both be paid.'

'Très belle.' She surveyed the players in the area. 'Paulette! Viens ici!'

Down a few storefronts, a tall, red-haired woman stuck her head out of a doorway, pulled the collar of her long coat up and stepped into the rain, walking with an unhurried stride. She gave Geiger a quick look as she came alongside him.

'Astrid . . .' she said. 'Quoi d'neuf?'

'Ménage à trois,' said the first woman. 'Speak English.'

The redhead smiled at Geiger. 'Good evening, monsieur. You would like to party?' She spoke French and English with an Eastern European accent

Geiger looked from one woman to the other. 'Party? No. I don't want a party.'

'But you would like to have us both, together?'

Geiger's fingers flicked at his sides. 'Yes, and no.'

'Pardon?'

'I will pay you both, but I don't want to have sex with you.'

The women shared a wise glance.

'Ah . . . You would like to watch us then?'

'No. This is not about sex.'

The redhead's smile was a ribbon wrapped around a secret. 'Chéri . . . It is always about sex – even when it is not about sex.'

'I need you for five minutes. Three hundred euros each.'

She'd been negotiating for years. There was nothing

new under the sun – only different ways of getting the same old thing. But the number stunned her.

'Three hundred – *each*?'

'Yes.'

'Bon. If it is not to have sex, and you do not wish to watch – then what?'

Through the sliding drops on the windshield, Dewey saw Geiger come out from the doorway with a woman in a silver jacket. She slid her arm inside his as they headed down the sidewalk in his direction, on the opposite side of the street. Dewey's breath slowed and he sank down a bit in his seat – but the couple stopped at a door of a narrow building next to a shop called 'Sex Time'. The woman unlocked the door and they went inside. Dewey straightened up.

'Make it last, man,' he said. He turned on the car radio, hit the scan button, and listened to the stations go by in three-second doses, hoping to catch an American song – something with a rough edge and a lot of guitar. Finding one was a rarity in this town. That's what he missed the most – some made-in-the-USA rock and roll.

The two taps on his window made him jump, and his hand slid inside his coat pocket as he turned. The red-head smiled at him from the other side of the speckled glass.

'Looking for me, handsome?'

Dewey waved her off with a scowl, and turned back to watch the door.

'A special tonight,' she offered. 'Fifty euros – whatever you like.'

'Not interested,' he said without turning.

'Twenty for a hand-job . . .'

'Just take a walk, okay?' He couldn't help grinning to himself. Fifty euros was a lot cheaper than Madrid.

'Want a look at what you're missing, handsome?'

Dewey sighed, turned round and lowered the window. 'Listen . . . Maybe some other night – but I'm *not* interested now. Comprenez-vous, babe?'

The hooker's smile held its place. 'You can look for free,' she said, and undid the top three buttons of her coat and spread it open, revealing full breasts in a skimpy, sequined bra. Dewey nodded.

'Nice rack. Truly fine, babe. Now take it someplace else – okay?' He noticed the almost imperceptible shift of surprise in her eyes as she closed her coat, and when he felt the touch of cold air on the back of his neck his brain instantaneously understood that the passenger-side door had been opened – and then four things happened in less than a second:

. . . he started to turn round . . .

. . . as the realization that he'd been set up began to take shape . . .

. . . then a fist slammed into the side of his neck, just below the jawline . . .

. . . and he heard the hooker gasp 'Mon dieu!' with utter sincerity just as his brain shut down the parts that managed cognition and consciousness.

20

His first thought, at the cusp of waking, was that he was not alone. There was the soft, rhythmic sound, a rustle like air through nostrils, in and out. It was so dark, he blinked a few times to make sure his eyes were open. He began to get a sense of his body – immobilized around the chest, arms and legs bound to something solid. His ass was on a flat surface, his back up snug against something, so he was fairly sure he was sitting in a chair. His mouth was taped shut.

The repetitive sound grew louder, and reminded Dewey of the hose-suckers they had him lying next to in the clinic after the Kandahar IED, and it made his heart sag. He tried to pull against his binds and found they had minimal give. It had to be some kind of tape. He didn't like the feeling of being immobilized. He never had. It made him feel weak. Then he remembered the hooker and what had gone down in the car, and his mortification hurt more than the pulsing pain in his head. The throb was like a Morse code message: You fucked up ... you fucked up ... you fucked up ...

When the toy piano joined in he realized it was taped audio. Fourteen tinny notes – over and over – some randomly out of sync and just barely out of key. Frè-re Ja-cques, frè-re ... *Jaaa*-cques, dor-mez ... *vooous*, dor-mez ... *vooous* ...

A third layer of audio began, a hardcore smoker's cough – a dry, cutting hack. The aural tapestry started making him see things in the heavy pitch-black – tiny pricks of light ... fuzzy, floating wraiths ... shifting shades of black on black. It didn't matter if he closed his eyes or kept them open. The circuitry of the brain ensured that when a sound registered it sought imagery, even when there was none to be found. It couldn't stop itself.

Geiger had decided to wait until the tape played out. The last eight of the thirty minutes was only one layer – hesitant, labored huffs of breath, the aftermath of some-one who is struggling for calm, and just when it seemed the sufferer would attain some peace, it broke into sobs again. On and on. When the tape ended, silence barged into the place like a mute beast – dense and heavy. Dewey had been relatively quiet through it all – clearing his throat half a dozen times and groaning once or twice – but the end of the ordeal brought a loud, gut-tural grunt of relief.

Geiger reached for the left lamp. Turning it on would take him back in time, and start it all again. Shining the light would deliver him to his darkest place. But there was no other way.

Geiger turned the lamp on – and a piercing beam illu-minated half of Dewey's face and made him turn away with a wince and mutter.

'Your license says your name is Dwayne Brock.'

Dewey's right eye squinted open, searching the black behind the light.

'It works best for me if I call you by your name. Nod if your name is really Dwayne.'

Dewey sighed, his head bobbed, and his eye closed.

Geiger's fingers stirred at his sides. He moved to the lamp on the right and switched it on. The lights were only two feet away from Dewey, and bleached his face into a death mask. The grey, two-inch duct tape that encircled his head at mouth-level had a thin, darkened line of moisture where his lips joined, and there was a large welt where jaw met neck that resembled an oblong port-wine stain.

'My name is Geiger. I'm not aware of how much you know about me and the man who hired you. His name is Dalton. Dalton and I worked in Information Retrieval. Our clients hired us to get information from people, and we were both adept at it – though our approaches and methodologies were very different. Dalton was violent, aggressive. I was more psychologically oriented – and understated, perhaps. They called me the Inquisitor.'

Geiger leaned to one of the lamps, bending the neck – a two-inch adjustment.

'I'm telling you this because it's important you understand the nature of this particular event. Point one ... I am working with very little time. In IR, we call that an asap. Point two ... I know very little about you – only what you do for a living and, because of your tattoo, that you served in Afghanistan – so the lack of time and personal data will limit what techniques I would usually employ.'

Geiger paused, aware his body was about to perform a very rare action – and he yawned. The sleep deprivation was making itself known – with him in the room, a Morphean presence tugging at his sleeve, offering dreams, softening the edges of focus. He headed for the wall. He hadn't planned on turning the overhead room light on this soon, but it might banish his visitor, for a while. He reached out in the dark, found the rough concrete, and ran his palms across it like a blind man until he found the switch and flicked it.

He turned, and they shared a stare. Dewey was stripped to his jockeys – taped to the chair around the chest, his legs taped to the chair's legs from ankle to knee, and his arms taped to the chair's from the wrists to the elbows. On the table was Geiger's iPad, connected to the two speakers, the knife, Dewey's clothes, neatly folded, and a pile of electronic innards that had been Dewey's cell phone before Geiger dismantled it to make sure it couldn't be traced.

Geiger started back toward his prisoner. 'Point three … In this session, I'm not just the interrogator – I am also the client. I am the one who needs the information … and I have never been in this position before. Taking all three points into consideration, what I'm saying is – I may end up doing things I never would have considered in the past. Honestly, it concerns me, deeply – because this session may be much more about pain than fear. Nod if you understand me.'

An indecipherable grumble came out of Dewey through the tape – and Geiger leaned forward, the fingers of his right hand stiffening to make a paddle as it flashed up –and swacked Dewey's left ear with a loud clap. The blow set off a deep gnarl while Dewey seized up from the face all the way down his body, like a chain reaction – muscles tightening, bungee cords popping up under the flesh. Then a rush of breath pouring out of his nostrils ended his noise and his body relaxed.

'Nod if you understood me.'

Dewey's head dipped up and down. Geiger counted the number of nods – two – and their speed – unhurried. Everything mattered.

'Good,' said Geiger, though he would have preferred at least three nods, at a faster rate. He stepped behind Dewey and undid the duct tape from around the mouth.

Dewey stretched his jaw open as wide as a cat's yawn, and then blew out a breath.

'Tell me your real name now.'

Dewey grinned. 'Okay, you got me. It's Darryl.'

Geiger grabbed a generous clump of Dewey's blond curls at the side of his head and started to twist it, clockwise. Dewey's jaw snapped shut, lips stretching back, teeth bared in an angry mutt's snarl. Geiger's fist continued its slow rotation – and Dewey's mouth finally sprung open.

'Okay! Dewey! Stop! Fuck! It's *Dewey*!'

Geiger let go, and Dewey shook his head wildly, like a man whose hair was on fire. '*Muhh–thurr–fuhhck!*'

Geiger's violence had been less strenuous than hammering a nail, but left a slight tremor in his hands. He folded the used tape carefully, again and again, trying to kill it.

'Dewey … Do you know who Harry Boddicker is?'

Dewey's reply was without hesitation, and matter-of-fact. 'Yes. One of the guys Dalton has.'

'Do you know who David Matheson is?'

'Yeah. The other guy. The Veritas Arcana guy.'

Geiger didn't care about these answers. They were like pre-test control questions for a polygraph where the tester already knows the true and false. He was getting a sense of Dewey's cadence, timbre, vocal tendencies.

'Dewey ... Who do you work for – Soames or Dalton?'

Dewey tilted his head like a cock o' the walk. 'Let me tell *you* something, dude. You're fucking with the wrong guy. I had the SERE training before I shipped out, okay? I know how to deal with this shit. Survival, Evasion, Resistance and—'

Geiger's hand came up and paddled Dewey's right ear. It sounded like someone slamming a door shut – and Dewey's roar started down in the pit of him, and grew in volume as it climbed some inner ladder and finally burst out like a shotgun blast.

'Ffffffffffffffffffuck, man!'

Geiger came around to face him. 'Dewey ... I can tell you with near certainty that your training will not play a major role in what happens tonight in this room.'

The wince slowly drained out of Dewey's face and he let out a long exhale, his cheeks puffing up like a blowfish. For the first time, he took a good look at Geiger ...

The guy was certifiably strange – he never blinked, and the odd walk, and the fingers flicking at his sides – but the weirdest thing was his voice. *Dewey ... I can tell you with near certainty that your training will not play a major role in what happens tonight in this room.* How do you say that deadpan straight-faced and without even a touch of *I'm fucking with you, Jack* attitude?

He watched Geiger go to the two space heaters and bring them back – placing one on each side of Dewey – and then turn them on. Their quartz hearts immediately started to glow. Dewey could feel it.

'We'll start with them on low,' said Geiger.

Dewey's head hurt like hell – and his lower back was knotting up – but most of all, he was mad. No one had bothered to mention that he was tailing a world-fucking-famous torturer.

Geiger took up a position before his captive, five feet away.

'Dewey, there are things I need to know. First, I need—'

'Fuck you, dude.' Dewey had the expression of a bored bartender, and the tone to match.

'First, I—'

'Fuck you.'

Geiger stepped toward him, and bent down until they could smell each other's sweat.

'Dewey ... It's best if you—'

'Fuck you, man,' and this time Dewey grinned. He felt better now.

Geiger's hands flashed up and applied swift, synchronized, sideways chops to both sides of Dewey's neck – something out of a magician's stage act without the 'Voila!' – and Dewey's head instantly drooped to his chest and his shoulders sagged, a marionette who's had its strings cut, gone from the waking world for a while.

Geiger went to the table, poured a cup of water, and drank it all down before he took another breath. Then he inhaled and poured a second cup. Something was catching up to him. Running him down from behind. He heard the smooth, solitary lope, knew the effortless breath. Soon it would pull even with him, stride for stride – and he would turn and look into his own face. The Inquisitor. He felt the faintest shiver wash over his shoulders. It was dread.

Geiger turned his head for the *click* but the bones would not accommodate the gesture. He tried the other direction, but instead of obeisance some defiant cervical faction fired a thin, hot squiggle up the back of his skull. The tail-end of the sensation tickled the back of his eyes – tiny minnows darting around the optic nerve – and then they swam away. A noise made him turn, and he watched another drop of water fall from the hot-water tank on the wall into the pail on the floor. *Plop!* He understood that the actual volume of the sound was lower than it seemed to him – that his brain was taking the aural information it was receiving and amplifying it – and he understood what that meant.

Geiger walked back to Dewey and started massaging the back of the man's neck, giving it a firm slap every five seconds. Dewey did a short, reflexive headshake as he came to.

'What the ... fuck, man?'

Dewey felt buzzed, a little wired – almost as if he'd had a couple of hits of really good grass – but not *high*. He felt *low* – the sense of something heavy slowly spreading out in his mind, weighing him down. That dream-sleep sensation when you're trying to run down the road but your quads feel like wood and it's all stumble and trip. Fear.

'How long was I out?'

'Approximately one minute.' Geiger slowly raised himself up on his tiptoes, stretching the calves, holding the position for a few seconds and then slowly coming back down, working the Achilles. And then up again ...

'Dewey ... I feel I know you somewhat better now.'

'Is that right? So we gonna go out for a drink later?'

Geiger settled down on his feet and began to stretch at the waist, side to side, to loosen the damaged hips.

'Everything in IR has meaning. What you say – and how you say it, and when you say it. Your facial expressions, body language, your breathing patterns.' He walked to the table, picked up the knife, and then started into his slow stroll. It would become a perfect circle, ten to twelve feet in diameter. 'And the converse matters equally. What you don't say, what you don't do. Unfortunately, as I said at the start – I don't have time to take what I'm learning and use it to shape an approach.'

The Inquisitor was beside him now, in step – a prodigal son, the necessary evil – ready to do whatever was required.

'There's a story about Dalton – that during Operation Desert Storm, the allies captured one of Saddam's henchmen, a very tough individual, and interrogated him for days without success – so they brought Dalton over. The first time Dalton asked a question the Iraqi didn't answer and Dalton sliced off his bottom lip with a rotary knife. Then he went to work with a nail-gun – and very shortly after that the man told Dalton what he wanted to know. Some say the story was hype – but Dewey, the point is – Dalton made a career out of proving there are ways to acquire information quickly.'

Geiger stopped before him. 'I need certain information – and if you interrupt me before I finish I will put you out again, and the next time you wake up you will be missing a part of your body.'

It hit Dewey again, a sudden gust – ice-cold, wrapped in elastic warmth. Geiger's voice. Like a perfectly programmed machine – no fluctuation, edgeless, without a soul – and to see it come out of a man's mouth made it all the more harrowing.

'You're on the clock now, Dewey. We'll go one by one. First ... Who do you work for – Soames or Dalton?'

'Soames.'

There were no signs of life in Geiger. Not a blink, not a breath. To Dewey, he looked like a life-sized cardboard cutout.

'I work for Soames, man. I'm on your side, asshole.'

Dewey replayed his answer in his head. The delivery sounded pretty good to him. He watched Geiger come closer – and turn the knobs on the two heaters. The soft gold of the quartz heating elements grew richer, brightening into a sun-flare yellow with a hint of orange. He felt the heat reaching him in a smooth wave, and his body – especially the sides of his forearms and calves – was starting to get that prickly, pre-sunburn feeling.

'What the fuck, dude? I told you the truth.'

'That's also a lie.'

'And what the fuck makes you so sure?'

'Did you notice before ... with the music – "Frère Jacques" – that a few of the notes were just barely out of key?' Geiger straightened up. 'That's what a lie sounds like to me.'

His forearm levered at the elbow and the side of his fist slammed into Dewey's upper thorax, with the second intercostal nerve the target. It was one of the Inquisitor's frequent maneuvers, and Dewey seized up – the neural explosion bringing his pulmonary activity to a sudden stop, lungs in abeyance, awaiting a sign to resume their duties – but Dewey was too distressed to give the cue. He would have doubled over but the tape round his chest held fast and would not allow it – yet his struggle was so forceful that the chair moved an inch on the floor.

The staggered, breathless *caaack! caaack! caaack!* spurting out of him was like gunfire from a small-caliber weapon, and the only thought his mind was able to start and finish – *I can't breathe* – vanished when Geiger put the point of the knife beneath his nose and rested it in the dent of the philtrum. Dewey froze, and the sudden shift in his focus was a reboot for his lungs. He tried not to move while he resumed breathing, and tried even harder to find a clue behind the slate eyes about what acts Geiger was truly capable of performing. The exposed hair on his arms and legs felt like it was about to catch on fire.

'Shall I ask you the first question again,' Geiger said, 'or move on and then come back to it?'

Dewey went cross-eyed trying to look down at the blade. 'Take it easy, Geiger. Eeee-zeeee.'

Geiger's grip on the knife tightened and a droplet of blood sprouted beneath Dewey's nose.

'If you work for Soames, then what is her plan – if she gets to Dalton.'

'I don't understand what you mean?'

'If Soames and you and Victor get to Dalton, who comes out alive?'

Dewey had seen guys mentally overload and never understood what it felt like – until now: a house of cards – one layer of fear on top of another, until you finally cave in from the weight of it all. The weird audio ... the darkness ... the pain ...

Geiger's grip was white-knuckled. A thin, crimson worm wriggled to life beneath the blade.

'Dewey ... If Soames gets to Dalton, what happens to Harry and Matheson?'

... the heat ... the immobility ... the glimpse of something cold and final hanging out on the corner of his vision, biding its time. Dewey tasted blood. It painted red-tinted pictures in his head that he didn't want to look at.

'Listen to me carefully, Dewey. You haven't lived very long, and you haven't made many important choices. This is about truth. That's what it always comes down to. If you tell me the truth, then you give yourself a thousand other choices after this. If you choose not to, then it may be the last choice you ever make.' Geiger lowered the knife. 'I don't know if you can hear the clock, Dewey – but it's ticking. Do Harry and Matheson live or die?'

'Listen ... I'm the low man in this thing – okay? If I talk, I'm dead. They'll kill me, man – even if you don't!' He wasn't used to hearing his voice at this high a pitch.

'Soames is not your main concern right now.'

'I'm not talking about Soames. Vic—' He snapped his mouth shut, but he was one syllable too late. He winced and his chin dipped to his chest. 'Fuck me,' he muttered.

Geiger's fingers were suddenly playing a mad concerto on his thighs. 'You said "Vic".' It was one of those out-of-the-blue IR moments – digging for gold and almost tripping over a nugget of silver. 'As in Victor?'

Dewey was shaking his head at himself, like a kid who's been put in a corner by the teacher for being bad. 'Fuck me ... fuck you ... fuck everyone,' he sighed.

Geiger resumed his circular route. He felt the touch of a shake in his steps.

'You work for Soames ... but you're worried about retribution from Victor ...' He could see a hint of a shimmer on the edges of his shadow as it followed him about. '... Why?' He stopped still – and his eyes locked on Dewey. 'Because you work for Victor, too.' He was like a philosophy professor in a lecture hall, stumbling on the answer to a dense theorem. And now he had it. 'And you and Victor both work for Dalton.'

Dewey's chin was tucked deep into his chest now. His sigh could have filled a balloon.

'What about Soames, Dewey?'

Dewey slowly raised his head. 'She doesn't know.'

'Details, Dewey.'

Dewey's sigh was drenched with a bitter acceptance of his status. 'The video gets sent out. Next day, Soames calls Victor. She's coming to Paris and wants him to help her take Dalton out – he's crazy, he's a threat. So Victor ... You're gonna like this, Geiger ... So Victor *tells her the truth*. He says he's on another job ... and has to ask his employer when he'll be done . . . and he'll call back. Victor tells Dalton – who says to take the job, cuz it's fucking perfect. Dalton was paranoid about the spooks trying to find him – and this way he's gonna have Soames on a string – and just pull her in. Sweet, huh?' His tongue came out and tried to lick away the blood dripping from his upper lip. 'So Victor calls her back and says yes – and you know the rest.'

Geiger was picking through it all – the pile of words and sounds and pauses – but they kept turning to sand in his hands, disappearing through his fingers before he could feel whether there was truth or lies in them. The aura was finally here, flashing its shimmering calling card – the bright tiny stars coming out and floating around him. The clock wasn't the only thing ticking. There was a ticking in his brain – from the bomb there, ready to go off. There was very little time before the migraine hit.

He moved toward Dewey – and the room moved with him. One more step brought his target into range – and Geiger's hand wrapped around Dewey's neck. He could feel one of their pulses raging. He wasn't sure whose.

'Dewey . . . Where is Dalton?'

'I don't even know what *town*, man.'

Geiger's grip slowly began tightening. 'Where is Dalton?'

'I told you, dude . . . I don't know! I've been there once – it's like . . . an hour from Avignon, and I didn't do the driving . . . we just delivered the two guys . . . and it was at night, too. Dark.'

'I'm out of time, Dewey. Tell me where Dalton is.'

'Just do me a fucking favor and bury me – cuz I'm already dead.'

Geiger's fingertips dug into the flesh – and Dewey began gasping, clenching his eyes shut, squeezing tears from them like juice from a fruit. His mouth opened – but he could not speak – and Geiger felt the heavens starting to open up inside his skull ...

'Tulette ...' finally tripped out of Dewey's lips.

Tulette. It could have been so many things. A wild flower, a lover's name ...

'Dalton's in Tulette. A little road.'

... a sugar-dusted pastry, a lively dance ...

'Way up a hill, at the top.'

... a melancholy epitaph ...

'A farmhouse ... only thing up there ...'

Geiger's mind turned the last 'r' into an unending purr, the cat sitting on his shoulder – *rrrrrrrrrrrrrr* – and then lightning broke loose in his brain and set it ablaze – a tempest without the promise of rain. His hands sprung to the sides of his skull, as if their pressure might keep it from blowing apart – the knife went skittering across the floor – and his sudden wail sounded like thunder from an approaching storm – and snapped Dewey's head up. Even in his own fog of pain, the spectacle put steel in his neck and opened his eyes.

'What ... the ... fuck ...?'

The burn in Geiger's skull was more lava than fire – seeping down in thin, molten rivulets – and his knees buckled and he hit the floor on them, moaning, head in hands. There'd be no black closet sanctuary, no music to feed on to slay the beast – only cold light and an audience of one. He slumped forward from the waist, forearms and forehead meeting the concrete – a mournful penitent without a priest.

Dewey thought it might be epilepsy. He'd seen a guy have a fit once, when he was in basic – but Geiger wasn't flopping around like a hooked fish on the bottom of a boat, so he didn't have a sense of how much time he had. It was the singular smell of singed body hair that made him look to the space heater on his left – its brilliant glowing innards seemingly afloat within the rippling, seared air around it. He tried to get a feel for the center of his body – then started jolting himself to the left in short bursts – and the chair started to move sideways, one quarter inch at a time.

The hammer came down on the anvil – *Whack! Whack!* Geiger's ears were amplifiers, turning every sound into a blast and bursting nova. *Whack!* The pain was weightless, bottomless, without borders. It was a night sky – starless and immeasurable . . .

Dewey gave a final shove and the side of the chair came flush against the fiery heater. A mad dog growl gathered behind his teeth as he watched the tape binding his left arm and leg start to melt, tiny bubbles rising in it – and fuse with his skin. He started levering his arm toward his chest – and the tape began to stretch, and finally the fibers started to shred, and give way, and with a last howl he tore his arm loose. He reached down, grabbed his ankle and yanked it up – and the heated tape ripped apart, freeing his leg.

'YES!'

He began pulling at his right wrist, and clawing at the thickly wrapped tape, without success. 'C'mon, you mother ...'

Geiger slowly raised his head, and saw Dewey at his task. Every atom in the air sparkled and swirled, a metallic blizzard. Then his eyes shifted ... and found the knife on the floor between them. He raised himself up onto his hands and knees – and began to crawl toward the weapon. The floor tilted like a raft on a river ...

Dewey glanced over at Geiger – and saw where he was headed. The gleaming blade on the floor. Dewey crooked his free arm and started hammering away at the inside of the chair arm with his elbow, punctuating each blow with a snarling cry. On the fifth strike the wood cracked and broke off. He anchored his free leg, then pushed back as hard as he could and the chair tipped over backward onto the floor with a thud. He raised his foot and began stomping at the seat. It started to loosen ...

Geiger needed the blackness and the music. He was desperate for it. He stopped moving and closed his eyes – and listened. The sound of Dewey's pounding rattled his mind – and then the growl of an electric guitar called out from far away, coming toward him like a night train down a long track. *Well, I stand up next to a mountain* ... the lightning bolts of sound were cool silver, slashing into the scorching white heat in his head ... *and I chop it down with the edge of my hand* ...

*

Dewey's foot smashed at the seat. From his position on his back, he craned his head around to see Geiger slowly rising to his feet like a drunk from the gutter. He brought his knee back till it met his chest – and pile-drove his shoe forward into the seat. With a loud crack the chair broke apart in pieces, and he rolled over and stumbled to his feet. A chair leg was still bound to his right calf, part of a chair arm was attached to his right forearm, and the chair's back was still taped to his.

To Geiger, Dewey was a bizarre creature – part-human, part-wood – as he came lumbering forward, getting linebacker low as he rammed into him ... and Geiger knew immediately, even before he hit the floor, that his left shoulder had dislocated. The immediate pain of the event was breathtaking, but solid, flesh-and-blood pain – a heightened version of the kind that had been a companion most of his life, that lived inside him, shared his days, hands-on pain that he could beat down. But there was a firestorm inside his head.

Dewey trundled to the knife, picked it up with a grunt, and came back to Geiger. He hurt too much to gloat. He raised the weapon.

'Relax, man – I'm not gonna mess with you. I should – I should really mess you up, right? – but Dalton wants you in mint condition.' He started carefully cutting the mass of tape round his chest. 'What's wrong with you? Epilepsy?'

'... Migraine.'

'Tell me something. You and Dalton. Why do you hate each other so much?'

Geiger took a breath – and slowly rolled off his back onto his good side. 'I don't ... hate Dalton.'

Dewey pulled the tape off, and the chair-back came with it. He flung it away, and stretched his back with a wince.

'Fucking back ...' He started cutting the tape from his forearm.

Geiger watched Dewey through the glittering whir. 'Dalton will have Soames ... killed.'

Dewey shrugged. 'Life's tough, man.'

'You have me now. Call Victor ... tell him to ...' Geiger had no sense of his voice coming out through his lips and into the room. There was someone inside him doing the talking. 'Tell Victor to slip away from her, come here ... and the three of us leave. Soames doesn't know where Dalton is – so she doesn't die.'

Dewey ripped the armchair off him and dropped it. 'No can do, man.'

The migraines were Geiger's master in many ways, but they'd never taken his power of reason from him. He knew he had one last chance. One shot. He tried to see it happen. Pushing off, one-handed – his left arm, useless. Leading with the right shoulder. Aim was a relative concept, but below the ribs if possible. And it would be all in the legs. Two strides to get to him. He flattened his palm against the floor for leverage, and waited – while Hendrix howled his confession and his scream of strings raced through Geiger like an electric charge. *I'm a voodoo child ... Lord knows, I'm a voodoo child!*

Dewey eyed Geiger's splayed posture. 'Shoulder's out?'

Geiger nodded. Dewey bent at the waist and, looking down, started cutting through the tape on his leg.

'We're gonna have to pop it back in, man. Like I said – *mint* condition.'

Geiger raised himself up on his right hand and pushed off the balls of his feet. He saw the energy of his movement part the swarm of tinsel molecules before him, and he got one solid stride in before Dewey glanced up – but then the room went into a roll, and he ended up ramming into Dewey's rib cage, as much with his head as his shoulder.

For a moment the impact seared away all sensation – just a buzzing whiteness – but the blow was powerful and momentum carried them backward before Geiger dropped. Dewey kept going in a stumble, and plowed into one of the water heater's two-by-four stilts. The old wood snapped in two, and the platform drooped as Dewey tumbled to the floor. The tank was without its support – and the bolts holding it to the wall began to lose their grip. Faint showers of dust puffed out of the concrete ...

Geiger was watching it all from his knees, a guilty bystander. Dewey was on his back, grimacing, one hand grabbing at his sacrum – and Geiger saw, in Dewey's eyes, the exact moment when he suddenly understood that the tank was going to fall ... and all that it would mean – then gravity stepped up to play its part, the tank broke loose with a metallic groan, and it landed with a crunch, sideways across Dewey's torso. All four limbs shot out straight in a grotesque, toy-like reflex – and then settled back onto the floor.

Dewey's lips parted, and his breath came out in slow spurts – thick and wet. 'Get it ... off me,' he gasped. 'Get ... it off ... me.'

Geiger shuffled over on his knees. He tried to push the tank with his good arm, but its weight had crushed the middle ribs and sternum and created its own concave resting place. He couldn't move it. He lay down on his back so he could use his legs, bent his knees, put his shoes against the steel, and thrust – and the tank slid off the body, hit the floor with a loud clank and rolled away.

A sound came out of Dewey – dry, fallen leaves being swept up by a soft wind and sent into a twirling dance. 'Jesus ...' he said. 'I'm ... gonna die.'

His head turned to Geiger, and the movement released the blood that had been pooling inside him. It slipped out of the corner of his lips in a thin scarlet thread and a puddle quickly began to grow on the floor.

'Oh God ... I'm ... dying ...' There were tears in his eyes. His shattered chest rose and fell, lungs filling and deflating, the time between each breath lengthening. 'It isn't ... fair.'

Geiger watched a few tears fall into the spreading pool of blood, dappling the dark burgundy with tiny spots of a paler rose. When he looked back up, Dewey's eyes had an opaque glaze. Geiger moved closer.

He had never seen death in someone's eyes. When he'd pushed the knife into his father, the fierce, cold eyes had closed – and being witness now to the magnitude of the change was compelling. Dewey had been rendered irrelevant – a complex mass of tissue, bone, sinew and electrical networks that was obsolete and meaningless. The heart beats, and then it doesn't – and the distance between that last thump and the absence of another was the most immeasurable and indefinable of things.

21

Geiger made it up onto his feet. Walking to the table was a slow, off-kilter trip full of tilts and squints. He wouldn't be able to get his shoulder back in by himself – he knew he needed help – and that recognition was a sense he'd rarely experienced. There was one person he could contact. Just one. There was no one else.

He picked up the iPad and knelt down, placing it on the floor before him, then pressed the iChat icon and the keyboard popped up on the bottom of the screen. The letters on the keys were wriggling about like tiny creatures dancing to a piper's tune. His fingertip hovered above them – and then descended ...

The nature of sleep had changed since July Fourth – it was never a deep state now, and he took short naps to fill in the holes in ragged nights – so he was dozing when the iChat alert's ding came out of his iPad, and he shot up so quickly that he spooked the cat nestled beside him and it leaped off the bed. He swung his legs round and hopped to the floor, heart thudding, because only two people knew his account name – his father and Harry – and that must mean they were okay. His mother wasn't home yet, but he ran to the door and closed it gently anyway, then dived to the iPad on his desk. The caller on the other end was 'guest' but he was too ramped up to stop and consider why.

Ezra clicked 'accept' – and the screen filled with a rough grayness. The first image that came to mind was concrete – maybe a sidewalk – then he noticed some kind of gizmo in the upper-right corner, a pinwheel shape, metallic. He leaned in … It was a small sprinkler head – for a fire system. He was looking at a ceiling.

'Dad? Harry? Hello?'

Something started sliding up into view from the bottom of the screen. A face. 'Ezra …'

Ash-pale, tight-fisted with pain. A ghost in limbo. It set off a chain reaction – charged neutrons racing into space at incalculable speeds, crossing thousands of miles in the skip of a heartbeat, like sticking a finger in a live socket, an emotional fission that made Ezra's eyes blaze and his body expand.

'Oh God …' said the boy. '… *Geiger*.'

Too many feelings and too many questions were causing a logjam inside Ezra – in his head and his chest. He couldn't nail down a thought. He couldn't seem to pull in a full breath. His parts weren't working.

'Ezra … I'm in a … bad situation. I need your help.'

'What *happened* to you?'

'Ezra …'

'Where are you?'

'You just need to listen, Ezra. I don't … know how long I can talk.'

'Okay. I'm sorry. Okay.'

'I'm in Paris. I'm hurt. I don't ... Write this name down.'

Ezra grabbed a pencil and one of his notebooks. 'Okay. Go.'

'Christine Reynaud. R – E – Y – N – A – U – D. Say it ... back to me.'

'Christine Reynaud. R – E – Y – N – A – U – D.'

'She is Harry's wife.'

'Harry's *wife*?'

'Ex-wife. I met her today ... she ... lives here.' Geiger squeezed his eyes shut, then opened them again. 'I need you ... to call her. Find her number ...' His face suddenly dropped out of view.

'Geiger?' Ezra's throat clogged with panic. He swallowed but he couldn't send it back down. '*Geiger*?'

'I'm ... here,' came the voice. 'Get the number.'

Ezra yanked his chair over, sat down and smacked his computer to wake it up. The screen lit and he went at the keyboard. It was good to have something to do – to focus on – to help put the fear at arm's length. Google gave him dozens of choices for 'paris france phonebook' – and he picked the first one and typed in the woman's name.

'Got it!' He heard the volume of his voice and looked to the door with a wince. 'I got it,' he said softly.

Geiger floated back into sight. 'Call her. Tell her I need her help. Ask her ... to come to 315 Rue Questel. Q – U – E – S – T – E – L. A boarded-up store. Back door. Call her ...'

Ezra stared into Geiger's eyes. 'Okay. I will – right now. Just tell me ... Did you find them?'

'I know ... where they are, Ezra. Make the call.'

Ezra nodded – and couldn't stop nodding – as if some mechanism was trying to convince him of his abilities. He picked up his cell.

'I can do this. I can absolutely do this.' Geiger had left the iPad screen again. Ezra was talking to himself. He dialed the number – and heard it ring. And ring again …

'C'mon … Pick up.'

… and again …

'Come – *onnnnnnn* …'

… and the ringing stopped.

''Allo?'

He flinched at the voice. 'Hello? Is this – Christine Reynaud?'

'Yes. Who is this?'

'Well … My – my name is Ezra – and I'm almost thirteen and I'm calling from New York City – and I'm a friend of Harry … and Geiger – and I know this is gonna sound totally crazy-strange but it's really important.'

'… Go on, Ezra.'

The smooth cool of the voice helped move him on.

'Geiger is on iChat with me right now … You know what iChat is, right?'

'Yes.'

'Good, good. Okay … Geiger said he met you today …'

'Yes, that's right.'

'Do you know why he's over there, Miss Reynaud?'

'Yes, Ezra. I know.'

'Well … Geiger – he's hurt … and he asked me to call you and ask you to help him … to come help him.

I know Geiger, Miss Reynaud – and I know he wouldn't ask for help from *anybody* if he wasn't in bad shape.'

The cat jumped up on the desk and lay down beside the keyboard, limbs stretched out to the max, awaiting a caress.

'Ezra ...'

'Yeah?'

'I need to ask you ... How do you know Geiger and Harry?'

The boy's glance swung to the iPad – to the silence and shot of the ceiling.

'They saved my life, Miss Reynaud.'

He could hear her breathing while she tried to meld the bizarre pieces into a recognizable shape.

'Where is he?' she said.

'He's at 315 Rue Questel. Q – U – E – S – T – E – L. In a boarded-up store. You can get in the back door.'

'What else?'

'That's all.' He gathered a breath and blew it out. 'I know you don't know him, Miss Reynaud ...' His voice bent like a bad note, and he wiped away a sudden tear. 'He's a really weird guy, but he's a good person.'

'It's all right, Ezra. I understand.'

'What should I tell him?'

'Tell him I'm on my way.'

Ezra sprung out of his chair like a jack-in-the-box. 'Thank you – thank you – *thank you*!'

'I'm going to hang up now, Ezra. Okay?'

'Yes, ma'am. Okay. Thank you.'

He leaned down to the screen. 'Geiger ... She's coming. You hear me? She's on her way. Geiger? Can you hear me?'

He sank back down in the chair. The only sound he heard was the cat's ridiculously loud purr. He picked the creature up and laid it across his shoulder, and began the wait.

Christine had never heard of the street, so she brought up Google Maps to see where it was. She'd been on the couch, sinking into a downhill half-sleep, far from peace, when the phone had rung – and she had known with odd, unsettling certainty that the caller was going to take her deeper into the hairpin turn her life had taken. And when she had hung up, she'd realized there had been no moment of choice, no 'do the right thing' element to consider, no decision. Her initial, intense desire to turn away from the boy was proof of that.

She stood up, grabbed her car keys off the coffee table and headed for the door, though she almost believed that once she got behind the wheel and turned the ignition she could sit back, hands in her lap, and arrive at 315 Rue Questel without issue – because someone else would be doing the driving.

22

His mind had been burning down – a cabin on fire, and he was inside the inferno. There was no music to hear or see or taste and draw sustenance from, only the baying flames, and wood crackling and spitting all around him. And the scorching heat. Finally he had lain down, curling into a ball in the center of the blaze, and waited for some kind of end. There was pain, but no dread – because he had no fear of this kindred spirit.

When he finally felt the air starting to cool, and the silence take hold, he stirred and looked up. The fire had finished its feast – and its appetite had been its death. The flames, except for a few orphaned wisps and flickers, were gone, and the charred husks of walls were cracking and falling to the floor in black chunks. But someone was with him – as clearly near as she was invisible ...

'Geiger,' she said.

He'd gone down the black hole enough times to know that when he came out the other side everything would be happening at seven-eighths speed for a few moments.

'Geiger ...'

He opened his eyes. She was kneeling at his side. She'd been studying him, and her face showed an internecine battle of feelings. Fear, bafflement, concern, mistrust ...

'Thank you for coming,' he said, as if he were the head psychiatrist welcoming an inmate's relative to Bedlam.

It hadn't been more than ten hours since she had met him, but the pain had frayed the edges of his voice, sucked the color out of his face and literally laid him low ... so whatever small sense she had of him – the tall, dark stranger on a dangerous mission – had been erased. He was a pale, wounded riddle.

'Geiger ... The man over there is dead.'

'Yes, he is. He's one of the men who kidnapped Harry.'

'Did you kill him?'

'No. The water tank fell on him. As a rule, I try not to kill anyone.'

It was her first taste of Geiger's singular way – the velvet, unironic delivery that could seem soaked with sarcasm. Geiger watched her gaze narrow. He'd seen the expression countless times. Harry used to call it the 'Listening-to-Geiger' face.

'It was an accident, Christine. I'd prefer that he were still alive.'

He started to sit up, forgetting the state of his shoulder and leaning on it for half a second before he slumped back down with a grimace.

'What's wrong with your shoulder?'

'Dislocated. I need you to pop it back in – if you can do that.'

'Tell me what to do.'

'I don't know.'

'You don't know ...?' Christine stared at the ugly, crooked joint. 'Jesus ...'

'I got it right here.'

Their heads swung toward the voice in the iPad ...

YouTube was on Ezra's monitor and he was typing quickly. H – O – W – T – O – F – I – X – A – D – I – S – L – O ...

'It's me. Ezra. I'm still here,' he said. 'One sec.' He hit 'enter', scanned the choices, and clicked on one. A handheld video started playing: the scene was a hospital emergency room. At the bottom of the shot was a chyron ID line – 'ST. MICHAEL'S MEDICAL CENTER/TEACHING HOSPITAL'. A doctor stood beside a gurney where a younger man lay on his back, one eye swollen shut, bare-chested, in a frozen grimace, his left shoulder clearly out of whack.

Ezra picked up his iPad and held it in front of the monitor. 'Here. Do what he does.'

Christine slid the iPad over to her side. On the screen, the doctor took hold of the patient's wrist.

'First, I'm going to raise the forearm ... about forty-five degrees ... while I put pressure on the upper arm here, at the elbow – to keep it anchored ...'

Christine duplicated his movements – holding Geiger's wrist, and grabbing the upper arm just above the elbow with her other hand. She brought the forearm up.

'That okay?' she asked, and Geiger nodded.

'Make sure to keep the arm close to the body – only a few inches apart. Now, I'm going to begin *rotating* the upper arm outward, very slowly, keeping the forearm *steady*.'

He started turning the upper arm toward him and the patient began to groan in short, loud bursts. Christine's face crimpled – as much in dread of her own actions as the compelling bellows.

'Try to breath evenly,' said the doctor, 'and don't fight the movements.'

'Go ahead, Christine,' said Geiger, and closed his eyes.

She began twisting the upper arm toward her, eyes darting back and forth to the screen to gauge her technique. While the young man's outbursts rose to sharp barks Geiger was silent, lips fused together in a straight, hard line.

Ezra was watching the video, locked in the betwixt-and-between state of fascination and repulsion – rapt, and flinching at every howl.

'Now ... When the arm's resistance to the rotation feels as if—'

'Ez ... I'm home!'

His mother's voice, from the other side of his door, punched up his heartbeat from rapid to panic speed. The door started to open and there was only time to lower the iPad and put it on the desk face-down before she stuck her head into the room.

'Whatcha doing?' she said.

'Huh? Uh ...' He tried to swallow. 'Nothing much.'

The patient's chilling cry brought Ezra's mother's gaze

to the monitor. 'Jesus ...' She came inside. 'What are you watching?'

'A video. How to fix a dislocated shoulder.'

Christine winced at the iPad's black screen. 'Merde!' The doctor's voice was muffled beyond understanding.

Geiger's eyes opened. 'Don't stop.' He reached across his chest with his other arm and gripped his damaged joint. 'Try and push the arm forward. Go on, Christine.'

She tightened her hold and slowly applied forward pressure. Geiger was trying to align the head of the humerus with the socket, making staggered noises without tone or texture – rough expulsions of air. *Hunh! Hunh!* Their expressions were nearly identical – twisted and tight – and without the sounds, a witness would have been hard-pressed to guess who was the one in pain.

'Harder,' he said.

Ezra's mother gawked at the monitor. 'Jesus, Ez ... This is brutal. And you're watching this *why*?'

'For, uh – for school.' He had no idea why he'd said it, and now he was going to have to think up something *and* pull off the delivery while keeping his heart from jumping out of his throat. 'It's a ... project.'

'*This*?'

'*More*, Christine. *Harder*.'

She let go of his wrist so she could get two hands on the upper arm, and pushed. A growl started forcing itself out through Geiger's clamped teeth. It sounded like he had an angry, wounded beast caged inside his mouth.

'Allez, merde!' she barked, and gave his arm a shove.

Geiger's sudden moan was an almost musical accompaniment to the *Pop!* of the bone finding its way back into the socket. He came to rest, in silence, and Christine sat back, shaking her head, slowly puffing out breath after breath.

Ezra waited, praying his mother had no further questions.

'A project?' she asked. 'What kind of project?'

'Well ... see ... We, uh, we – we have to show a way that the internet has changed how we, y'know, live and stuff.'

'And this is what you chose?'

'Well, yeah. Like ... Like if – if you were stuck on a mountain or something with a dislocated shoulder and you had an iPad or a smartphone – you could watch this and fix it – and, y'know ... you couldn't do that before the internet, right?'

His mother cocked her head at her son. 'Know what? You're absolutely right. Cool choice, Ez. Truly strange – but cool.' She leaned down and kissed the top of his head, then walked back out the door, shutting it behind her.

Ezra stopped the video and flipped the iPad over. 'Hey ... You there?'

Christine leaned into view. 'Yes.'

'Sorry, sorry. My mom came in. Should I play it again?'

'No. It's done. It's all right now.'

He clicked off the video. 'He's okay?'

Christine's smile floated across her weariness. 'Yes, Ezra. Geiger's okay.'

'Can he talk?'

Christine nodded, the image swerved, and Geiger's face replaced hers.

'Thank you, Ezra.' He sounded like a marathoner speaking his first words beyond the finish line. 'You did really well.'

Ezra smiled. 'God, it's so great to see you.'

'It's good to see you too.' He turned his head to the right. *Click*. 'But I have to go now.'

'. . . Now?'

'Yes.'

'You're gonna find Dad and Harry?'

'Yes.'

'. . . Okay.'

Geiger's head screwed left. *Click*. His constant stare blinked, once. 'Goodbye, Ezra.'

Geiger's image blurred slightly in the screen, like a lens going out of focus – and Ezra realized it was the effect of his imminent tears. July Fourth had been a crash course in hell – fear, betrayal, death – and extinguished part of the boy in him. The phoenix that had risen from the ashes possessed wisdom at odds with his youth . . . and understood that there were a thousand things left to be said – and nothing more to say.

'Goodbye, Geiger.'

He turned off the iPad. On the desk, the cat lay waiting for a scratch, his eye trained on the boy. Ezra complied, then slid his mouse along the desk until the cursor reached the monitor's iPhoto icon, clicked, and then clicked again on one of the small photo squares. It zoomed up to full-screen – eight-year-old Ezra standing on a small stage in a suit and bow-tie, holding a violin in one hand and a framed certificate in the other, his proud, smiling father standing beside him. On the curtain behind them was a red banner with bright gold letters: N.Y.C. JUNIOR VIOLIN FESTIVAL.

Ezra reached over and picked up his instrument and bow, closed his eyes and began to play – Bach's 'Air on a G String', sweet and somber – shoulders dropping, feeling the vibrations flow from string to flesh ... and deeper, letting it soothe him, giving himself over to it.

The door opened slowly, silently, and his mother leaned in, listening – the music and memories of a past weaving their way into her. When she saw the photo on the monitor the hot-cool rush of anger and melancholy came up in her again, and she blew out a sigh to dispel it.

Ezra stopped playing, and lowered the violin to his lap.

'You haven't played that in a long time, Ez.'

The boy raised his head to her.

'What's wrong, Ez? Something's wrong.'

'Nothing.'

'Ezra ... There are some things you can't lie to me about. What's wrong?'

Ezra pointed at the desk. 'Top drawer. The letter.'

She went to the desk, opened the drawer and took out the sheet of paper, and read. *Now you know. But tomorrow I am leaving here, going out of the country, and will not return. I am going to try and help your father and Harry. They are in trouble.*

'Who wrote this?'

'Geiger.'

Her eyes snapped up. 'Geiger? Geiger's dead.'

'No he's not. He's in Paris, trying to save Dad and Harry.'

'Save them from what?'

'I dunno, but it's real bad or he wouldn't have gone.'

Her gaze dipped back down to the letter, but part of her mind was already at work on something else.

'When did you get this?'

'Two days ago. I lied about the cat. I didn't find him in the street. Geiger brought him here, with the letter.'

'But you didn't see him . . .'

'No.'

She folded the letter neatly. She was nodding to herself, agreeing with a private decision. She started out of the room.

'You aren't going to school tomorrow.'

'Mom . . . What are you gonna do?'

She was already gone, into the hall, out of sight.

'Mom! What're you doing?!'

Her growl was so loud he heard her quite clearly.

'Goddamn *bastards*!'

23

Geiger sat up and tested his shoulder, slowly rotating the joint. It felt swollen, but he didn't think anything was torn. The pain was thick and warm, and he tried to move it around his body, spreading it out and diminishing it at the same time.

Christine stood up. 'How is it?'

'It hurts. I'll be all right.'

'You should take some Advil, or Doliprane.'

'I don't use drugs.'

She smiled faintly. 'Drugs?'

'I have other ways to deal with pain.'

Christine looked over at Dewey's crushed body. 'What are you going to do about him?'

'After I've left the city, I will notify someone.'

'*Someone*?'

'Christine, I understand your reaction to all this, but—'

'My *reaction*? Geiger, I'm looking at a *dead body*.'

'If you called the police, Christine, what would you say – when they started asking you questions?'

'That's not the—'

'What is your relation to the deceased? Who is he?

Do you know how he died? Were you here when he died?'

She turned back to him. She knew he was right. She wasn't thinking things through to the end – because she couldn't even catch up to the here and now.

'You would have to tell them about me, Christine, and that would not be helpful.'

Geiger picked up the iPad and slowly got to his feet. It was as if the planet had undergone a massive subterranean calamity and gravity's pull had somehow doubled. He felt like he was made of lead, and when he wobbled Christine reflexively grabbed his uninjured arm.

'It's okay. It always happens.' He started tentatively toward the table. Slow, short, half-slide steps.

'What does?'

'I get migraines. When they're over, it takes a moment to get anchored.' He put the iPad in his bag, zipped it shut and looked up at her. 'If you could drive me to a hotel – whatever is nearby – so I can pack my shoulder in ice and get a few hours' sleep before I leave ...'

'... Yes. All right.'

She watched him head for the door – bag in hand, covered with the floor's gray dust from head to foot – and she was struck by an image of a man trying to straddle different worlds – an acrobat moving from one tightrope to another, adjusting his balance and purpose with each step. But whoever he was – savior, avenger, killer – he didn't seem to *belong* anywhere at all.

He walked through dense woods between sheets of angled bronze light that shot down through the canopy, his bow and arrow held chest high. He was seven or eight years old, but had the mind of a man who knew he was dreaming – suspended in that dim corridor between true sleep and wakefulness. He could smell the sap from the trees and, at the same time, felt the smooth rumble of the car's tires on the street.

The boy stopped. Fifty feet away, a small fawn sat between two trees, the sun bringing out the rust and gold in its dappled coat. It turned its head to face the visitor – eyes brown, glistening jewels, big ears twitching . . .

. . . Geiger felt a spatial shift – the car swerving slightly – and heard a horn's short bark that seeped through one layer of semi-consciousness into another. It could have been the cry of a hawk above the forest, sensing something helpless below . . .

. . . The baby deer started struggling to rise, knobby legs aquiver, but no sooner did it accomplish the feat than it sank back down in a tangle of skinny limbs.

The boy whispered. 'How old do you think it is . . . ?'

'Very young,' whispered a deep, sonorous voice nearby. 'Almost new.'

'It wants to get up. Can't we help?'

The boy's father stepped to his side. 'No,' he said.

The boy turned and looked up into his father's dark tunnel eyes. 'Why?'

'Because it would be unnatural.'

'I don't understand,' said the boy.

His father's crooked, scarred carpenter's fingers went to his thick, black beard and scratched.

'Son ... There is a natural way to things. If it were older – we would kill it for the meat ...'

'But it looks so weak.'

'That is of no matter.' He put a hand on his son's shoulder. 'Why do you think we live as we do – up here, away from everything and everyone? Weakness in the world is not our concern. What matters is that we become strong *inside ourselves*. That is what works best for us.'

... Geiger could feel the motion of things slowing, the hum of the car engine dropping in pitch, the spinning planet accommodating the changing speed of the wheels' rotation. A traffic jam ...? Red light ...? Another sharp squawk of a horn ...

... The boy looked up to the sky. A golden eagle glided across the sun, wide and stark as a fighter jet in a war zone. The boy jabbed a finger at it.

'Father ... Look.'

The short, white streaks in the great bird of prey's wings brightened as they tipped and it started downward.

'It's coming down, father.' The boy turned – but his father was gone. All that was left of him was the potent, bitter scent of smoke. The boy's head snapped back to the fawn – but where it had lain was a newborn human infant swaddled in a black cloth, arms stretching, impossibly tiny fingers exploring the warm air.

... There was a tug of war in Geiger's brain – the throb in his shoulder a reminder of real life, trying to pull him out of the dream, but he didn't want to leave – not yet ...

The boy watched the eagle descend into the woods like a dark angel, long talons stretching open, its wing-spread so wide their gleaming tips sliced clean through branches on each side like scythes through wheat. As limbs fell all around the boy, the bird swooped down with an undulating, plaintive cry, snatched the baby up in its claws, swathe and all – and flew for the beckoning sun with its prize ...

Geiger opened his eyes. The world was waiting for him with a thousand lights – stacks of soft white windows, gaudy neon signs, scattered headlights and brake-lights in the sparse traffic, glowing streetlamps. They were driving down a wide boulevard, the asphalt polished shiny black with the remnants of the rain.

'How long was I out?'

Christine glanced over. 'Not long. Two or three minutes.'

The picture of the eagle and infant lingered, growing dimmer as they soared higher and farther away – and Geiger tried to put himself in Corley's office, lying on the couch, describing the dream ... and wondered what Corley might say.

'Let's talk about the eagle, Geiger. What does it make you think of?'

'... A bird of prey. A predator.'

'That's interesting.'

'Because ...?'

'I don't think most associations with an eagle are

*about predation – hunters, cold, remorseless – like a
hawk ... or a buzzard. I think more often eagles are
thought of as noble creatures.'*

'And ... ?'

*'And maybe – and it's just a maybe – but maybe the
eagle wasn't taking the infant as prey. Maybe the you in
the dream wanted to save the helpless baby.'*

Up ahead, Geiger saw a bright green sign that said
HOTEL RONDO – and Christine turned left onto
another street.

'There was a hotel just up the street, Christine.'

'I'm taking you home to my house.' There was a heft
to her voice Geiger hadn't heard before. 'You need help
packing your shoulder. And I'll make you a meal. Then
you'll sleep. Then you'll go.' She turned to him. 'And I
have questions that you're going to answer.'

Geiger nodded at her. 'All right,' he said.

Victor punched off his cell. 'Still not answering.'

Zanni nodded. 'I don't like it.'

They were sitting in their hotel's street-level bar in
front of a window that looked out on the street and
Geiger's hotel. Victor had a cup of tea before him,
Zanni stared at an untouched glass of red wine.

She tapped the glass with a trimmed fingernail. *Tink.
Tink.* 'There are two reasons why he isn't answering.
One – something's wrong with his cell. Two – he *can't*
answer.' *Tink. Tink.* 'And if he can't answer, there are
two reasons why. One – Geiger found him and compromised him so he could get away clean. Two – Geiger
has him somewhere and is ... *asking* him questions.'
She looked up at Victor. 'That's what Geiger does.' She

picked up her wine and took a sip. 'I shouldn't have brought him in on this one.'

'But you have used him before – yes?'

'In Madrid, last year. But that was just a two-day drive-around, with me in the backseat playing video-tag with a mark. First-grade stuff.' She shook her head. 'Not enough experience – not for a mark like Geiger. I thought about it – that he wasn't seasoned enough – but I did it anyway. If something's happened to him, it's on me.'

Victor slowly turned his teacup around on the saucer, a few degrees a nudge, while his other thumb went to the cleft in his chin. Thinking time.

'Pardon, Zanni – but … You did not sleep with him, did you?'

Her mouth wrinkled up like a lemon-sucker. 'No, Victor. I didn't sleep with him.' Zanni raised her wine again and drank.

There was something in her voice Victor hadn't heard before – a thin, delicate thread of sentiment, just the faintest trace.

'Zanni … How long have you known Dewey?'

She put the glass down softly – and met Victor's gaze. 'Since I was five and a half.'

Victor sat back like he'd taken a good shove in the chest. 'Oh Zanni … He is your *brother* …?' He was shaking his head now. 'Zanni, Zanni …'

'I know … I *know*. Never family. I said I fucked up, didn't I?' Her shrug and sigh were inseparable – one rueful action. 'I mean – we weren't close, really – but he came back from Afghanistan messed up and broke – couldn't get a job …' Her face widened with memory.

'They used to call him "No-Can-Dewey" in school – but
he was great with cars. He started calling, asking me to
get him inside – for one chance, as a driver. Calling all the
time. He was making me crazy – so I finally said yes –
and it turned out fine. He started getting gigs without
me. He just wanted money to buy this joint back home,
fix it up and pour shots all night. After this one he'd be
close to getting out …' She grabbed her glass and drank.

Victor watched her, poker-faced. 'Do you want me to
go look for him?' he said. 'To where he was last time he
called? To look around?'

Zanni kept sipping until the glass was empty. 'Yes. I'll
stay here in case Geiger comes back.'

Victor stood up. 'But you do not think Geiger will
come back, do you?'

'I don't know. Probably not.'

Victor headed for the door. Zanni turned toward the
room, raised a hand and snapped her fingers. A waitress
looked up at her.

'Un espresso, double!' Zanni turned back to the
window. She was using one of her most valuable traits –
digging into the situation, tightening the clamps down
on her emotions …

Their bond had always been defined more by genet-
ics and proximity than temperament or interests – and
they had let much of that slip away once she left for college. More texts than calls, e-mails every few months,
Skype a few times a year. When he'd come back from
Afghanistan and started calling, she'd felt as much irri-
tation as sympathy. And now she felt equal parts
concerned … and fallible. Victor's head-shaking 'Zanni,
Zanni' had said it all.

She started breaking things down into possibles, with odds for each. Had Dewey been mugged? Ten percent likelihood, tops. Did his cell phone battery die? Twenty to thirty percent. It happened on stakeouts and tails. Even with a charger in the car, you forget sometimes . . .

The waitress arrived with the order, set it down, and left without a word.

Zanni shifted to the scenarios with Geiger, based on the near-conclusion that he was gone. She'd always known he might disappear – try and go it alone at some point. She'd even said it to his face back in Brooklyn. Had he put Dewey out of commission long enough to ensure a getaway? She didn't have trouble seeing it play out – thirty percent chance . . . maybe forty – but it felt like too much work. Geiger was good enough to slip away without a confrontation.

She picked up her cup, brought it to her lips – and froze. Across the street a taxi was pulling up in front of Geiger's hotel – and she felt the cat-and-mouse tingle start up in her fingertips. The cab's back door opened and a young woman in a red evening gown stepped out and walked into the lobby. Zanni took a slow sip of espresso and put it down. Her pulse had been a dead give-away. Her mind might be working on the premise that he'd slipped the leash, for good – but clearly her heart was still hoping otherwise, and she didn't like her body confronting her with that conflict.

There were other scenarios.

Geiger figured Dalton had someone keeping an eye on him – so he might have picked up Dewey tailing him, and on the chance he was Dalton's man set him up somehow, overpowered him, and taken him someplace for a little IR. The more she thought about it, the more it felt like Geiger – and the angrier she got. She hadn't considered it. What else had she missed . . . ?

She became aware of someone arriving . . . and hovering close by. She glanced to her left – and a man smiled at her when her gaze found him. A thirty-something in a shiny, expensive suit with a pleasant, practiced smile and a glass of white wine.

'You've been sitting here alone for a while,' he said in perfect French-tinted English. 'Could I buy you—'

'Fuck off.'

If the command had been a knife it would have cut him in half.

'Okay,' he mumbled, and walked off.

She took in a slow breath and let it out smoothly, helping her shoulders to sag. This was the biggest chance of her life – and she was starting to feel like Geiger was up front driving the train and she was sitting back in the club car, sipping her coffee, watching the countryside roll by – and not knowing when it would stop.

And where the fuck was her little brother . . . ?

The taxi entered Place Pigalle, circling, and Victor leaned forward from the backseat.

'Arrêtez ici,' he said, and the driver pulled over in front of the Cupidon Theatre X. Victor handed him a ten-euro note, stepped out, and headed up the boulevard. One of the strip clubs had a speaker above its doorway – and Johnny Hallyday called out across forty years from another world. 'C'est une honky-tonk woman. Fini, fini, fini le honky-tonk blues . . . ' Victor grinned. In the 1960s, what kid hadn't wanted to be Johnny Hallyday? He had started trying to grow those long sideburns as fast as he could – until his father came home from two weeks away, proclaimed – 'Rock'n'roll est merde!' – and personally soaped up his son's cheeks and shaved them.

He wasn't going to give the whores and hucksters Dewey's description and ask them questions, because if the kid was dead – and the cops came round asking about him later on – there was a tiny chance he and Dewey could be tied together ... and tiny was big. He would just walk and look for the car.

Zanni's admission had stunned him – a rare event in itself. He'd learned long ago that blood was indeed thick, and could muddle the mind and lead to foolish decisions and far worse – but for Zanni to make that choice, cold and diamond-hard as she was ... It had a double-edged effect on him. He would have to do a fast reassessment of certain aspects of her – but more important, an investigation of his own instincts were in order. He'd dealt with them both, brother and sister, and missed it all on each end.

He crossed to the pedestrian divider of the boulevard so he could see the cars on both sides, parked east and west, and moved on, doing his due diligence – but whenever he conjured up an image of Dewey it was not of him sitting in the car watching the street, or strolling down a sidewalk a safe thirty yards behind Geiger, or at a bar having a drink ...

It was still possible, though unlikely, that Geiger would call in, and that they might head for Dalton together without Dewey – the three musketeers on a final adventure. *Un pour tous, tous pour un* ... But each of the variables, the many uncertainties that defined this job from the start, suddenly seemed more present. They were like weeds in a bed of flowers, capable of strangling all that had been carefully designed and planted – so his job now would be that of a merciless gardener. He would have to keep a keen, diligent eye on the participants – and, if necessary, be ready to pull them out by their roots.

First, he'd have to find a club that would let him in for a piss without paying the door charge. His prostate was fucking with him for a change.

24

When Geiger had stepped outside to the patio for a cigarette, the first thing he'd done was take off his shoes and socks, and the cool, rough smoothness of the flagstone beneath his feet was sending a soothing, loosening effect up his whole frame. He sent a long, cottony stream of smoke into the night, and watched it curl in on itself like a bashful snake. Hanging from one of the patio's posts was a mobile of tiny brass bells, motionless in the still air. He raised a hand and tapped them with a finger – and they sang softly to him.

He was thinking about Dewey, watching the final sequence play out. Bodies colliding, the random stumbling, the sound of old wood cracking ... The utter melancholy of Dewey's last statement – *'It isn't fair ...'* – then life giving up on him like a long-suffering lover finally saying goodbye. Geiger kept rerunning it over and again like a film loop – trying to render it mundane, to strip it of its power through repetition. He had learned what he needed to know ... to possibly save a life – and it had cost a life. *It isn't fair ...*

'Do you want a drink?'

'I don't drink.'

Christine was in the open patio doorway. 'Ice packs are ready.'

'I'll finish my cigarette.'

She stepped out beside him, a highball glass in her hand. 'There's never a sound out here when it's very late, except for the bells.' She took a sip of her drink, and then stared at the amber elixir. 'Bourbon. Harry's favorite. But he liked the cheap kind. The kind that burned going down.' She sat down in one of the pair of wicker chairs. It gave out a small squeak as she settled in. 'He said he'd stopped drinking. Did you know him when he drank?'

'For one night. When I offered him a job, I said he would have to stop.'

'*You* got him to stop drinking?'

'No. It was his choice.'

Christine was beginning to feel the weight of her confusion. Just being around Geiger was disorienting. He was like a magnet causing nearby compasses to go haywire.

'Harry worked for you?'

'With me. We were partners.'

'In what kind of business?'

Geiger sent another plume into the air. 'Information Retrieval.'

There was something about the term that brought a faint tingle of goosebumps to her forearms.

'I don't know what that is.'

'Clients paid me to acquire information from a third party.'

'You mean – some kind of ... research?'

Geiger turned his head for the *click* – and got it. 'I interrogated people.'

'I still don't understand,' she said, but was afraid that she did. She didn't realize her uneasiness had made her shift in the chair until she heard the old wicker creak.

Now Geiger's head went left, twenty degrees. *Click*. 'I tortured people to get them to tell me the truth.' And he blinked. Slowly. Once.

There was a surge in Christine's brain – a cavalry of chemicals trying to deal with the incomprehensible ...

'You are ... a torturer?'

'Not anymore. I was.'

'And "Information Retrieval" is just another name for torture?'

'Yes. It is.' Geiger felt the growing heat of his cigarette between his fingers as it burned down close to his flesh. He flicked it into the flat darkness of the yard, took out his pack and jiggled another loose.

'Give me one,' said Christine.

He handed her one. His lighter flicked, she leaned in, and when her eyes looked up at him for a moment, Geiger saw the flame encased in both of them. It seemed as if it had always been there.

He lit himself up and took a few steps onto the grass, out of the light. Christine drew on the cigarette. She'd never liked the taste, but the sensation was pleasing. Geiger was a lean blur in the black with a tiny, glowing orange dot. A sudden breeze set the bells ringing.

'Harry ran the business side,' he said. 'Research, transcribing, book-keeping, the website ...'

'Website ... ?' She watched the hot tip rise like a firefly and suddenly glow brighter. 'Jesus, Geiger ... A *website*?!' There was a grating mix in her outburst – pure astonishment, outrage, and acknowledgement of the absurd all tumbling out together. 'How in God's name does ...? I mean – is there a school where you learn this? Torture 101?'

Geiger stepped back into the light. 'Actually, there are training programs. Governments have them ... the military. But it was instinctual with me. I have a lot of experience with pain.'

Christine looked at the cigarette between her fingers as if she had no idea how it got there ... and tossed it away.

'Is that what you were doing with the dead man?'

'Yes. To get information about Harry and Ezra's father.'

'And ...?'

'I know where they are now.'

'Where?'

'It's best you don't know that.' Geiger slowly rose up on the balls of his feet, stretching the calves and Achilles. Then down, then up again. 'I understand some of what you're thinking, Christine.'

'Do you?'

'Yes. I do. That's why I stopped ... last July – until now.' He took a long pull on his cigarette. 'You are repulsed by torture – and ashamed that you're glad I was able to find out where Harry is by those means.'

She felt revealed, naked.

'You're the first person I've talked to about any of this, Christine.'

'You didn't regale people with it at dinner parties, huh?'

She heard the mordant underside of her tone – and wondered why she wanted to hurt him. She watched him drop his cigarette to the grass and grind it out with the bare heel of his foot. Then he looked back up at her. The sarcasm had made no impression. Not in his placid expression, or his stony eyes.

'I don't go to dinner parties,' he said, and came toward her, and then past her into the house.

Geiger sat at the dining table, shirtless. His shoulder was swollen, but not discolored, which meant there hadn't been any internal tears. He was studying the place – the dining room, living room. He felt a sense of stasis around him. Everything seemed firmly set in its place – furniture, the paintings on the walls, vases, curios – as if nothing had been moved, or switched, or replaced for a long time. And there were no photographs of anyone – no evidence of connections, no proof of the past. It was as if consciously or unknowingly her purpose had been to create a space in which time had no role, a haven where change was irrelevant.

Christine came in from the kitchen with her arms full – three Ace bandages and two large zip-lock plastic bags filled with ice cubes. She dumped everything on the table.

'Where should they go?'

He tapped the top of his collarbone at the joint. 'Balance one across here first. Wrap a bandage around a few times, under the armpit, and then around the chest once.'

Christine positioned an ice bag and Geiger slowly raised his arm twenty degrees to allow the bandage through. There was a looseness in the joint that concerned him more than the pain, but the cold was a balm. Christine began wrapping, over the bag and under the armpit, round and round.

'Too tight?'

'No.'

He needed to lock down a schedule. It was almost 2 a.m. He'd need a small meal, a shower, and two hours' sleep before he left.

'Around the chest now?'

'Yes. Twice.'

Christine watched things in him tense and ripple as he leaned forward from the waist, away from the chair's back. His sleek, lean body reminded her of a perfect machine, except for the star-shaped scar in his pectoral.

'Is that a bullet wound?'

'Yes.'

'What happened?'

'It's a long story. Last July.'

She started going around his chest and back with the bandage. 'You keep mentioning July . . .'

'Harry . . . his sister . . . Ezra . . . his father . . . myself. We found ourselves in the middle of something. People died.'

Her hand brushed against his bare skin. It was cool and tight, and she felt hard muscle beneath it.

'Some men kidnapped Ezra . . . in order to get to his father. His father had some very sensitive, classified videos the government wanted to stay hidden. I took Ezra from them – to get him back to his mother. The man who has Harry and Ezra's father now – Dalton – he was involved.'

Geiger let his eyes fall shut. He hadn't had time yet to focus on what to do about Soames. If he tried to contact

her, to alert her to Victor's duplicity ... It didn't feel like
something he could tell her on the phone – and person
to person could create a multitude of entanglements. If
he chose not to tell her and go on alone – she'd be a certain casualty, a sacrificial lamb whether she got to
Dalton's or not. He suspected Victor preferred a blade
to a bullet.

'Are you all right ... ?' she asked.

The sudden smell of lavender, riding in on a breeze.
The question came again. She was very close.

'... *Are you all right?*'

So close the softness of her voice was like a feather
tickling his ear.

'*Yes, Ma. I'm all right. What should I do?*'

'*You can't do anything, sweetness,*' she said. '*There's
nothing to do.*'

He had the heart of a boy, and it beat against his ribs
like a captive animal flailing at the bars of its cage.

'Are you all right?' A warm hand came to rest on his
forearm. 'Geiger ... Are you all right?'

He opened his eyes. Christine was watching him with
a tilted look.

'I asked three times if you were all right. You didn't
hear me.'

'I heard you. But I thought you were someone else.'

Geiger looked like a weary sailor who'd navigated
through a thick fog back out into familiar waters, and
Christine decided that he was the strangest and saddest
person she had ever met.

'Where does the other ice pack go?'

Geiger tapped the outer arm below the shoulder joint.
'Here.' He took an ice bag and held it against his

deltoid, and Christine picked up another bandage and began.

'I have a question,' he said.

'Yes?

'What does *soleil couchant* mean?'

Christine slowed in her movements. 'It means sunset.'

'Why did you name the café Soleil Couchant?'

She did two more circuits with the bandage and tucked the end in.

'Watching the sunset was something my daughter and I loved to do together. It was her favorite thing.' The hour and angst was catching up to her, tugging at her to slow down. 'Are you hungry?' she asked.

Geiger nodded. His eyes followed her as she went into the kitchen. He tried to summon an image of her and Harry and their little daughter – sitting in a room, walking in a park, sharing a meal . . . a unit, content to be as they were, together – and he had no difficulty seeing Harry wearing a comfortable, easy grin like a favorite, old sweater. When Christine opened the refrigerator, she bent down and the silver door blocked his view of her – and he saw his own, blurred reflection in the burnished steel instead, the melted features drained of color and expression. The irony was not lost on him.

25

Dalton gave the back room a final looking-over. It was like staring through a magic window back into the past. He closed the door, and with thumb and forefinger put the key in the old lock and turned it. Mid-action, he had to alter his grip before he could turn it far enough to get the click of the chambers. Some hand movements were still difficult to perform successfully without adjustments.

He took out the key and moved down the hall toward the kitchen. The old planks muttered beneath his shoes. Sometimes he heard the words they were saying ... but not tonight.

There was a glass of red wine he had poured earlier waiting on the counter – a rich Margaux from Bordeaux that Victor had brought as a gift the first time they had met. He picked it up and continued through a darkened doorway to the study, flicked on the light and sat down at his computer. The monitor's screensaver was a single silver word in a large, ornate, three-dimensional font – floating, turning, tilting randomly. *GEIGER*.

He tapped the space bar and the screensaver flew

away, revealing a page of his memoirs. He took a sip of wine as he read his latest entry.

CHAPTER 27

Sometimes I have felt like a reporter delving into the
past of a stranger, but I have told it all – every
interrogation, from the first – 1986, in Nicaragua – to
this week, in Tulette. I shall make a final decision on
the status of Harry Boddicker and David Matheson
very soon. It is an odd realization – that holding the
power over their fates feels almost trivial in the
larger scope of things. But I have not lost my sense
of the pragmatic, and will make my choice based
on what might serve my own needs best.

Dalton looked to a window. The deep silence had made a pact with the blackness, weaving itself into it, allies now, creating a fibrous, impenetrable wall of night. It shut out the pinpricks of starlight and the cries of hunter and prey. He began typing.

Because the future is undefined, I will e-mail the
manuscript to Lars soon. It is strange, and perhaps
thrilling to think this could be the last chapter of the
book – that Geiger will arrive tomorrow, or the next
day, and I may never write another word. But that is
not to say that this memoir would remain
unfinished, because what is a memoir but the story
of one's life . . . until it ends. If this is the last
chapter, then there is nothing left to tell – and I am
complete.

He closed the document, leaned back in his chair, and the screensaver – *GEIGER* – returned to the dark monitor. Dalton reached for his glass – as the floating, silver word came to rest in the center of the screen and morphed into Geiger's placid, unblinking face. It was as if they were looking at each other through a tinted window.

'Ah … Bonsoir, mon ami.' Dalton took up his glass. 'Tchin-tchin,' he toasted, tilted the wine to his parted lips and drank slowly. 'Getting close, aren't you?' He put the glass down softly. 'But not as close as you think.'

Dalton's forefinger rose and began to tap his lip.

'What I realized, back on that day, when you were in the chair and I was cutting you up … is that you *don't know who you are*. You're like a blind man with incredibly attuned senses – but the fact still remains … You can't *see*.'

Geiger stared back at him, unmoved by the diagnosis.

'You *think* you can see – but you can't.' Dalton leaned to the monitor. 'And that is why I am here. To help you. You think this is about saving lives – Matheson, Harry – all for Ezra, in a sense. But you *can't see*. This isn't about anyone else's life but *yours* – and *mine*. I'm in your head, Geiger. In that beautiful brain of yours. And I am going to give you sight.' He raised the wine again. 'And then all shall be revealed.'

Dalton drained the glass, then held it out before him, turning the bowl in his fingertips, left and right, so the light wrapped round its equator like a thin, gleaming ribbon. His fingers tensed slightly, slowly, the pressure increasing in minute degrees – and the glass shattered in his hand.

'Voilà,' he said.

Christine rinsed a plump Belle de Pontoise apple under the kitchen faucet, then sliced it into quarters and put it on a plate beside spears of raw asparagus and stalks of broccoli. Geiger had told her he only ate raw food.

She didn't have to look around to know the long-lost troll was near. She could hear the sniffles and sobbing, the taunting dare to come join in the remorse. The size and power of all she'd been dragged into was beginning to hit home, and she needed to keep doing things. Geiger was in the bathroom washing the dirt and dust off. She'd put his dirty clothes in the washer. The events of the past few days, and the last twelve hours – they'd been picking the locks of her vault, and she felt her sad, precious treasures and horrors were about to come tumbling out.

She turned. Geiger was coming down the hall, cleaned up, wearing a pair of gym shorts. The swelling in his shoulder had diminished, but her eyes immediately went to the three horizontal marks on his left quad. She felt the urge to ask – but stopped herself.

Geiger sat down at the table. Christine brought the plate and a fork and put it down before him.

'Are you sure you don't want me to cook any of this?'

'Yes.'

She sat down across from him. 'Do you want salt?'

'I don't use it.' He picked up an asparagus spear with his long fingers and took a bite. It made a loud crunch. 'Thank you, Christine – for your help.'

'You're welcome.'

They stared at each other. Christine felt a trace of a tug – the aftermath of a shared calamity between victims ... witnesses ... accomplices. She tried to imagine him smiling – but the image wouldn't come to her.

'If you know where they are now, why not bring the police in?'

'Because I would lose whatever control I might have. Police don't necessarily make good choices in these situations. If they tried to negotiate ... or stormed the house, Dalton might decide to kill them both ... if he had time. It's impossible to know. But the deal was to make a trade – them for me – and if I show up as planned, he might let them go. Or if I arrive secretly and get the upper hand, I might be able to save them ... if they aren't dead already.'

'But you don't know what you're going to do ...'

'No. The only way to know is to get there.'

The simplicity of it all made it scarier for her to contemplate. The only concrete element was death – that people would die. It was a very strange thing to be certain about. She reached out and took a piece of apple from the plate, and nibbled off a small chunk. The tartness gave her a tiny rush.

'What did Harry tell you about us?' she said.

'Nothing.'

The word was an unexpected crisp jab – and Christine wondered why it hit her as sharply as it did.

'Nothing?'

'No. He never mentioned you until the day he was leaving to come here.' Geiger took a bite of broccoli.

Snap. 'And he said you had a daughter. He used the past tense – so I made the assumption she is dead ...'

Somehow, his unadorned tone cast the statement in italics. *I made the assumption she is dead*.

'... and that her death destroyed the marriage.'

Christine felt a flinch deep down. It was another lock being picked, another chamber clicking into the open position.

'Tell me something, Geiger. Do you ever stop to think about *how* you might say something before you say it?'

He swallowed. 'Was I mistaken about anything?'

She slowly put the apple down on the table. 'No,' she said. The way his eyes took her in – she felt like a book in his hands. More and more, she was understanding why he was so good at what he did.

'You were the one who left,' he stated.

She kept her gaze with his. 'Yes.' She didn't want to look away.

'Why?'

'Because I couldn't look at him without seeing her ... and I couldn't be with him without feeling her *not* being there. So I left.'

'Have you missed him?'

'Very much – but I became adept at putting that feeling away.' Her smile had a small, bitter crimp to it. 'Like fixing up a guest room for it all. Someplace I can open the door and have a quick look at sometimes if I'm blue enough.' She let out a long breath, as if she'd been holding it for some time.

Geiger pushed his chair back and stood up. 'I need some water.'

He started toward the kitchen – and that was when

Christine saw the back of his legs, and the perfect lat-
ticework of slender scars from his thighs all the way
down to his ankles. Their degree of precision, and what
that signified, made them all the more horrific to discover. She watched him find a glass in a cupboard above
the sink, fill it up and drink it all, then refill the glass
and come back to his seat.

'Who did that to you?'

'My legs?' The fingers of his right hand began to rise
and fall on the tabletop in a rhythmic ritual. The images
were never far from the moment ...

*Lying face down, naked, on the bench before the
hearth, staring at the cabin's floor – an astonishing work
of art, a recreation of Bosch's* Garden of Earthly
Delights, *the thousands of inlays a testament to his
father's virtuosity and obsession.*

'My father did it.'

'For how long?'

'Years. Since I was five or six, I think. I'm not certain.'

*His father stood over him in faded denim overalls,
holding the pearl-handled straight razor.*

'What do we know, son?' he said.

'Life makes us ache for things we think we need.'

'And ... ?'

'And the pain makes us weak.'

'Why did he do it, Geiger? Do you know why?'

'To teach me about pain. To make me strong.'

'So what must we do, son?'

*'Embrace the pain, a little each day, and grow
strong.'*

'But *why?* Did something happen ... to make him
start?'

'I don't know.'

His father laid the blade down on the quadriceps. *'Say it with me, son,'* *and they chanted together softly.* *'Your blood, my blood, our blood ...'*

Geiger put the visions away. He could feel his body's messages. He needed to sleep. Christine leaned to him.

'What about your mother? Where was she when – when this was happening?'

'I don't remember my mother. I don't have many memories of things as a boy.'

Christine's new knowledge changed the way his face appeared to her. He looked ... younger.

'I'm sorry, Geiger,' she said.

'We all carry things with us, Christine.' He picked up his glass and slowly drank. 'I'm going to stop talking now. I need to sleep for a few hours.'

'The bed in the guest room is made up. Clean sheets. Last door on the right.'

Geiger rose from his chair and headed down the hall. She turned and watched him – the slight tilt to his walk odd but not inelegant, the marks of madness shifting slightly with each step. She tried to picture it, the terrible ritual – perhaps it would help her grasp the unspeakable – but when the images came she couldn't bear to look at them.

She took hold of the breakfront's center brass knob and pulled. The drawer stuck. It hadn't been opened in a long time. She gave a tug and it slid open. She pushed some of the contents aside – half a dozen candles, a pack of napkins with floral designs still wrapped in cellophane – and found what she was looking for. She lifted the thin leather album out, took it to the coffee table and sat down on the sofa.

She opened the album and leaned over it. The first page had three photographs attached to it, beneath a protective plastic sheet: she was in her hospital bed, her brand-new baby in her arms, its tiny white skullcap perched at an angle; Harry sat on a beige couch, smiling, cradling the infant in one arm, feeding her a bottle, Christine beside him, her hand on his thigh; Harry sat in a wide, overstuffed chair, two-year-old Sophie on his lap, the two of them staring at a *New York Times* he held open in his hands.

A tear fell onto the plastic sheet. It looked like the first drop of a rainstorm landing on a window. Then the heavens opened up and it began to pour ...

26

He had left the light on, and was lying on his back instead of his usual fetal position because of the pain in his shoulder. He heard her come into the room and stop at the bedside.

'Geiger . . . ?'

He opened his eyes. She stared down at him, a shining line of tears on each cheek. Geiger watched their slow descent. He had always been intrigued by the act of crying. Tears were unique, triggered by every kindred and opposite emotional state. He'd made a list once, put it in one of his binders and studied it for hours, watching the connections grow between the words like routes on a road map to destinations he'd never known – fear and joy, apprehension and anticipation, loss and fulfillment, despair and pleasure, grief and rapture . . .

'Can I lie down next to you . . . just for a little while?' A faint quiver threaded through her voice, and her arms were wrapped across her chest – as if she were cold, or afraid she might come apart.

'Why?'

'I feel very sad.'

Geiger moved a foot to his left – and Christine lowered herself onto the bed and slowly lay back, leaving six inches of the blue comforter between them. Crying always made her chest tighten and breaths feel unfinished – so she clasped her hands on her stomach and tried to breathe deeply, slowly.

'I was looking at some pictures.'

He could feel her body rising and falling beside him, with a slight tremble in the valley of her breaths, as if she had been through a hard spell of sobbing.

'I loved them so much – and I loved the *feeling* of loving them. Do you know what I mean?'

'I've never loved anyone, Christine. I'm not made that way.'

'What does that mean – "not made that way"?'

She felt his fingertips begin tapping the space between them in a waltzing beat. *Tap* – tap – tap ... *Tap* – tap – tap ...

Christine's head turned on the pillow, and she studied him. His features looked less angular in profile – less vulpine.

'Then why are you doing this?' she said.

'I was an instrument of suffering – for a long time – and now Harry and Matheson are suffering because of me. And if they die, Ezra will also suffer.' He turned his head to her. 'And I have much less to lose than they do.' The finger-tapping stopped. 'I need to sleep.'

Geiger closed his eyes. His breathing changed within a few seconds, an engine shifting down from drive to neutral, settling into an even idle. The thoughtless, heartful part of her wanted to touch him, let her fingertips brush against his cheekbone just above the sharp

304 Mark Allen Smith

line of his beard. It was not the flesh she wanted, but the sense of connection ... for a moment ...

Her hand slid across the comforter till it found his. When she rested hers in his open palm, there was no response. She couldn't tell if he was already asleep – or simply being true to himself, remaining unconnected. With tiny increments of movement, she found a position that felt lasting and natural, and entwined two fingers in his as a kind of anchor. Then she closed her eyes and hoped to dream.

He had left the waking world behind him, and was in the antechamber to deep sleep when he felt someone take his hand – and pull him into a place where he was both present and observer ... and instantly aware that the vision was not a dream ...

... His six-year-old ghost, barefoot in faded overalls ...

The cabin was the work of a master carpenter, the walls and cathedral ceiling made of massive split logs, windows set oddly high so all that was seen of the world were lush treetops and infinite sky.

He sat in the sun-washed great room beside an off-kilter cot where his mother lay beneath a dog-eared sheet, her long, thick braid of black hair stretched across the pillow. Her pallid skin shone with sweat, her gray, almond eyes gleamed with a warm but fading light – and the scent of her lavender water was in his nostrils.

The linen rose around her swollen belly, and at her inner thighs the fabric held the glistening proof of her distress. One hand lay flat and still upon her chest and the other at her side, fingers interlaced with her son's. A string quartet's concerto sprinkled down from the rafters and, to the boy, seemed to shift in mood with the slow rise and fall of his mother's chest.

'Are you all right?' she asked.

'Yes, Ma. I'm all right. What should I do?'

'You can't do anything, sweetness,' she said. 'There's nothing to do.' More than her words, the fuzzy hush in her tone and sibilant breath through parted lips gave the boy his answer.

'Ma ... I could go try and find a doctor.'

'You can't go off the mountain. You know Father's rule.'

'But this is ... different.'

'No. No doctors. It would end up being much worse for you – later on.'

Tears spread out along the rims of the boy's eyelids, and then spilled over.

'And wipe those tears away before your father comes back.'

The boy used the back of his hand to erase the evidence. Pain suddenly stretched his mother's lips into a flat horizon.

'Why is it doing this to you, Ma?'

'It isn't the baby's fault, sweetness.'

'But it's hurting you,' he said. 'I don't want it to hurt you anymore.'

'It'll stop hurting. But I may have to go away.'

'Go away where?'

Her smile was late arriving. 'Don't worry, sweetness. It will all make sense.'

'What will?'

306

306

'Just stay here with me now. I'll sing to you.' She squeezed his hand tighter. 'You are the sunshine of my life ...' The song was more than melody and words. It transcended sound and meaning. It was a chord of life that had joined them, warm and soothing, since his birth, in sleep and wakefulness. 'That's why I'll always be around ...' But it had become more fragile, tremulous – and now seemed an echo of itself.

'Ma ... If you go away, are you going to forget me?'

He heard her breath catch – and felt her fingers tighten around his.

'I won't forget you, sweetness. That's the best part about loving someone. You never forget them.'

The crunch of a metal latch being lifted screwed his head around as the room's only door swung open. His father stepped inside, a steel bucket in each hand, and milk spilled over their edges onto the floor as he walked toward the wide, cast-iron cooking stove.

'She gave plenty, Mother,' he said.

'That's good,' said his wife.

He set the pails down on the stove and rubbed his palms dry on the front of his overalls. He had the look of a domesticated creature – born wild, trained to live in a world of people and cabins and dogma. He held his massive hands up to his face, examining the crooked fingers, bent by a thousand slips of a hammer, then shoved them down into his overalls' pockets and stared at his pale wife.

'Do you still feel it moving?'

'Yes,' she said softly. 'Some.'

'Stay strong, Mother. It isn't time yet.'

'I know. I will.'

His father's gaze moved to the boy. 'Are those tears, son?'

The boy knew that crying was a failing. But lying was unthinkable.

'Yes, Father.'

'Then we need to remember to talk about that, later.'

'Yes, sir. I won't forget.'

'Good.'

He got out his pack of Camels and loosed a cigarette, took a wooden match from the jar on the stove, scraped it across the iron top, lit up and sent a rich bloom of smoke into the room.

'I'm going to warm some milk for you, Mother. You need to drink more milk.' He looked over at the large stone hearth. 'Shall I light a fire? Are you cold?'

When no answer came, both father and son turned to her. The boy had forgotten that he still held her hand, and realized now that her fingers had stopped gripping his. His father's cigarette dropped to the floor. The boy wasn't sure whether he meant to do it or not.

'Mother ... ?' his father said. He walked slowly to the cot – and laid two fingers on the white, smooth throat.

'What's happened, Pa?'

The great, dark head slowly slumped downward. Something had given way within him. The silence in the room was a visitor commanding that no one speak. The boy thought it reigned over the world too. He heard no chirps from the birds, no hum of wind or chatter from the leaves on the trees. Even the sonata seemed chastened.

The boy stood up. 'Ma?' He put his hand on his mother's shoulder. 'Ma?' He gave her a soft nudge. 'Did she go away, Pa?'

Slowly, his father glanced at him. 'Is that what she told you?' Embers suddenly flared at the center of the coal-black eyes – and he looked back down to the body. 'Is *that* what you told him?!'

The boy could almost taste the bitterness laced in the question, though he didn't understand its presence. He didn't understand anything. He felt adrift, in between places. He watched his father's fingertips run slowly across the length of her braid, then move to her face and gently trace a line along her cheek.

'You will be missed, Mother, terribly,' he said, 'but damn you for your weakness. You've left me with a miserable job to finish for you.' He pulled a hunting knife from a sheath on the tool belt round his waist, and grabbed hold of the sheet. 'Move away, boy – and look away.'

The boy turned and found a small, solitary cloud beyond the trees to watch. It was creeping across the sky, moving east, toward the top of the mountain like a lamb searching for the flock. Sounds were rushing back into the room, and he was being wrapped in an odd melange – the crisp, light strokes of the classical players punctuated by the tympani of his father's grunts of effort, and the soft squish of flesh giving way to honed steel. He knew the sound from the many times he'd watched his father gut a deer. Then he heard the knife hit the floor, and looked over at it. The sunlight flashed bright red on the wide blade – and he understood whose blood it was.

A noise came out of his father, bearish but muted, and some primal urge – shock, or grief, or anger – prodded it to a higher pitch before it slowly died down and out, revealing another intonation beneath it. A quiet stirring. At first the boy thought it was leaves nuzzling against each other in a sudden breeze, but the sound was inside with them.

'Is that the baby?' he asked.

His father's breath came out of his nostrils in short, staggered puffs. 'Get two towels.'

'It's alive, isn't it?' the boy said.

'*Do as I tell you!*'

… The bludgeoning force of the command almost knocked Geiger back into consciousness – but his mind refused to let go of the vision. He would not leave it. He would stay until the end …

The boy ran to a tall armoire against a wall, flung the doors open and grabbed a pair of towels from a shelf. As he started back, his father turned, blocking the body from sight with his own. He held out a bloodied hand. Drops formed at the blunt edges of fingernails – hanging like small, ruby berries, then giving in to gravity and falling.

'Give them here. Don't come close.'

He took the towels and turned back to his task. The boy watched his arms shift in concert with muscles in his wide back, pistons in an engine performing a grim service. Something was growing in the boy's chest, weeds snaking out, getting tangled round his heart …

His father turned around, holding the swaddled

newborn. The boy couldn't see the infant, but a rheumy, irregular wheeze drifted out from inside the towel.

'It *is* alive,' said the boy.

'It will not live long, son.'

'Why?'

'... Because it isn't meant to.'

'Can I hold it?'

'For a short while. Sit.'

The boy sat down in the chair beside the cot.

'Put your arms like this.' His father demonstrated the cradling position, the boy prepared his arms, and his father placed the bundle in them – and then walked to the stove, struck another match and lit another cigarette.

The boy was surprised by the lightness of what he held. The weak murmur was slipping out through a narrow opening in the wrap – and he slowly widened it with a finger ...

It was the smallest living thing he had ever seen, and the oldest – wrinkled and ashen, yet somehow unfinished. Its only movement was the slow, stuttering rise and fall of its chest. The eyes were closed. The boy wondered if they would ever open.

'It's sick.'

His father spoke from behind a dense haze of smoke. 'It's dying.'

'But ... it's just *born*.' Something was taking hold of him – far beyond understanding – a sense there was a great spirit, even more powerful than his father, able to make terrible things happen just by deciding it should be so, and its reasons would always remain unknown.

He nudged the tip of his forefinger into the infant's hand – and the impossibly tiny fingers slowly closed around it. His mother had asked him many times if he wanted a brother or sister. He had always said he didn't care which. He looked over at her. His father had pulled the sheet up to her neck. Her blood had turned the mid-section of it dark red. Her face was smooth and white – cool, elegant marble. He felt a pulsing start up in his ears.

'Father ... I think I'm gonna cry. I'm sorry.'

His father walked over, slightly hunched. To the boy, it looked as if the original, untamed beast in him was coming alive. He bent down and picked up the hunting knife – and when he straightened up the boy saw his face head-on. It had turned rigid, as if flesh had petrified to stone beneath the thicket of beard. And death had paid a visit to his eyes, bringing condolences and darkness ... and taking the light with it when it left.

'Go on then – cry,' he said. 'Then there will be no more crying. And there will be no more *weakness* in this house. No more *frailty*. I will see to it.' He wiped the blade off on a pantleg of his overalls – slowly, one side, then the other. 'You will have no brothers or sisters now – and I'm going to find a way to make you strong. Stronger than your mother. Stronger than *me*. So cry now, for the last time.'

He started for the door.

'Where are you going, father?'

'To get a shovel.' He swung the door open, stepped through and slammed it closed behind him.

The boy looked down at the infant. Father was right – it didn't look like something that belonged in the world. It reminded him of a baby bird born without wings, a sad, nonsensical thing with no place to be. He looked over at his mother.

'Don't forget me, Ma,' he said. 'Please don't.'

And he began to weep – for the last time …

Geiger's eyes opened. There was a slight, soft tremble in his breath rippling across the grain of his heartbeat, and within it was an ache. He was the student and master of pain, his and others, but he didn't know this sensation. It was not a product of force, of cruel acts, of the darkest of human intentions. It was not of flesh and nerve-endings and muscle and joints. It was a revelation.

Christine was asleep, nestled against him, one arm lying across his chest.

He glanced at the clock on the night-table. Eight-forty. He'd been asleep for over five hours. He'd never slept that long before. He wiped his tears away – and then gently tapped Christine's arm. One sleepy eye opened, regarding him languidly … and then awareness kicked in – of his identity, and her position, and the precarious tilt of the world. She turned onto her back, and they watched the ceiling together.

'I have a question,' he said.

'Yes.'

'Is it there all the time?'

The question settled down in her, like a lapdog, waiting for a response. She didn't need to ask for clarification. She knew what he meant.

'Yes, it's always there.'

'What do you do with it?' he said.

'I keep it at arm's length. Close enough that I can see it out of the corner of my eye ... but far enough away that it can't sneak up on me.' She turned to him. 'But you don't do that. You do something else.'

He turned to her. They were close enough that he could see a few tiny specks of hazel in the blue irises.

'I ... embrace it,' he said. 'I let it fill me up.'

'And then there's no room for anything else.'

She suddenly became acutely aware of her body – how it rested in the mattress, the blouse's silk on her skin, the insistence in her pulse ...

She wanted something from him – wanted to let go of herself and *take* something from him. Flesh, touch, breath, motion ...

'I need to leave soon, Christine. I'm behind schedule.'

She sat up and ran her hands back through her hair. 'Yes,' she said, and straightened her blouse. 'I'll make coffee.'

'Black.'

'Sugar?'

'No.'

Geiger watched her go. She left like someone who was late for an appointment. His right side, where she had lain against him, was still warm. He would ice his shoulder once more before he left. There was no reason to go back to the hotel room.

'Are you hungry?' she called.

'No.'

He scrubbed the steam off the mirror with his palm – he had lingered in the hot shower so the beard would be soft and pliant.

Five a.m., 3 July – the last time he had shaved. Almost nine months to the day – when he firmly held the reins of his life, deaf to echoes of a past, numb to sins of the present ... when the walls between the inside and outside were staunch, uncompromised ... and there was no Ezra, no betrayals, no revelations ... no vengeful quests, no dead-eyed body in a shuttered store ... no stirrings, no father and mother staking claim to their place amid tumbling memories ... no pristine sense of intolerable wrongs awaiting redress ...

Carmine's words came back around to him.

'... *Life owns your ass – from day one, cradle to grave. You don't get it. You think you can choose whether you're in or not ... but you can't ...*'

He raised the razor he'd found in the medicine cabinet – the plastic disposable kind in a box of ten – to his soapy cheek, and started working the blade, half-inch downstrokes, slowly uncovering his face. There was no longer need for camouflage of any kind.

Outside the dining-room window the sky's coy shimmer was a hint the rain had moved on and would not be coming back. Christine put Geiger's coffee before him in a blue ceramic bowl – and he stared at it until Christine sat down with hers, cradled it in her palms and brought it to her lips.

'Two hands,' she said. 'When in France ...'

He copied her technique and sipped. She watched his newly revealed face for a sign of pleasure or satisfaction, but his features gave no evidence of either.

'Feels good – without the beard?'

'Cleaner. Lighter.'

Christine lowered her bowl. 'Can I ask you a question?'

'Yes.'

'Beneath the surface, on the inside ... Do you feel different things – at different times?'

Geiger blew softly on the coffee, curling the steam. 'Christine ... I have nothing to tell you about myself.' He took another sip. 'I'll tell you something Harry once said. I overheard him speaking with a client. The man asked what I was like – and Harry told him it would be a waste of time describing me. He said – "Geiger's like a mirror. What you would see isn't what I see ... or anyone else would see."'

Christine put her hands on the table before her, entwining her fingers as one might as a preface to prayer.

'Is that how *you* see yourself?'

'That's the point, Christine,' he said. 'I don't see myself.' He took a long drink of his coffee and put the bowl down. 'May I see your knives?'

'My knives?'

'For cooking.'

Christine's lips parted. *For cooking*. The near-weightlessness of the words had the force of a slap across the face.

'They're on the counter, next to the stove.'

Geiger stood up and went into the kitchen.

She turned her bowl slowly in her fingertips. The pictures she was seeing were terrible. She had held them off until now – but with things coming to an end, she could no longer keep them at bay. A fast-running stream of images – violent, bloody, vicious – different versions of suffering and brutality in some farmhouse in a tiny town.

Geiger returned and put a knife on the table – a short-bladed carver with a beechwood handle. The sight of it made Christine's spine straighten.

'Jesus ... Is that what you are going to ... to *use*?'

Geiger gave her only a second's glance – and took out a roll of duct tape from his bag and sat back down.

'I'm concentrating on what needs to be done, Christine. It's one way Harry and I are alike. "Stickler for detail" is how he puts it.'

He began to wrap the handle – each revolution of tape precise, the application thicker and raised at both ends of the handle so the hand would settle easily and securely into the center. She watched his long, elegant fingers at work, calmly customizing the everyday for the most extreme of purposes.

'Geiger ... ?'

His hands came to rest, and he raised his gaze to her, and waited.

'Have you ever killed someone?'

'Yes,' he said, 'but not the way you mean.'

'Then how do you know you can – if you have to?'

She caught a moment's shift in Geiger's face. She couldn't tell where it came from – the lips, jawline, the eyes.

'You've come here to *save* lives, so how do you—?

'Christine ... This has been an intense experience for you – but it would be a mistake to feel you know me ... at all.'

'Or – perhaps you aren't as unknowable as you think.'

'... Perhaps.'

Geiger stood up and went to his bag.

'What are you doing?'

He returned to the table with his iPad and began to type. 'Harry kept everything in a secure data storage facility. Financial records, dossiers, session transcripts and videos.' He finished typing, turned the tablet around and slid it over to her side. 'Click on a file labeled "S.D.V.D."'

The display showed a listing of 'S.D.V.D.' files – dozens and dozens of them, each with a pair of letters and a date.

'Which one? There are so many ...'

'One hundred and twenty-one, not including Ezra. It doesn't matter which one you choose.'

She scanned the entries. They started in 1999 – 'S.D.V.D./JM/6-29-1999.' The quantity alone was chilling to behold. *One hundred and twenty-one people.*

'Why do you want me to do this?'

Geiger picked up his coffee and took a long sip. 'You asked me how I saw myself. I'm trying to let you see who I am.' He put the bowl down. 'They called me the Inquisitor.'

Christine looked up at him. 'These are videos – of you?'

'Yes.'

There was a hot infusion into her blood, a swift jet of anger her heart pumped into her veins. The world was too full of pain. Bursting at its seams with it. She had borne witness to it long enough on her own. She did not need his help.

'That's a miserable goddamn thing to do, Geiger.'

She pushed the iPad back to him. 'I'm not going to look at these – and you can go to hell.' She grabbed her bowl and marched into the kitchen.

Geiger's gaze went down to the screen.

'WS/3-17-1999'.

WS … Warren Sloan. He asked God why he had forsaken him.

'PK/7-9-2002'.

PK … Paul Knowles. He fainted at the sight of the straight-edge razor.

One hundred and twenty-one moments when truth was dug up and dragged into the light, kicking and screaming in all its muddy, battered glory – and each at an indescribable cost. What atonement, how many tests and proofs, what *sine qua non* would lift him high enough to clear the reefs and make it to open water?

'NB/10-20-2005'.

NB … Nico Bartelli. He kept repeating, 'Do you know who the fuck I am?!'

'EG/11-4-2009'.

EG … Edie Garson. She said she would fuck him anyway he liked if he didn't hit her in the face.

He wondered if he could remember every name …

Christine's voice sounded tempered and careful. 'Do you want more coffee?'

'Yes,' he said, and picked up the knife and resumed his task.

He was outside on the patio smoking a cigarette. From her seat at the table, Christine could see his reflection in the glass of the patio door. Geiger's leaving would transport her to a limbo of doubt and hope. She might spend the rest of her life wondering if they were all dead – turning at every jingle of the bell atop the café's door to see if it was Harry walking in.

Geiger came back inside. 'Time to go.'

'Are you sure you don't want me to drive you to the metro?'

'Yes,' said Geiger, and picked up his jacket. He put it on, being measured and methodical with his shoulder.

She stood up from the table. 'Does it hurt?'

'Yes, but it's not a hindrance.'

He picked up his bag. She wondered if there was a gun inside. She suspected not, but was surprised to realize she was hoping there was.

'What happens now?' she said.

'I take the train to Avignon. There are instructions for me at the station there.'

Christine started shaking her head back and forth, but her eyes never left him.

'You going into all of this – having no idea what could happen ... It's *insane*. Can you see that?'

He zipped up his coat. 'I see a beginning, middle, and end, Christine.' He headed for the door – and she followed after him.

'And what does *that* mean?' She heard the edge to her question.

'It's how I see things – beginning, middle, end – and I focus on where I am in the process.' At the door, he turned round to her. 'It's not insane, Christine. Thinking that you ever really know what's ahead of you is an exercise in folly – so I don't focus on the end till I get very close to it.'

*

... He remembered his mother reading to him – seated in her lap, his skinny, bony back nestled into her chest, her arms extended out and around him, holding the book before them, the scent of lavender and sense of peace inseparable from one another – and when she turned a page, her head tilting down so her lips could kiss the rim of his ear lightly ...

'You looked like you had a very faint smile just now,' Christine said.

'Did I?'

'For a moment – yes.'

Geiger nodded. 'I'll have to take your word for it.'

She stepped in close to him – and her hand rose and rested on his smooth cheek. She was taking a long careful look at his face. It wasn't often that you knew, in the moment, with complete certainty, that it would be the last time you ever saw someone – and after today, when she thought of him she didn't want memory to smudge his features ... or feelings to alter them. She wanted to remember him as he really was.

Geiger's hand slowly came up to hers, and gently closed around it. The warmth of her skin was nearly narcotic.

'I have to go now.'

Their hands descended together, entwined for a moment – and then she took a step back. He opened the door. The crisp morning air slid past him like a cat coming in from the cold.

'Be safe, Geiger.'

'Goodbye, Christine.'

She didn't take her next breath until he'd gone and

the door had shut with a soft click. She felt chilled from the cold, and the weariness, and the fear in her veins. She walked into the living room and picked up her sweater from the couch. As she put it on she stared at the old photograph she'd put in a frame last night and placed on the coffee table. It was of two people, taken from behind them at dusk – silhouettes of an adult and a very small child sitting side by side in a park, watching the sun go down behind dark hills across a river. It had always been Harry's favorite shot of the two of them.

Part Three

Part Two

When he'd left Christine's, he'd walked past the nearest metro station and continued on – wanting movement and the air's chill.

... He remembered that the baby had died in his arms, a last fuzzy sigh signaling the end to its brief hours, and he had wondered if it knew it had lived at all. He remembered that his father had buried mother and child together, wrapped in the same sheet ... and no words were spoken at the grave ...

Something was heating up places inside him, bending them, like a blacksmith urging the hardest, coldest of things into new shapes. His mother. Gentle and bloodied and within him and lost.

... He remembered the pungent smell of gasoline and smoke when his father burned all her clothes in the fifty-gallon drum behind the cabin. He remembered his father's decree – that neither mother nor sibling be mentioned again ... that to speak or think of the weak was to invite weakness into their lives – and he remembered that his father had started building the special closet for him to sleep in the very next day. He wasn't certain when the ritual of the razor had begun – but it had been soon . . .

He spent the rest of the walk to Gare de Lyon station trying to decide about Soames. It was like trying to hammer a nail into a blob of mercury. Making the call to her would mean keeping Victor close – but it could also limit his maneuverability down the line. If he didn't make the call and went on alone, then soon enough Victor would have no reason to keep her alive . . . and an image barged into his mind – Victor stepping up behind an unsuspecting Soames, grabbing her by the hair, his arm swinging round and sinking a knife into her chest – and it slowed his steps to a dead halt. This wasn't about fine-edged thought and strategy. It was thicker, messier – from the heart, not the head.

He heard Corley's voice – *Geiger . . . Do you feel disconnected from people?* – and his answer had been – *Martin, if you've never been plugged in, you can't be disconnected.*

Something had changed.

The *swoosh–swoosh* of the jump rope kept at a steady pace – four snaps a second. Fast enough to push her heart without going to the level where she got zoned and thoughtless. Beyond the window, there was hardly any traffic on the street. Only three of the windows of Geiger's hotel were lit up.

Victor had called to say he was on his way back. He hadn't found Dewey or the car. As soon as Zanni hung up she had decided, big picture, that nothing would change. They'd go a man short and play it out ... assuming Geiger wasn't already looking out a window thirty thousand feet up in the sky. For now, she was going to put her brother in a box, along with her dread – she had seen what Geiger could do – and the pictures in her head. If and when the job was done, if Dewey hadn't shown up she'd look inside it – but until then she had to have a lockdown on her focus.

She switched to an alternate-foot speed-step to double up the work. Feet touching lightly, the scene out the window bouncing up and down before her, her huffing in her ears. Hard as she tried she couldn't see Geiger as a killer. Not by nature – and not situationally. If he had compromised Dewey, why murder him? Where was the need? And then she thought of Hall and his men going after him ... and no one came back.

She had put the Nextel cell on the window sill directly in front of her – and when it rang, she dropped the jump rope in mid-swing and stared at the phone, chest heaving, pulse knocking in her temples. She let it ring a second time, tamping down her breath, and then picked it up.

'Geiger ... ?'

'Yes.'

'Where are you?'

'I'm about to get on the train to Avignon.'

'So – we're going to do this together?'

'That was the plan, Soames – wasn't it?'

The question squeezed Zanni's gaze into a squint. 'Yes, it was.' She wiped the sweat away from her eyes with her free wrist. 'When do you get there?'

'One fifty-six.'

'We'll leave right away. It takes twice as long by car.'

'I'll call once I get the instructions from the locker.'

'Okay.' She was digging through her emotions to figure out why she didn't feel relieved.

'You didn't think I would call, Zanni.'

'I wasn't sure. I saw you go out last night ...'

'I know.'

'... so yes – I wasn't certain if you were coming back.'

'I saw some of the city. I've never been to Paris before.'

She allowed herself a thin smile. 'Anything in particular you enjoyed?'

'I have to get on the train. I'll call from Avignon.'

'Okay.'

She clicked off, headed into the bathroom and turned the shower on – and took a moment to study herself in the mirror. The violet eyes shined back at her. Sometimes when she looked at her image she could still see the tomboy – driving the tractor, outrunning all comers, beating up Dewey whenever she felt like it just because she felt like it.

She pulled off her T-shirt and shorts and got into the shower, and made the water as hot as she could handle. She was one step closer.

Victor came into his room, tossed his coat on the bed and sat down, and started massaging his knees. All the walking had kicked up the arthritis. He could see his father in his rocking chair, doing the same ritual nightly. *Le fléau de Bran*, he used to call it. The de Bran curse. One of the many things he'd passed on to his son ...

*

He rose with a grunt and opened the connecting door, and heard Zanni's shower running. Steam drifted out from the open bathroom door.

'Zanni ... I'm back!'

'Go get the other car and bring it around front! Geiger just called. He's on the train to Avignon!'

He walked back into his room. His thumbnail took up its post in the cleft of his chin, up and down, as he parsed the information. Geiger was going to play this out after all – and Victor did some rearranging of the main unknown.

Dewey.

Was Geiger involved in his disappearance? If yes, then it created more unknowns. How much might Geiger have gotten out of Dewey? Did Geiger know the true nature of things? If yes, that created still more unknowns. Is that why Geiger had called? Keep your friend close and your enemy closer?

His scuffed old traveling bag lay open on a small bench. Morocco ... 1987 ... at a bazaar in Tangier ... the German banker who'd skipped with millions ... tossed off the roof with a phony suicide note in his pocket. Victor looked round the room, picked up his vest, lay it on top of the neatly folded clothes in the bag, and closed the ties. He was always ready to leave someplace. He headed for the door with it, then paused, and put his bag down.

'I am on my way! Two minutes! I just have to take a piss!'

The train to Avignon was a sleek, slope-nosed TGV Duplex, and Geiger had gone to the upper level and settled into an aisle seat with a view of the stairs. There were a dozen riders in the car with him. During the ride south, he'd paid little attention to the view outside, but stared at the patterns in the seatback in front of him and considered scenarios for a future that he was racing toward at a smooth two hundred miles an hour.

He stepped off the train onto the platform to be met by his own reflection in the curved glass and steel walls of the Gare d'Avignon terminal. The sun was a burning white blotch on the glass and the sky was clear. He hoped the weather held.

He doubted Dalton had anyone on the train with him, but as he neared the entry he knelt down with his bag and feigned a search of its contents, catching the reflections of those who disembarked as they went into the terminal – a young mother with a pair of cranky boys in tow, a bald old man with a tobacco-stained moustache, three glum teenaged boys going back to their school ...

Inside, the main hall was flanked by towering walls that curved gracefully inward and met to form a cathedral-like arch of glazed glass. Strips of sunlight coming through the steel slits lay across the floor like bars of glowing paint. Geiger stopped and looked up, slowly turning in a circle, giving himself the gift of a moment to take in the striking, elegant angles – then headed down the corridor. There were plenty of people about – hustling for trains, huddled beneath the large schedule board, lined up at a café for bread and coffee – and then he sensed a body moving toward him from behind.

'Monsieur? Pardon, monsieur ...'

The flat, nasal voice had a French accent straight out of Rosetta Stone. Geiger turned. The man wore a checkered flannel shirt and khaki slacks that said – or meant to say – Farm Belt tourist. He had a jacket with its red '*CHURCH OF CHRIST BOWLERS*' logo slung over his shoulder, a camera round his neck, and looked very unhappy.

'Uh ... Est-ce que vous – uh – savez où est ... Uh ...' His vocabulary failed him, and with a mutter he pulled an English-to-French dictionary from his back pocket and started paging through it, licking his thumb as he did. 'Pardon ... Un moment ...'

Geiger was letting it play so he could get a read. The man looked fit and hard for forty-something, and his nose had been badly broken at some time in the past. He was a definite possible.

'Ah!' said the man, tapping the page. 'Bureau des *objets trouvés*!' He looked back up hopefully. 'Objets trouvés, monsieur?'

'I don't speak French.'

The man's face split open with a toothy, jack-o'-lantern grin. 'American! That's great! Oh Lord, thank you!' He reached out and gave Geiger's arm a short, brisk shake of camaraderie. 'Calvin Haas – Bellevue, Nebraska – *really* pleased to meet you. Praise God.'

Geiger nodded.

'Listen ... What I was trying to say was – do you know where the *Lost and Found* is? I left my wallet somewhere, or dropped it ...' He flashed a mortified grin and shrugged. '... or the pick-pockets saw the dumb tourist coming a mile away – right?'

It was the salt-in-the-wound grin and shrug that sold Geiger. The man was the real thing. A sad-sack with a big heart and small vocabulary. And no wallet.

'I believe I saw a sign, Calvin.' Geiger pointed down the hall. 'That way.'

'Yeah? Well thanks, man. Really.' He smiled, and started away. 'Wish me luck.'

'Good luck, Calvin.'

Geiger was looking for a sign with the term he'd found online – *consigne à bagages*. The arrow pointed left. He felt loose-limbed, smooth, in the flow of things. Soon the speed of time would start to shift – racing faster, slowing to a crawl, stuttering to a dead stop, revving up again ... It would be like rodeo riding – trying to stay in the saddle, react to the beast with body and mind, and not get thrown.

The lockers, six rows of three compartments painted a bright teal, were in a shadowed, recessed stretch of wall. Geiger took the red-nubbed locker key from his pocket. Locker 27 was at the end, the middle compartment. He turned to have a look around, and waited till the vicinity was relatively person-free, then put the key in and opened the locker. Inside was a letter-sized envelope and a small wooden box – the kind one would find on top of a bedroom dresser filled with earrings or rings. Geiger took out the envelope and pulled a single sheet of typewritten paper from it.

Geiger,
Go to the 'Taxi Provençal' counter. They are expecting you, under the name 'Ezra'. The driver

will have instructions where to take you.

But first, open the box. Consider the contents a reminder of the sincerity of my threats. I apologize for my heavy-handedness, and I have tried to atone for my lack of style with style – a 19th-century French 'snuff' box. Appropriate, no? And quite expensive. I find it charming.

Geiger reached into the locker and took out the box. It was made of polished teak, three by two and a half inches, the lid decorated with an intricate oval mosaic of tiny nacre and sapphire diamond-shaped inlays. He ran his fingertips across the design. The craftsmanship was superb. The artisan had been a patient, passionate man – a stickler for detail, as Harry liked to say. Geiger turned the box upside down. Etched into the bottom in gold were three initials – DJS – and a date – 1815. What would DJS think – that two centuries later his beautiful creation was being admired by a kindred soul ... and filled with some cruel, unthinkable memento?

Geiger grasped the lid between thumb and forefinger and lifted it off. The inside was lined with chartreuse felt, worn in spots – and laid out on it in a row were four circles of skin, each about the diameter and thickness of a penny. Geiger could tell they were from a human palm by the pronounced creases in the flesh. Some were parts of life-lines. Each circle had a letter etched in it, in gold, much like the bottom of the snuff box. Read left to right – U ... S ... U ... S.

Geiger put the top back on and slid the box in a pocket, then took his iPad out of his bag and Googled 'usus'. It was Latin, and there were many usages – legal

term, form of matrimony, participle, and the most
common – a noun, whose first definition was 'skill,
advantage, expertise'.

Expertise.

The thing that bound them together. The skill and
practice of a dark art. The echoes of suffering forever
drifting in their heads. The willful tainting of the spirit.
Dalton sought a final session – and who else could it be
with? In a very real sense, Dalton *needed* him. It could
be no one else. Geiger understood that Dalton's madness had clarity, a creature dwelling in a house built
with detail and purpose, but the angles were all askew –
tilted walls and sloping floors, halls that dead-ended,
doors that opened onto nothingness ...

He tore the paper into pieces and dropped them into
a refuse bin. It would be at least three hours before
Soames and Victor arrived. He'd get coffee and a piece
of fruit, and think for a while. Now that he had his
instructions, there were a few things that would need
tending to.

Matheson was seeing it all in crisp, Technicolor play-
back – Ezra up on the stage like a miniature man in his
little suit and bow-tie, eight-year-old fingers coaxing
sweetness and soul from the violin's strings. Bach, 'Air
on a G String' – and now, as then, Matheson's eyes grew
warm with tears and he felt a fullness and sense of grace
he rarely knew ...

... and Harry's clogged snoring suddenly kicked
back in and Matheson looked over at him. He was
lying on his side on the mattress. The swelling in the
cheek and temple seemed to be going down, but the

mean, purpled splotches refused to follow suit, and Matheson wondered if some infection had taken root. In the last few days he'd thought about dying more than in the whole of his life – ways to die, how much pain might be involved, how fast or slow the process, the order of their deaths ... and whether he'd want to be first or last. *'After you, Alphonse.' 'No, you first, my dear Gaston ...'*

To gain some traction in a mind slippery with pain, he'd kept forcing himself to examine a two-part question: In the end, if Geiger arrived and Dalton agreed to set one of them free, and *only* one, who should it be? And if the moment arose when it was in anyone's power besides Dalton to decide, who should make that choice? Matheson had tried to come at the dilemma from different starting points, but always arrived at the same conclusion.

He slowly raised his leg and, once again, studied the fetter and chain round his ankle – and the stories of wolves and coyotes gnawing off a limb to free themselves from a steel-jaw trap paid another visit. And there was the man pinned down by a boulder in a canyon who cut off half his arm ... They made a movie about him, but Matheson couldn't remember the name.

For years he'd thought it a high-percentage bet his death would be a private affair, carefully and anonymously planned by strangers, and undiscovered. Veritas Arcana would go dark, and there would be some slow-simmering concern, whispers and rumors, perhaps speculation in the media – but no resolution would arrive, no evidence would be found. Ezra would be the last hold-out, as much out of obstinance as hopefulness, but as the days without his father's e-mails and apologetic IMs stretched out the boy would come to accept the truth – because he'd learned too well, and much too young, that there is power that corrupts and destroys without hesitance. This was the legacy his father had left him.

He lowered his leg to the mattress, and the chain's clank opened Harry's swollen eyes. Harry licked his lips.

'Christ …' His eyes found Matheson. 'I feel like hell.'

'You're basically purple, Harry.'

'… Purple, huh?' He grunted his way up into a sitting position against the wall. 'Would you say closer to violet … or plum?'

'… Plum, with splotches of eggplant.'

'But it's a good look, right? Plum is a good color for me.'

'Yes, it is.'

'I have a plum sweater. I'm a knockout in it.'

Matheson watched Harry's wisp of a blue smile come out. It had been years since he'd shared enough time with someone to have a sense of who they really were, let alone care about them. He and Harry would've made a good team …

'Gotta piss,' said Harry, and swung his legs around so his feet reached the bare floor. He planted his good hand against the wall and started to get up.

'Careful, Harry.'

Harry rose unsteadily, took a deep breath to help his blood find a new rhythm, and shuffled to the portable toilet, his chain jangling on the floor.

'Jesus … Look at me. I'm fucking Jacob Marley.' He pulled up his smock and started to piss.

'We need to talk, Harry.'

'About what?'

'Ezra.'

'Nope,' Harry said.

'Nope ...?' Matheson's brows tilted like a seesaw. 'What the hell is that supposed to mean?'

'Just what I said. I'm not going there.'

'Where exactly is the "there" you think I want to talk about?'

'You want me to promise I'll help look after Ezra if you die and I don't – and it's bullshit.'

'*Bullshit*? Well fuck you, Harry.'

Harry shook off the last drop, let his smock down and turned.

'Listen up, man!' The sudden punch in decibels made the room feel much smaller. 'Christ ... Either Dalton's gonna kill us both – in which case I'll be hard-pressed to make good on my promise ...' A sudden wince from unknown origins made Harry pause and take a breath. '... or he's gonna let us both go, like he said he would – in which case you can go back to your son and try to atone for your fucking sins by yourself.'

Matheson nodded slowly. 'Right.' The sole word had the flat sound of a nail being hammered into something hard.

Harry looked to the window and stared at the two-inch vertical opening between the boards. The perspective took away all sense of depth – it looked like a still-life, the bottom lavender and striated forest on the top. He started toward it, until the chain stopped him. The pulse in his temples was piston-heavy. He didn't want to die here. He wanted to do some damage.

Break something. Growl at the top of his lungs. Rip something apart. He looked down at his chain.

'Motherfucker ...'

He bent down to it, grabbed it in both hands – and began smashing it against the floor.

'Muh – thur – fucker!' The loud clang accompanying his outbursts was like tympani from hell. Up, down, up ... Harry's very own Anvil Chorus. '*Muuuh – thurrr – fuuuucker!!*'

Matheson had the look of a bystander watching a multicar pile-up on an icy highway – one sliding vehicle crashing into the back of another – and another – and another.

'Fuck!' growled Harry. Wham! '*Fuck!*' Wham! '*MOTHER–FUCKING FUCK!*'

Harry slammed the chain down one last time, tottered, and flopped down onto his ass, chest heaving, spewing gusts of air from his mouth, spent.

Matheson didn't know what to say, so he said nothing. He was thinking Harry resembled one of Notre Dame's gargoyles – but then decided he looked more like a truly crazy person – a character out of *Marat/Sade*, or *Cuckoo's Nest*.

Harry looked over at Matheson, and let loose a final, satisfied sigh.

'David,' he said, 'I think I'm finally starting to get in touch with my anger.'

They regarded each other with the equable look of philosophers putting a point of existential theory to bed – but the comment was a lit fuse, burning its way to the truth of their situation. Jet-black humor could only deflect the reality of things for so long ...

It was Matheson who lost control first, with an explosive, harsh guffaw that set Harry off – and their brittle laughter rose, unable to be contained. That there was no trace of humor or pleasure in the sounds made the effect all the more jarring – but they couldn't stop.

Geiger was staring at the Taxi Provençal counter fifty feet down the hall. He had the scene worked out. It had weak spots, but there was no helping that now. He headed for it – and noticed Calvin sitting on a bench to his left, staring at the floor. He stopped.

'Any luck, Calvin?'

Calvin looked up with a dark face. 'Oh, hey there. No – no luck. Not a stitch. I can't even use the friggin' ATM.' His sheepish grin returned. 'I believe I am now officially, royally screwed. But thanks for asking.'

Geiger could feel thought lines in his mind quickly shifting, rerouting, connecting dots into a different picture. It happened in IR sessions all the time. New input equaled new construct.

'Calvin … How much do you need?' he said.

Calvin squinted, and then waved the idea off with both hands. 'No, no. You're a great guy for asking, but I can't let you do that.'

'Why can't you let me do that, Calvin? It was my suggestion, not yours.'

Calvin shrugged. 'True. But still, I just couldn't—'

'Where do you need to go?'

Calvin frowned. 'Closest American Express office is back in Paris …'

'So you need one hundred twenty euros.'

The man from Nebraska sighed. 'Yup.'

'Here is what we'll do, Calvin. I need to go to the taxi service – over there, for a car. I don't have much cash on me – I was going to have them charge my credit card for some euros anyway. You wait for me over there ...' Geiger pointed to the wall directly across from the taxi counter. 'We'll get you back to Paris. All right?'

Calvin stood up. 'You're a very nice man, mister. A godsend.'

Geiger pointed again. 'Right over there, Calvin. I'll see you in a few minutes.'

Calvin went off toward his destination. Geiger took a moment to put the finishing touches to the scene ...

The striking young woman behind the Taxi Provençal counter was on the phone. She smiled at Geiger, held up a finger and silently mouthed, 'Un moment.' She was dressed in a crisp, white, man-tailored shirt and a snug blue vest that she tugged down to accentuate her figure for him. He watched her eyes wander over him, pleased with what she saw. It was a look he'd seen many times, from women and men. It started with a simple glance, and then something about him – the tunnels in his eyes, the angles of his face, the stillness that made him stand out on the landscape – turned it into a stare that lingered, curious and often carnal, until the lack of any kind of signal from him sent the looker's gaze elsewhere.

The counter woman hung up the phone. 'Bonjour, monsieur.'

'I don't speak French,' he said.

'Ah, an American. I speak English. I was in University of Miami one year.' Her playful smile slipped out. 'The sun. And *waterskiing*.'

'There's a car and driver reserved for me. The name is Ezra.'

The counter woman took a second's notice of his disinterest, looked down at her monitor and poked her keyboard. 'Yes – here it is. "Ezra". I'll call the driver. His name is Bruno. And – if you will just read this and sign.' She put a pen and one-page document on the counter and dialed her cell. ''Allo, Bruno. Céleste.' She turned away from Geiger and lowered her voice as she continued talking.

Geiger picked up the pen and leaned to the paper – and the action combined with the counter's height set off a dull throb in his shoulder, an alarm clock reminding him to stay awake about the injury. He signed as the woman turned back to him.

Bruno will arrive quite soon, just outside by the taxi line. A red Renault.' She turned the paper around to examine the signature. 'Mr. – Jones, is it?'

'Yes. Ezra is my first name. Your name is Céleste?'

Her flirting smile made a comeback. 'Oui.'

He leaned forward a few inches. 'Céleste ... I am assuming there are directions in the rental order ... to notify the renter, my friend, when I arrive for my ride. Am I right?'

'Yes.'

'I need you to not make that call, Céleste.'

'But monsieur ... It is—'

'I would like to surprise him. It is – like a game he and I play. You understand?'

Now it was her turn to lean in. Her smile ebbed to purely professional.

'Monsieur Jones ... This is a – a *difficult* position that you put me in. I am sure you understand this, no?'

'Yes, I do, Céleste. But this is not a request.'

'... Excuse me?'

The fingers of Geiger's right hand began a smooth, easy drum roll on the counter.

'The truth is, Céleste – it is crucial that my friend not know of my approximate arrival time – and that's why you cannot make the call.'

'Monsieur ... This is – a joke, perhaps?'

'Céleste ... I have never told a joke in my whole life. Do I look or sound like I am now?'

Her stunning head did a ten-degree tilt. She reminded him of a deer hearing a twig snap in a forest.

'There is someone watching us right now, Céleste. Your photo has already been taken.'

'My *photo* ... ?'

The Inquisitor watched her eyes reflexively dart away from his and scan the area. He turned halfway around – and found Calvin leaning against the opposite wall, ninety feet away. Geiger nodded, and Calvin gave him a short sideways wave.

Céleste saw the gesture. 'But ... *why*?'

Geiger turned back to the woman. One of her hands was pressed against the counter, and he gently covered it with his own.

'Céleste ... Look at me.'

The command was soft and light as a summer breeze, and pulled her gaze back to him like a pair of strong hands.

'I realize you don't understand any of this, that it seems bizarre, or as you said – even some kind of prank. The simplest way to put it is … it's bad timing for you – that you were on duty when I arrived – but you are now part of something very serious. Life and death serious. Is your English good enough to understand what I said?'

A score of actors might have recited the speech to no effect … or scorn … or dismissal, but while she stared at him Geiger could see parts of her face – the jaw, brows, eyes, the temples – shifting and resettling as the outrageous morphed into her moment's reality. She finally nodded.

'Good,' he said. 'Céleste … When I arrive at my friend's house, it will be clear whether he was expecting me or not – and I will know if you notified him. If you did, I will tell that man over there, the one with your picture, to find you. And he will hurt you, Céleste. That's what he does. There really are people in the world who do that for a living.'

Their faces were six inches apart, and she had no more ability to move away from him than the moon from the earth.

'So again … I want to make sure you understand. It's very simple. If you don't make the call, your life goes on as it has. Nothing changes. If you make the call, there will be terrible consequences. It's crucial you believe me, Céleste.'

She nodded again. 'I won't call. I promise I won't.'

Geiger took an envelope from his pocket and put it on the counter. There were ten hundred-euro notes inside.

'This is for your trouble. Thank you, Céleste.'

Geiger picked up his bag, turned, and walked away.

'You're welcome,' she said, but so softly that he couldn't have heard her.

Geiger put four fifty-euro notes in Calvin's palm, one at a time, and Calvin started shaking his head as the pile grew.

'Dear God ... Please ... This is too much. I'm already—'

'Calvin ... I need you to stop talking now. You should have some money in your pocket after you pay for the ticket.'

Calvin's mouth crumpled up with emotion. 'Thank you. Really. Thank you. And I want to say to you ... I don't know if you're a man of faith, and what that faith might be—'

'I don't believe in God, Calvin.'

Calvin's smile came out, calm and patient. 'Well, my friend ... You are a generous soul, and in the book of God it doesn't get any better than that.' He put the bills in a pocket. 'If you give me your name and address I can send you the money when you're back home.'

'That's not necessary, Calvin. And the truth is – I don't expect to be going back home.'

'So this is a hit the road and see the world kind of trip, huh?'

'Something like that.'

Calvin put his hand out. 'Well ... If you're ever in Nebraska ...'

Geiger took his hand and they shook. 'Goodbye, Calvin.'

'Goodbye. And God bless you, mister.'

Geiger glanced over at the taxi counter. Céleste had been watching it all. She looked as white as her blouse. He picked up his bag and walked off.

Geiger waited inside, by the glass wall, while he took himself for a Google Maps virtual drive on his iPad – away from the terminal, toward the road to Tulette ...

He saw the red Renault cruise up alongside the terminal and stop. The driver's door opened and a man stepped out. He looked to be in his mid-fifties, with a wide slab of shoulders and the face of a Shar Pei, and as he tugged down the sleeves of his navy-blue suit Geiger saw that the elbows were faded. The man took up a post beside the car and, with one hand, held up a one-foot-square piece of cardboard with 'Taxi Provençal' printed across the top and EZRA written below it in large, crude letters, while he combed his fingers through his graying, steel-wool crop of clipped hair with his free hand.

Geiger stepped outside and walked toward the driver. 'I'm Ezra,' he said.

The driver smiled and did a short, choppy bow. 'Bonjour, monsieur. I am Bruno.'

He opened the back door and Geiger got inside the car. There was the faint but cloying aroma of synthetic pine. The driver came around and got in the front, put the Renault in gear and eased the car away from the terminal. Geiger put one of the windows down to dilute the smell.

'Do you speak English, Bruno?'

'A little – some. Pleasure for you or business, monsieur?'

'... Business.'

'First time?'

'Yes.'

Geiger was looking straight ahead, to the windshield – one eye was on the road and one was on the rearview mirror, studying the reflection of the driver's face as he spoke.

'You have your instructions, Bruno ... to take me to Tulette?'

'Yes, monsieur. Not to worry.'

'I'm not worried, Bruno.'

They were on a two-lane road heading northwest. Geiger turned halfway round and looked out the back window. There were no cars in sight – and he turned back around.

'Do you do this full-time, Bruno?'

The driver glanced up at Geiger's image in the rearview window. 'Pardon?'

'The job. Driving. Do you do this all the time?'

'Ah, oui. Five years. For long time I am chef. But no more. No work.'

Geiger was getting the rhythm of the man's normal, unstressed speech, like a hoofer listening to a piece of music's nuances before beginning to dance.

'Do you like it?' he asked.

The driver's grin was fast coming, and crooked. 'Ça craint.'

'I don't speak French, Bruno.'

'Pardon. It sucks.'

Up ahead, Geiger saw what he had been waiting for – a narrow gravel turn-off that looked like it went nowhere. He reached into his bag and took out

Christine's customized kitchen knife, holding it out of Bruno's view.

'Bruno ... Pull over – up there on the right.'

The driver's eyes bounced to the mirror. 'Monsieur ...?'

Geiger leaned forward. 'Pull off the road here. Turn.'

'Take you to Tulette, no?'

Suddenly the knife had risen into view, and came to rest with the blade flat against Bruno's upper chest.

'Bruno ... Don't make me tell you again.'

There was something about his voice nearly as unsettling as the knife – that it could be velvet-soft and steel-hard at once – and Bruno slowed the car, turned the wheel, and pulled into the turn-off.

'Go to the bushes, then stop.'

The driver obeyed the order, and then put the car in park. His gaze didn't leave the face in the mirror.

'I have forty euros ... and take the car. Please don't hurt me.'

Geiger got a read on the unadorned sound of the man's fear.

'I'm not robbing you, Bruno.' Geiger took the knife away and sat back, keeping the weapon visible, resting on his thigh. He checked the view from the back again. They couldn't be seen from the road. 'Turn around to me.'

The driver undid his seat belt, and turned round. The Inquisitor watched what looked like confusion gathering in Bruno's sad eyes.

'Bruno ... Do you work for Dalton?'

The question put a row of ripples in the driver's forehead. '... Pardon?'

'Are you working for Dalton?'

'Not understand. Work for Taxi Provençal.' His stare kept making a detour to the knife before finding its way back to Geiger. 'This name – Dalton. Not know this name. Please, monsieur. You make ...' He scowled, searching for the proper word, and his hand went to his tie and pulled the knot loose. 'Ah. You make *mistake!*'

Geiger took out his pack of Lucky Strikes. He'd seen and heard enough.

'Do you mind if I smoke, Bruno?'

'... No.'

Geiger lit up, and then put the knife back in his bag. 'It was necessary for me to scare you, Bruno. I'm not going to hurt you. I want you to calm down – and listen closely.'

'I smoke too.'

Geiger held out the pack and Bruno took one from it. The cigarette shook in his hand as Geiger lit the end.

'You are taking me to a very dangerous place, Bruno. You understand "dangerous"?'

'Yes.'

'And depending on what happens – some people may prefer that you were dead. You understand "dead"?'

'*Dead?!*' His eyes scrunched into slits – like a myopic trying to read a street sign. He unbuttoned his collar. 'Why?'

'Do you know the phrase "loose end" in English?'

'No.'

'It means an unfinished part of a job – something that needs to be taken care of before the job can be considered done. Understand?'

The driver nodded. 'Oui. Details.'

'... and some of the people I'm involved with don't like loose ends.'

'Me – because I contact with you ... ?'

'Yes.

'They *okay* with killing?'

'When you were a chef – were you okay with killing the chickens?'

Bruno began shaking his head pensively, side to side – one of those moments when a gesture means the opposite of what it seems. He looked baffled, stunned – but he understood all too well.

'It could happen when you drop me off, Bruno – or tomorrow – or a week or month from now – or perhaps never.' Geiger flicked his butt out the window. 'I suggest you leave Avignon. Park the car in a garage and take a train someplace where nobody knows you. Stay a few weeks. You understand?'

Bruno ran his hand firmly down his face. The Shar Pei wrinkles stretched with the gesture, like a gloomy sad-sack in a cartoon.

'Impossible.'

Geiger unzipped his bag, took out a large wad of euros and started counting some off. With each bill, the furrow between Bruno's brows deepened.

'Here.' Geiger held the money out. 'Three thousand euros. It should last you a month.'

Bruno frowned at the offering.

'Take the money, Bruno.'

'Why?'

Geiger's eyes blinked – once. 'Take it.'

Bruno's hand suddenly flashed up in an angry wave.

'C'est délirant! Crazy! You say "go away". You say "take it ... take it". But why *give* it?'

Patience had always been an ally, but now Geiger could sense it standing off to the side – a bystander just out of sight, hesitant about joining in.

'Bruno ... Let's just say – it works best for me.' He dropped the money on the front passenger seat and zipped up the bag. 'You need to go.' He opened the door. 'You have the address you were taking me to?'

When Bruno sighed, his shoulders hitched up around his ears. He reached up to the driver's visor and slid out a piece of paper, and handed it to Geiger. It was three sentences of typed text.

> *Tournez à droite vers D51/D51A.*
> *Quand vous arrivez à une fourche, prenez la route sur votre droite.*
> *Allez tout droit jusqu'à l'impasse.*

'Simple,' said Bruno. He looked at the pile of money on the seat. Its presence made as much and as little sense as anything else that had just happened. 'You strange man, Ezra.'

'People have told me that. Goodbye, Bruno.'

Geiger got out of the car, closed the door, and watched the Renault turn around and head toward the road. He could gear his head toward the next phase now. He'd taken care of Céleste and Bruno. No innocent bystanders would suffer.

Standing in this dead-end path with the sound of traffic in front of him and a train approaching in the distance at his back, he had reached the last dot on the map where he could turn off and make his way alone.

When her Nextel dinged, Zanni and Victor gave each other a look.

'We play this his way,' she said. Victor nodded – and Zanni clicked on.

'We're here,' she said. 'Three minutes from the terminal in a hotel parking lot. Where are you?'

28

A gun-metal BMW 3 sedan cruised toward him, gravel crunching and grumbling beneath its wheels. The windows had a dense charcoal tint that sucked in and snuffed out the sunlight, and Geiger couldn't see who was driving.

There would be a number of things to keep track of in his presentation, various layers of interplay moving through the maze. From here on, Soames and Victor would interpret almost everything he said in very different ways – Victor knew where the endgame was and Soames didn't – and what Geiger knew, and how and when to dispense it, would determine who survived.

The car stopped and the front doors opened – Soames stepping out from the driver's side and Victor from the passenger's seat. Victor immediately lit a cigarette. There was a moment – when bodies finally arrive in the same physical space for the first time – that movement is briefly suspended while minds take measure of real flesh and bone. Size, posture, power.

Zanni leaned against the door-frame. 'Bonjour, Geiger ...'

'Hello, Zanni.'

Victor walked toward Geiger, his arm rising in the ritual offer of a hand. Geiger filed away a few observations: the man was fifty-something but rock-hard, and had bad knees – more likely arthritic than an injury.

'Geiger,' Victor said, 'good to meet you … in the flesh.'

Geiger grasped Victor's hand and shook it firmly – and settled on a seventy-five percent likelihood that Victor was left-handed.

'Hello, Victor.'

Their reflections were in each other's gaze like funhouse mirrors – one image born of another, tunneling deeper and deeper. Geiger had looked into the eyes of killers too many times – and had rarely glimpsed that maniacal spark or lurking evil poets often found in residence there. Eyes held a thousand secrets and truths, but they could lie like tongues.

'Geiger,' said Zanni, 'this is your show. Do you know where we're going?'

'We do now.' He held up the directions Bruno had given him. 'From the taxi driver. In French.'

He handed the paper to Victor and waited till his gaze went down to it, watching him read. The eyes moved minimally – and vertically, not horizontally. He was scanning information he already possessed.

'Have you ever been there, Victor?'

'Tulette? No,' said Victor. 'I've heard something of it, though.' Geiger was certain the tell was coming. Victor's hand rose, and his thumbnail began its ritual, up and down in the cleft of his chin. 'Small – a decent local wine, I think. There are many villages like it in Provence.'

'Let's go,' said Zanni. She dipped back into her seat and closed the door. Victor walked to the passenger door and gestured for Geiger to get in.

'You sit there, Victor. I'll sit in the back.'

Victor nodded. 'Certainly,' he said, flicked away his smoke, and sat down in shotgun.

Geiger picked up his bag and slid into the middle of the backseat. He took out his iPad. On the screen was a Google map of Provence, the route from Avignon to Tulette traced with a violet line. He leaned forward and handed it to Victor.

'This is the route. It's just under an hour's drive. And I bookmarked the satellite shot of what I presume is the house.'

'Excellent,' said Victor.

Geiger handed Dalton's note and the snuff box to Zanni. 'These were in a locker at the station.'

Zanni read the note, handed it to Victor, and gave her attention to Dalton's gift.

'A *snuff* box,' she said. 'How clever.' She opened it and eyed the contents. '*Usus* . . . ?'

'It's Latin. It means expertise,' he said. 'Something he and I discussed when he worked on me. Our bond, if you like.'

'Can we talk about how you see this thing?' she said. 'What you've been thinking about?'

'I need to sleep for a little while first. Twenty minutes.'

Geiger settled back and closed his eyes. Zanni frowned, put on her sunglasses, then spun off a perfect reverse-to-drive maneuver and headed for the highway.

He could smell her lavender scent.

*

He hadn't been sleeping, nor had he needed to. He'd wanted to take himself out of the three-way for a time and have a chance to hear the tone of simple back-and-forth between Zanni and Victor – but there had been few exchanges. He opened his eyes.

'Did you look at the satellite shot?'

'Yes,' said Victor. 'No other houses nearby. A good thing.'

They were on a two-lane road, going through a tiny village – a small café, a boulangerie, a single narrow street to turn on lined with a dozen two-story, faded pastel houses – and they were past it in less than a minute.

'Here are my thoughts,' said Geiger. 'We drive up the hill toward the house, pull off out of sight, leave the car and go on foot to a higher vantage point. We watch the house, see if anyone comes in or out, perhaps we can see movement inside.'

Up ahead, arching plane trees on each side made a tunnel of the road – their branches curled over the road and clasped above it.

'Then, I see two choices. I walk in alone – and at some point, you move in. Or – we go in together. We don't know the interior layout ... so we don't go in at night – we wait until first light tomorrow. Either way – the reason I'm here is Harry and Matheson. I know your job is to take Dalton out – but my only concern is keeping them alive.' His hand went to his jaw, to scratch at his beard, and he realized it was no longer there. 'Your thoughts.'

He and Zanni found each other via the rearview mirror – their faces frames with blank canvasses.

'If you go in alone – you're putting whatever plans he has for you in motion. Maybe he wants to swap war stories over a bottle of wine, maybe he wants to see how much sushi he can make out of you. I don't know, Geiger. If we go in together – the benefits are textbook. More interior coverage in less time – more discovery in less time – if he has guards in there, more decisions for them to make, more stress ...'

They came out of the cave of trees and quilts of farm-land stretched away on both sides, hues of a painter's palette – tan and light and darker greens, spotted with trees, solitary exclamation points of cypresses, clusters of umbrella pines and sycamores, white-flowered almonds, huddled groves of olive trees. Geiger had a flash of the house in Brooklyn, filled with his creations and the rich scent of woods and oil. They were already orphans. Who would be the one to adopt them?

'Key point, Geiger: Is Dalton going to let them go if you show up alone? My feeling is no – but it wouldn't shock me if he did, either. He's that crazy. If you believe he's going to make the trade, then maybe you should go in alone ... and we'll bide our time. But – I think we should go in together.'

Geiger nodded. 'Victor ... Your thoughts.'

'I agree with Zanni.'

'Nothing else?'

Victor turned round to face Geiger.

'Do you gamble, Geiger? Play cards?'

'No.'

'There is a saying – in English it would be "the dealer gets to cheat first".' The crimps at the ends of Victor's pale smile were like battle scars, testaments to time served. 'So, like Zanni, I should rather act than react. Always.'

He turned back around in his seat. Zanni glanced at him. 'The dealer gets to cheat first. I like that, Victor,' she said.

'My pleasure,' he said.

Geiger watched her profile grin very faintly. She didn't have doubts about Victor. She would be surprised to find herself dying by his hand – if she had a moment to consider that fact before she did.

They came into Tulette on Avenue de Provence and slowed at the small town center, where a Roman-numeraled clock stood on a ten-foot wrought-iron post. Place du Cheval Blanc was two parallel, one-way streets with a stretch of parking between them, flanked on both sides by rows of bare-branched, knobby-trunked trees. A dozen two-story buildings of old mortar and stone ran the length of each street, most with pastel shutters, some with narrow wrought-iron balconies, their ground levels housing shops – a brightly colored épicerie, a gift shop, a pâtisserie, a boucherie with an impressive window display of fresh crimson and brick-red meats. In the center was a fountain surrounding a statue of Ceres, the goddess of crops and fertility, who had only a few people to watch over from atop her six-foot pedestal.

Zanni pulled into a space in front of Café du Cours. Its green-awninged sidewalk terrace had eight small tables and chairs. One of them was occupied by two men in thick, high-collared sweaters reading sections of a shared newspaper, their cold espresso and idly burning cigarettes forgotten before them.

'Geiger,' said Zanni, 'what do you want if you get hungry?'

'Fruit, vegetables. Raw. But not very much.'

'Victor … A baguette and cheese for me. And water for all of us.'

Victor reached for his door. 'Café?'

'No,' said Zanni.

'Yes,' said Geiger. 'Black. No sugar.'

'And Victor …' said Zanni. 'Chocolate. With nuts if there is.'

'This, I already know,' he said.

He got out and walked toward the épicerie. Geiger's gaze followed him all the way to the shop's front door and inside.

'Zanni … There isn't a lot of time. Look at me.'

A dark presence had moved into Geiger's voice – and it made Zanni turn completely around in her seat. She took off her sunglasses.

'Go on,' she said.

'Victor works for Dalton.'

One of Zanni's brows rose, arching into a question mark above the bright violet eyes. Sharpshooter's eyes.

'What the hell are you talking about, Geiger?'

'The man you had tailing me told me. Dewey.'

The pictures came crashing into Zanni's mind like waves over the top of a storm wall. Her brother strapped into some kind of chair … Geiger holding something utile and blunt … his queries delivered in the silkiest, most even tones … No-Can-Dewey trying to hold his own with bravado against a force he could in no way appreciate.

'And you're sure he was telling the truth?'

'I'm right about these things.' From another's lips there might have been a ring of arrogance, or a ripple of false modesty with a faint smile, but it was prototypical Geiger. 'Concentrate, Zanni. Why would I make this up? What purpose would it serve me?'

Zanni shook her head. 'But I *know* Victor. We've worked—'

'Listen very carefully. I'm going to play something back for you. You came to pick me up at the turn-off near the station. When I handed Victor the directions he started to read them ... and I asked – 'Have you ever been there?' – and he answered, "Tulette? No." Remember?'

'Yes.'

'But I never said Tulette. I just said, "Have you been there?"'

'Christ, Geiger ... He was *reading the damn directions.*'

'Yes, he was – but there is no mention of Tulette in them.'

That awful feeling started to grab at her. She used to get it when she was racing, when she had the lead, set in her stride, top speed – and she sensed someone coming up, closing the gap, and she'd think to herself – *I'm in my groove ... I'm flying ... I put it all together just right – so how can this be happening?* She wondered if Geiger could see it in her face.

'Look at the directions, Zanni. There are route numbers and, I assume, places to turn – but the name of the town – Tulette – isn't there. Go ahead. And hurry.'

Zanni reached up to the passenger seat's visor and

pulled the paper out, and searched the lines for the name – hoping he was wrong ... but already knowing he wasn't.

'It was a natural slip on his part, Zanni. He's known where we were going from the start.' He glanced out the window. 'You've been set up.' The épicerie's door opened and Victor came out with two bags. 'Put it back. He's coming.'

Zanni slid the paper back in the visor. 'How did *you* know we were coming to Tulette?'

'Dewey told me. He was working for Dalton, too.'

The past tense – '*was* working' – made Zanni's pulse twitch.

'Is he dead?'

'Yes.'

'Did you—?'

The opening of the door shut her lips. Victor got in, put the larger bag on the floor between his legs, and took two coffees from the smaller bag and offered one to Geiger.

'Black. No sugar.'

Zanni watched Geiger take the paper cup. Both men pulled their lids off and took sips. There were too many things to focus on, too many feelings to tamp down, and her heart felt twice its size, cramped inside her chest with little room to beat. She pulled back inside herself – something one of her instructors had taught her years ago. He called it 'circling the wagons' – a way to dial everything down for just a second or two, if you needed to catch your emotional breath ...

Victor was talking to her now, lips moving, but she hadn't heard what he'd said.

'... with hazelnuts,' he finished, and cocked his head at her. 'Zanni ...?'

'... What?'

'The chocolate. It has hazelnuts in it.'

She nodded. 'I like them.' She glanced at Geiger, and he raised his eyes from the steam of his coffee to look back at her. 'Time to go,' she said, put on her sunglasses, and slowly pulled out into the street.

Victor could feel Geiger's stare on him like a tap on his shoulder. He turned to meet the gray, unblinking eyes for a moment, and then settled back in his seat. In the time it had taken to do his shopping, some new element had shown itself and left behind traces. He could sense it.

He took the directions out from the visor. 'Everything is good?'

'Everything's good,' said Zanni, and got back onto Avenue du Provence, heading away from the town center.

Victor took another sip of coffee and let it linger in his mouth before he swallowed. He was near-certain of one thing. Everything was *not* good.

They were pulled over on the side of the road, one hundred yards from Route 51. Across the intersection, the dusty, narrow way turned to gravel and started a steep climb. The higher the road went, the thicker the forest on the east side grew.

Victor looked up from the directions in his hand and pointed. 'We go across, and up the hill and stay right, and the house is at the very top.'

Zanni was looking down at the iPad in her lap – at a

satellite image of the area and its solitary rectangular house – bordered on one side by woods and three sides by vineyard fields, their rows of vines stretching out in long, even lines. Superimposed on the shot was a digital grid with numbers at each junction of its bright blue lines. The absoluteness of it was helping to fence in her thoughts, as they turned more wild.

'The house is seventy-six feet long, twenty-two feet wide,' she said. 'There's a break in the forest a hundred yards up the road – we'll pull in there as far as we can and walk the rest of the way up through the woods. The closest point from the treeline to the house is sixty-one yards.'

Geiger was listening – but he was thinking about killing, the specific act of it. From the start he'd made the decision to keep the subject tucked away and unconsidered until the relevant moment, and now it was time to bring it out and explore the possibilities – the timing, logistics, and the repercussions. The situation had become mathematical in its purity, as logical as a geometric equation – and whether or not Zanni believed what he had told her was not part of it. Victor had to die, and Geiger would arrive at the answers to how and when by slipping inside Victor's mind.

Victor's true function would be moving into the foreground very soon, an actor taking center-stage for his big scene – delivering Geiger safe and sound ... and disposing of Zanni. Dewey's absence would add to his load and pump up his stress – certainly, Victor had been reworking how things would play out since Dewey disappeared – but that wouldn't slow him down. Geiger knew the man. He had met Victor many times over the last dozen years, in cities all over the world. The trackers, the finders, the snatchers of Joneses, delivering and then retrieving them – and sometimes the last faces a Jones ever saw. Victor was the kind of man who, on occasion, killed people as part of his job ... and slept soundly in his bed, perhaps waking after a pleasant dream. They went about the business with different techniques, in different shades of darkness, but they were alike in a particular way – they were all missing the one, same cluster of neurons in their brains that produced the singular spark of compassion, and the sense of kinship with their own species. Maybe it had been burned or beaten or cut out of them – with a hot iron, or a fist, or a razor. Maybe they had been born without it. But the lack of it made them very good at what they did.

And Geiger knew this because he had been a close cousin to them all for much of his life.

Zanni hit the gas. There were no cars coming either way, and she drove across the intersection and reached the road. The gravel started chattering loudly beneath the tires and she shifted down, and they slowly began the ascent.

29

They had pulled off the gravel road onto the dirt path into the woods and been able to drive in fifty yards deep before the tall, lean Scots pines became more crowded and barred their way.

Now Geiger and Zanni stood staring at each other across opposite sides of the hood while Victor, at the open trunk, took items from two cases and put them in a black canvas tote. Geiger had been allotting half his thoughts to what Victor was thinking. With no word from Dewey for so long, the man likely assumed he was no longer alive, and that there was a good chance Geiger was the cause of death. So Victor's main concern would be – what, if anything, did Dewey confess before he died? What did Geiger know? And the supreme irony that had to have occurred to the Frenchman – if Geiger tried to take him out, Victor could not respond with equal intent. His job was to bring Geiger in alive, unharmed.

Victor picked up the tote and closed the trunk. 'Ready.'

Zanni pressed the key in her hand, the car locks clicked shut, and without a word she headed up the hill. The two men followed after her, a very soft crunch to their steps on the carpet of needles underfoot. A few voices took turns trilling from up in the high branches – sweet, short bunches of notes. Geiger looked up. The sound reminded him of something, but he couldn't nail down what it was …

Zanni glanced back. 'We go to the highest vantage point first and see what that angle gives us …'

… and then Geiger knew. The tiny bells at Christine's patio – and his memory swerved to the bedroom. Christine lying asleep and warm beside him, her hand in his, as if one lonely piece of her had found a place where it belonged …

'… then we make our way back down to the closest point at the treeline.'

… while his mother came alive within him – and with her resurrection the knowledge that he had been cherished …

'If we find we have a kill-shot somewhere, at least we know we have that option.'

… and that his simple presence had given another joy.

'Yes,' said Victor. 'That would be good to know.'

Zanni stared at Geiger, waiting for a response. 'How do you feel about a kill-shot, Geiger, if the opportunity presents itself?'

'As you said – it would be an option.'

They were like identical twins who speak to each other in their own secret language. And they weren't talking about Dalton.

Zanni nodded, and the trio continued up the slope, weaving through the pines. Geiger heard a muted grunt come out of Victor. His knees didn't like the climb.

*

'Scuze me. Sorry,' said the man in the gray suit as he pressed up against Ezra. The subway had already been crowded when Ezra and his mother got on at Eighty-sixth Street, and now the Forty-second Street horde was pushing in the car, not to be denied a ride no matter how slim the space or the odds.

'You okay?' asked his mother.

Ezra's dark scowl met her. 'Yes, Mom. I'm okay.' His expression had set in before they'd left the apartment and had become a permanent fixture on his face.

'You can lose the scowl, y'know,' she said. 'You made your point.'

'This is a bad idea. A *really* bad idea.'

'Ez ...'

He shook his head wisely. 'Mom ... Going to talk to these people. Giving them information. Telling them stuff they may not know. Yeah – maybe they can help. Or maybe they come after all of us ...'

'You don't necessarily know the right answer to this.'

'Maybe not – but Geiger does, and if he thought it was a good idea he would have gotten in touch with them.'

'Geiger is always right?'

'As a matter of fact – yeah, he is. He always knows what to do.'

The train started up again with a sudden jolt, and the mass of bodies swayed a few inches – but there was no reason to worry about losing one's balance.

'Ezra ... I can't just leave this to a man I've never met – not if it's about your father's safety. And Harry's too. There are people who know how to deal with this.'

'Yes, they do – but that's the point, Mom. We don't

know if they're gonna be the good guys or the bad guys. We could end up helping guys like Hall find them ...' He tried to scrunch around a few degrees, but couldn't. 'And the good guys wanna put Dad in prison anyway.' He knew it was a lame comment, but he was running out of ways to try and dissuade her.

'I can't *not* do anything,' she said. 'And if it's a choice between your father going to prison or dying, then I'll take that chance.'

'Well, since when do you care what happens to Dad?'

His mother flinched. It wasn't so much the force of the blow as the tender spot it hit.

'That is a really shitty thing to say, Ez – and you know it.'

He hadn't meant to hurt her. He wasn't really even mad at her. But he knew he was right and it was making him crazy. He felt like a war vet trying to explain the nature of battle to one who'd never served. He'd been in the midst of it. He'd seen men die, he'd learned the cold rules of treachery.

He couldn't quite relinquish his scowl, but it wrinkled with contrition. 'You're right, Mom. I'm sorry I said that.'

She cocked her head, and then gave him a soft smile.

'Ez ... I've never made believe I understand what you went through – not for one second. You thought you were going to die ... and he saved your life – and I don't know what that feels like either.' She pulled her hand up out of the crunch and ruffled his hair. 'Just so you know I think about it.'

'I know you do, Mom.'

'So let's do this and see what they have to say.'

Ezra sighed, and shook his head. 'I love you, Mom – but you don't get it. What they *say* doesn't count.'

The laser rangefinder in the binoculars read '257 FT/44 DEG' – focused on the only window of the south end of the farmhouse, three feet wide and four feet high. Inside, all that was visible was a small wooden table with a vase full of lavender against a wall of time-yellowed mortar.

Zanni lowered her binoculars. The three of them were standing atop the hill between two trees.

'The south window could be any kind of room,' Zanni said. 'I can't tell.'

Victor continued peering through his binoculars. 'Front door looks like old wood. Casement windows.' At this stage, it was the Inquisitor's ear that listened to each statement Victor made – and he could hear the echo of polished guile like a single, barely skewed note in a symphony of a hundred players. And he wondered how Victor would have fared in a session – and decided it would have been a long, exhausting event.

The house was old, made of pine, a single level. There was a twenty-foot-wide apron of grass around the front and sides. A few yards from the back of the house was a small shed, a square garden and then a field of heather – and stretching out to the north, south, and east the forsaken vineyards, their four-foot-high rows of dead, twisted plants like markers in a graveyard. Once the trio came out of the trees, that would be their only cover – and they would have to crouch or crawl to make use of it.

'Most likely,' said Geiger, 'there are five or six rooms,

three weight-bearing interior walls. A house this old, the inside walls are probably mortar with thin wood slats eighteen to twenty-four inches apart. They might not stand up to a good pounding at the right spots.'

He lowered the binoculars and turned to see both Victor and Zanni staring at him with matching, cock-eyed expressions.

'I know how to build things,' he said, and handed the binoculars back to Victor.

Zanni put her pair around her neck and pointed. 'I'm going a little west to see if there's a better view of the back.'

The two men watched her walk away. Victor took out his Gitanes.

'She doesn't allow me a smoke near her,' he said, and offered the pack to Geiger. Geiger slid one out, Victor took one, flicked his lighter and lit them up. Geiger watched Zanni's graceful form disappear within the trees.

'You've been at this a long time, Victor.'

Victor's smile was like that of a mourner speaking fondly of the deceased. 'I sometimes think *too* long – but then they come to me with another job.' He shrugged. 'We do what we know, yes?'

Geiger took a deep drag on his smoke. 'Have you ever met Dalton? Made a delivery to a job he was working?'

'No. But one hears of him over the years ... as I had of you. The Inquisitor, yes? Zanni has told me what he did to you – and what you did to him. It strikes me, Geiger – it is a most courageous thing you are doing. How many men of ten would make this choice, I could not say.'

'Choice is not a word I would use, Victor.'

'No?' Victor studied Geiger openly, his interest clearly sincere. 'I would not have thought the Inquisitor would act out of sentiment.'

'I'm retired.'

Geiger took another pull on his cigarette. Each time he raised his hand to his lips, he felt the very slightest pull of the two six-inch-long strips of duct tape he had fixed horizontally across his chest to hold Christine's knife in place, in the dent of the sternum between his pectorals. He'd put on a sweater when getting dressed this morning to help hide the customized handle.

Victor dropped his cigarette butt and started mashing it into the pine needles. 'May I ask . . . ? Why did you crush Dalton's fingers?'

'I decided that he should retire too.'

Victor looked back up at him. Any hint of antipathy or irony was not to be found there. Nor in his voice.

'Well,' Victor said, 'it would seem he is – how do you say? – back in business.'

The surrounding quiet bordered on silence. There was a small congregation of thin, flowing clouds in the sky. The sun looked pale and tired, nearing the end of its shift, and above it, to the west, was the moon's ghost. It would be a bright, huge golf ball in the night sky.

She could see the back of the house clearly from here. Three windows with their curtains drawn, two others that were boarded up, a back door, and an overhang with a small, grey Peugeot parked beneath it. The little shed was corrugated steel.

Zanni lowered the glasses and leaned against a tree. Her mind was like the inside of a hive – a thousand thoughts buzzing, coming and going.

Dewey was dead.

Cause of death – Geiger.

She was waiting to be hit with something primal – but felt only a light, fuzzy melancholy settling around her. It was true they had shared very little for a long time – that things other than love connected them – need on Dewey's part, and an odd sense of obligation on hers that she'd never taken time to understand. But he was still her brother. Shouldn't there be something more? Had she become so skilled at censoring her feelings that she couldn't feel them at all? A cold wave of grief? A pang of outrage?

And what of retribution?

What had Geiger done to him – before killing him? The question brought back flickering pictures of the Inquisitor at his dark trade – and she clamped her eyes shut, wiping them away. All that would have to wait. She knew where her focus had to land.

When her cell had rung in the hotel room and she'd heard Geiger's voice on the line, she'd felt that cool rush of reacquired control, of misplaced pieces settling back into their proper spots. But Geiger had worked some sort of alchemy – turning the hard, precise angles of the scenario pliant and unpredictable. Now there was a decision she would have to make quickly, almost on the run – because time had become an unstable element, about to reach critical mass.

As had Victor.

*

They had moved deeper into the woods, in the cover of the pines, as they came back down the hill.

'The two windows in back that are boarded up ... Strong possible that's where he has them,' said Zanni. She checked their progress on the iPad's blue grid and stopped. 'Closest point is here.'

She turned and walked in the direction of the house, went into a crouch for the last ten yards and then lay down on her stomach near the edge of the trees. The men joined her, one on each side. Geiger felt the ground press the knife's taped handle into his chest.

The sun was on the horizon, and dusk was soaking up the light from the sky like a sponge. It would be dark in half an hour, and the moon was already growing light-bulb bright.

Zanni and Victor raised their binoculars to their eyes.

'Geiger,' she said. 'What about a kill-shot if we have one?'

'I don't like it.'

Zanni brought her glasses down. 'Go on.'

'Dalton didn't snatch Matheson and Harry on his own. He has at least one, maybe two or more people working for him.' He leaned forward and looked past Zanni to Victor. 'Doesn't that sound right to you, Victor?'

Victor lowered his binoculars. 'Yes,' he said. 'Absolument.'

'And where are they?' said Geiger. 'Almost certainly – inside. Right?'

Victor nodded. 'I would think – yes. It only makes sense.'

'Zanni ... Taking down Dalton from out here could mean the next thing that happens is someone inside kills Matheson and Harry. Victor ... Isn't that what you would do?'

'Perhaps, yes. That could also make sense.'

'If they'd seen your face, that would be reason to kill them ...'

'Yes.'

The two men could have been discussing their preferred stitches for knitting a scarf.

Geiger's gaze settled back on Zanni. 'That isn't why I came here. You know that.'

Zanni watched the stone-gray eyes. There was no hint there that he'd just put a brazen play on Victor – literally an in-your-face performance, pushing buttons, toying with minds. Having a discussion with Victor – *about Victor*. It made her wonder how long it had taken Geiger to make Dewey give up his secrets.

'All right,' she said.

Geiger sat up. 'We move in separately from three different entries. As you said, Zanni ... It will give us the most coverage and discovery in the shortest time. But ...' His fingers came to life on his knees, playing a slow beat. 'If either of you finds Dalton – you are not to kill him.'

He turned his head. *Click*. Then he took Zanni's binoculars from her, lay back down, and trained the glasses on the house.

Harry was making a list. The Top Ten Best Days of his life, in no particular chronological order. The first five had been easy.

... Losing his virginity at eighteen with his girlfriend, Abby, at her parents' apartment while watching *Raiders of the Lost Ark* on HBO. His performance had been light years from stellar, but he felt terrific that he'd finally gotten it out of the way.

... Watching Sophie come into the world at Lenox Hill Hospital after Christine had twisted and growled 'Merde!' through twenty-three hours of labor. Around hour thirteen he'd started begging her to agree to a C-section, or at least an epidural, but she'd refused – and, between extraordinarily inventive curses, had informed the kind and fretful obstetrician that she would pull out his liver with her bare hands if he listened to Harry.

... His finding out, four months into his first post-college job – as a researcher at the *Times* – that his elders had given him the nickname 'Shovel' in honor of his remarkable talent for digging up information. He could never have guessed how that skill would serve him in the future.

... The night early on in the courtship, when he and Christine were sitting in his small, cluttered living room at Seventy-eighth Street reading different sections of the newspaper. He had looked up to discover her staring at him. 'What?' he'd said. 'I had a hard time at work today,' she'd answered. 'Why?' he'd asked. 'I missed you, Harry. All day long. Tu m'as manqué.'

... The night in Central Park when Geiger had come out of the rain and saved his life – and made him realize, as pitch-black, fucking miserable and self-destructive as he was, that he really didn't want to die.

'Harry ...' said Matheson.

Harry opened his eyes. Matheson was on his feet,

turning and stretching and bending as best he could, trying to loosen up his stiff, aching body.

'Yeah? What is it?'

'Nothing. The position you were lying in, I couldn't tell if you were breathing. I just wanted to see if you were alive.'

'I was making a list. The ten best days of my life.'

Matheson leaned back against the wall. It looked as if he'd have fallen down if he hadn't.

'And the reason you're making this list . . . ?'

'Feels good. Makes you think about all this great stuff. Gets you back there . . . you remember things – how something felt, how somebody looked . . .'

'Are you getting ready to die, Harry?'

'Yeah, guess I am.' Any amount of talking made him want to swallow, so he did, knowing it would hurt like hell – and he was right. 'Christ, David . . . I feel really fucking stupid, and pissed off – and I don't want to die feeling like that – so I'm doing my Top Ten Greatest Hits. Why not go out with that stuff – right?'

'Makes perfect sense to me.'

Harry's hand rose and gingerly tapped at his face. 'My face feels like a loofah. Is that what it looks like?'

'How long were you married, Harry?'

'Seven years. You?'

'Eight.'

'How many were really good?'

Matheson shrugged. 'Maybe four. You?'

Harry sighed – and slowly, a shadow of a smile came to his lips. 'All of them,' he said.

The door opened and Dalton stepped inside.

'Good evening.' He sniffed the air, his nose wrinkling.

'Getting ripe in here, isn't it? Not to worry. This may be your last night here – so I've come to ask what you'd like for your last dinner. There are beef tomatoes, squash, leftovers of that delicious ham, and some veal.'

Harry pushed himself up into a sit. 'That mean you're letting us go?'

'Or ...' said Matheson, '... not?'

'Don't worry, boys. You'll be leaving here.'

Harry gave a sick little smile at the answer. 'Is Geiger here?'

'Not yet – but I think he's very near.'

Matheson started walking. His jangling chain let him get four feet from Dalton before it went taut. The two men regarded each other without expression. Had Matheson leaned forward and reached out, his blood-ied fingertips might have brushed Dalton's flannel shirt.

Dalton pushed his glasses up on his nose. 'Something on your mind, David?'

'I just wanted one last look at you – up close.'

'And what do you see? Tell me.'

'... Something that shouldn't be alive.'

Dalton nodded slowly. 'All in good time, David,' he said. 'All in good time.' He turned and headed toward the door. 'I'll bring you two a little of everything. The veal is a bit tough, but tasty.'

He opened the door and went out. Matheson turned to Harry.

'I never wanted to kill anyone before. It's a real bad feeling.'

Harry nodded silently. He knew exactly what Matheson meant – and had nothing to add.

Matheson went back to his mattress and resumed his

post against the wall. His eyes dropped closed. At this point, it was easier than keeping them open. Exhaustion felt like a virus. And the pain and shackles had unlocked something in him – anger in a new, mutant form. It jumped in his veins. Skittered about in his brain. His purest anger had always been a righteous element, finding its footing on the most basic of creeds – *Tell the people the truth … Just tell the goddamn, fucking truth* – but this fury that jabbed at his insides – it was primal, coarse, mean. Of the blood. It was his life, Harry's life, Geiger's, and Ezra's, too. And nothing was unthinkable now. Nothing was impermissible.

He let himself slide back down the wall till his ass hit the mattress. His hands slid across the surface and came to rest at the mattress's edge, at the rounded ribbing. His fingertips played at it. He opened his eyes. The ribbing ran all the way around the top edge of the mattress. It was half an inch in diameter.

'Harry … ?'

'Yeah?'

'What do you call this? The border thing around the mattress?' He tapped the ribbing.

Harry brought a weary eye to Matheson's bobbing finger. 'That? That's called the border thing around the mattress.'

'Harry …'

'Jesus, David … What the fuck does it matter what it's *called*?'

'Fuck you, Harry – and let me rephrase the question: Do you happen to know what's *inside* the border thing around the mattress?'

Harry looked at the edging of his own mattress.

He reached over and squeezed it between thumb and forefinger.

'Feels like a cord inside a cotton sleeve.'

'That's what it feels like to me too, Harry.'

Harry looked up at him. It was something of an effort to shift his mental gears into a constructive mode, but he was making progress. He moved his other hand into play, grabbing the ribbing tightly, and started to tug. The stitching that connected it to the mattress stretched but didn't tear. Not yet.

'We can pull it loose,' he said. 'Definitely.' He repositioned himself for better leverage, making clamps of his fingers, and pulled hard. Slowly the threads gave ground, and daylight started to show between the ribbing and mattress. 'Coming ...' Harry said – and an inch-wide length of the ribbing gave way. 'Got it.' Harry gave a good yank and the edging started to tear off with a *scrunnnnch*.

'Gonna take me longer, Harry.' Matheson held up his bandaged hand. 'No fingertips on this one. Do you know how to make a lasso knot?'

Harry kept pulling. 'No.'

'I'll show you. It's easy.'

'You were a Boy Scout?'

'No. A summer on a dude ranch when I was thirteen.'

Harry was doing some calculating. 'About eighteen feet of it around the top, eighteen around the bottom. That's a lot of rope, David.'

'More than enough. What's that old saying?'

Harry had most of it free. 'Give a guy enough rope to hang himself ...'

'Right,' said Matheson. 'That's the one.'

30

When the sun had taken its leave, the sky quickly let the night in and turned an inky blue-black – and in minutes the moon became a witness to it all. It was that midmost time – when creatures on the dayshift had punched out and the nightshift was coming on board – so living sounds were few and far between. In the farmhouse only two windows, front mid-center, were lit.

They sat in a row, facing the farmhouse, twenty yards in from the treeline, eating silently. Geiger took small bites of a pear. He had two carrots and a bottle of water in his lap. Zanni and Victor each had a baguette and a chunk of brie, an apple, and water.

While Zanni had a bite of cheese and either tore off a chunk of bread to go with it or took a chomp out of the apple, Victor was more ritualistic – slicing his brie and apple meticulously, just so, with a spring-loaded hunting knife, wielding the blade as if he'd been born with it in his hand.

Not once had they seen movement or proof of life inside a window.

Victor closed his knife, put the remainder of his

baguette and cheese back in the tote and tossed the apple core away.

'Geiger ...' he said. 'Cheese, bread. You do not like these?'

'I don't eat things that have been cooked or processed.'

'A smart man. Me ... I cannot resist. You will live longer than most of us.' Victor got to his feet. 'Now, another vice – a cigarette – which Zanni does not allow close enough to be smelled.'

He strolled off farther into the trees.

Zanni's head slowly turned, bright eyes like a lighthouse beam in a black night, watching Victor go. She had worked it out in her head – covered all the angles. That didn't mean she was certain of every move she'd make, but right this moment that was not a burning concern – options would present themselves. She waited patiently until Victor faded into the dark – then turned back to Geiger.

'Tell me exactly what Dewey told you. Fast.'

'You called Victor and offered him the job – to back me up ... and kill Dalton. But Victor was already working for Dalton – he and Dewey snatched Matheson and Harry. Victor tells Dalton about your offer ... and Dalton says take it. We know from his video that Dalton was worried about one of Deep Red coming with me. Now, he'd know where you were every step of the way – walking right into your own execution. That is what Dewey told me.'

'I don't know, Geiger. All right – that's what Dewey *said*. But what are the fucking odds of Victor working for Dalton the same time that I offer him a job? I mean – Christ ...'

'Why did you call Victor? Because you needed an experienced contractor who was fluent in French and English and knew his way around Paris.'

'Yes.'

'And Victor is the best in that category?'

'Yes, he is.'

'All right. And who would Dalton be looking for at his end?'

Zanni did something with her lips that made them crimp at the ends. It looked childish to Geiger. It reminded him of Ezra.

'An experienced contractor,' she said, 'fluent in French and English who knew his way around Paris.'

'And the reason you're trying to stop yourself from accepting what seems clear – is that you trusted Victor. It's as much about your failing as his betrayal.'

Zanni's eyes suddenly flared with tiny, shimmering violet flames. 'Fuck you, Geiger. Save the psycho-analysis. I don't need it.'

One of the two shining windows of the farmhouse went black. Zanni took in a long, slow breath – as if she were trying to stoke something inside her ... or gathering strength to keep something inside from getting out. She pulled the zipper of her jacket down, slid a hand inside and took out a silver Beretta nine millimeter, then reached in a pocket for a coal-black silencer – and fitted it into the gun's muzzle. Geiger took the last bite of his pear as he watched her start screwing the silencer in.

'Why did you kill Dewey?' she asked.

Geiger had spent years exploring the different approaches and deliveries of a question – because, in the end, that is what IR is about. That is the moment when things can crystallize – and the tone, engagement and timing might say as much about the asker as the question. Her voice had been cool and flat, but there was something animated and twisting below its surface – like an easy-going river whose hidden undercurrent could prove deadly to an unwary swimmer.

'I didn't kill Dewey,' he said.

She looked up at him. Her hand made a final turn of the silencer.

'I took him to an abandoned store. He was able to work free of his restraints. We fought. We stumbled around. A water tank fell on him – and crushed his chest.'

He watched her working her way through a maze of feelings and logistics. She had choices to make.

'What are you going to do, Zanni?'

She raised the weapon and extended her arm into a firing position, then squinted to check that the silencer was in line with the barrel. The gun's line of sight was an inch left of Geiger's face.

'What are you going to do?'

She lowered the gun and put it in her jacket pocket. 'I'm going to ask Victor if it's true.'

'I'll go with you.'

'No you won't. This isn't about you, it's about me – and I do my job just as well as you do yours.' She got to her feet. 'So you'll stay the hell out of it.'

She looked hard as stone, and her anger was in the air around them like sudden heat. She zipped her jacket back up, turned, and walked into the woods.

*

Victor heard the footsteps crushing pine needles and turned, and blew a perfect smoke ring as he watched her approach. Zanni stopped fifteen feet away from him. The trees let a drizzle of moonlight in.

'Did you ask him about Dewey?' Victor said.

'Dewey's dead.'

Victor frowned. 'I am sorry, Zanni.'

'But before he died, he told Geiger something.'

'What was that?'

'He said that you were working for Dalton.'

Victor nodded mechanically at the news. 'I see.' He sighed. 'I must confess – when Dewey went missing, I feared that might happen if Geiger had him.' He took a long drag of his cigarette. 'Take no offense, my dear – but your brother was not made for this work.'

He dropped his smoke, and very slowly ground it out with his heel. His thumbnail went to his cleft, up and down in consideration of the situation. He finally looked up at her.

'So, Zanni ... What are you going to do?'

Zanni's hand came out of her pocket with the Beretta. She raised it.

Victor's slow smile was proof he could still appreciate fate's twisted sense of humor. He stared at the mouth of the silencer. There was not the slightest tremble in her grip. She was close enough that he could see her finger tighten on the trigger.

Geiger heard the faint, muffled *ffffp* of the shot – and got to his feet. He moved quickly toward the sound – and slowed to a stop when he saw her, thirty yards away, her back to him, standing over the motionless body as she fired again.

She put the gun in her pocket and headed back toward Geiger in a steady, unhurried stride. As she came even with him she met his gaze.

'Let the animals have him,' she said, and kept on walking. 'I'm going back to the car. Getting cold.'

He sat at the kitchen table and slowly drew the blade of the antique scalpel back and forth across the hone, each stroke identical to the last. The ritual's repetitious nature, coupled with the soft, rough murmur – *swiff* ... *swiff* ... *swiff* – was soothing. He sharpened the tool every day for half an hour, using a striped-gray Belgian coticule whetstone, timing the movements to the beat of his pulse.

And this was often the time when the madness arrived – his wizard accomplice stopping by for a visit, casting a spell – changing the field of lavender into a tribe of bloodthirsty serpents ... turning the large whorls in the tabletop's wood into plaintive faces, desperate souls trapped beneath the ice of a frozen lake ... transforming the bottle of dishwashing detergent into a tiny nun, hands clasped at her waist, reciting her prayer in sweet, devout tones – *I abandon myself into your hands, do with me what you will, I am ready for all ...*

Dalton remembered the two doctors entering his room in the clinic after the second surgery – faces stiff and lips pursed to mask the futility. They came and stood at his bedside like mourners at a wake – and he heard the unexpected undercurrent in Dr. Ling's voice when he finally spoke. *'There is something we wish to discuss with you. Something to consider ...'*

He put the scalpel and whetstone down on the table, and raised his hands to his face. In so doing, his gaze caught a glimpse of something beyond them. He lowered his hands as his optical gears involuntarily refocused, and stared at the chair directly across from him, on the other side of the table. Its arms were human, its hands folded together on the table, fingers entwined, flexing calmly – and it had acquired a head atop its flat, lacquered pine back.

Geiger's head. The unblinking slate eyes perused him.

As always, during the visions some straggling rational element of Dalton's mind came along for the ride.

'Not even here yet – and already back again?'

'Why are you doing this?' said the head.

Dalton sighed. 'As the poet said – "How do I *hate* thee? Let me count the ways ..."' He leaned back in his chair. The old wood squeaked. 'And I don't think it's presumptuous to say I've done very well by you, Geiger.'

'How so?'

'Well ... I envisioned a scenario with an effective dilemma for you – constructed it in such a way that you felt it accessible ... that you could devise and invest in a strategy, and preparation ... Am I wrong?'

'No. But you didn't really answer my question.'

'It isn't really *your* question. You're just an hallucination. So it's really *my* question.' Dalton's elastic grin stretched. 'Why am I doing this? Because, thanks to you, I've become a disciple of suffering in a very new way – and I am going to blow your fucking mind.'

Geiger nodded. 'I see.'

Dalton shook his head slowly. 'No, you don't. That's the whole point.'

Geiger's hands began cracking their knuckles, one by one, but after each *pop!* the deft, elegant fingers continued applying pressure – until the digits snapped at the base joints and hung loose, splayed, crooked – just as Dalton's had when Geiger had finished with them last summer.

'That's a neat trick,' said Dalton.

The hands collapsed into a tangled, wriggling heap of fingers on the table. Some decided to leave the pack and strike out on their own, and Dalton watched them inch-worm off in different directions. A few headed toward him, and he smiled like a patient shepherd.

'That's right. Good boys. Come to Poppa.'

Harry was on his knees on the mattress, the knotted cord in hand, practicing playing cowboy. His water jug was on the floor, six feet away – and he was flipping the looped end of the cord at it, trying to lasso it. He'd been keeping count. So far he was five for twenty.

Matheson was sitting cross-legged on his mattress, blinkless in thought.

Harry flicked another shot, and missed. He looked at his palms. They were each missing two circles of skin that Dalton had sliced out, and the tentative scabs had come off. They hurt. They burned.

'I suck at this.'

'We need blood.'

'Huh?'

Matheson looked up. 'To help sell it.'

'What are you talking about?'

'Blood on the floor. So it'll look real.' He pulled up his smock and sleeves and stared at his limbs. 'Where's a good place to cut yourself to get blood – where you can stop it before losing too much?'

'I once got a bad gash in my ankle – that really bled.'

'How'd you stop it?'

'Compression. Holding it up.'

Matheson ran a fingertip over the edges of the steel shackle around his ankle – and scowled.

'Too smooth . . .' He slid over to the edge of the mattress, bent his leg so the shackle rested on the floor, then took hold of it and started scraping it back and forth against the rough concrete. After a dozen strokes he stopped and felt the edge.

'Is it getting sharp?'

'It'll get there,' he said, and went back to work.

Zanni watched Geiger through the windshield. He was leaning against a tree smoking a cigarette. Neither of them had said a word on the walk back to the car, and once inside they'd sat silently for thirty minutes.

'I'm going to have a smoke,' he'd finally said, and stepped outside.

She couldn't get a handle on him. There was something primal there – stripped down, with little want, without artifice, a closer cousin to an animal that belonged in the forest than a worldly man . . .

. . . and there was the Inquisitor – the steel-trap mind, the nerveless, sleek machine, cold prescriber of pain . . .

. . . and there was the man who chose to try and save her life . . .

*

Geiger was drifting in a sea of women – their scents, silken touch, the tug of secret knowledge. He closed his eyes. Their music was swirling in his head, the voices floating on the water in golden strands – sad ballads and lullabies and siren songs ...

A rough, wet snort opened his eyes. Ten yards off to his right, a massive 300-pound wild boar was staring at him with milky eyes, its sharp tusks picking up the moonlight. Geiger straightened up – the animal took a step forward – and Geiger slowly headed for the car ...

From where Zanni sat, clearly the beast was not satisfied with Geiger's pace – because it suddenly charged at him. Geiger kicked into a sprint, reaching the car and swinging the passenger door open, and slipped inside and pulled the door closed a second before the boar rammed into it. The car shook.

'Jesus ...' whispered Zanni.

They watched it through the window. It seemed unfazed by the impact, and not particularly angry.

'Wild boar?' she whispered.

'Yes.'

'That's the ugliest animal I've ever seen.'

'And much faster than I would have thought.'

She glanced at him. One might have expected a grin to accompany the remark, but not with Geiger.

They watched the boar start away with another snort – the tankish body moving slowly over the forest carpet, its large snout rooting for food.

Victor's absence was as distinct as his presence had been. The last entry on his lengthy resumé of sins would be one of the classics, the fraternal trinity – greed, fed by arrogance, delivering betrayal. Carmine called it Zombie Poker, because once you'd made that particular bet the odds were you were already one of the living dead. Geiger thought of all those who had made the same play and ended up in his session rooms – and he wondered if wild boars ate dead, human flesh.

Zanni let her seatback down six inches. 'I want to ask you something, Geiger,' she said.

'Go ahead.'

'You'd planned on doing this solo. From the start, even back in Brooklyn – right?'

'Yes.'

'And this morning, you were free and clear – but you called me ... to bring me back in ... even though you don't trust me.'

'I don't remember saying I didn't trust you.'

'Even though you *know* my job is to kill Dalton ... and to that end you and Harry and Matheson were expendable.'

'Yes.'

'So you brought me back into this why?'

'It became clear to me that Victor would murder you, eventually,' he said. 'I actually saw an image in my mind of his killing you. With a knife.'

Zanni's head did a twenty-degree tilt at him. It was one of the strangest things anyone had ever said to her. '*I actually saw an image in my mind of his killing you ...*'

'So you called to save me?'

It was a toneless question seeking information. A bank teller asking a customer what denomination of bills he would like. She had distilled the question like smooth

Scotch. Whatever feelings she had about the subject were undetectable.

'Zanni ... Let's just say – I know what works best for me.'

'All right,' she said. 'And don't worry, Geiger. I won't tell anyone. Your secret's safe with me.'

She looked away, past her window. As the night stretched out, more wild voices were talking to it, and sets of golden eyes blinked.

'Geiger ... Why do you hardly ever blink?'

'Remember I told you that I spent my nights in a small closet as a child?'

'Yes.'

'I never slept very much. I listened to music on a cassette player all night. It was pitch-black, and I got used to not knowing if my eyes were open or closed. It was all the same. I think that's why.'

'Why were you punished like that?'

'It wasn't punishment. I didn't realize that until last night – when I had a dream. My father was trying to make me strong.'

I'm going to find a way to make you strong. Stronger than your mother. Stronger than me. So cry now, for the last time.

Geiger shifted in the seat. The sudden yanking open of the door had set his shoulder throbbing. It had been twelve hours since it had been iced.

'And I have a question for you,' he said.

'Ask.'

'The anger.'

'What about it?'

'It's there all the time?'

She turned to him. 'Keeps me sharp, Geiger. In my job I can't be the strongest, so I have to be the sharpest one in the room.'

She reached into the backseat, took something out of one of the grocery bags and put it in her lap. She opened the white paper wrapping and spread it back to reveal a three-inch-square piece of lustrous chocolate.

Geiger watched curiously as she broke off a chunk and put it in her mouth – but she didn't chew. She just let it lie there inside her. Every ten seconds or so her cheeks would draw inward as she sucked on the treat, and then she would swallow.

The next step in the ritual was a nod in silent tribute to the pleasure – and then she began to chew what remained in her mouth.

'Good,' she murmured, and became aware of his stare. 'Want some?'

'I don't eat chocolate.'

'Does that mean you don't like it?'

'It means I've never tasted it.'

Zanni looked as if she'd just received news of a grievous crime. 'Ever?'

'I don't think so. No.'

'Would you like a taste?'

Geiger didn't see it coming – because it was not something he'd ever looked for . . .

Zanni leaned to him, and took his face in her hands, and kissed him.

Her mouth was warm and wet – and sweet – and set off a ripple of cool waves across his shoulders that cascaded down his back like an electric waterfall.

The kiss was a slow, easy dance. Simple steps.

Curiosity, restraint. And Zanni wasn't in a hurry. She let her mouth linger against his. He felt the breath from her nostrils on his face – tasted the chocolate ...

She ended it with a nip of his bottom lip.

'Did you like it?' She felt no need to specify what 'it' was.

Geiger swallowed. 'Too sweet,' he said.

Even in the middle of this train wreck – cars going off the tracks front and back, bodies piling up – Zanni felt her smile coming. She slid across the center console and straddled him, her knees at his waist, and pulled the seatback's lever so it went down until Geiger was almost prone. She studied him as she unzipped her jacket and took it off, then pulled her thin sweater off over her head.

Something about the way her arms moved and her body stretched reminded Geiger of the cat. And the two had something else in common. They both made it very clear what they wanted, and when.

'FYI,' she said, 'I like you better without the beard.'

She leaned down toward him – and he grabbed her shoulders and held her there.

'The timing is questionable, Zanni.'

'The *timing*? Geiger ... There's a real chance that in a few hours I might die – and if so, I'd like to have the two things I enjoy most in life before I do.' She pulled his jacket's zipper down. 'And I've already had the chocolate.'

Zanni came for him. This time the kiss was hard, an accompaniment to other urgent gestures, fingers working at buttons, hands searching for things, bodies turning, making adjustments in the cramped space ...

'Careful,' he said. 'I have a knife taped to my chest.'

She stopped, and raised herself so she could have a better look at him. 'If that's your way of talking dirty, Geiger – it's working.' She yanked his shirt up, exposing the weapon, and tore it off, tape and all, in one pull. He winced.

'Hurt?'

'Yes.'

'Good.'

Geiger pulled her back down to him. The scent of lavender filled his head. His hands were tangled in her hair. There was a sudden heat in his chest, an incandescent bloom, as if his heart had become a sun. He was as close to painless and thoughtless as he had ever been – and that state felt more pure than any he had known ...

And when her first, throaty gasp came, almost a growl, it was the most honest sound he'd heard her make since they'd met.

31

She snored.

The sound barely met the definition's requisites – it was a fuzzy flow and ebb, a fluttering of wings, and had he been asleep it would not have awakened him. He felt her warm stream of breath brush his cheek with each rustling.

Zanni lay half atop him, one leg and arm resting across him, her head next to his on the seatback. She'd been asleep for twenty minutes, and he'd been able to reach his jacket and hers without waking her and drape them across her slim nakedness, from the waist down to her socks.

He'd used the time to try and envision the finale. *Beginning – middle – end.*

He and Dalton had been in the business of using torture to gain information, and by its nature the process was impersonal – certainly in the way Dalton went about it – but whatever Dalton had planned, there was an aspect of it that transcended physical pain. He wanted more than suffering.

Vengeance was a key element, but there was something else floating around it, portentous but so sheer

Geiger couldn't see it. You stand on a city street corner, surrounded by aromas ... The exhaust from a passing bus – a piquant dish drifting from a window – hot tar spread in a pothole – and there's another scent mixed in with them all. You can smell it, almost taste it on your tongue. You tilt up your nose, turn in a slow circle. It's right there with you. It's knowable. But you can't give it a name.

He heard Zanni's breath shift into waking mode, and she sat up. She looked at her watch, then at Geiger.

'I fell asleep.'

'For about twenty minutes.'

The exchange was the first words either of them had spoken since she had put him inside her. It had been a long, rolling rush of sounds between silence – some of them comments, appraisals, some questions, some answers – but not one word.

Geiger saw the almost imperceptible movement of her bottom lip – just the faintest pulling away from the top. It was a tell he'd seen a thousand times on the faces of a Jones. She had been about to say something else – and had stopped to play it out in her head, and then decided to leave it unspoken.

She grabbed her panties and slacks from the floor and opened the door. 'Have to pee.' She got out, and went a few paces before she stopped and crouched down.

Geiger stepped out and walked east, ten yards or so, until he could see a good-sized chunk of sky through the trees – and then found the faint, smudged dividing line between the inky blue and the heavy black of the adjacent hills. The sun had at least another hour of climbing to do before there'd be a hint of it on the horizon.

He was rerunning Dalton's video in his mind, trying to get a glimpse of the game within it. He would not factor Zanni in. If her presence ended up affecting things, he would deal with it at that point, but not now. He had one piece to play with, a single chip to get the men out alive: that what Dalton wanted, only Geiger could provide – and Dalton could not *take* it from him. Geiger had to *give* it to him.

There was a knock on his door.

'Ez ...' His mother's voice sounded thin, and tired. 'You're still up, aren't you?'

'Yeah.'

Ezra was sitting on the sill of his open window, his feet on the fire escape, the cat on his shoulder, staring at the windows of the brownstone on the other side of the communal garden. His door opened and she stepped inside.

'It's very late,' she said.

'I know. But I'm not going to school again tomorrow – right?'

'Right.'

'So it doesn't really matter when I go to bed.'

His mother walked to his bed and sat down. She could hear the cat's motor running.

'Jesus ... What a purr. That's the funniest cat.'

'He likes shoulders. It's his favorite place. Geiger used to walk around with him on his shoulder.'

'Why do you call him Tony?'

'Cuz of the scar – his eye. *Scarface* – Pacino – Tony Montana – Tony.'

She knew that slow delivery – the hollow center to it. It jabbed at her heart.

'Gotcha. I like it.' She ran her hand across the bed-spread. It was thinning in spots. She made a note to get a new one. 'Ez ... Look at me a sec.'

He turned round to her.

'I'm so sorry, Ez. For all of this, for everything – and that I can't just be brilliant and make it all better. I love you so much – and I'm just so sorry.'

'I know, Mom. I really do. I love you too.'

She leaned toward him, and he leaned toward her – just close enough for her to put a kiss on his forehead.

'Don't stay up too late.'

'I won't.'

She got up and left the room, closing the door. He turned back to the night. His hand rose to the cat's scar and went to work with a hard scratch. The animal's hum rose a few decibels – from contented to blissful.

'I should do it, right? I *have* to – right?'

He grabbed his iPad from the bed, hopped to the fire escape, put the cat down and slowly, quietly closed the window.

Geiger walked back to the car. Zanni was dressed. One of the bags was on the car's hood. She smacked a new magazine in the Beretta, then took a sight out of the bag and slid it onto the gun's frame rail. She tapped a button and a neon green laser came to life. She raised the weapon and slowly moved the thin beam across the dark trees.

'I assume you won't take this – right?'

'The only reason for me to have a gun is if we both go in shooting.'

'But remember, Geiger ... Dalton may not know it, but he's down two men.'

'All he needs is one man with a gun on Harry and Matheson – we go in firing – maybe they die.'

'I could try and call in some help. We'd have to wait ...'

'Two guns, five guns. It doesn't matter. Our numbers wouldn't change what I just said.'

Zanni nodded. 'You're right.' She punched the laser sight off and put the gun into her jacket pocket.

A *dinging* jingle sounded, and they both turned. It was coming from the backseat of the car. It sounded again.

'That's an iPad. FaceTime,' she said. 'Someone's calling you.'

Geiger opened the back door, reached inside and took his iPad from his bag. The screen said that Ezra was calling.

'Ezra ...' said Zanni. 'Matheson's son?'

'Yes.' Geiger stared at the 'accept' and 'decline' options. Green and red, like stop and go lights.

'He knows you're in France?'

'Yes.'

'And looking for his father?'

'Yes.'

He glanced at her. She looked somewhat surprised and clearly displeased with the information – and she looked like she had more questions to ask, but just stared back at him. The iPad rang again. And again.

'Well ... ?' she said.

Geiger tapped 'accept' and Ezra's weary face filled the screen. Zanni took a step back out of camera range.

'Hi,' Ezra said. 'It's me. I—'

'You shouldn't be calling me, Ezra. This isn't good.' He could feel Zanni's eyes on him.

The boy winced. 'I'm sorry. I – I had something I had to tell you.'

There was no space left in Geiger for more information, no time for any more interactions. He was full up.

'What is it, Ezra?'

'I – I screwed up.'

'How did you screw up?'

Ezra's wince grew an inch wider. '... Mom read your letter.'

Zanni lifted a brow at the statement.

'Ezra ... I told you no one was to read the letter.'

'I know – but she came in my room, and I was upset – and she could tell something was wrong. I mean – she just *knew* ...' His lips scrunched up like a pair of pipe-cleaners. 'So I showed it to her.'

Zanni watched muscles harden in Geiger's face. It was the closest thing to a show of emotion she'd seen him display.

'Go on, Ezra.' It was more cold instruction than conversation.

'She, uh, took me down to the FBI office and showed them the letter. She was *really* pissed – y'know – that somebody might be screwing with Dad again. She wanted answers – from them, or the CIA, anybody – or she'd make a lot of noise ...'

'Go on.'

'The guy said he didn't know anything. He said he'd look into it and call her back.' He shook his head dolefully. 'Geiger ... I told her from the start they wouldn't say they knew even if they did. But now – if it's the same guys that are after Dad and Harry again ... Well – now they know you're coming after them.' His sigh pulled his shoulders up around his ears like a collar. 'Sorry I messed up – but that's what I wanted to tell you – y'know – so you'd ... know ahead of time.'

He blew out a breath and his shoulders fell down. He was done. He looked spent.

Zanni's eyes went right to left, left–right, right–left – from the rueful face on screen ... to Geiger's granite stare ... and then she saw it soften.

'Ezra ... Don't worry about me. This time they're the good guys.'

'For real?'

'For real. Now I have to go.'

'... Okay.'

They took a last look at each other. Somewhere on a Manhattan street, a car horn blared. To Geiger, it sounded like it came from a million miles away.

'Geiger ... Whatever happens, you're not gonna come back – are you?'

'No.'

Ezra nodded. The bright green eyes filled with tears. 'Bye.'

Geiger nodded, and then tapped 'end' and the screen went black. He turned to Zanni. In his work, he had become closely acquainted with almost every expression a face could convey – but he couldn't find the story or feeling in Zanni's expression. There were too many angles – like a Picasso face, hard edges and soft, slanted planes.

'You wrote him a letter – that you were doing this?'

'Yes.'

'Doesn't seem like a smart thing to do. Why would you do that, Geiger?'

'Because if Matheson and Harry don't make it back, I didn't want him to think he'd been abandoned.'

He put the iPad back in his bag. It was time to put everything away except the next few hours in the farm-house.

Zanni let his answer settle – another piece of Geiger that didn't fit into any kind of big picture – and she was not going to try and understand it now.

'Okay. What're you going to do?'

'I'm going to knock on the front door. I'll wait until the hint of first light. You'll be able to see a bit more – outside and inside. You wait till I'm inside for a while. Maybe some lights get turned on. Maybe you can get some sense of the layout – or how many he has in there with him. Then you find a way in.'

She zipped up the bag. 'Right.'

'Zanni?'

'Yes?'

'Victor was supposed to take out Dalton ...'

She turned to him. 'Are you worried about me, Geiger?' She opened the car door and tossed the bag inside. 'Would you worry about me if I was a man?'

'I'm not worried about you, Zanni.'

'Good. You just put your Inquisitor's hat back on and I'll handle my end.' She looked to the sky. 'I'd say we've got about an hour before dawn. Time to move up.' She leaned into the car again, picked up something from the floor – and held it before him. His knife. 'Still want this?'

He nodded. It was a disconcerting moment. He'd forgotten all about it.

They moved through the narrow rows of the dead vineyard in a low crouch, Geiger in the lead, the crooked, stubbed branches grabbing at their pants and sleeves. One hundred feet from the house, he stopped. Zanni came up beside him. The single illuminated window tossed a pale splash of light on the front yard.

'I'm going around the back while it's still dark,' she said.

They turned to each other. The remarkable violet of her eyes looked richer in the night. When she blinked it was like the flicker of neon lights. It wasn't a color someone would associate with a human. It was animalistic – stripes in the wings of a bird of prey, or iridescent scales on an exotic snake, or the feathers of a peacock. It would be almost impossible to forget.

'I'll wait for the sun,' he said.

Zanni nodded. 'See you inside,' she said, and moved off to the left, staying low. In a few seconds her silhouette went from black to invisible, like a magic trick the night kept up its sleeve.

Geiger lay back on the ground. The stars' shimmering created an illusion of movement – shiny ornaments hung on the sky, twisting slightly in a celestial breeze ...

... He saw Dalton standing over him, the overhead lights of Geiger's session room spreading tiny stars along the torturer's glasses. The sparkling display was an odd partner to his solemn look. He leaned down to Geiger, strapped into the barber's chair.

'I'm not going to bother with any head games – not that head games are my strong suit, and not that they'd work on you in any case. No, I'm going straight to the pain. That's my humble expertise – that's what I do ...'

... But Geiger knew neither of them were the same now.

He sensed the change in himself, but as a child becomes aware that this day he is different than the days that came before. The hows and whys play catch-up. They will reveal themselves, but not yet. All Geiger truly grasped was that he was not the same – fuller, denser from the resurrection of the past and this endless baptism of being in the world.

So who would be the Geiger that sat down with Dalton to honor this dark contract?

Zanni walked to the back of the house and sat down against it. She took three slow breaths, put two finger-tips to a wrist and looked at her watch for twenty seconds, then did the multiplication. Seventy-two. Her resting pulse was sixty. Not bad, considering.

They were coming around the last turn now – and she felt like she had a final kick in her. She would not take even a quick look back yet. She would finish strong. She would deal with what she'd left in her wake later.

Bowe was at his desk, eyes on his laptop reading a report on BBC Online News about a street protest in Riyadh. He always worked late. He usually got more done from 9 p.m. to midnight than he did the twelve hours before.

He picked up his Starbucks and swiveled round in his

chair to stare out the window at the Washington Monument. He knew it was corny, and he kept it to himself, but after all these years the sight of it, lit up at night, still gave him a rush.

His assistant walked into the office. 'Sir . . .'

Bowe came back around to the room. 'What're you still doing here, Marie? It's late. Go home.'

'Just dealing with the new mail system, sir.' She came to the desk and put a manila folder down before him.

'This came in from New York on the code line a little while ago,' she said, and stepped back, lacing her hands together at the waist of her navy-blue skirt suit.

Bowe opened the folder. There were two pieces of letter-size paper inside. He slid one toward him and began to read – and his left brow began to rise, reached its zenith, and remained frozen in place.

'Is Mac still here?' he said without looking up.

'I'll check, sir.'

'If he isn't, I want him here – now.'

Bowe's assistant had been with him for nine years, and over that time she had developed a recognition and filing system for his tones of voice. Though the differences were often subtle – perfunctory, engaged, passionate, frustrated, angry, nuclear – she was almost always successful in her readings, but at this moment, she was stymied in her attempt to categorize the character of his last statement.

'Yes, sir,' she said, and walked out.

Bowe put the first sheet aside, slid the second sheet to him and read on. A trio of horizontal ripples set into his forehead. The door opened and McCormack took two steps inside and stopped. Basic procedure.

'Wanted to see me, sir?'

Bowe tapped the desktop with a finger. 'Read.'

McCormack stiffened inside. One-word commands from Bowe were never a good sign. He came to the desk, and Bowe slid the first paper around. McCormack bent to it, and as his eyes scanned the printed lines his head tilted slightly, as if he thought he heard a strange sound from far off – but wasn't entirely sure.

From: Felson/NY

For: Bowe/DEEP RED ONLY
Today, 4/04/13– 11.06 AM, NINA WAYLAND, DAVID MATHESON'S ex-wife, and their son, EZRA, arrived and produced attached letter re: MATHESON & HARRY BODDICKER, claiming it was written and delivered to her son by GEIGER (Is Geiger alive?!), and demanded to know what we knew about content of letter. She was angry and aggressive.
The boy was monosyllabic in his answers to questions and clearly unhappy about being here. I told her we knew nothing (which is true).
Are you boys having another go at those three?
FYI – if you are, I don't want to know ANYTHING about it – and, if you are – you're fucking crazy.

Bowe slid the second paper around to McCormack. It was a copy of Geiger's letter to Ezra. McCormack bent lower to the desk, as if the paper possessed a magnetic force. He read aloud.

'"Tomorrow I am leaving here, going out of the country, and will not return. I am going to try and help

your father and Harry. They are in trouble."' McCormack looked up. 'That could mean a thousand things,
sir. Veritas Arcana and Matheson have enemies all over
the world.'

Bowe's fingers started their drum roll on the desk. 'I
understand that. But Geiger wrote the letter – so that
makes three out of three of them from last July involved
in this – and three out of three makes me feel on-edge –
and you know on-edge is one of my least favorite feelings.'

'Yes – I know that, sir.'

'So Mac ... I want you to tell me if you know *anything* about this that I don't.'

'No, sir. After the Hall disaster you were quite clear
about hands-off on all of them, especially the boy. I
know of nothing active with any of them.'

Bowe sighed. 'Is Soames here?'

'No, sir. Still on vacation.'

'Where is she?'

McCormack braced himself for the explosion. 'I
don't know, sir. A family get-together of some—'

'I don't care if she's playing gin with the fucking
Pope! Find her – and get her on the fucking phone!'

'Yes, sir. Will do,' said McCormack, and gratefully
hustled out of the room.

32

The concept of suffering was and had always been more compelling than the concept of death. Suffering could be complex, protean, in the blood, the flesh, the mind – open-ended, life-changing. And – suffering could make you wish for death, but it didn't work the other way around – because death was an immeasurably brief, one-dimensional experience. *I am* ... then, nothing. Not even the awareness of nothing. In terms of meaning and substance, it was the shallowest of human events.

That was what he brought with him as he walked across the yard, because that was what today would be about.

Geiger stepped from the grass onto the stone path and went to the door. He knocked, three times. The wood spoke with a deep, wise voice – and then the door opened ...

A stranger might have thought, on first glance, that there was a faint smile on Dalton's lips, but there was a hardness to their line that crushed any possibility of humor or warmth.

'Geiger ...' he said. 'It's very good to see you. Come in – please.'

Dalton took a few steps back, putting ten feet between them, and Geiger came inside, into a foyer that was the nexus of three hallways. There was nothing on any of the walls or floors – and a strong, heavy aroma of coffee.

Their gazes' intensity was low wattage, and low-key. They might have been long-lost friends at a reunion trying to sense if they still had anything in common. Once again Geiger was struck by the loss of weight. The cheekbones and nose and brows were far more prominent now. He reminded Geiger of the death's head on a Grateful Dead album cover.

'Nine months and one day,' Dalton said. 'If you were wondering.'

Geiger glanced down the hallways – and Dalton grinned.

'Wondering where my guards are? Don't worry. They're around.'

'I want to see Harry and Matheson.'

'Of course you do. You want to see they're alive, and all right. I understand. In a short while, Geiger. First, we'll talk – for a few minutes.' Dalton gestured toward a hall. 'This way. There's fresh coffee.'

Dalton waited till Geiger started walking, came back to the door and closed it, and then followed Geiger from a few paces behind.

'All the way to the end, and have a seat.'

Geiger entered the kitchen. The sun had just cleared the horizon and the room was coming alive with light from the eastern window. On the two-burner stove was an old-fashioned pressure coffee maker – and on the counter beside it, two large coffee cups, two spoons, and porcelain milk and sugar pieces.

There were three chairs at a rectangular table and two tall cabinets. On the table was a thick stack of typed paper, with yellow tabs sticking out from various pages. Geiger sat down in a chair that gave him a view of the doorway. The table was very old oak – wide-plank with an elegant grain and few knots. *The world was in the wood*. He ran his fingertips over it. *Completion was in the wood, waiting to be found …*

Dalton came in. 'A little musty in here.' He went to a window and opened it, then walked to the stove. 'How do you like your coffee?'

'Black.'

'Sugar?'

'No.'

Geiger's fingertips started a slow roll on the table – and then he put his hands together before him, fingers laced. He needed stillness. No movement. The only part of him he should sense was his heart, and he wanted each beat to be identical to the last.

Dalton brought the bowls and put one down before Geiger, then sat across from him. His back was to the entry.

'Careful,' he said. 'I expect it's hot.' He raised his hands a few inches from his coffee. 'I can't tell temperature with these very well.'

Geiger wondered how many surgeries had been performed on them. The procedures had left the skin hairless, and abnormally smooth. Perhaps skin grafts had been performed. Geiger picked up his bowl and had a taste.

'My own mixture,' said Dalton. 'Sumatra and—'

'Blue Mountain.'

Dalton's eyes crinkled behind his lenses. 'Very good. A connoisseur. Why am I not surprised?'

'It's not a good pairing. They work against each other.' Geiger took notice of Dalton's fleeting frown, put his bowl down, and pushed it to the side. 'I want to see them, Dalton.'

'And I told you – *in time*.' Dalton took his glasses off and started cleaning them with the tail of his flannel shirt. 'They're alive, Geiger – a little worse for wear, yes ... and you'll see them when I decide it's the time to do so.' He put his glasses back on. 'Don't make me tell you that again.'

Geiger nodded, while the Inquisitor took note.

Dalton had spent a great deal of time, thought and effort turning fantasy into reality. Obsession was addictive. He'd played out this moment and those to come countless times – his psychotic expectations had become future fact – and each moment that didn't sync with them would be a tremor beneath it all. The bedrock truth was that Dalton owned the bank and Geiger had come hat in hand – but Dalton was crazy.

'What have you been doing with yourself, Geiger?'

'I work with wood. I make furniture.'

'Furniture. Sounds satisfying.' He cocked his head, and nodded at something. 'Yes. Your father ... He was a carpenter – right?'

'Yes.'

'Like father, like son. I'm sure he's very proud. Oh, but wait ... You told me he was dead – correct?'

'Yes.'

Dalton picked up his bowl and drank, rolling the brew around in his mouth. He shrugged.

'Perhaps less Sumatra, more of the Blue Mountain.' He put the cup down precisely. There was a touch of the mechanical to the movement. 'Geiger ... Do you remember, last year, I told you that someday I was going to write my memoirs?' He reached to the stack of papers and slid them in front of him. 'My agent already has three bidders. He's especially excited about the European markets.' He eyed the pages' yellow tabs. 'I thought this would be a good time – perhaps the only time – that I could share some of it with you. How does that sound?'

'It sounds psychotic.'

Dalton's peculiar, ambivalent smile came back to him. He grasped one of the tabs between thumb and fore-finger. Geiger found the action slightly more methodical than normal. Dalton turned to the page, cleared his throat, and began to read.

'"It was thrilling to see him before me. Geiger, the Inquisitor, the legend, king of our craft. Even strapped into the barber's chair, nearly naked and stripped of power, he seemed to be the one in control."'

It was easy as stepping through a doorway for Geiger to get back there.

... His own session room, the deep whiteness of it, summoning the music in his head for the trial to come, hearing the heavy footsteps of buried memory coming closer, sensing the nearness of his father and the black truths he carried ...

'"As I worked on Geiger, with a white-hot awl, then a baseball bat, and finally his own antique straight razor, I began to understand I was in the presence of a true alchemist. But instead of changing copper into gold, Geiger could transform pain into something that transcended suffering. It was a revelation."'

Dalton picked up his bowl and took a long sip, then put it down and took hold of another tab. He turned to the page and read.

"'Perhaps I was off my guard. Perhaps I was relieved the session was over. Perhaps I was in awe, watching him stitch up the long cuts I'd put in his quad without one wince or sound ... But his fist fractured my jaw and knocked me to the floor, as two teeth flew out of my mouth and went skittering across the floor like bloody dice."'

His left brow did a quick pull-up, as if he was hearing the tale for the first time.

"'Bloody dice". That's good, isn't it?'

Geiger could see it – slamming his knee into Dalton's groin and then hammering his face. It was, by far, the hardest he had ever hit someone. Then – he thought he heard something in the house.

'Do you mind if I smoke?' he asked.

'Be my guest.'

Geiger took his time getting his pack from a pocket and lighting up. He was trying to clear out a patch of empty air, listening for sounds beyond the room. But none came.

Zanni stepped into a hallway, gun in hand by her side. She could hear voices. She moved toward them ...

Dalton looked back down to the page. "'As I lay on my stomach, Geiger straddled me, and what happened next – maybe he'd planned it, or maybe it came to him then and there in a blaze of passion – the crushing, the breaking, the demolishing of my fingers and hands. Geiger said to me – 'Early retirement, Dalton. Teach yourself to type with your toes and you can start writing your memoirs.'"'

Dalton looked up. 'And here we are,' he said. 'What do you think? Does it have a ring of authenticity to it?'

Geiger tapped his ash into his coffee bowl. 'There was no blaze of passion. I don't have those.'

'That's a pity. They can be very satisfying.' Dalton sat back, muscles at his jaw-joints flexing a few times. 'Maybe I can help you with that.' He stacked the papers together and pushed them to the side.

And Zanni came into Geiger's view in the doorway, gun pointed at the room. She met Geiger's stare without hesitancy, her extraordinary eyes clear and cool.

There are moments when the mind suddenly retrieves something that seems, at first, irrelevant to the situation – a *where did that come from?* memory that might unveil its pertinence if there is time for the brain to connect the dots ...

Soundlessly, Zanni stepped into the kitchen behind Dalton.

... and Geiger's mind did a loop-de-loop – Brooklyn, the first time they met – and he remembered a decision he'd made that night. He had told himself that he couldn't believe anything she'd say.

'Hello, Zanni,' said Dalton, without turning.

She lowered her gun to her side.

Dalton grinned. 'How about it, Geiger? Do we have a blaze – of *anything*?'

There was a steady thump starting up in Geiger's

temples, and a sharp, bitter taste flooded his mouth – the flavor of lies. She'd held out a poison apple and he'd taken more than a bite. And battered by his migraine, he'd even taken Dewey's fiction for truth and swallowed it whole.

Now Victor came into the room. The dead man's Beretta was pointed at Geiger. The world was a chessboard, with four pieces, and he was the only pawn.

'Bonjour,' said Victor.

Geiger shifted in his chair so his body faced Zanni. 'Your idea,' he said. 'Making Matheson the bait . . .'

'A moment, please,' said Dalton. 'Her plan, yes – but I'm the one who told her, after she debriefed me, that if she ever received information about your whereabouts, I would pay a lot for it. I planted the seed – so please, a little credit where credit is due.'

Geiger nodded. 'No one in Deep Red saw the video . . .'

Zanni nodded. 'No one.'

'And no one knows you're doing this.'

'No one. Now take the knife out and put it on the table.'

Victor shifted his aim a few degrees. Geiger reached inside his shirt, pulled the knife free and laid it down softly, tape and all.

'Any others, Geiger?' said Victor.

'No.'

'Shall I frisk him, Zanni?'

'No.'

'You are sure?'

'Yes, Victor. I'm sure.'

Zanni and Geiger's eyes hadn't left each other's since

she arrived. Flat, untelling stares. The wisest of seers couldn't have guessed what they were thinking.

Dalton pushed back from the table and stood up. 'He can see them now – just for a minute – and then bring him to me.'

Zanni turned and walked out. The spent cigarette was warming Geiger's fingers. He dropped it in the bowl. Victor stepped to the entry.

'Please. You first.'

Geiger rose from his chair and walked out of the room. Victor followed, three steps behind him. They reached the foyer.

'Turn right,' said Victor.

Geiger headed down a hallway. He could see Zanni waiting at the end, and he knew he had to kill the hot kick in his blood. Like sucking the poison out of a snake bite before it spread. He needed pure focus. If he hadn't called her yesterday morning and come here on his own, he would have discovered her duplicity just the same – so nothing that had happened in between mattered. If it had changed him in any way, so be it. *Nothing else had changed.* He couldn't allow himself to see it any other way. Not now.

Zanni motioned at a door with her gun. 'Here,' she said.

Geiger stopped, and turned to watch Victor halt six or seven feet away, gun up.

'They are chained to the walls,' said Victor. 'Do not go more than a few steps in the room. Do not touch them. You understand – yes?'

During the length of Victor's statement, Geiger had eyeballed the distance between them all, the width of the space, their posture, the position of the guns – and decided an attack would almost certainly be unsuccessful, and quite possibly worse than that.

'I understand, Victor,' he said.

Harry was flat on his back, staring at the old beams set into the ceiling, trying to find the place within him where he could get a true sense of whether or not he could kill someone. Certainly the anger was there, a mother-lode, shiny, fiery red – but anger was only the flint. What element must it strike to set off the act – and was it in him?

At the same time, he was aware of a part of him that just wanted to slide into a sleep that didn't end. There was something appealing about the concept of utter thoughtlessness. And that part of him wasn't choosy. All he wanted was to know that the last thought he'd have was, in fact, his *last*. Just a heads-up that he was finished using his brain. A sort of farewell to self just before a bye-bye to everything else.

He looked over at Matheson, who was sitting up, cross-legged, still applying pressure to the self-inflicted cut in his ankle with a blood-soaked gob of toilet paper.

'Did it stop?' asked Harry.

'Just about, yeah.' Matheson held up his plastic water jug with his free hand. He'd poured out the water, and managed to get about half an inch of his blood dripped into it. 'I think that's enough, huh?'

'I guess.'

Matheson leaned to his portable toilet, put the jug and compress inside and closed the top, and the door opened, and Geiger walked in.

Matheson and Harry were like ragged marionettes on

the same set of strings, slowly rising to their feet – and Geiger felt his fingers curling inward at his sides, balling into fists so tight that his forearms almost shook.

'Good to see you, Geiger,' said Matheson.

Harry started toward Geiger, off the mattress onto the floor, and then four shaky steps, chain jingling, as far as he could go. Five feet away.

'Hello, Harry.'

'Hi.'

'Why is your face purple, Harry?'

Harry smiled, but some of it was lost in the swollen flesh. 'The Asian giant hornet. I've become very well informed on the subject. According to our host, they have the most toxic venom in the insect world. Cool, huh?' Harry wagged a finger. 'And it's not purple – it's *plum*, according to Matheson.'

Matheson nodded. 'Definitely plum.'

Harry's heartbeat was a jackhammer, breaking up things inside him. 'Can I ask you a question, Geiger?'

'Yes.'

Harry's face hardened like fast-acting superglue. 'What the *fuck* are you doing here?'

His voice had a thin, rough coat of anger. It was new to Geiger, and with all the balls his mind was already juggling, it gave him pause.

'I . . . came—'

'Jesus, man . . . You're a human goddamn sacrifice! That's *all* you did by coming here – put yourself on the altar of the almighty Dalton. And the fact that he'll probably *still* kill me and David anyway isn't even the point. Christ . . .'

Harry had a faint awareness that the brake on his

emotions had given way, and they were barreling down-hill, picking up speed – and that the rant wasn't just about Geiger's outlandish, selfless act, but about other things, too many to try and grasp.

'I'm not cool about you trading your life for mine. Okay? It's not right, man. It feels really wrong.' He huffed and ran a hand through his matted hair. 'Goddamnit, Geiger ... If this was some kind of atone-ment for your sins, there were plenty of churches in Brooklyn! You should've stayed home. Whatever the hell it was you thought you—'

'I didn't want you to die, Harry. That's why I came.'

It wasn't the emblematic velvet cloak of tone – Harry knew it as well as his own voice – but the communion wrapped inside it that muted him and glazed his eyes with tears. His head started shaking side to side in tiny degrees, like a pre-Parkinson tremor.

Victor was listening, thumbnail stroking his cleft. He turned to Zanni, leaning against the wall. She was star-ing straight ahead, barely a rise to her chest as she breathed.

The bass drum pulsed in Geiger's ears. He looked to Matheson. 'I spoke with Ezra. He asked me to tell you that he loves you.'

Matheson sighed. 'Then he knows – about all this?'

'Not the details – but that there's trouble, yes.'

'Is he ... okay?'

Zanni stepped into view. 'Time, Geiger.'

'Who are *you*?' said Harry. She didn't answer. 'Geiger ... Who the hell is *she*?'

Geiger glanced at her, framed in the open doorway, the morning light alive behind her. She looked different to him now, but he chose to not investigate that perception any further.

'Now, Geiger,' said Zanni. 'Time to go.'

Geiger turned back to the two captives. He owned all of this – everything here, everything that had happened, every notch of fear and loss and pain was because of him. This was the Inquisitor's doing. They might just as well have been two of his Joneses.

'Goodbye,' he said.

Matheson nodded silently.

'See you around,' said Harry. In his present state there was little he could trust of his senses – but as Geiger stared at him one last time, Harry thought there was something in the gray eyes that had never been there before. Some very pale, warm light.

Geiger turned and walked out. Zanni was waiting at the far end of the hall. Victor pointed that way and then fell into step a few feet behind Geiger.

'I have to say, Geiger. Before, when I came into the kitchen, you looked – how to say? – so *disappointed* to see me. You would rather I had still been dead.'

'Yes. That would be my preference – that you were still dead.'

'I understand. There are others too who feel the same way. I would think there are many who feel the same way about you.'

Geiger stopped, and Victor did too.

'Do not be foolish, Geiger.'

Geiger slowly turned round to him. The gun was raised and ready.

'I'm not a foolish man, Victor. I just have something to tell you.'

'Yes?'

'Don't hurt them, Victor. This isn't about them, it's about me. Do you understand me?'

Victor smiled. 'Geiger ... Please, take no offense – but you are not in a position to make threats.'

'I agree with you, Victor – and it wasn't a threat.'

Geiger turned and headed away, leaving Victor's smile to slowly dissolve.

As Geiger came her way Zanni's pistol rose, but there was no hurry or concern in the motion. There would be no last-second, unforeseen zigs or zags. The race was all but done. In minutes she'd be breaking the tape ...

She'd wait for the deal's back-end transfer to show up in her account – then an hour and a half south on the A7 to Marseilles – park the car in the long-term lot – change into the skirt suit, put on the wig – then get the shuttle to the international terminal, and onto the plane.

She'd thought about asking Geiger about her brother's last minutes – but decided she wasn't going to take that with her – or Geiger's granite stare – or Dalton's insaner-than-thou dissertations. She wasn't going to leave with anything that would weigh her down. The horizon was a tightrope she would tiptoe across – and at the end was a place where it all started over again.

'Far enough,' she said when Geiger was ten feet away, alongside another door. 'You're going in there.'

'And then you're done?' he said.

'And then I'm done.'

Geiger nodded. 'The sharpest one in the room.'

'That's right,' she said. 'Go on in.'

His pulse's thump refused to calm. Some new element in him was fueling it, and it was immune to his old methods.

He turned the knob and went inside.

33

'Welcome home,' said Dalton.

The room was a three-quarter-sized replica of Geiger's session room on Ludlow Street – a dedicated effort, or as Carmine was wont to say, close enough for the blues.

Every surface was gleaming white linoleum, there were a dozen recessed three-inch pin-spots in the ceiling, and in the center of the floor was a chrome, leather and porcelain barber's chair like Geiger's that had five metal-mesh straps attached to it. Beside it was a folding chair, and a chrome cart with a towel on top – and various shapes were visible beneath the fabric. On a metal desk were a plastic jug of water and a stack of paper cups, and a DVD player and monitor. A second door was across the room in the opposite wall.

Dalton waved a hand around his creation. 'A modest facsimile, I know – but I was trying to create a feel of continuity for our reunion. What do you think?'

'You have a good memory,' said Geiger.

'Some things you never forget.'

Geiger heard what he could only think of as a hush of melancholy in the undertones of the madness – and he knew this much was true: no matter how different he and Dalton might be and had been, how disparate their reasons for choosing the trade, how opposed in their methods – they were joined in ways no other pair on the planet could be.

'Have a seat, Geiger.'

Geiger walked to the barber's chair and sat in it.

'Comfortable?'

'Yes.'

'It took months to find one in mint condition. Give it a whirl.'

Geiger gave a small push off the floor with his foot and the chair spun smoothly. He stopped after one revolution.

'You went to a lot of work,' he said.

'Yes, I did. And it's fascinating ... Have you ever noticed how anticipation changes the nature of time?'

'In what sense?'

Dalton pulled the folding chair over and sat down five feet from Geiger.

'All these months, it felt like each day pushed July Fourth further and further into the past – that it all happened so long ago – and now that you're here, it feels like it was yesterday. Do you know what I mean?'

'I understand that today means a lot to you.'

Dalton stared back at him, and then he sighed. 'Don't humor me, Geiger. It doesn't suit you.'

'I'm curious about something.'

'What about?'

'The psychosis.'

'... Yes?'

'You do realize you're deeply psychotic ...'

Dalton shrugged. 'It's a catch-all term – but go on.'

'Are there times when you feel out of control? When you're at its mercy, so to speak?'

'No. I feel quite ... What's the right word?' Dalton gave it thought. 'There's no inner struggle, if that's what you mean.' He was warming to the subject. 'The madness usually shows itself in hallucinations. Very compelling events. At first they were unsettling – even frightening – but I came to terms with them as I moved to a higher state. It's like being on a rollercoaster ride.'

Geiger needed to keep him talking – to gather as much psychic information as he could. He'd have nothing else to work with.

'In what way?' he asked.

'When you're at the very top and you start down – and the speed grows quickly, and the car is rattling, you feel that *pull* ... It's very scary – right?'

'I've never been on a rollercoaster.'

Dalton nodded. 'And again, why am I not surprised? Well ... You're barreling down the track, the torque is yanking at you, the deafening noise, your pulse is exploding, you might even be screaming ... and you're terrified – because your systems, your primal self, is telling you that you won't make it through – you're going to die. But—'

'But you know the ride is going to end.'

'Yes! Exactly right.' Dalton nodded eagerly. 'The higher state knows the ride will end even before you even get on – but then *fear* overwhelms us.' He stood up and began to pace. 'So now, when I look at someone and see their head explode, or watch the serpents rise out of the lavender and devour each other ... What I've

learned to do – is to remember that *the ride will end*.
And it does.' He turned to Geiger. 'That's what I learned
to do with the pain, too.' He held out his hands. 'With
these. And I owe it all to you.' He sighed with palpable
satisfaction. 'I knew you'd understand. I am so pleased
that you came, Geiger. Really.'

Dalton walked to the desk, poured himself a cup of
water and drank it slowly. Geiger couldn't see a play
anywhere – and he decided to stop looking, for now.

'Thirsty?' Dalton asked.

'No.'

Dalton crumpled the cup and let it drop to the floor.
'Time!'

Zanni and Victor came in. Victor went to the barber's
chair while Zanni held her gun on Geiger.

'Now,' said Dalton, 'Victor is going to secure you.
Take off your jacket and shirt first.'

Geiger obeyed the command and handed them to
Victor, who folded them neatly and put them on the
desk. Then he returned and started securing the straps –
first, around Geiger's chest, then the ankles.

'Put your wrists on the chair arms,' Dalton said.

Geiger placed his forearms down flat on the leather
padding.

'Merci,' said Victor, and strapped Geiger's wrists
down.

'Good,' said Dalton, and started out. 'Be back soon,
Geiger. Victor ... Zanni ...'

Victor followed, and Zanni came to Geiger's side.

'I'll be going soon,' she said.

Geiger nodded. 'They'll find you, you know.'

'Why so sure?'

'Because that's what they do. You found me, didn't you?'

She nodded. 'Yes, I did.' She leaned down to his ear and whispered. 'Full disclosure: Dewey was my brother.'

Geiger's head turned to her. The list of things he'd missed was growing longer. The short, subtle flick of her lips was not a smile or a scowl. It looked lost, as if it had wandered onto the wrong face. Then she cradled his cheeks in her palms and kissed him. The tenderness of it was unexpected.

She straightened up. 'Goodbye, Geiger.' She gave the chair a firm push and started it spinning, and then she left.

As he went round and round, Geiger closed his eyes – and started making a list of the music he would play in his head ... when the time came.

When she walked into the study, Dalton was standing at his desk and Victor was across the room, staring out a window. She had the Beretta down at her side, against her thigh, but her finger was on the trigger, because this was fertile ground for betrayal.

As a physical threat Dalton was an unlikely candidate, but back at the very start she had fashioned a scenario and held it close, like a lucky keepsake – that when and if everything played out successfully there would be a moment, this moment, before she got paid, when killing her would be a smart cost-cutting move on Dalton's part. That if he had offered Victor a tenth of her fee to take her out, her French friend would do it with a melancholy flick of his knife. And it would not be a betrayal in his eyes. Betrayal's partner, by definition, was trust – the former could not occur without the latter – and in their line of work there was no such thing.

Dalton pointed at his laptop. 'It's all ready. Just put in your account number.'

Zanni sat down. 'Dalton ... A few steps back.'

He nodded. 'Of course,' he said, and backed away half a dozen feet.

'Victor ...' she said. 'Come over here with Dalton – so I can see you while I do this.'

Victor turned – and saw the Beretta – and he sighed. 'Zanni ... Zanni.' He shook his head sadly as he walked to Dalton's side. 'This mistrust. It is disturbing. I worry about you.'

'Good. Keep worrying about me until I'm gone.'

Dalton shrugged. 'She's just being thorough, Victor. I sensed that about her the moment we met. Very thorough.'

The screen showed a bank transfer setup. She typed in the numbers, which showed up as dots in a thin rectangular box. A second box appeared below it and told her to re-enter the same information, and she performed the task.

'Hit enter,' said Dalton.

'Hit enter.' The words had a pleasing sound – solid, simple, nearly anthemic. In God We Trust. Don't Tread On Me. *Take your marks. Set* ... She raised a finger and hit the key. 'TRANSFER IN PROGRESS' began flashing at the bottom of the form.

'Zanni ...' said Dalton.

'What?'

'I understand that Dewey was your brother.'

Zanni looked to Victor. 'You're like an old woman sometimes – you know that?'

'Don't be upset with Victor. I only wanted to say that—'

'Shuttup, Dalton.'

She looked at the screen. The message was still blinking.

'It was a questionable choice on your part, Zanni. And your secrecy raises other issues, too – but luckily for all of us, in the end it was of no consequence.' He removed his glasses and held them up to the light. 'Except, of course, for Dewey.' He was satisfied with the state of the lenses, put them back on, and sighed. 'C'est la vie.'

Her eyes slowly rose to him. She remembered what he looked like with his jaw swollen and wired after Geiger had broken it. She wanted to do it again, with her own fists.

'When do you let Matheson and Boddicker go?' she said.

'That depends on Geiger. But I suspect it will be soon. Don't worry, Zanni. Victor will take care of them. I'm sure they'll be in Paris before night.'

She checked the screen. There was a new message. TRANSFER COMPLETED. 'Done,' she said. She clicked on 'log out' and stood up. She was primed. She'd never felt more ready to leave someplace. She stared at them silently – and Dalton showed his dreadful smile.

'Goodbye, Zanni. And thank you. Live well.'

Victor did a little half-bow. 'Goodbye, mon ami.'

It was an odd thought that came to her – that these two were very likely the last people who *knew* her that she would ever see. And even with that, she realized she had nothing to say. She turned and walked out of the room.

'Extraordinary woman,' said Dalton.

'Yes,' said Victor. 'She is.'

'Angry.'

'Always.'

It was colder outside than inside, but the sun was a few rungs up its ladder, and it made her warmer than she'd felt in the house. She didn't stop to look back until she was into the trees. From the start she'd been adept at staying on point – make it about the trip, not the arrival. And not the consequences. She would never know what happened inside the house, and she would find out how much she wondered about it down the line. 'Later on' was the operative phrase now. For everything.

She turned around and headed for the car . . .

Dalton came in holding a hinged teak case the size of a large shoebox that he put on the cart's lower shelf. With his back to Geiger, blocking the view of the cart, he lifted the towel.

Geiger was trying to measure Dalton's body. His pants were bunched at the waist, and the seat was baggy. He must have lost at least thirty pounds . . .

'Just keep in mind . . . Victor is nearby, just out in the hall. Not that I expect you to cause trouble . . .'

And Dalton came out swinging, whirling around – his

left hand adorned with a bright red boxing glove – and smashed Geiger in his right pectoral. The blow's shock-wave was more potent than the pain, rattling him down to his ribs and up to his neck. The men's grunts were a chorus – like parts of the same machine.

'This isn't about *hurting* you,' said Dalton, and wound up and hammered Geiger's left pectoral. This time pain took center-stage – dancing into the spotlight, then rolling up into his wounded shoulder and pulling a sharp growl out of him.

Dalton stepped back, sucking air. 'I'm helping you get an adrenaline rush going so we get that dopamine and endorphins into your bloodstream …' He pushed his glasses back on his nose. '… to help when the *real* pain comes.'

Geiger blew out a slow purge of breath. 'Thoughtful of you.'

Dalton couldn't help but smile. 'I have to ask,' he said. 'It's never sarcasm – is it?'

Geiger performed minor adjustments to his upper torso, as best he could, shifting things to round up the pain and drive it out of the damaged joint. It was his most vulnerable spot right now, and anywhere else would be preferable. Dalton had plans – so the rationing of energies would be crucial.

'Dalton … When do Harry and Matheson get to leave?'

Dalton pulled off the glove and tossed it away. 'That's still to be decided.'

'I'm here. Where you wanted me. That was the deal.'

'I think you mis-assumed something.' Dalton turned back to the cart. 'Is that a word – "mis-assumed"?' He bent down, took the teak case out and turned round. 'I think you made an incorrect assumption about all of this – which is certainly understandable – but your presence is only a prelude. And it's not up to me when they go free. It's up to you.'

There are rare times when a voice speaks one truth and reveals another – but the listener must possess an equally rare sense to hear it. The Inquisitor heard it – and Geiger saw him from the corner of his eye, plucking Dalton's words out of the air and peeling off a layer to find their second meaning. The unexpected was present.

Dalton laid the case down across Geiger's quads. 'Something for the Inquisitor.'

Dalton opened the lid of the box. Inside, resting on a lining of red velvet, were a pair of amputated hands. The flesh was gray-brown, shriveled and mottled, and they wore the signs of failed surgeries – thin, darkened scars and dots of suture holes. The right hand was missing the forefinger and the left had no pinkie.

To Geiger, they looked like something unearthed at an archeological dig – ancient relics from a punishment exacted for theft, or adultery, or an affront to God.

Dalton began to prowl the room. 'After the third surgery they said fine dextrous skills would not be restored. The damage was too extensive. I could pick something up and hold it ... I could dress – but no buttons ... using silverware would be likely after therapy ...' He realigned his glasses at the bridge with a long, smooth finger. 'But I wouldn't be able to peel an orange ... or sign my name ... take a cork out of a wine bottle ... or use a razor – for whatever purpose ...'

He stopped at the desk and tapped on the power of

the DVD player and monitor, then turned to Geiger and the Cheshire Cat smile blinked again. 'Or *type* – if I should want to write something ...'

Geiger was retracing his assumptions, sensing there was much he had missed. Being fallible was starting to feel commonplace.

Dalton was on the move again. 'When they brought up the alternative ... "We can give you new hands ... " I mean – this was make-believe stuff. Movie stuff. You know – those movies where the accident victim gets the hands of a killer ...'

'I don't watch movies.'

'They showed me videos. Up to eighty-five percent fine motor skill recovery after therapy and training. It was one of those moments. Simple math. Inescapable logic.' He raised his hands. 'They even put in the creases on the knuckles.'

He pulled up his sleeves. A few inches above the wrist, the prosthetics' sleeves became heavier and darker toned, and ended halfway up the forearm.

'Neural interfaces, myoelectric signals and impulses. Incredible. They don't just do what they're told ... they even give me feedback. I can *feel* how tightly I'm holding something.' He pulled his sleeves back down. 'The underside of the nails' tips are a bit difficult for me to keep clean. I've let the engineers know they should have another look at that. But I've bought stock in the company.'

Geiger stared at the madman – and one by one, tiny lights were coming on in his mind, like windows in a city as the night moves in.

Dalton returned to the desk. 'I want to show you

something. I downloaded it from the internet. I can't tell you how many times I've watched it.' He pressed a button on the DVD player and video bloomed on the monitor.

The scene was a brightly lit concrete, windowless bunker, and in the lower right corner there was a digital display of the video's running time and the date – 2/16/2004.

A bearded man was strapped into a gurney – naked except for his boxers, his face and body spotted with welts. His dark, nervous eyes were following Geiger as he strolled the room.

Geiger's appreciation for Dalton's obsession was growing. Here was what had put everything in uncontrollable motion, the Cairo sessions – the secret post-9/11 video that Matheson acquired – a runaway train that brought Hall and Ezra and Dalton to Geiger ... and left dead bodies and broken hearts in its wake before it went out into the world on the Veritas Arcana website. The worst of him, at his very best.

'There will be no more beatings, Nari,' said the video-Geiger. 'Crude brutality wasn't working. That's why they brought me here.'

'I tell you again,' the man said. 'I am not lying. I swear to almighty God.'

Geiger's fingers started rolling out a rhythm on his thighs. 'I don't believe in a god, Nari – but if yours exists, I can tell you with complete certainty that he won't have a say in what happens here. It's a godless room. It's just you and me.'

Dalton nodded at the screen. '"Godless room ..." Wonderful.'

Video-Geiger came to the man's side, and the battered body visibly stiffened. Geiger raised a hand and put it against the man's cheek, so his curled fingertips rested in a line just below the ear.

'You're not my enemy, Nari. Your political views, religious beliefs, they're unimportant to me. I don't care about them.'

His fingertips began to slowly press inward where the vertical line of the jaw meets the neck.

'Listen carefully – because it's important you understand me.'

Geiger remembered every word.

'My job is to retrieve information ...'

... *and the tools I use* ...

'... and the tools I use are fear and pain.'

No matter which of a hundred sessions Dalton might have put in the DVD player, Geiger would have remembered every word.

'Suffering is a result of the pain, Nari – but not the purpose or the goal.'

As Geiger's fingertips pushed in deeper, the man's lips stretched out and thinned like rubber bands from the pain – and a low growl gathered in his throat. As soon as the cry burst out Geiger took his hand away.

'Starting now, we are partners ...'

... *but not equals* ...

'... but not equals, because you have what I need – the truth – and in the end the choice is yours, not mine.'

Dalton stopped the video. '"In the end the choice is yours, not mine."' He looked to Geiger. 'Et voilà.'

Dalton came and picked up the teak case. 'It started out as pure, simple vengeance – twenty-four seven.

Pound of flesh, retribution ... It consumed me. Completely. But the longer I yearned for it, I began to sense that when it arrived the satisfaction might be fleeting – and I worried what would be left in me once it was gone. To spend so much time and feeling and effort ...'

He put the case on the cart and picked up the antique scalpel and whetstone.

'And then I had one of my hallucinations – but this was more a vision. You were an angel, falling to earth with your wings on fire. But you were smiling. Yes – *you*, smiling. Content. And I knew what I would do. I won't deny revenge was still a part of things – but there would be more now. Something with meaning. Something lasting – for both of us.' He turned to Geiger. 'Sacrifice.'

He started stroking the blade against the stone. *Thwwwkk* ...

'Sac–ri–fice.' *Thwwwkk* ... 'It has a lovely sound, doesn't it?' *Thwwwkk* ...

Geiger couldn't tell if Dalton was talking about the word or the sound of steel on stone – but he was getting a clearer sense of the man's lunacy. There were no seams, no sharp edges or rough patches. It fitted him perfectly – like a second skin.

Dalton put the whetstone down, then uncapped a bottle of alcohol. 'As you said – "Starting now, we are partners." It's a win–win, Geiger. For both of us.'

'What is?'

Dalton stuck the blade in the bottle and stirred it in the liquid. 'Sacrifice.'

Dalton removed the scalpel and gently put it down on a napkin, then turned, tilted the bottle and poured alcohol on Geiger's right hand, then the left. It was only now Geiger noticed how the overhead pin-spots put a soft gleam on the latex skin that flesh would not have reflected – and the observation jabbed at his curiosity.

'Are they heavier?' he asked.

'A little. But you get used to it. Anything lighter would feel strange to me now.'

'What does that mean, Dalton? That sacrifice is a win–win.'

Dalton put the alcohol down and picked up the scalpel. 'Let me ask you first: Why did you come here?'

'Harry and Matheson are here in my place. They don't belong here. I belong here.'

Dalton nodded. 'Yes, you do – in more ways than one.'

34

Dalton grabbed a hand towel from the cart, pulled the folding chair over and sat down before Geiger – and took a deep breath. It was a sound marking a commencement – the start of something anticipated and worked toward for a long time. He held up the scalpel.

'Horatio Kern – eighteen sixty-seven,' he said. 'Left ... or right?'

Geiger didn't need further explanation. He was already in preparation, summoning his tools – the always-fresh memory of a blade cutting into him, and a final choice from the jukebox in his mind, to listen to, to taste and see and wield against the pain. Mahler ... Dylan ... Hendrix ... Bach ...

'Left or right, Geiger?'

Geiger fixed his gaze on the cold eyes in the skullish face. 'It doesn't matter.'

'All right. We'll start with the left.'

Dalton looked down and laid the scalpel across the joint of the index finger, just above the knuckle where the digit joined the palm.

'The metacarpophalangeal joint. That's a mouthful,

isn't it?' Dalton looked back up to Geiger. 'You smashed mine so hard that you pulverized some of them. The doctors said they'd rarely seen anything like it.' He refocused on the blade. 'Don't move now.'

Geiger turned off his lights. He was in the dark, where it made no difference if his eyes were open or shut, and wakefulness and sleep joined hands, where it was always easier to see the music's colors ...

He watched the grip of the mechanical fingers tighten – and with a surgeon's care Dalton drew the scalpel very softly across the joint, barely cutting the flesh, leaving a thread-thin, one-inch line of blood.

'There,' said Dalton, and reached over to the belt at Geiger's right wrist and flicked open the clasp, releasing the lock – and then sat back in his seat.

They regarded each other like chess players after a bizarre opening move.

'When the blade is that well-honed,' said Dalton, 'you hardly feel a thing, right?'

Geiger didn't move. His thoughts were racing elsewhere – trying to recreate the labyrinth of Dalton's madness inside his own mind – so he could find his way to the heart of it ... and understand what was happening ...

Dalton folded his hands in his lap. 'So ... You ask – what does it mean – "Sacrifice is a win–win". Well ... I told you I was in your debt – and so I'm offering you a gift. A rare opportunity. The chance to make a *sacrifice* – a pure, selfless act – an act that will open you to yourself ... and cleanse you ... and banish the Inquisitor.' He pointed a mechanical finger at Geiger. 'You want that. I know it. To be free of him once and for all. And as you said about the truth ... "In the end the choice is yours, not mine".'

Dalton rose – and held the scalpel out to Geiger.

'This is how they go free.'

Geiger peered around another corner of Dalton's lunatic maze – and now he understood. The grin that spread on Dalton's face was as sharp and cruel as the blade.

'As we say in France ... touché.'

Geiger looked at the offering. The lights turned the pale silver steel nearly white, like a shiny sliver of paper. He reached out and took the scalpel. It had a cool, pleasing smoothness in his palm.

Dalton grinned like the proud owner of a vintage touring car. 'Perfect balance, right?'

Geiger nodded. 'Perfect.'

Dalton headed for the desk. 'And *my* sacrifice?' He poured another cup of water and sipped at it. 'I give up the chance to make you suffer with my own ... hands.' His face darkened, and his breathing slowed to a near-stillness. For a moment, it looked as if there was nothing alive in him. Then his hand squeezed into a steel fist and swung out like a wrecking ball, smashing into the monitor and sending it flying across the room.

Victor's voice came from the hall. 'Is it all right?'

'Yes, Victor.' Dalton sighed. 'As I said, Geiger ... A win–win.'

Geiger saw the triumph behind Dalton's glasses slowly grow to full flame. The madness had served him well. It had sculpted hatred and obsession into a work of art.

'Take your time, Geiger. Get up and stretch if you like.' He headed for the door. 'I'll only be gone a minute or two. The back door is unlocked, if you decide to leave.'

Dalton left the room. Geiger undid all his binds, but didn't get up. He felt unbalanced, wobbling in his orbit. He had prepared for the pain, and damage – this was only about him and Dalton, and no one else should suffer for it. That was clear and simple as child's math, and had been from the start. But ...

Dalton had turned life inside out, brilliantly. He had become the patient psychological manipulator and master – he had become the *Inquisitor* – and if Geiger had a chance of saving anyone, it would mean savaging himself. He would have to become Dalton.

The waiter came out to the sidewalk and put the second demitasse on the small square table. The stunning American took no notice. She seemed to be staring intently at the little town's modest octagonal fountain, where Avenue de Gaulle and Avenue Jean Jaures met. There was barely any traffic, hardly anyone about, and almost all of the buildings' muted blue and teal shutters were closed.

'Madame ... manger? Eat?'

A single, short shake of her head.

'Good,' he said, and went back inside the café.

Heading south, Sainte-Cécile-les-Vignes was the first town Zanni had come to, and a minute in she'd had a choice of two cafés, one across the street from the other. She'd decided on Café du Commerce because there was no one seated at the half a dozen outdoor tables.

She picked up her coffee and took a slow sip. Her field of vision was in soft focus, the foreground and background mixed together like brushstrokes in a blotted watercolor. Her breathing gears had shifted down for the first time in weeks, and the rev in her pulse was almost gone. She was coming down, feeling looser, more like herself – except for the regret. She had picked up its scent – and she wanted to look in its eyes. She wanted to be clear on everything going on inside her before she cut this life loose.

Dewey, her dumb sweet brother lying alone, dead somewhere … That would stay with her for a while, and she would ride that out.

And Geiger, more a fool than he ever suspected, who couldn't seem to stop himself from being someone's savior – first the boy, then Matheson, and Harry …

But why her?

The question made her angry, and wondering about the answer – even angrier. She didn't want it in her mind. He'd put it there – without intent – but she was furious at him for doing so. It was baggage she hadn't planned on taking with her.

She took another sip of coffee. It was already getting cold. She put a ten-euro note under the cup, stood up and walked across the street to the car.

'Merci, madame!'

She turned. The smiling waiter waved the money at her.

'You're welcome,' she said, got in the car, and started the engine. She eyed the dashboard clock – she had plenty of time. The reality of days without names stretching out before her made her breath catch for a moment. She settled back, checked her mirrors and pulled out onto the street. When she saw the street sign for Avignon, she turned. Soon she would be on A7 heading to Marseille.

Geiger stared across the room at the back door. It may have been open, as Dalton claimed, but he was locked in just the same. Nothing anyone else might say or do or want was a factor now. The choice was pure and exclusive.

Dalton came back in, having changed from his flannel shirt and jeans into a gray sweatshirt and khaki pants.

'Still here. Good,' said Dalton. 'Understand, Geiger ... If at any point you decide to try and reconfigure things – assault me, use my life to make a trade, that sort of thing – Victor has orders to shoot you, without regard for my safety ... and then kill Harry and Matheson.'

'I understand.'

'You know, Geiger ... There's an element to all of this – an irony I find especially satisfying. A sort of cosmic finishing touch. I don't know if it's occurred to you – and I'd hate for you to miss it.'

'I'm listening.'

'I've used knives, awls, razors, scissors ... I even used a box-cutter – when my switch-blade broke. But you've never used a blade. You've been cut again and again – but the Inquisitor never drew blood. And now, if you do – it will be your own.' Dalton smiled. 'To be honest ... I can't wait to use that line in the last chapter.'

Geiger looked down at the graceful instrument in his hand. Eighteen sixty-seven ... He wondered how many times it had been used to save a life. To cut out something that festered on the inside.

'I underestimated you, Dalton.'

'Did you? How so?'

'The depth of all this. I didn't think you had the mind for it.'

'I didn't – not until after July Fourth. I told you, Geiger – I owe it all to you.'

'The psychological layers ... It's remarkable.'

'Thank you, Geiger. That means everything to me.'

Dalton picked up a one-liter plastic bottle of Cosmoplast 500 from the cart.

'Superglue. German brand. Very fast-acting. Excellent product,' he said. 'Tell me something. Did you feel anger towards them?'

'No.'

'Never?'

'No.'

'I did. All of them. The anger was what kicked me into gear – and kept me going. That was my money-maker.'

Geiger was aware of a change. The thud in his ears – it was gone. His heart was calm.

'There was no anger,' he said. 'It was just the work. And when the truth would finally come out ...'

Dalton cocked his head. 'Yes?'

'Completion.'

Dalton nodded. 'You know, Geiger ... I believe you – and I don't.'

His fist rose and slugged Geiger in the side of his

head. Geiger shook off the blow and shot to his feet – and Dalton's smile froze him like a glance from Medusa.

'Angry?'

Geiger's fingers tightened around the scalpel. A flick of his wrist would sever the external carotid artery. Unconsciousness within seconds, dead within the minute. He glanced behind him – Victor was in the doorway, his face was stony, indifferent, his gun aimed at Geiger's head. Geiger lowered himself back down into the barber's chair and Victor stepped out of view. There was an aching static in Geiger's skull now.

Geiger met Dalton's curious stare, and planted his left hand flat on the chair's arm. He would summon no music. He would keep the lights on inside. There would be no alchemy, and no sliding back into memory. He would anchor himself in this moment.

Dalton could taste his hate, a bitter surge on his tongue – and the sweet anticipation of vengeance being served was almost its equal. He would be done with it soon enough.

Geiger laid the point of the scalpel down across the thin, crimson guide on his knuckle and filled his lungs with air so he wouldn't have to take another breath until it was over.

'Win–win,' he said, and pushed the scalpel in.

The flesh parted evenly, giving a glimpse of the joint, and Geiger pressed harder, sinking the blade down between the bones. His howl began.

Dalton's lips parted. 'Yes,' he hissed, but neither man heard it.

The evolution of the pain was swift – a fine electric

sting erupting in a heat blast that rocked and scorched him as he cut through vein and tendon. The borders of the sensory realm began to melt and expand – his jaw locked down, teeth grinding like millstones – jimmying the blade through the joint . . .

There was never a moment when his mind lost sight of his purpose, or questioned it . . .

. . . and he gave one final push and the scalpel stopped flat against the porcelain. He dropped it, and there was a sudden whiteout in his mind as blood spurted in a thin, arcing stream around the room, painting the white floor with crimson drizzles.

Dalton watched, uncertain if shock or pain or the sight of the extraordinary visual display kept Geiger frozen – then he grabbed Geiger's wrist tightly and raised the arm straight up. The bleeding paused and Dalton squeezed a tablespoon's worth of superglue onto the raw stump. It instantly began to harden into a pink-ish glaze.

'That was stunning. Flawless.' The rush in Dalton's veins was unlike anything he had ever experienced. 'Just another twenty seconds or so.' It was the ride of his life. 'Did you hear me, Geiger?'

Geiger was staring at his index finger, lying on the chair's arm in a small apron of blood. By itself, it looked different to him than it had when it was part of his hand – longer, somehow – as if severing it had made it grow. The sensation was ferocious. A blowtorch.

'Yes, I heard you.'

Dalton lowered the arm and let the hand rest in Geiger's lap. 'The pain's incredible, isn't it? Trans-formative.'

In a sense, Dalton was right. It was turning into a soporific, so strong that it was starting to numb Geiger's senses. He worked at keeping his breaths slow and deep. He wanted to close his eyes, but he was afraid he would pass out if he did.

'Let them ... go now.'

Dalton picked up a towel and started wiping off his hands. 'We're not finished, of course – but yes, I'll get the process started. Victor – get one of them ready!'

Victor reappeared in the doorway. 'Who first?'

Dalton put the blood-stained towel down. 'Geiger – you have a preference?'

'No.'

'Very well. Victor ... Make it Matheson.'

Victor went down the hall. With things seemingly moving toward an end, he was considering whether or not to ask Dalton for Dewey's back-end. He was doing the work of two now, but there was an unwritten clause in every contractor's deal: Dead men don't get paid. He decided he'd wait till it all played out.

On the wall, dangling from a hook, were two silver keys on a ring. He put them in a vest pocket and continued to a door, took out his Glock pistol, opened up and walked in the room.

'All right. I am here to—'

Harry was lying on his back, on the mattress, asleep. Matheson was sprawled on the floor, face down, his head in a pool of blood.

'Merde ...' grunted Victor. He walked to the body, stopped two feet away, and trained the gun on Matheson.

'Matheson ... Matheson!'

Harry stirred. 'Huh?' He raised his head, bleary eyes slowly opening ... then the lids springing up. 'Oh God ...' He propped himself up on his elbows. 'David! Jesus, no ...' He looked to Victor, lips pulling back – an angry dog. 'What the hell did you do to him?!'

'Be quiet now. I just got here.' Victor slid a foot forward and gave Matheson's ribs a solid nudge. 'Matheson ...' He came a half-step closer and kicked him. 'Matheson!'

Harry shook his head. 'Christ ... Is he dead?'

Victor sighed. Dead could be a problem. Dalton might not be pleased. It was impossible to guess how the madman would react to *anything*. He crouched down, and with the gun at Matheson's temple, grabbed a fistful of hair and raised the head. The pale face was coated in blood. Victor lay the head back down and frowned.

Harry's belief that rare moments of symmetry might lie waiting within the endless mayhem of life had never been more fervent, and desperate – the one split-second in a trillion that was earmarked for a purpose, fashioned for it, and must be exploited before it dissolved into the past and life went on its merry, absurd way, tripping over itself and wreaking havoc ...

'Jesus, man! At least see if he has a fucking pulse!'

Victor's head did a 45-degree turn to Harry. 'I said – Be quiet.'

'Yeah? Well how do you say "Fuck you" in French?'

Then real life shifted into a slow-motion ballet before him ...

In a combined, clumsy effort of motion, Matheson rose up on his knees and lunged forward, raising the length of ribbing hidden underneath him, wrapped three times round his hand – with a noose at its end . . .

Victor's peripherals kicked in, head turning, gun hand swinging round and thudding into Matheson's chest – as the noose slipped down over Victor's head . . .

The blow knocked Matheson backward, but his grip held firm, and the momentum of his fall pulled the slipknot tight around Victor's neck. Matheson hit the floor and gave a vicious tug, jolting Victor down to his knees – his hands jumping to his neck, clawing at the noose, Glock clattering to the floor, a clogged choke bursting out of his mouth . . .

Harry's brain leaped back to full-speed – he pulled his own lasso from beneath him, crawling as fast and as far as he could toward Victor. He tossed the noose out like a rodeo wrangler of the most amateur level. It hit Victor's back and fell to the floor – and Harry frantically reeled the cord back in . . .

Victor took hold of the taut rope with one hand, and then the other, like a man in a tug of war – negating Matheson's leverage – and something between a grin and a death grimace stretched his lips as he started pulling, hand over hand – and Matheson began to slide toward him on his back. It was no contest.

Harry gripped the loop and flung it again. It floated in the air, a vengeful halo – and dropped down over Victor's head. Harry yanked hard, the noose sliding closed – and brought Victor down on his back. They had him from both ends now. They were exhausted, but this desperate adrenaline – fast-acting and short-lived – was helping. Separately, they were no match for Victor – but together they made one dangerous enemy. For a second, they found each other's face. Partners, committed to a killing.

Victor twisted on the floor like an animal in a trap – eyes bulging, sandpaper gasps. Panic was becoming his third enemy – hands flying about, gripping and clawing here, then there, unable to stay faithful to one task. Then one of his hands disappeared inside a vest pocket.

Matheson saw it. 'His hand, Harry! Something in his pocket!'

The hand came back out in a blur, holding something – thumb pressing a button, the sleek blade springing out of the handle as the wrist flicked and the knife was launched, slicing through the air ... until it buried itself in Matheson's neck.

Matheson's breath caught, and his eyes widened. He looked concerned, and saddened by the sudden turn of events. But he wouldn't let go of the rope.

'Harry ...' he said. 'Pull ... hard.'

Victor's head swiveled back and forth – a muscular reflex to trauma, or a show of disagreement with Matheson's command, or just a final, simple plea.

Harry and Matheson were mirror images of each other – the grim features etched in hard faces, the unsteady bodies trying to brace themselves – and then, the identical movements, the arms jerking back ...

The *crunnnnch* was a sound of irreparable damage – its meaning underlined by the silence that seized the room. Victor was suddenly a still-life, a body in crooked repose. The keys were visible, dangling out of his vest pocket.

Matheson dropped to his knees, and then fell over on his side – and Harry started reeling Victor in.

'David ...? David ... Can you hear me?'

The fingers of Matheson's left hand fluttered a response.

Victor was heavy, but Harry's adrenaline was spiking off the graph. With one more heave, he brought the body to him. He didn't bother to find a pulse – the angle of Victor's head ruled out all possible physical states but one. He pulled the keys from the pocket and flopped down on his ass. His hands were burning and it was a struggle getting a key into his shackle.

'Fit, you mother ...'

It slid into the slot, Harry turned it, and with a click the shackle opened. He pulled it loose and crawled quickly to Matheson's side, gently rolled him onto his back and then raised him up in his arms about fifty degrees. The knife was in so deep there was very little blood escaping, just a wet, red collar slowly growing around it.

'David ... Can you—'

'Don't ... take it ... out. Lose blood faster.' Matheson's eyes opened. 'Read that ... somewhere.'

Matheson's hand made its way to Harry's and rested there. His breath came so softly that Harry's huffing almost drowned it out.

'Don't worry, David. I won't.'

Harry felt their presence. His ghostly congregation, sad-faced, faithful, warm hearts. They were arriving to share in the suffering, to pay their condolences. And they would not judge him harshly for a murderous act. They understood that any and every moment was only a breath away from the last.

'Harry ...'

'What?'

'You're a … good man.'

'You shouldn't talk, David.' Harry heard the hollow echo of grief in his voice. He was already in mourning. From the corner of his eye, he picked up an image of something on the floor. Victor's Glock.

'I'm sorry, David,' he said, and his sigh rose up from the deepest place in him.

Matheson's eyes closed again. His sigh was very different from Harry's – almost weightless, winged. And then he stopped breathing.

35

Dalton swirled the scalpel in the alcohol bottle, giving the liquid a hint of pink. He'd put the amputated finger on a gauze square on the cart. He came back to his chair and sat down, and studied Geiger. The face and body didn't match – his limbs stretched out and at rest, his head still, leaned back against the headpiece ... but his face was compressed with pain, muscles shifting and tightening, etching lines in the flesh and then erasing them.

'Geiger ... Tell me how you feel.'

The feeling was new, and saturating. Geiger was lying on Dr. Corley's couch, and waited for the wise, sad voice.

'Tell me how you feel.'

'I ache, Martin. Everywhere.'

'From your hand?'

'No. The hand hurts, but this is different.'

'Can you describe it?'

'It's not the kind of pain I can control.'

'Do you think it's sadness?'

'I don't know, Martin. How can I tell?'

Dalton poked Geiger on the knee. 'Geiger ... Tell me what you're feeling.'

'I hurt, everywhere.'

Dalton nodded. 'Good. That's good. Anything else?'

Geiger's eyes opened. 'I'd prefer to not do that again.'

Dalton nodded again. 'Even better.' He held out the scalpel. 'Same hand – or the other one?'

Zanni came up out of a crouch and looked into the open kitchen window, then climbed through and dropped down to the floor without a sound, Beretta at her side. Her head was in lockdown. Get in, get done, get out. No other thoughts till then.

She moved down the hall on cat's feet – and slowed when she saw the door was open. She raised the gun and stopped at the edge of the doorway, then swiveled into it – and took in the grisly tableau.

Victor was sprawled on the floor, pop-eyed and blue-faced, hands clutching at the cords embedded in his neck. Matheson lay on his back, arms folded on his chest, blood still seeping from him. Harry was gone.

She took a slow breath. The body count was rising. A bloody tide.

Geiger tapped his lacquered stump with the scalpel. It was rock-hard.

'You're right,' he said. 'Excellent product.'

All his systems had found the same place to dial down and still function – just past halfway between shut-off and full capacity. Mind, senses, tolerance, reflexes.

'You know,' said Dalton, 'the military used to use superglue in Nam, to stop the bleeding till they could medevac somebody to a hospital. This stuff's even better.' He sat back and crossed his arms. 'So ... what shall it be, Geiger? Which next?'

'That depends. Can you give me an idea of how many I have to lose?'

'How *many*?' Dalton's smile was as slow and cold as a winter river. His finger started its tapping on his lip. 'Let's put that issue aside for now and take it one at a time. Start cutting.'

Geiger had been trying to mathematize the dilemma. Was it better to lose a few fingers on both hands ... or all of one? But Dalton's response implied there was no reason to continue with that pragmatic train of thought.

He switched the scalpel to his left hand and, as Dalton had done with the forefinger, made a cut across his right pinky's knuckle that just broke the skin. Blood rose on the line.

'Nice choice,' said Dalton. 'Less work, less pain – and no great loss, comparatively speaking. There've been studies. We use it much less than the rest.'

Geiger looked up at him. Dalton was leaning forward in the chair, a Roman in the Colosseum waiting for the festivities to resume ...

This time Geiger opted for speed over craftsmanship. He let out a ragged, extended bellow as a preface to action – and sank the blade in deeply, point-first, then levered the scalpel down fast and hard. The finger jumped free of his hand in a jet of blood and fell to the floor – the pain turned molten – and the growl slowly faded to a thick, breathy huff.

Dalton repeated the process – a vice grip around Geiger's wrist, raising the arm, the application of the superglue. They were like figures in some twisted ritual of anointment.

'Well done,' said Dalton. 'Really. You don't disappoint me, Geiger.'

He let the hardening time pass, put Geiger's hand on his thigh, and bent down and picked up his trophy – and when he straightened up he was staring at Zanni, standing in the open doorway.

Dalton's expression had a touch of the beatific. 'Forget something?'

Zanni walked in. The chair had swiveled so she couldn't see Geiger. But there was blood, spray splashes. A lot of it.

Dalton put the little finger down next to the other. 'We're in the middle of something, Zanni.'

Her gun rose and flicked to the right. 'Over there. Against the wall.'

'... What?'

'Move, Dalton.'

'Exactly what is happening here, Zanni?' His confusion was sincere. 'Geiger and I have much more to ... *talk about.*'

'Later on you can set up a Skype account together. Now go over there.'

Dalton's angry breath became audible in his nostrils. 'Should I assume Victor is aware of this?'

'Victor is no longer aware of anything.' The gun flicked again. 'Now *move!*'

Dalton started across the room, shaking his head. 'Betrayal is such a cheap sin. The melodrama ... It's beneath you, Zanni.'

'So is shooting you in the head, but I will.'

She moved deeper into the room, so the three of them formed a triangle. She had a view of Geiger now – his pale face, the slow rise and fall of his chest, the hands. He reminded her of a Raggedy Ann doll she'd had when she was a very little girl.

'Jesus ... Geiger ...' she said.

Geiger's head slowly straightened – it was an uphill battle – and he opened his eyes and found her. Zanni saw no sign of surprise at her presence, no gratitude or relief. Just the classic Geiger stare. And that was a good thing. Keep it linear. Get it done. Leave.

Dalton leaned against the wall. 'Can I ask what you think you're doing?'

'This is finished,' she said. 'Lie down on the floor, on your back.'

The tendons in Dalton's neck suddenly sprang out like cords. 'We are not *done*! Tell her, Geiger!'

Zanni fired – and a bullet plowed into the wall inches from Dalton's scowling face.

'All right,' he growled, and lay down on the floor.

Harry was still in his soiled smock and socks, wandering down the hall. When he heard the shot he turned, the Glock held tightly in both hands.

Geiger watched Zanni. She kept the Beretta on Dalton and came to Geiger's side. The faint scent of lavender brushed against his senses – but he couldn't tell if it lived in the present or the past.

'I'm interested in the answer too, Zanni,' he said. 'What are you doing here?' He watched the angles of her face shift. 'Answer me, Zanni. What are you doing here?'

She measured out a sigh slowly. 'Let's just say: "I know what works best for me".'

Harry stepped into the doorway – the strongest and most constant parts of him used and spent, running on fumes, the Glock chest-high, fanning it slowly across the room.

Geiger saw Zanni's eyes widen – and he slowly turned his head toward the door ...

What we learn through time is both blessing and curse. It alters the mind – bestows the gift of options ... and weans us from instinct. For Zanni, years of training kicked in. Someone enters a scenario, intent unknown, brandishing a gun ... You raise your own weapon – identify and measure the threat – play out the seconds, one by one ...

Her gun came up in her hand.

For Harry, the novitiate, fear and reflex were all he brought to the moment. A bumpy racing in the blood, a desperate urge to stay alive, the primal drive to protect those dearest to you. He watched Zanni's Beretta rise ...

As Harry slid into Geiger's sight, dominos of thought started to fall in his mind. 'Harry ... no,' he said.

Someone pulled a trigger.

Harry grimaced, and the Glock dropped from his grip.

Zanni stumbled backward a step, listing.

Harry's aim, unsurprisingly, was off the mark. The shot had entered the far right side of her waist. Had the entry point been an eighth of an inch higher, it might have gone right through her and caused minimal internal damage – but the bullet clipped the top edge of the pelvis, and took off inside her like a pinball, veering up and inward – and because it came to rest in her heart, ripping it open, she died before she hit the floor.

Dalton sprang to his feet, hustled to the back door, pulled it open and was gone.

Geiger dropped to his knees beside Zanni. The violet eyes had already paled. He put two fingers to her throat, but all he felt was the clanging of his own fury. He whirled on Harry.

'Do you know where Victor is?'

Harry was a cheap knockoff of himself – poorly stitched together, coming apart at the seams.

'Dead,' he mumbled softly. 'Matheson, too.'

Geiger awkwardly picked up Zanni's gun and rose, and reeled so precipitously he had to grab the chair-back to keep from falling. He closed his eyes and slowly sucked in air, trying to equalize the pressure. He was summoning the things that had always killed the feel-ings, petitioning the Inquisitor to come back one last time.

'Stay here,' he said, and headed for the open back door with a weave in his step. He needed to let the pain spread and set him on fire, and then draw the power from it – a blazing furnace to stoke a locomotive, to keep the pistons churning.

He went a few paces outside and stopped, listening. The day was as glorious as it was dreadful – a polished, spotless, blue-glass sky and the lavender untroubled in the breezeless air. A postcard from Provence day. Having a wonderful time. Wish you were here.

He heard a car door close.

*

Dalton reached up to the driver's seat visor and grabbed the car keys. The twisted righteousness of his anger was flooding him. He'd been fair and true to his word, right from the start. Geiger had come of his own free will, made his own choices each step of the way . . .

He put the key in the ignition and turned, the engine coughed itself to life and the locks clicked shut. He grabbed the stick shift . . . and movement caught his eye – through the windshield, in the field of lavender. The rainbowed serpents were rising again – but this time there was no internecine battle. The cunning eyes were all gazing his way. They shared one mind, one desire.

'That's right. Come to Papa.'

And they did – curling out of the lavender, flowing like long-tailed kites in the wind, terrible and majestic, coming to him, fangs gleaming in the sun. The first to arrive was the most beautiful of all. Monster and angel, regal and cruel. And it could speak . . .

Geiger brought the gun up in both hands. 'Get out of the car,' he said.

Dalton stared at him through the glass. 'You don't kill people, Geiger. Go away.'

Geiger pulled the trigger.

The bullet shattered the driver's window and pas-senger window, showering Dalton with thousands of tiny, edged glass missiles – and his face broke out in a rash of bloodied dots.

Geiger leaned in and put the gun's muzzle to Dalton's forehead. 'Get out.'

He backed up three steps and Dalton came out – leaning back against the car, dazed by the shot's percussion, a dozen ruby rivulets coming slowly down his face. He wiped some blood off his cheek and stared at his hand.

Geiger could tell by the soggy feel of his legs that he needed more adrenaline. A junkie in serious need of a fix.

'You said we weren't done,' he said.

Dalton looked up at him. 'I know.' He rubbed his sleeve across his mouth. 'So tell me how it ends?'

Geiger tossed the gun away.

Dalton grinned. 'Good. Very good.'

Geiger stepped to him and drove his fist into the center of Dalton's chest as hard as he could. Every part of Dalton seemed to give way, except for his mouth – which opened into a large circle.

The pain in Geiger's hand was a constant rush, like a river in a downpour – so strong it had a sound to it, a rumble in his ears. But he reloaded and hit him again, and again – and stood back as Dalton slid down against the car to the ground. A dry, dusty noise came out of him, in irregular intervals. *Huhsssss … Huhsssss …*

Geiger slumped against a post of the lean-to. A new kind of fuel was pumping through him, combustible, hot. It was fury. He'd never known it before. And the blending of it with the pain felt like it could blow him apart.

Dalton tipped over onto all-fours and spit blood. 'Is that it? All the anger, the pain … You're lying, Geiger. There's more in there. Much more.' He grabbed the handle of the car's back door and pulled himself up to his feet, laying his cheek against the steel, then took a long, ragged breath.

'Geiger ...'

'What?'

'Is she dead?'

'... Yes.'

Dalton turned his blood-smeared face around. 'Make sure to tell Harry I said thank you.'

Geiger felt the match being struck – saw it flicker to life behind his eyes – and then thought and pain and reason were obliterated by the blast. In the second it took to reach Dalton rage had risen from the flames like a phoenix – and he grabbed him, swung him round and sent him crashing into the house with a bony clunk, crumbling in an ungainly heap on the grass.

Geiger hoisted him back up by the shirt and slammed him against the wall.

There would be no stopping. Not yet ...

He pounded Dalton into the house again.

Not while the fire still raged ...

He yanked him close and then slammed him back against the old wood. Dalton's head dropped forward like a tapped-out drunk.

'Not yet!' growled Geiger.

Not until there was nothing left to burn, and the fire consumed itself and died ...

Geiger pulled Dalton back and shoved him into the house again – but he was starting to flag. Dalton was growing heavier by the second. He kept the body pinned against the wall while he waited for strength.

'No more, Geiger. It's enough.'

Geiger turned to the haunted voice.

Harry stood ten feet from him. 'It's enough.'

Geiger's forehead dropped onto Dalton's chest – and he let his breath and mind slowly come back to him. In the sudden stillness, another presence made itself known – an uneasy, troubled whirr. Geiger looked left.

The wasps' massive nest – more than two feet in diameter – was five feet away, nestled beneath an eave. The series of shocks against the house had set off insectan alarms, and a dozen of the creatures had come out to investigate, hovering in a tense buzz around the entry hole.

Geiger was not the only one aware of their displeasure. Dalton whispered in his ear.

'Hear that? They're mad.' The drooping skull slowly rose. The eyes opened. 'Not ... finished.' It was like a death-bed voice.

Geiger looked into the eyes. He could see himself. He was in there, with Dalton.

'Look at you, Geiger. I set you ... free.'

... *Beginning* ...

'You ... owe me.'

... *Middle* ...

'Finish it.'

... *End* ...

Geiger's grip tightened – he pulled Dalton away from the wall and hurled him toward the nest. He hit it face first – and it broke into three large pieces as it came loose from its mooring – and body and nest fell to the ground together.

There were hundreds of them – a single mind and purpose, their communal anger as loud as a race car's engine, the sun turning them into a gleaming, trembling veil as they gathered. They had no interest in Geiger. They knew who the enemy was. And they descended, and attacked.

Dalton's face and upper body disappeared beneath the swarm. Geiger watched the legs flinch, and the arms wave about feebly, the hands twitching like living things. If Dalton was making a sound, it could not be heard over the vengeful drone.

And a hand closed around his arm.

'Come on,' said Harry. He gave a gentle pull but Geiger was a statue, hard and heavy as marble. 'Hey ...' He gave a firmer tug. '*Geiger* ...'

Geiger turned to him. Harry caught a glimpse of something in his eyes – a change, distinct but indefinable. If it was a reflection of the soul, Harry couldn't tell if something had been gained or lost.

'All right,' said Geiger, and he walked toward the back door.

They had arranged the bodies side by side on the floor of Dalton's den. Befitting the task they had gone about it in silence. Then Geiger had sent Harry down the road to see if Zanni had left the car where they had parked it when they first arrived.

The only one who looked at rest was Zanni. Victor had a bluish glaze and a crooked grimace to go with the crushed neck. Matheson had bled out to a ghastly white. Dalton's face was so swollen that his features were barely visible – it looked like a loaf of risen dough ready to be baked. But Zanni could have had a beating heart, asleep with a dream, waiting for the summer to give some color to her pale, smooth skin.

He felt heavy, and sodden. Drenched to the bone with death.

He heard the car coming near, and then the engine shutting off.

He had been tracing it back from the start. Zanni, Victor, Dewey – they had been his chaperones. Keeping an eye on the unpredictable guest of honor, letting him go his own way, being on hand if needed. Just as long as he came to the party …

Harry got out of the car with a small suitcase in hand and headed into the house. His gait was slow, tentative, like someone lost or unsure of where he wants to go. He came into the den. Geiger was seated in Dalton's desk chair. Harry held up the suitcase.

'This was in the car. I looked inside. It's hers.'

'Put it anywhere.'

'Passport says "Deirdre Gold". Is that her name?'

'No. That's a fake. Her name was Rosanna Soames.'

Harry put the case on the floor. 'Did the patch work at all?'

'Yes.'

Harry had rummaged through the house and found some of Dalton's old fentanyl patches. They were past their expiration date but, very much to his surprise, Geiger had agreed to wrap one around his hand for fifteen minutes.

'Your bag is still in the car.'

'All right. Take it out and leave it by the front door.'

Fogged out as Harry was, he assumed he had misunderstood.

'Whaddaya mean?'

'When you leave. Put the bag by the door.'

'When *I* leave? We're not going together?'

'I need to do this by myself, Harry. And you need to go.'

Harry knew that tone better than anyone else, so he knew the discussion was over before it began. He'd be talking to no one. Geiger was already gone. He just hadn't left yet.

'Where are you gonna go?'

'I don't know, Harry. I haven't thought about it yet. Do you have money?'

'A little.'

'There's plenty in my bag. Take some.'

'Okay. I will.'

Geiger stood up. 'You should head out now.'

Harry understood what Geiger's presence in this house meant, what it spoke to without need of words – this strangest of bonds – so he chose to remain wordless about it himself.

'I need to ask you a question first,' he said.

'Go on.'

'When I came in the room – when you were in the chair, with Dalton and her ... I had the gun up and you said, "Harry, no." Why did you say that?'

'Harry ... I don't want to talk about—'

'Geiger ... I *killed* her. I need to know. Why did you say, "Harry, no"?'

'... Because she was trying to save me.'

The air turned arctic around Harry. A cruel, biting cold.

'But – but she was one of them.'

'Yes.'

'Then why would she do that?' There was a whisper of despair in the question.

'I can't answer that, Harry. I don't know why. I don't think she did either.'

The thought came to Harry like a lonely orphan. 'She wasn't going to shoot ...' He looked over at Zanni. 'Jesus ... She wasn't going to shoot.'

'Harry ... Let it be – for now.'

Harry's eyes slowly came back to Geiger. 'How do I do that?'

They stood there. Brothers at a mass funeral – then Geiger took a large, thick manila envelope from the desk and walked to Harry.

'Take this with you.'

'What is it?'

'Dalton's memoirs. You can throw it away – or you could put it up on Veritas Arcana. I think Matheson would.'

Harry nodded, and took the manuscript.

'Harry ... Christine knows. Go see her.'

And then Geiger walked out of the room.

Harry listened to the footsteps on the old floors grow fainter, deeper into the house, until their sound was gone – and then he headed for the front door.

When he neared the crest of the woods he put his bag down and lay back on the crisp pine needles. It was very still here, but up above a breeze jostled the trees' tops and the high branches swayed back and forth across the sun, chopping it into gold slivers over and over again – left to right, right to left ...

The pain was constant – dense and kinetic – but

oddly enough, if he didn't look at his hands, it felt as if the fingers were still part of them. The phantom limb sensation. He'd read about it, and suspected that, at the start, it might be more troublesome to deal with than the actual physical loss.

Then the scent of pine smoke reached him – and he sat up.

Down below, the house was ablaze, flames reaching higher than the roof. The fire he started in the den had spread quickly. Old wood burned fastest – time had patiently prepared it – and the can of kerosene found in the backyard shed held just enough to splash each room and hall's floor with a thin, wet strip. He wondered if Tulette had a fire truck, or if once the smoke was spotted someone would make a call to a nearby village.

He lay back down and closed his eyes.

Drawing the truth from himself was something very different from drawing it out of others. He would have to learn how. He could see Corley sitting in his chair, sad, dark eyes, notebook in his lap, the brief smile flickering each time Geiger came into the office.

Martin ... I think I know what the feeling is.

The sadness?

Yes.

Tell me.

Grief, Martin. Grief.

36

Christine rubbed away a tiny smudge on the bar with a fingertip, then brought her coffee to her lips. As was her new custom, she looked to the door every time its bell chimed.

For a second, the angle of the morning sunlight burned out the visitor's image as he entered. After two steps, he stopped – and she slowly put her cup down and got up from her stool. She had come to assume that if one of them came back, it meant the other was dead – and an ache was blooming that drew as much from joy as dread.

She walked across the floor to him. Something was broken. A part inside him that no doctor could fix or replace. She put her arms around him and pulled him into her. She felt his body give in, as if he'd somehow been hollowed out.

'I'm not all right, Chris,' said Harry.

'. . . I know.'

She took his hand and led him back to the office, closed the door and took his jacket off.

'Sit.'

He sat on the couch. His gaze wandered, but he didn't seem to be looking at anything.

'I wanted to see you – before I went home ...'

'Harry ... Tell me what happened.'

It was hard to look at him. His face was haggard and had odd, faint splotches. He'd lost weight. He looked like a survivor of some tragic disaster. She pulled a chair over and sat across from him, and took his hands in hers.

'Do you want something to eat – or drink?'

Harry shook his head.

She wanted to sit, calm and silent, and let him come out with things in his own way and time – but she couldn't stand it any longer.

'Harry ... Geiger was here.'

'I know.'

'A week ago. Trying to find you. I know about Dalton.'

'... He's dead.'

The two words were a pair of hands around her throat. She couldn't swallow. She let go of him and sat back in her seat. She had that sensation – of slipping away, the glimmering, crystalline sadness for things beyond her reach ...

'Dalton ... Matheson ... They're all dead – except for me and Geiger.'

... and then the sudden feeling of abeyance – breath, blood, the infinitesimal molecules in the air. Life in a freeze-frame.

'Harry ... Geiger is *alive*?'

'Yes.' He looked doubtful about his grasp of things. 'I just said that, didn't I?'

Her body kicked back into motion with an electric jolt. Her breath was cool in her lungs. She realized she'd been gripping the chair's arms, and put her hands in her lap.

'I'm sorry,' he said.

'Sorry for what?'

'It must've been hard – sitting, waiting, not knowing.'

She wasn't going to ask anything else. What happened to him ... where he was. This would be enough. They were both alive – and there were different hues of melancholy to surround herself with, some more pleasing than others. She got up and sat down next to him.

Harry's sigh sounded like someone's last breath. 'It's that feeling, Chris.'

'Which one?'

'When something happens – and you know you're never going to be the same. No matter what you do, or how much time goes by – you already know you're never going to be the same again. Right?'

'Yes.'

'I had to do things ... *Had* to. Things I'm having a lot of trouble with. Real bad stuff.'

She raised a hand and started smoothing his hair with her fingertips. He'd always loved that.

'Harry ... You don't have to go home right away. You should stay with me a while. We'll try and make it a little better.'

'Y'think?'

'Yes. I think.'

He leaned back into the cushion and closed his eyes. 'Okay,' he said. 'For a while.'

She kept running her fingers through his hair, and watching him, until some of the demons that had him in their grasp let go, and the lines in his face lost their edge. Then she settled back beside him, close against him.

The image that came to her was of Geiger walking away, transforming his limp into that singular grace. She couldn't see what it was he was leaving behind, but he wasn't looking back at it. It wasn't something he would do.

The cat was lying on the window sill, a faithful audience of one.

Ezra stood on the fire escape, playing his violin – a melody made up, a slow, plaintive strain he'd found inside of him days ago and added to each night outside his window. The neighbors hadn't complained about it, yet. Someone in a nearby apartment had even applauded once.

Time had reinvented itself – renouncing ancient conventions, casting off the constraints of hours and minutes, liberating itself, expanding, shrinking, exploring its supple nature. Now Ezra measured time by feelings. A flight of reverie. An orphan instant of hope. A short, bumpy ride of sleep. Stretches of despair ... and resignation. A moment of peace. They all ran together, one after another. His mother was the time-keeper. 'Ezra ... Time to get up.' 'Ezra ... Dinner.' 'Ezra ... Time for bed.'

The cat's one eye opened, a shiny gold coin – and Tony rose in a slow, back-bending stretch and then slunk down onto the metal grating. The boy watched as it walked to the square opening and climbed down the three rungs of the raised ladder. It always came back home, just as Geiger said it would, but each time it left on a nightly journey Ezra had to kick the ass of a panic gremlin that popped up in his brain.

'See you later, Tony.'

The cat jumped to the ground and strolled off, disappearing into the darkened courtyard.

Ezra hadn't given up hope, but he'd put it on a shelf where it was growing a coat of dust, like a broken toy he couldn't bear to throw away. Dr. Corley once said that grief was both the toughest and simplest feeling. He said that love and hate are different for every person, that there can be a million reasons why you love or hate someone, and you might not even understand why – but grief is pretty close to the same for everybody, and we all know the reason why we feel it. Lately, Ezra had wondered if it was something you got better at ... with practice.

As he finished drawing out a tremulous A flat, he saw a shift in the darkness below – it lasted less than second, black on blacker, shadow on shadow. From a thousand nights of solitary staring he knew the courtyard's every silhouette. There was something out there now that had never been there before. By the west fence. A tall smudge on the night. His mind did a back-flip – to his mother and him in the subway.

Mom ... Going to talk to these people – telling them stuff they may not know. Yeah – maybe they can help. Or maybe they come after all of us ...

Then the cat meowed.

'Tony?' Ezra put the violin down on the sill and leaned out against the railing. 'Tony ...'

Another meow started up – and was stifled before it

ended. The truncated sound made the back of Ezra's skull tingle.

'Tony! C'mere!' His voice ping-ponged off the opposite brownstone and died.

'Don't yell, Ezra. He's with me.'

The sound of the satin voice was so electrifying it rendered the words meaningless. Ezra was down the three rungs of the ladder and dropping the six feet to the ground before he'd taken another breath. The rage of adrenaline made oxygen unnecessary.

'Where are you?'

'Over here.'

Ezra pivoted – and across the courtyard a wall of shadow seemed to bulge, a part breaking free from it and coming forward, becoming a separate dark presence, and stopping in a pale gray slash of light. Ezra saw the blink of a golden eye atop the silhouette's right shoulder.

He'd never run so fast in his life, afraid he might explode before he reached him. The last five feet became a lunge – and he threw his arms around Geiger and held tight. The cat dropped to the ground with a displeased grunt, and Geiger's arms completed the embrace, one of his gloved hands holding Ezra's head to his chest.

Their silence was not about finding the right words to say. Geiger had no urge to speak at all, content to stay as they were – and the only words on Ezra's mind were a question he was terrified to ask.

'Tell me,' Ezra finally said.

The answer came without hesitation.

'Harry is alive. Your father died.'

The prelude to Ezra's weeping was a single nod, and

then the tears gathered and spilled – a segue without turmoil or sobs. To Geiger, it felt like an act long anticipated, and brave – the choice to embrace grief instead of running from it, or disavowing its dominion, or armoring the heart – as a fool might take refuge from a hurricane in a paper house.

Perhaps the boy could teach him.

The city's humming midnight drone was an engine that never stopped running. It was something you couldn't get away from. It was always with you.

Geiger tightened his hold around the quivering body. 'I'm here, Ezra,' he said. 'I'm here.'